The Heart
of the
Fire

The Heart of the Fire

A Novel

by

CERRIDWEN FALLINGSTAR

CAULDRON PUBLICATIONS
SAN GERONIMO, CALIFORNIA

Published by Cauldron Publications
P.O. Box 282, San Geronimo,
California 94963

Book Design, Production & Cover Graphics by
Sky & Rainbow Canyon, Aspen, CO 81612

Cover Art & Title Design ©1990 Susan Gliss,
Wine Country Graphics, Sonoma, CA 95476

Library of Congress Catalog Card Number: 89-085678

Printed in the United States of America

First printing: May, 1990

ISBN 0-9621470-0-1

90 91 92 93 / 10 9 8 7 6 5 4 3 2 1

Printed on Recycled Paper

To
the memory of Gran,
my Grandmother Tindy
and all our Grandmothers. . .

To
the Goddess and the God
within us all.

Acknowledgments

This book has been the labor of seven years and I have many people to thank, including:

My editors, Wendi Kallins and Rachel Margolin, who waded through many confusing shifts from past to present.

Sky Canyon, producer and midwife of this book, and his wife Rainbow Canyon, for her invaluable and loving support.

Deborah Ann Light, whose grants enabled me to research *The Heart of the Fire* in Scotland.

The Holy Terrors, my coven sisters who supported me faithfully through the initial terror and the long years of work that followed. Particular thanks to Cathi Wickham/Merlyn who assisted me through many hypnosis sessions to gather material until I developed the confidence and self-guiding techniques necessary to work alone.

Ruth Barret and Cyntia Smith of *Aeolas*, for their inspiring, magical Celtic music. Many chapters of this book have been written with their voices in the background.

Patricia Sun, Chad Walsh, and Bruce Cockburn, who healed

my hatred of Christianity and helped me understand its true value as a heart teaching.

The Alive Tribe, whose teachings greatly expanded my power as a Sourceress.

June Brindel, author of Ariadne and Phaedra, for her encouragement and her example.

My parents, Michael and Jane Lesh, who loved me in spite of all my peculiar ideas.

Edward Farmer and Arbuthnott Farmer, my grandparents, who encouraged my writing when I was young and gave me a model of living an artistic life.

Isis Coble, my dear Mina, who remembers.

Elie Demers, whose financial support and love enabled me to nourish our child and my creative dream throughout this project.

My son, Zachary Moonstone, whose presence challenges me to be impeccable in each moment and to continue on the highest evolutionary path possible.

Theo Bailey, minstrel, who inspires me with his music, his creative fire, and his commitment to the truth.

All Witches and Shamans and Sourcerers walking a path with heart, sisters and brothers creating the world anew.

Foreword

The Heart of the Fire is an historical novel which chronicles the life of Fiona McNair, a young Witch living in the 1500's who is academically ignorant, but apprenticed to an old system of knowledge including wortcunning (herbcraft), healing, time-travel and other forms of magic. It is not fiction, but posthumous autobiography, or 'far memory' of my own past life experience as a Witch in 16th century Scotland. I have confirmed the details of my memories with traditional research, including two trips to Scotland in which I located and explored the site of Glen Lochlan, the village in which Fiona had lived. Writing this book has been a process of reclaiming this lost part of myself, as well as a lost part of our collective history

As Fiona, I spoke not Shakespearean English, but Gaelic. There are places where I have used Scots-English words, Shakespearean English or magical terms to convey the "flavor" of our thinking and conversation as best as my twentieth century mind and language could approximate. There is a glossary of possibly unfamiliar words at the end of this book.

Witchcraft[1] in the 16th century was what remained of the
Celtic-European Shamanic traditions which had thrived among
those peoples for thousands of years before the advent of Christianity. It has been falsely portrayed as the worship of evil and
the practice of psychic manipulation. In reality, the essence of
Witchcraft is the essence of the earth, nature, the dance of female and male, the birth, growth, life, death, and rebirth of
plants and animals. Witchcraft honors the spinning world as it
weaves its patterns of darkness and light and dances in a circle
through the seasons. At first, Christianity incorporated many
Pagan customs into its own beliefs and practices. But as the
Catholic Church consolidated its power over the next thousand
years it became gradually more monolithic and corrupt. All
Christian sects with differing interpretations from the domi-
nant one were branded heretic and millions of people—whole cities and subcultures—were slaughtered. Gradually the Inquisi-
tions spread to include Witches; the Pagan healers, midwives,
herbalists, Priestesses and Priests of the old shamanic forms of
worship. In the 300 years between 1350 and 1750, millions of people, about 85% of them female, were murdered. The suppression
of Witchcraft was a political struggle between a tradition which
saw God as being distant and transcendent, apart from the world
and harshly judgemental of the world, and a tradition which saw
God as a birth-giving Goddess and her Mate, who were one with
the world and loved the world as a mother would love her children. The suppression and denial of the feminine, will-oriented
aspect of spirituality was successful at that time. The great
light of the Renaissance era cast a correspondingly dark shadow,
a shadow our culture has, up until now, chosen to deny.

It is my hope that *The Heart of the Fire* will leave the reader
with the realization that "everything lost is found again."[2] That
nothing is lost forever. Our brilliant microcosmic brains contain
all the history, the knowledge, the creativity and awareness humans have ever experienced—and we are learning to tap these
sources at will. No matter how many books and people have been
burned, the truth is imprinted in our genetic code and passed on.

This is the story of a life that I lived, almost four hundred
years ago in a little village in Scotland which is no longer there.
This story, and the desire to tell it, has been inside me since I

1—For an excellent overview of the worldview and practices of tradi
tional and contemporary Witchcraft, I recommend *The Spiral Dance*,
by Starhawk, Harper and Row
2—From 'The Kore Chant' by Starhawk

came into this lifetime, and I offer it to you now in the hope that it will heal some part of you that has been wounded since this part of human history was obliterated and this aspect of the human spirit was so damaged that it became unconscious. The intuitive, the feminine, the Goddess and the God of the earth are spontaneously arising again within us. Whenever any of us tells the truth about our feelings, our perceptions, our experience, a piece of the web of life is healed, and the healing is made easier for all of us.

To each of you who is willing to read this book as more than a novel, using it as another tool to facilitate your own healing, I thank you for your courage and your vision.

— Cerridwen Fallingstar
Beltane (May 1), 1990

"Unfortunately, the witch herself—poor and illiterate—did not leave us her story. It was recorded, like all history, by the educated elite, so that today we know the witch only through the eyes of her persecutors."

— *Witches, Midwives and Nurses,*
by Barbara Ehrenreich and Deirdre English

"Not created, but summoned."

— Zen Koan

Chapter 1

My adversary confronts me with lowered horns and paws the earth. Annie and I stop, clutching hands. If the goat would stay where he was, we could go around him. But we know from past experience that he is unlikely to let us pass without butting us into the ditch. I wish McTavish would keep his goats penned; they are forever foraging and getting into trouble in other people's gardens. But when Annie asked McTavish once to take his goat out of our path he snorted and growled in his gruff voice that he only wished it was a bull. I can't tell if he hates me because I am Annie's friend or hates Annie because she is mine, but his cross red face has never brought anything but trouble for us.

Annie is half a year older and half a head taller than me, but she hangs back behind me.

"Say something to him," she whispers.

"Like what?" I demand.

"I don't know," she says crossly. "Everyone says your grandmother is a Witch. Has she taught you nothing?"

"She's taught me nothing about *goats*," I reply.

"Well, Witches are supposed to be able to talk with the animals," Annie says, swallowing hard. "Aye, and the trees and the plants too. She must not be a *real* wise woman if she hasn't taught you anything of that sort."

"My Gran is the wisest woman in the whole village," I retort, stung. "She says I'm too young to be learning yet."

The goat makes a little half-charge and we cower back a few paces, dropping the herbs we have gathered in the mud.

"We'll never live to be old at this rate!" Annie is trying to act as tough as she usually does, but her voice quavers.

She picks up a couple of dandelions. It is spring, the earth smells fresh and sweet and there is plenty of fresh greenery all about so the goat cannot blame his cantankerousness upon hunger. She ties the dandelions together and tosses them to the goat.

"Go, goat, and I'll give you a groat," she chants hopefully.

The goat nuzzles the dandelions and then stares at us with his baleful eyes, almost as yellow as the fresh flowers of the sun, but with none of their warm promise.

Suddenly I feel a rage rising in me, remembering the last time we came through the village and McTavish's goat knocked us both into the ditch, leaving us to run home crying with our scraped knees and elbows. He has no right to be so mean like this.

"Go, goat, and I'll give you a groat," I growl, "but if you will not go away, then ever after rue this day!"

"Don't make him angry," warns Annie.

"You're almost seven," I snap. "You shouldn't be afraid."

"You're the one who knows the magic!" she snaps back.

Aye, I think to myself, raising my chin. Would my Gran be afraid of a goat? In a flash I see her prominent cheekbones, frown marks like angry waves across her forehead, black, flashing eyes—no, Gran has never been afraid of anything. She is not very tall for a woman, nor broad, but the strongest men in Glen Lochlan bow their heads and acknowledge her when she passes by, and the women curtsey. No, Gran is not afraid of anyone. Everyone in the village owes their loyalty to Lord Lochlan, but even in his presence she is as haughty as a queen. It is my Grandmother, or her best friend Mina, the people come to when they are sick, and it is they who know everything there is to know about plants and how they may help us. And it is John and William, Gran's friends who are also in the coven, that everyone comes to if they have a sick animal. Even the Laird respects John's opinion over anyone else's where his horses are concerned, and William is the shepherd for the Laird's great flock.

The coven is secret, but tis a strange secret, that everyone knows about, yet pretends not to. Rose, the oldest woman in the village, near twice as old as my Gran, is in it, and almost half the people in Glen Lochlan are related to her, if not directly, then through marriage, for she had eight living children, all of whom bore children in turn. Gran says I am too little to be trusted with secrets, but often on full moon nights I cannot sleep, and often the moon has led me, bare-foot and shivering, to the coven's gatherings. So I know that it is three grandchildren of Rose's, Sarah, the midwife, her husband Peter, and Mari, reputed as the best baker in the shire, who complete the circle of wise ones in my Grandmother's coven. I sometimes feel that I can hardly bear being a child and endure the long years that stand between me and being as wise as the grandmother I adore.

I stiffen, feeling my Gran's regal disdain straightening my spine. Stupid McTavish and his stupid goat! They will not hinder me on my path!

Grabbing Annie by the arm, I march past the goat, who for a moment stares with disbelief at our display of fearlessness. But soon I hear fast-moving hoof-beats biting into the earth behind me, and Annie crying, "Fiona, look out!"

I turn, and without thinking my fist shoots out just in time to connect with the goat's nose. Then I am on my bottom, in the mud. McTavish's goat sways, takes several steps, first to one side, then to the other, and then topples. I stare with amazement and hold my aching hand. Annie's mouth drops open, white teeth sparkling in her gypsy dark face, her black eyes enormous.

"Did you see that?" Incredulous laughter comes from the side of the road. I look up and see Mari's husband, Galen McClinnock. I've never seen Galen at a coven meeting, but he and Mari are both good friends with my mother, and often at our croft, and I trust his warm arms and his big laugh. He is leading a jennet mule carrying a cart full of decayed midden to hoe into the communal fields.

"I was just about to help you lasses out of your predicament," he laughs, "but I see you've helped yourselves! Fiona, brawling with a goat? What will your mother say?"

I struggle up out of the mud, feeling with dismay how my skirt clings soddenly to my legs, thinking in anguish of all the time it will take me pounding it in the stream before my mother deems it wearable again.

Galen calls loudly to the men coming behind him with more loads of midden, and they all stop and laugh and exclaim over the goat, which is just now starting to twitch slightly. To the right of us, the bairns from Jack and John Turner's crofts pour onto the road, staring at us with amazement.

"I could have done that," boasts one of the boys our age.

"Could not!" a smaller lad pushes the first.

"I could so! She's only a girl. I could have done it."

"Is the goat dead?" a little girl quavers.

"Naw," says Galen, patting her on the head.

"You'd best clear out of here," he whispers to us. "McTavish catch you, you're in trouble."

We run as quickly as we may through the gloppy March road, through the village, passing the fields where the men are planting barley and flax, peas, oats and wheat. We run past the dozen crofts that lie along or shortly off of this main road. We run past the Bluebell Inn, a large structure of wood five times larger than any croft, past the Smithy without stopping to chat with Ewan, a boy only a little older than us, one of the few boys who doesn't seem to feel obligated to yank on the girls' hair and throw mud at them. We run panting past the castle, magnificent with its four round towers and the vineyards, orchards and rose gardens that surround it. Gran, who has traveled, insists that it is not much as castles go but I can scarcely imagine a huger or more elegant building than this, made all of gray stone, with its doors taller than the tallest man in Glen Lochlan. The castle kitchen, big as a whole croft with its huge hearths for baking and roasting, sends clouds of wonderful odors rolling onto the road.

Out of breath and with a stitch in my side I stop and yank at Annie to stop also. Her brown skirt is also muddy from our run, but her mother does not seem to care so much, and Annie is, as usual, dressed in a rag-tag collection of garments, mostly adult clothes which have simply been torn smaller and basted roughly together. They do not fit well and prettily as mine do, but rather bag and sag, one of her little brown shoulders exposed, a ragged cloak so dirty it is hard to say what color it was to start, flapping around her ankles. Lately when Annie has come to our house she has practiced a great deal with her sewing, helping mother teach me and my little sister Eostre, who is four. I hate sitting still and sewing but Annie will often do nothing else, insisting that as soon as she can, she will sew her own clothes and not be ashamed to be so ragged as her mother dresses her.

We look anxiously over our shoulders, but of course there is no goat nor anyone else pursuing us. Annie and I slow our pace to a walk. We come to Annie's croft, just on the outskirts of Glen Lochlan, a couple of miles before we get to mine. Her croft is one of the nicer ones, and they have more land than most; her grandfather even has a barn and his own small flock of sheep, as well as a good-sized garden. Her grandfather has been one of the guards and retainers of the old Laird, Lochlan's father, so I do not see how it is that they are so poor that Mairead, her mother, must dress her so shabbily.

"I wish I didn't have to garden and help with the soap making today," mopes Annie. I almost wish I could stay and garden with Annie; I love working with dirt and the plants. But Mairead is so sharp-tongued that I never feel welcome there. For us to be together, Annie either comes to my croft or we go to play together on the hills or by the sea.

We part sadly, our triumph with the goat forgotten as each of us faces the prospect of a scolding mother.

Annie's croft is at the end of the little valley where Glen Lochlan nestles. Mina, Gran, Peter and Sarah and my mother all have crofts near each other in the next valley over. I leap down the lightly wooded slope into the small forested valley, really no more than a small trough between two hills. Here my mother's croft, and Gran's, and Mina's, are all within a mile of each other. I would like to go over to Mina and Gran's and see if they need any help gathering herbs or tying them into bunches to dry, but I know that I must go to my own croft and get the soap from my mother to wash my skirt.

I open the gate in the rough brushwood fence that keeps the

deer from pillaging our garden, and run to the door of the croft.

My mother is holding my littlest sister, Elana, on one hip, while she stirs the stew over the fire. Elana is starting to fuss and search through my mother's clothes to find the lunch that is more to her liking.

"What did you find?" my mother asks, and then turns to look at me. "Fiona!" she cries in dismay. "Are you a child or a frog?"

I shrug, regretfully, showing her my muddy but otherwise empty hands.

"McTavish's mean old goat tried to butt us again," I say. "I hit him in the nose but we lost the potherbs in the mud when I fell down. Annie was scared and dropped hers too."

Elana starts to cry. Mother gives her a breast and sits on the bench, obviously tired.

"Fiona, go stir the pot—no, wait—go wash your hands. And take off those filthy clothes and put on your other skirt. After lunch you can go wash that one. Leave it outside for now."

"Can I go see Gran later?" I beg.

"Not today. I've had you out long enough and I'm needing your help." She hands me the baby. "Go change the baby. You can take her naps down to the stream when you take your skirt and get them all clean for me."

"Ohhh—" my shoulders slump. If there is anything I hate worse than sewing, it is cleaning baby naps. "That is the most disgusting task in the world!" I complain.

"Aye, so it is," Mother says briskly. "And the one that needs the most doing."

After lunch, Eostre and I carry a load of dirty nappies down to the river to be washed. Soon my hands are red from the harsh soap and the cold water and my back hurts from carrying the heavy load and pounding it over and over again with heavy rocks to get out the stains. I think longingly of when I will again be able to visit with Gran and Mina, asking them questions and watching the magic work they do that is so much more exciting than the drudgery of cooking and cleaning and sewing that my mother does. When I grow up, I'm not having babies, I think rebelliously. I think of my mother's fat belly and how she has told me that soon there will be yet another little one sharing our croft.

"I'm cold," Eostre complains. She puts her red little hands on her thighs and sits there pouting, blue eyes reflecting the sky, blonde hair tumbling over her shoulders.

"Aye, leave it all to me," I grumble, brushing a strand of crimson hair out of my face. Four year olds are useless. I sigh with exasperation at how muddy my clean skirt has become while washing the old one.

When I grow up, I think to myself firmly, *I will not have children. I will learn everything Gran and Mina know about herbs, everything Sarah knows about helping babies come. And whatever the men in the coven know, yes I'll learn that too. And when I walk by, people in the village will nod to me and drop their eyes as they do with Gran. And Annie and I will live right close to each other like Mina and Gran do and we shall play together whenever we like without anyone's aye or nay to decide for us.*

Chapter 2

The storm rocks the house. The big wooden doors shudder; the thatch roof hisses and trembles as if it would open into wings and escape into the thundering air. Easily, as if it were part of their conversation, Mina rises and takes the black handled knife from the sheath at her waist. I watch intently as she draws a circle around the house, making magical signs at every opening, narrowing my eyes until I can see the thin streams of blue fire trailing the blade. Is that blue fire the blood of the severed air? I know that the black dagger, the athamé, is one of a Witch's most powerful tools, but I still do not understand its workings. The coven never uses it to cut meat or bread; for fashioning magical tools and inscribing runes on stones and branches only the little penknife with a handle of white bone or shell can be used. Everyone in the Coven keeps the biolline or sgian dhu strapped to an ankle so it would be there when needed. But the athamé is worn at the waist, and never in public view.

"But what is it for?" I had asked Gran, "And why is it black?"

"From the black place in the mind where there is nothing comes the clear sharp edge of thought," Gran had replied.

Try as I would, I could not find any such black place in my mind.

"When the red rose blooms in your belly then the black place between your eyes will open as well," she assured me. I sighed. Would I never grow to womanhood and learn all the secrets that women know?

I turn my attention from the elusive black place in my mind back to Mina. She pulls the water bucket to the center of the room, lays the knife down before it. Her hands hover over the water like birds borne up by a current of air.

"Blessed be thou, creature of water." She takes a handful of salt and cups it reverently before letting it sift into the bucket.

"Blessed be thou, creature of salt." She takes up the knife, resting the blade flat across the fingers of both hands.

"Blessed be thou, creature of the Art." She brings the blade down to pierce the water. I shut my eyes and shiver, knowing the meeting of blade and water is powerful without knowing why.

As she stirs the mixture with a circular motion of the blade, the house shudders under the impact of rain. Inside, Mina sprinkles a gentler shower of salt water. It sizzles in the smoking hearth, clots in muddy balls on the hard dirt floor, sparkles off the pots and pans and hanging swatches of herbs. She flutters some through the air over Gran and gives me a mischievous splash. She slings open the door and hurls what remains in the bucket into the howling wind. She scatters three handfuls of grain after it, calling:

"Dear wind
Be not so wild
Take this grain
To feed thy child."

The wind gusts up more strongly than ever, seizing the grain before she can cast it. Then there is a great sigh, and it eases. The trees subside from wild tossing to a gentle rocking. The clouds still hover black and swollen with their burden of water, but the rain has ceased.

Mina stands sniffing the air, head cocked attentively as if the storm whispered to her. I realize, not for the first time, but with surprise, that she is taller than my Gran and that her face is as stern as a hawk in repose. It is just that her face is so rarely in repose; she laughs and jokes so much no one can keep solemn or awed about her, so it is easy to forget her power, whereas Gran is so dignified and quiet that even when I feel closest to her my love walks on eggs. Gran has but to clear her throat or slant her eyes sideways at me and a lump the size of a large toad will be squatting in my throat, eating my giggles before they can rise to my mouth. I am sure it is the same huge and hideously warty toad that lives under her doorstep.

Once when I asked why she kept such an ugly familiar she cuffed me and snapped, "Handsome is as handsome does!"

I burst into tears and ran out to hide in the fields. Remorseful, I brought the toad a small wriggling beetle and dropped it onto his lightning tongue. Gran came to the door. I handed her my peace offering of cornflowers and poppies and wild grasses. She smiled and bent to stroke the toad's carbuncular back.

"This Beval Spindleyshanks is teaching me the mysteries of old age," she said quietly. Beval sat quiet as a knob on a stone, entranced by the sun and my Grandmother's touch. A gray moth bobbled drunkenly out of a poppy. Beval did not appear to move, but with a flicker of wings and a flash of white maw, the insect was gone. "And how not to waste time," Gran added with satisfaction.

"Speaking of wasting time, Fiona—who do you suppose is milking the cow this evening?" I jump a sole and a palm into the air, startled that Gran has read my mind, embarrassed to have forgotten her admonition that I must cover and clothe my thoughts if I wish them not to be naked to her. Mina turns back nodding from her silent conversation with the elements.

"Aye, she will rage some more. Go now to your mother's house while the wind rests," she says.

I scuff my toe in the dirt, not wanting to leave. "But Mina— wait—I—why do you say 'creature of water' and 'creature of salt'? Is water really alive, are fire and air really creatures like animals, like cats and dogs and such?"

Mina gives Gran a secret smile.

"I believe the bairn is ready for the passage of water," she says.

"You'll spoil that child to death," grumbles Gran.

"Oh please, oh please!" I cry, hopping with excitement. I have no notion of what Mina is referring to, but I want it—anything that has to do with magic I want more passionately than berries in winter.

Gran can not quite hide her smile.

"As you see fit," she tells Mina.

"Now scat!" she growls at me, and I run home faster than any storm could ever chase me.

Chapter 3

Blessed be thou, powers of the East. Accept this noble sacrifice."

The sun streams into my hands, making the offering cupped there look like it is woven of gold. Slowly I turn to the South, then the West, repeating my invocation. The field of dandelions and marigolds shimmers under the shifting light. Surely the Gods are present.

"Blessed be thou powers of. . ."

Skirl of the North wind whirling out of the Cave of Glass, twisting like a serpent up from the earth's core. Raven and rock and the deep winter silences, She appears. Anu.

Gleaming crescent of the reaping sickle at her waist, the black-cloaked old woman folds her arms and narrows her eyes.

"What do you think you're doing?"

"I'm offering this dolly for the sacrifice," I say, handing her the doll assembled from the yellow flowers.

"That dolly's not the only thing that'll be sacrificed if you can't keep your mind on your work!" She takes the dolly as if to throw it, then gives it back to me.

"Where did you come by such a notion?"

I can only shrug meekly.

"I don't know."

As the anger leaves her, she seems to grow smaller, my Gran only, rather than the angry caller of winds and serpents.

"Well, this basket needs filling. When you're done, come help me with the moss."

I take my dolly apart, put it in the basket, and set to picking the yellow blossoms. Yellow dandelions and marigolds mixed with mullein make a good remedy for winter cough. Soon a pretty orange butterfly distracts me from my work. I follow it from flower to flower, softly, on my hands and knees, so as not to startle it. She does a little greeting dance around each flower before lighting and unfurling her long spiral tongue. As the butterfly laps beads of nectar the soft strands at the flower's heart reach out, stroking pollen on her belly. What good friends they are, the flowers and the butterfly. I don't want to pick any flowers she has visited, for fear she would mourn them. How nice to be a butterfly. . .

Clothes are easily shed; nose and chin, flat nipples and thighs and belly are soon wallowing in the blossoms. My tongue is not skinny enough to lap up the sweetness, but I feel the sun on my wings. . .

"Christ's rotting body!"

I jump up, trip over my feet and fall over. Gran clasps her hand to her brow.

"Standing stones, give me patience! Now what rite dost thou practice, that thou shouldst be gathering these flowers but instead thou art rolling in them?" Her exaggerated politeness makes me cower.

"I was pretending to be a butterfly."

"Aye, a very butterfly indeed, lighting on one thing, then another." She pulls me up by the arms and drags me over to the basket. "But tis an imrock* I require. One with a mind to its work." I put on my clothes quickly.

"Gran teach me this, Gran teach me that!" she mimics. "How canst I teach thee anything an' thou will not attend to it? Now it is not so hard, every third blossom. You can count to

---

*Imrock—an ant

three?"

Shamed, I nod. I'm a big lass of seven. I can count to thirty.

"Have this basket full and bring it to me in less time than it takes to boil water, or I'll find me another assistant."

I hurry through the field, muttering, "One, two, three, forgive me! One, two, three, forgive me!", decapitating every third flower that comes to hand.

Rushing into the woods with the filled basket, my haste turns tippy-toe when I see that Gran is digging roots, deep in concentration. As I move close to her, something turns over behind my eyes. When the dizziness passes I can see my Gran casting her mind out in ripples, like a bell without sound. Wherever the ripples touch the earth the dark ground becomes transparent as air, each web of root she seeks distinct to the finest hair. With a claw-shaped instrument called a griffin, she exhumes each root whole and uninjured. We have come seeking the elusive mandragora, but she takes other roots as well—comfrey, mallow, dock. The roots come from the earth easily. As each one emerges, the soil that cradled it again goes dark. She brushes the dirt away, puts the root to her forehead, mutters a prayer and places it in her basket. She pats the dirt back so the earth does not appear wounded and rests her hand there a moment as if to heal the place. Each rite takes only a few moments to complete, but her whole being is absorbed in it.

"Could I please try it?"

"No."

"Please, I can see them as well as you."

"I'd sooner let a mole run amuck in my garden. You'd be digging up everything."

The woods are too enchanting for my disappointment to flourish long. I find a flock of tiny mushrooms growing out of the cleft of a broken tree.

"Oh look, look at these! Might they not be good for something?"

Gran comes over to inspect my find.

"Aye, poisoning very small people." She cups my drooping chin in her hand.

"You can be of help. See this moss, growing about the north side of the oaks? Go and gather as much as you can."

Relieved that my bounce and supple bones have some use, I clamber happily up the trees, tearing off big clumps of the dry moss she desires.

"What's this for?"

"For blood."

"Stops bleeding?"

"No, it catches it."

"But what use is that?"

"Plenty of use, when you're grown to be a woman." Gran frowns at my look of puzzlement.

"I've told you; when you are grown the moon will open your womb. Once opened it will open every moon, and for a few days you will bleed. Unless you're with child."

"How long do you bleed?"

"Oh, a few days. When the time comes, I'll show you how to bind yourself up with a cloth and some moss."

"And do we use the blood for magic then?"

"It may be used for that. If you have no fit purpose for it, then we rinse the moss in the river and let the blood flow back to the sea, where all blood began."

"Blood began in the sea?"

"Keep picking the moss. Aye, all life began there."

"I thought the Earth was our Mother."

"Aye, and most of the Earth is water. Seen from the heavens, this world is as blue as a robin's egg." I do not ask how Gran came by this knowledge. If she says tis so, then tis so.

Gran arranges some cloth over all the baskets once we're done.

"Very well then. How shall we get these baskets home?"

"We'll have to walk," I say glumly.

"Aye, we'll have to walk. But we can lighten our load. Imagine I've just tucked a wee cloud into each of the baskets under the cloth. Imagine all you have to carry is the basket with a little cloud in it."

I start to lift them.

"It still feels heav—."

"Here now." She presses her forehead against mine. "Imagine what a cloud feels like—light, soft, the spirits of water are become one with the spirits of air. . ." Effortlessly the place between my eyes opens. Blue sky floating fat clumps of fluffy clouds streams into my skull. This time, the baskets lift much lighter.

"And now we sing a bit of a lightening song as we walk, and every word lightens our load," Gran says. "The wind pushes them here and there, the wind pushes them here and there, the clouds do no work, yet they travel everywhere. . ." Soon we are the clouds; a little wind comes up and pushes at our backs. I'm so happy, a small cloud traveling beside my grandmother cloud, who is dark about the edges, grumbling with thunder and occasional flashes of light.

In this way, with no more effort than one would make in a dream, we get to Mina's house.

"Ah, bless you," she cries when she pulls the cloth off the baskets containing the moss. "I thought I was done with this business last year this time."

"This is likely your last, so honor it," Gran admonishes. "I find I miss it."

"Ah, the red's too much trouble. I'm ready for the black," Mina responds. She sees a bruise on my arm. "Och now, who's playin' so rough?"

"She was turning into a butterfly. I had to pull her right out of the air."

"Oh, Ann!" Mina gets some salve and rubs it on my arm, clucking like a broody hen.

"You were never a child," she reproaches Gran, "that's why you have no understanding of them."

"Aye, and you never stopped being a child," Gran says darkly, "and never had any either. So dinna fesh me with this 'understanding'!"

Mina gives me a kiss on the forehead.

"Trot on home to yer mommy and thank ye for all yer hard work."

"Hard work and a copper horseshoe!" says Gran. "This child's mind is as scattered as a floatabout. I'll make a Priestess out of her when I've wove a hog's ear into silk."

My lower lip is trembling. I didn't think I was so bad as all that. Mina hugs me again.

"There now, Ann is just tired, run along then."

I close the door and scuttle underneath Mina's window.

"Yer too hard on that child, Ann. She means well—"

"If that bairn is to survive she must be strong. I have seen, Mina, I have seen—her innocence will kill her! If she learns not bending, and quickly, too, the world will break her!"

"Anu, Blessed Mother—leave the future be. It gives you no content to see it."

And it gave me no content to hear them talking. I ran—not to my croft—but to Annie's. Annie fears nothing, I think, not even Gran. Hanging by our knees from an apple bough in her mother's orchard, we munch stolen bannocks, trying to swallow while swinging upside down. Our giggles shake flurries of fragrant white blossoms into our skirts and hair. I don't care if I am a hog's ear, as long as Annie is the other one.

Chapter 4

In summer, entering Gran's croft is like walking into the inside of a giant herb packet; drying plants hung from the ceiling and bubbling potions and ungents steaming over the fire. In winter, her croft, like everyone else's, smells chiefly of mud. In such wet weather it is impossible even for one as neat as my Gran not to have the smell of the wet earth predominate.

Like most crofts, it contains but one large room. The bed is a pile of rushes matted together, with coverings and blankets on top. This is where she and I most often sit when we're sorting herbs or stuffing them into little packets. Two stools and a few sections of tree trunk are arranged around the small, bee-hive shaped hearth. A few cooking pots and utensils, and a chest containing clothing and blankets completes Gran's sum of visible possessions. The house is more pear-shaped than rectangular, the single door at the narrow end of the pear, the hearth at the other end. But it is not just the pear-shape of the croft that makes it different from the others. It bears a double thatched roof with a secret space within. This is where she hides her precious things like her magic book. Frequently now she sends me scuttling up the ladder to fetch whatever magical tools she needs.

Today she has charged me to fetch two white candles. I replace the secret trapdoor and kneel, waiting for my eyes to adjust, inhaling the dusty fragrance of old bundled reeds. A tiny opening under the eaves admits a small patch of filtered light. I feel, before clearly seeing, the candlesticks—some carved of different woods, a few of brass. Stacks and stacks of candles, most made during the three day fest of Bride[1]. Some are made with real beeswax which is so precious I have yet to witness a rite in which one was used. Most are tallow, sometimes mixed with crushed herbs to deepen their power. Beside the candles, a whole section of the secret space is filled with dried herbs wrapped tightly in bundles, the color or other sign on the cloth telling its contents.

My heart beats at the array of ritual objects. Unusual shells spilling over each other like Marianna's[2] treasure. A necklace made of the black elf-bolts, and another with white arrow tips the like of which I have seen no where else. Different colored crystals, the round white stones called moon-drops, and Ashtar's Eggs that are a peerless cure for barrenness in beasts or humans. A cloth shrine in the east corner contains a wealth of feathers, including an owl mask. A collection of beautifully carved wands look as if they are all John's work. I had once thought they all belonged to Gran, but when I touched them the picture of each one's owner came to me instantly. Gradually I learned that almost all of the coven's magical gear is stored here, though Mina holds the chalice, sword and cingulum used to cast the circle, as well as the calling conch and most of her own talismans. Mina relies on her ability to make things invisible for concealment. Gran seems not to want to put her trust in that art.

"There are some that see with their eyes that do not see with their hearts. May none such ever venture here, but I trust not to luck more than I need to."

Chief among my Gran's personal treasures is a black mirror-bowl used for scrying[3], resting on an intricately carved stand. Standing guard beside it are a pair of fancy hide boots that lace up nearly to the knee, lined with fur. And draping down from the upper part of the thatch, a hooded cloak decorated with white ermine tails. The cloth itself is faded purple. I wonder where she

---

1. Bride—Also known as Bridget, is the Celtic Goddess of poetry, smithcraft and healing, and of fire and water. She is honored at the Celtic festivel called Oimelc, or Bridget, celebrated around Feb. 2nd. 2. Marianna—Goddess of the sea. Mannanon MacLir is her mate and male counterpart. 3. Scrying—Seeing visions of past, present or future by gazing into water, flame, or a reflecting object.

came by it, for no one that I know kens how to get such a color from any of the plants in our district. It is reserved for the royal in any case, being as rare as it is. The Laird himself could not presume to wear such. As a younger child I used to fancy that cloak meant my Gran was really someone of the blood who for some reason fled a queen's life to live as a peasant. But while her bearing is that of a queen, I know that my Gran would never have left a life of richness and power. The cloak is only one of many of Gran's mysteries. My eyes linger longingly on heaps of unknown objects covered with cloaks which I dare not disturb.

In choosing two of the plain white tapers I cannot resist handling the beeswax ones. They smell so good, my mouth waters, thinking of honey. John says the tears of the sun are sweet, and it is sun's tears the bees gather when they visit the flowers. The moon weeps salt, the moon has wept the seas. Rivers, lochs and wells, veins of the earth, run with clear water.

"Salt, sweet and clear—we need them all for life. We could not live at all without the clear waters—but what is life without a bit of sweetness and savor?" asks John.

I like John. He is about Gran's age, red-faced and cheery, bluff and strong. He always has a kind word for any child and he speaks to me seriously when I ask him questions about magic. He is kin to Rose, and to the Laird himself; he has been in the coven since he was a boy. His wife, Maire, is not well enough to be in the coven; people say she went mad with grief after the death of their last child and has been strange and ailing ever since. But there is nothing sick or sad-seeming about John; he is as sturdy and solid as the oaks he loves. Part of his gift is that he sees shapes in branches.

"Just as if," he described to me, "I saw an animal frozen in ice and I had but to chip away the ice from its body to have it come alive."

One of his carvings crouches near my foot, a toad with a bumpy back which is the image, exact, of Gran's familiar Beval. A small sleeping cat, also carved by his hand, represents Mari's familiar, Questing. After a familiar dies, their carven image may serve as a link so that the familiar can be contacted in the spirit and asked to work for us again in that form. William's wand is his walking stick, the head of it carved like a ram. John has carved the form of a thistle at the top of his own wand. You have to look closely to see the snake under the thistle.

I take the candles and descend. Once the little hatch in the ceiling is shut the space cannot be distinguished from any other bundle of thatch. No one who had not seen it open could guess it was there. The ladder is naught but the trunk of a young tree with some of the branches left on, the sort of thing anyone might have in their woodpile.

Outside, the rain begins again. Gran holds her hands before the fire, massaging the slightly swollen knuckles. She hangs her small black kettle over the fire. The mixture of herbs wrapped in muslin darkens the water, sending up clouds of pungent steam. I like not the smell of it. Sharp scented evergreens and cohosh dominate over the more subtle scent of nettles and comfrey. She adds some tincture of pennyroyal. The stench of bruised leaves steeped in whiskey pervades the room. I would have to be very sick, I think, to consider taking this potion.

"Who's coming?"

"Jonet McCandless."

Hard to imagine Jonet coming to see Gran. She is one of the most faithful of the Papist Priest's followers. I try to picture the woman's face but see her always with her head bent; eyes cast down as she stands beside her husband; eyes cast down as she kneels to the Priest.

Gran sets the three-legged stool back beside the hearth, cozened in amongst the wood pile. She sits me down, folds my hands in my lap.

"Now," she says, "you must be still. Totally. . . . silent." She looks straight at me. Enormous black pupils swallow all but the thinnest ring of green around them. And I also am swallowed by that blackness, enveloped by a well of night-black sky. My heart almost stops in obedience to her command for silence. I have forgotten entirely how to make noise or move, no more capable of it than the stool on which I sit. Slowly she draws her gaze back from me. The enchantment is like a heavy sleep, yet my eyes and ears are open.

Palm outstretched flat before me she draws a curtain of black, gauzy material from the ceiling down to the floor. Deep as a shadow, but transparent, I know it is a fabric woven of her will only.

Gran pulls the other stool up to the wall near the flickering candle, a spindle wrapped with grey wool thread and a pair of shears in the basket beside her. At that moment I hear a woman scraping her feet outside the door. She stands there silently, afraid to knock.

Gran pulls long strands of wool from the spindle, holds it to her eye, measuring, winds some back. She makes no move towards the door. At last the woman—whose shadow I perceive as clearly as if it were but a curtain rather than a door she stood before—raps softly. Gran's eyes examine the yarn as if she were scrying from it.

"Come in," she calls gruffly.

The door opens; Jonet sidles in. Thin as she is, it is easy to see that she is with child. She twists her hands together, biting her chapped lips. Her eyelids are puffy and bruised-looking. She bows her head before Gran, scraping her feet in deference. At last she raises her head with a piteous look. Gran does not speak to her, nor does she gaze on her directly, but keeps her attention on the threads which she draws out, considers, and snips, the severed yarn dropping like grey worms back into the basket.

"I've brung some eggs," Jonet says. She withdraws the brown ovals from a deep pocket in her dirty black skirt.

"And a farthing—tis not enough, I know—I'll give ye more, I promise—but I need yer help now."

Gran continues her work. Jonet flushes a deeper red.

"I. . . ah. . . my legs." Jonet pulls up her skirt, revealing legs so swollen and purple there are no indentations to show the location of her ankles or knees. Her feet, wrapped in wet rags, look red and swollen also. "I'm past the third month but everything I smell sickens me—I can't hardly eat for myself," her voice sounds hoarse and teary. "I'll not survive it this time. I had eight...not my fault I lost all but three. The three I've got are not so very healthy. . . Lord knows what they'd do without a mother. I don't want to kill it but if it kills me 'twill die anyway—it's sucking the life out of me—Mother—I—"

"There does not have to be a reason for it. Sit!" Gran commands, pointing to a stump. The woman drags the piece of wood over and sits at the spot Gran indicates as if her legs could not have borne her for much longer.

"Have you the courage to do it then?"

"Havna choice," says Jonet. "I tried—I tried something my Ma told me about once but—it didn't work and—" she sighs, lifts her washed-out blue eyes to Gran's black ones. "Yer my only hope. Believe me, I'll pay what ye ask—it maybe takes me some time— I'll not forget it."

Gran gets up and nods to Jonet to give her the cup she carries on her belt, pours in some of the mixture she's been steeping over the fire and hands it to her. Jonet takes it to her lips.

"Let it cool!" snaps Gran. "We're not trying to burn it out."

"Will this do it then?"

"You're going to drink the contents of this whole pot now. And I'll give you a packet—" she fetches three packets from under her bedding, "—here. One of these tonight, one tomorrow morning and one tomorrow night. Boil it in water until it smells almost as strong as this does now. It won't get this strong, but close."

"I cannot do it tonight with my goodman home. He'd kill me if he knew."

Gran sighs with exasperation. "Well then, tomorrow morning and tomorrow afternoon before he comes home. Hopefully that will be enough. If not, the next morning after he leaves for the fields."

"But the harvest is in," whines Jonet, "He'll not go to the fields."

"Well, send him to fetch wood if he'll not go to the fields! What does the man do after harvest? He must do something besides threaten to kill his wife if she saves her own skin!" Gran snaps disgustedly.

"Perhaps I could send him for wood. Perhaps the Laird'll—I could tell him—some of the men have been doing some work for the Laird—I could ask him—for the money—because of the— baby and all."

"There's another matter," says Gran. "I don't want you confessing this to the Priest." The woman starts, splashing a little tea on the floor.

"It'll not work on the floor," says Gran. "Drink it now." The woman takes a sip, gags. "Oh Christ, Mother, must I drink it all?"

"Aye, the whole pot!" says Gran. At Jonet's look of reluctance she adds, "If you'd rather die in childbirth, the choice is yours. But waste not my time. For you're right you know. You will die if you continue with this confinement. And as I said, the choice is yours. It makes no difference to me."

Jonet drains the cup. Gran ladles her a second.

"I have an ungent for you as well," she says. She hands her a very small box. The contents smell even more foul than the beverage.

"Rub this around the mouth of your womb—and let not your husband come near you—tell him you're ill, tell him you have the pox, tell him whatever you need to tell him!"

"Mother. . . it smells so bad. . . he'll surely know."

"Have plenty of other smells in the house. I doubt me that Sean McCandless is so sensitive of nose as to know what is going on, providing you don't tell him with your trembling and looking all about the room as if you're just waiting for him to guess something is amiss. Now, about the Priest. I want your oath that you'll tell him not."

"But tis a sin," Jonet whispers, "I must confess it or I'll have no—hope of redemption."

"Christ's rotting body," curses Gran. "By the bloody palms." She stands up, shakes her head in disgust. She takes back the packets and the ungent and makes as if to throw the rest of the tea on the fire. "Die i' the faith then."

"I swear," says Jonet, "I swear. Please. Take it not away."

Gran thrusts the things back into her hands, sloshes some more tea into the cup. "If you are foresworn, be assured, this death shall find you. You understand?"

For a moment I think Jonet will pass out with fear. Instead she nods and chokes down the tea. Gran pours the last half cup.

"It is no sin to say no to a spirit that you cannot survive bringing forth," she says to Jonet, holding her gently by the shoulders.

"It is no sin Jonet."

Jonet swallows, casts her eyes down and nods. But I can tell that she believes it not. Gran also knows. She shakes her head. Her skin looks almost gray—perhaps it is only the curtain that gives it such a cast.

"Well then, may I serve you in any other way today?"

"Oh no. Oh no," says Jonet. "I give thee my thanks. I will do as thou sayest. Give. . . my. . ." she edges towards the door, struggling with the words, "thanks. . . to the Mother." she ends hurriedly, opens the door and shuts it after her.

Gran quickly makes a cross on the floor. For her I know it is the sign of the crossroads, the changing place that she invokes, and the Crone who rules it.

"Crone of the Crossing, Old Woman—Chooser of Paths—Turn aside any bitter fate. Turn aside any ill luck. Turn aside any ill chance. Turn aside any accident. Turn aside any fear." She makes motions at each of the four ends of the cross as she speaks the charm. I see the cross turn, bearing the wheel, following the motion of her hand.

"Choose for me a lucky path
Choose for me an easy path
Choose for me a sacred path
Choose for me an open path
Running free and clear."

She puts her palm down on the cross and rubs it in circles until the cross is erased and a circle stands in its place.

"So mote it be."

She covers the circle with the dried grasses carpeting the floor.

She comes up to where I am sitting, and with her other hand, her left hand, draws the curtain back up from the floor to the ceiling. I look to see if I can see that dark translucent fabric somehow hidden on her palm, thinking it would cling to her hand like a dark stain, but I see nothing.

Again I can move. I squeeze my hands together, trying to massage them back to feeling. Abruptly she knocks them apart.

"Dinna go wringing your hands together like that woman. Never, ever, ever. Keep your palms open," she says, holding my hands out, "and good fortune will fill them. Leave this wringing and praying and clasping of hands together for idiots and once-borns. The woman has not the mind of a sheep," she hisses, "not so much intelligence as a ewe."

I shake my head meekly.

"One wonders if humans were so stupid before Christianity or if Christianity has made them so. I seem to recall that at one time in the world there was more good sense than there is now. Perhaps my memory plays tricks on me. Perhaps not. I'm sure there has never been a time when there was *less* common sense in the world." She leans up against the wall and sighs.

"Put on a bit of fresh water," she requests. "We'll have a cup of reviving tea. Surely we deserve it."

I put on the water. She draws out a packet of herbs from under the bed for me to add to it. I wash out the other pot outside. The rain is coming down slowly so I am not too soaked by the time I get back in. I pour the tea into our cups. We sit together drinking it. The very first sip makes me feel awake. The second sip tingles my fingers. The third goes down to my toes.

"Ahhh," we sigh together.

"Did you understand that?"

I nod.

"When you're of age I'll teach you how not to conceive until it's your time to have bairns. For women may choose these things and you will know how to choose. You will never be—as that poor wretch is. Not unless," she laughs, "you're a great deal more stupid than I suppose you to be." I shake my head no.

"Your mother chooses to fill her womb whenever she can. Of course, she has the health for it," she sighs. "I don't understand it. Your mother had such promise when she was your age—ahh, they say the gift skips a generation—I suppose it is too much to hope for to have a daughter who follows you—but I am well pleased to have a grand-daughter. So perhaps it is well for her to bear as many as she can for perhaps there will be more in her brood that have the use for the art which she has not."

Chapter 5

The corn dolls dance and pirouette in the air, as far above the snow-powdered ground as our chapped fingers can hoist them. The rags wrapped around our hands make us more awkward, but our fumbling and stumbling only makes us more drunk with glee. Even my sister Eostre, normally sober and self-contained, is giggling uncontrollably, weaving and slamming up against Annie and Sean and me. Elana clings to Annie's hand; she is small for a two year bairn and is so lost in Annie's voluminous skirts I forget she is there until we tumble into the croft.

Baby Colin lets out a delighted squeal when he sees us, thundering over on all fours to tug on my skirt. I scoop him up in one arm and have my hands full to keep him from grabbing my precious dollies. Mother is sitting on a bench before the fire, her blond hair hanging loose to her waist, face as pink as the new lacy frock the Laird had given her. The Laird hugs her close; his green and yellow tartan draped around him makes him look so grand. He smiles at our invasion, his teeth white and straight, his eyes blue, hair as blond as Mother's.

The smell from the big black pot over the fire is wonderful. It's so fine to come home to this; the fire snapping in the hearth, the soup steaming, the warmth of those two together. Our croft is not smoky like most, for the Laird built us a chimney of mud bricks that sucks the smoke right up. Most crofters have but a hole in the roof and live murky in winter. My father must have planned to sire many bairns; our three room croft is one of the largest in Glen Lochlan. But when I was two and Eostre but new born he left to visit his family to the south and returned no more. Whether he fell to brigands or illness or other mishap we never knew.

No one in the family spoke of it, but I knew from village talk that my mother had borne a son to the young Laird when she was but fourteen. She was too young to bear; the child died and she nearly lost her life as well. Gran forbade her to see the Laird after that, but when my father disappeared four years later she took up with the Laird as if there had never been parting or grief between them. I always called him 'the Laird' for everyone called him that, but I had no memories of any father but he.

Elana solemnly holds out her wee doll for the Laird's inspection. Sarah had given her a scrap of wool to keep it warm. Elana's mouth purses in concentration as she unwraps her wee bairn for the Laird's approval.

"You make fine babies," he praises her, "as your Mother before you."

She looks at him with solemn gray eyes.

"Bess," she lisps.

The Laird holds his hands over the dolly in benediction.

"By the gracious will of God and his Mother, so shall your bairn thrive."

"I had not thought to be made a grandmother so soon!" says Mother. "Come sit on my lap so I may see her—tis a girl is't not? Ahh—so bonny she is—fair like her wee mother."

Elana snuggles contentedly in Mother's lap, Sean offers his sun doll to the Laird. One of the simplest dollies to weave, it is nonetheless as ratty as a last year's bird nest. The Laird laughs in a friendly way at the straws poking awkwardly out from the sphere.

"Tis a fiery sun indeed—what a fireball you'll be lad, we'll be hard put to keep up with you," he ruffles Sean's ducked head.

I cannot think of any one less like a fireball than Sean; he is so slight and shy, more a shadow than the fire that casts it. I give the Laird my gift—the simple braided corn dolly that looks like a small broom, but holds Mother, Maiden and Crone in her design.

"These are fine," he says, holding Sean's sun in one hand and my braid doll in the other. "I shall hang these over the Great Hearth in my Hall, and so the Goddess and the God shall reign there, yet none will be the wiser. For if any do ask, I shall say that they are but toys my children made for me. No one would deny a man a token of his children's love. Now remember—" he whispers conspiratorially so we all giggle, "if any ask we shall say your arts be all in fun—none but us shall know the truth of it."

"Annie made the best of all," I say. She displays her sun with its perfect spokes, and a complicated spiral dolly that represents the spinning whirlwind at the heart of all things. She shrugs and slips them quickly back into the lining of her cloak, examining one of her long black braids as if the pattern there were far more interesting than anything she could make.

Sean presents the little straw heart he made to my Mother. I quickly offer mine.

"I made mine first and he copied it," I say. His shoulders slump and he looks so small and forlorn that I immediately regret it. He is the Laird's only legitimate son, but his mother died soon after he was born and he lives alone in a cold room in the castle. Sometimes I think it would be fine to have my own room like that, but when I snuggle with my sisters at night I feel sorry imagining him shivering in his big bed by himself. Mother pulls him toward her and hugs him—I see his face color under the white-gold of his hair. Mother praises both our gifts, cuddling him and smiling at me, and I feel happy.

Eostre is only six, but her braided dolly is woven tighter and neater than mine.

"Mine shall go over *our* hearth," she says.

"Help her put it up lad," the Laird says to Sean.

"I'll do it myself—tis *my* hearth, not his!" asserts Eostre. She stands tiptoe on the stool to fix it in place, walks back from the hearth to survey her handiwork and nods with satisfaction.

"Mine is the best."

"Annie's is the best!" I say.

"Annie the best," chimes Elana. Elana adores Annie, has followed her like a puppy since the time she could crawl.

"Might we put your dollies on our door, or will you be wanting them for your mother's croft?" Mother asks.

Annie shrugs, "Oh, you can have them if you want. I could have made better but I had to help Elana."

It troubles me that Annie seems not to hear when we praise her. Already she makes all her own clothes, yet when Mother compliments her needlecraft she makes that indifferent shrug of her shoulders saying, "Tis good enough for the likes of me." Perhaps if scolding Mairead were my mother I'd be as deaf to the opinions of others as Annie seems to be.

"By the God that is seed and our gracious Mother the Earth, blessed be this food and all our company," the Laird says.

Mother sits at one end of the table, the babe in her lap holding her breast in one hand and a hunk of bread in the other. The Laird sits at the other end, and the warmth flowing over the table between them makes it like sitting between two hearths.

"How I dread this visit from Ross and Lindsay," the Laird says. "What a bitter bargain to trade this cozy house for a cold hall and talk among men." He sighs and raises his glass to mother.

"A fortnight of this bitter business before I come home again."

When I dare, I make faces at Annie and Sean across the table. I neither know nor care what the Laird's business is. He says something about a sickness the sheep have.

"Did William say anything about the sheep when he brought your goats by this evening?"

"No, but he had a long face," Mother replies.

"I wonder if William is getting too old to care for them. But his son is an idiot, and I'll not have an idiot minding my sheep." He turns to Sean, ruffles his head fiercely with his palm.

"How would you like to learn shepherding?"

Sean looks at his plate.

"I'm going to be a smith."

The Laird laughs.

"Tis an honest profession at least. In truth lad, iron's more fitting for a man's hand than corn husks. Leave the dollies to the girls next time and perhaps young Ewan will be kind enough to teach you a bit of his craft. He's scarcely more than a lad himself, but give him a year and he'll be as fine a smith as his father."

"God rest his soul," whispers Mother.

The Laird cuffs Sean playfully on the shoulder.

"Make me a horseshoe next year and I'll put *that* over my hearth." He turns back to my mother.

"That damn Priest has been after me to tell my men not to put horseshoes over their barns! Can you imagine? I told him I could not remember the commandment that says a horse's foot is an evil thing." He mimics the Priest's whine, " 'Tis not a horse's foot, but a female pudenda that men think of when they put a horseshoe over their barn.' "

"*I* said," he takes a quaff of ale, quite enjoying the telling of it, " 'Father, would I had so much pleasure going in and out of my barn—I would put thirty horseshoes about the door!' "

Mother blushes. So does Sean. I can't see what relationship a horseshoe has with a woman's parts, or what's in it to blush about.

The Laird laughs so much that he grows red as well. He runs his tongue along the top lip in a way that says that he likes my mother blushing. He takes another drink.

"I'm going to build that Priest a wee kirk. He's like a snail without a shell. Then he'll have enough on his hands caring for his own place and not go worrying about what my good folk put on their barns and over their hearths. Keep him busy—that's the way to handle his kind."

His tone drops as he becomes more serious.

"The Separationists have gained so in the south some say they will drive the Papists clear from these shores. But I doubt it. Not that it would grieve me if the gloomy crows all departed, but if the old Priests are crows, these new Priests I hear are more like carrion birds. They have not even the grace to worship Mary. How would they have men be born without women to bear them?"

He clasps Sean's hand.

"Learn well your Latin and your ciphers, but trust not what the Priest says of women. A man who dwells not with women has no understanding of them." He shakes his head.

"Would that the minds of Priests would be as open as the sky wherein God dwells."

"God does not live in the sky," I say.

"Where does he live?" asks the Laird.

"In the big oak tree in the meadow. He does, I saw him there!" I insist to the Laird's amused smile.

"Did you lass! And how did you know him?"

"He had horns on his head."

"A deer," says Sean.

"No! A man with horns, but he turned into a deer and bounded off when he saw me."

Seeing a fight brewing, the Laird lays a conciliatory hand on each of us.

"The God may dwell in many places. Would I were as a God, that I might dwell in two places at once. Then could my heart rest here always." He sighs, caressing my mother with his gaze.

"Easily I could suffer Priests and nobles with my mind, could my body and heart be always here."

Mother gets up and puts the baby to bed in her room. The Laird rises.

"To bed, my pretty ones."

Sean sulks.

"Tis early yet."

"Your mother and I are going for a walk. When we return, all must be clean and all of you tucked in."

"It *was* a deer," Sean hisses as soon as they are out the door. I start to circle him like an angry cat. He shrinks back.

"I cannot fight a girl!"

"I'll not be doing these dishes by myself!" snaps Eostre.

Sean sits with his arms folded.

"That's girl's work. Besides, 'tis *your* croft, not *mine*,'" he mimics. We girls all look at each other.

"There's a bad smell in here," snips Annie. As one we tilt our noses in the air and march outside to wash the trencher boards. We get silly over the washing and spend a long time dropping trenchers in the mud and washing them all over only to drop them again. When we return, Sean has laid another chunk of peat on the fire and swept the dirt floor clear. We make peace and lie all together giggling until the grown ones return and we dare giggle no more. I drift off to sleep, soothed by the crackle of the fire in the other room and the Laird's voice. I can make out few words, but just before sleep I hear him say clearly, "Ah, dear Anna, on such a night I am the happiest man alive."

Later I wake, startled by a cry that was not owl or cat. But it is only my mother's love cries. I turn over smiling and fall back asleep.

Chapter 6

At last the day has arrived for the first passage into my training as a Witch, the Passage of Water. It is a brilliantly sunny day, my heart radiant and expanding as the sky. Larks singing, "Fiona Fiona," welcoming me. The trees are sparkling. Not much wind but I can hear them whispering anyway, "Welcome, welcome." Each one of them acknowledges me, sends me a wave of recognition, warm as fur, and I send an answering wave of warmth to swirl around each trunk. The forest is a song; each plant and tree a note, all playing together. Huge crowds of tree and bush beings saluting me and paying attention to me as I walk by on the path that runs along beside M'hira, the river that flows into Loch Inbhir.

Mina trudges along ahead of me, panting, her walking staff leaving little depressions in the moist earth. Frequently she stops, takes out a handkerchief, mops her brow and puts her hand to her chest.

"Go ahead, fly away from me. See how far you get," she grumbles. "This heart wants to be the heart of a bird instead of a hu-

34

man."

She has admonished me to keep solemn silence, so I do not speak—yet within that silence, everything is speaking to me. The grass that I walk on is willingly bowing itself down to the ground so I can pass over without hurting it. The rocks are smiling at me from under the glossy skin of the water. The sibilant murmurs of M'hira as she polishes the stones, swishes by the rushes—the croaking of frogs:

"Here comes Fiona."

"She here?"

"Here comes Fiona."

Sudden streams of birdsong from the woods—cuckoo, mockingbird, oriole and finches splashing their songs like bright yellow and red color into the blue silence of the sky. The loop of a grass snake slides over a tussock of grass and winds down into an invisible crevice. The stalks of grass quiver here and there—mice and voles—nothing is quiet in this silence.

The walk is long, slow enough to accommodate the pace of Mina's erratic heart. Over a bit of a rise and we are there. The large emerald pool at the bottom of the main falls gleams; above it, a smaller pool brims just out of sight, though sprays of white foam from the upper crest of falls are visible. Mina stops, fanning herself with a fern. The cloth she uses to mop off her neck and face is limp with perspiration.

"I was a great walker when I was young," she says bitterly.

Her hair is straggling down from its knot. She takes a bristle brush from the purse at her waist and brushes it smooth, still vain of its length though it is now all gray. I never see her with it long like this except on coven nights. I watch, fascinated, as she begins to take off her clothes. I've never seen her naked and don't know if it's polite to look, so I turn my eyes away, sliding them back to peek when I think she's not looking at my looking. Her long pendulous breasts almost graze her navel; the flesh on her back bulges and sags but the muscles beneath look still firm. The hair covering her cleft is still golden brown as her head must have been once—just the edges of the triangle curling white and gray.

Naked, she walks over to the pool, stepping gingerly over stones. She swirls the middle three fingers of her right hand in the water, saying, "Bless me Mother, for I am thy child." She touches the water to her feet, cleft, her navel and breasts, her mouth and the place between her eyes, and then dives into the water. I gasp, never having seen anyone do such a thing. Young Jack Turner died last year playing at stepping stones—slipped and fell and was carried away by the current.

Standing at the edge of the pool biting my lip I hold my breath, fearing that she will not come up. Suddenly she bobs to the surface, and the way she pops up reminds me of selkies* I've seen off the coast in Loch Inbhir where they come sometimes for the mussels and clams on the rocks off the point. She flashes me a smile of wickedness and delight, swims over to the falls, stands under the water snorting and sputtering and shaking like a wet dog—and dives back into the green pool. I watch now with delight as she twists and turns in the water, the sun sparkling off the whiteness of her body. She seems so graceful and at home there, as if it were much easier for her to be swimming about like a fish than it was for her to be walking up here huffing and puffing and mopping her brow. I could almost imagine her as a woman my mother's age, so strong and sure she seems to be as she coasts, first on the water, then diving under it, then up again. At last she floats, lying on her back on top of the water, her hair streaming around her like a gray water wort. She wiggles her fingers in the water, releasing a sigh of satisfaction. Just barely paddling with her hands and feet she comes back to where I am.

"Och. Fetch me my plaidie." I bring it to her—she bunches it up so she may sit comfortably on the pebbles bordering the pool.

She says, "Very well then. Off with yer clothes and in with you."

I take my clothes off quickly, excited that I will get to do this wonderful thing. My skin prickles a bit with goosebumps—how much from the chill mist of the falls and how much from excitement tis hard to distinguish. Mina nods. I try to dive in as I saw her do—but I scrape my knee on the pebbles and the water comes up my nose. Thrashing and waving all around, the more I thrash the more I go right down under and the water is up my nose again. Before I can get my mouth clear to call for help, her arms are under me, pulling me out. I'm sputtering, snuffling, coughing.

---

*Selkies—seals

"She tried to drown me!" I cry. Mother has always warned us never to go in the water, especially so since Jackie was lost. After I finish sputtering, Mina regards me calmly, brushes hair out of my face.

"This is the Passage of Water. You must trust the water."

How can I trust it when it comes up my nose and tries to choke me? She looks at me, brown eyes ringed with gray.

"We think of ourselves as being of the earth, yet most of us is water and we grow in water in our mothers' wombs. The power of the fish is the first passage a growing human knows—and this is why this is the first passage we teach. Find a black stone."

It takes some looking, most here by the pool are white or gray.

"Now, close your eyes and put all your fear into the stone. And put all yer Mommy has told you into the stone, and put all that you have heard anywhere about water harming you into the stone." And so I concentrate very hard, eyes shut tight as my hands. The stone seems to grow heavier and colder in my hands as I fill it with my fear.

"Now! Cast it, be free of it!"

I cast it into the middle of the pool. Instantly I feel lighter, my shivering quiets.

"Now," she says, "come with me." She holds my hand and leads me into the pool. When it is waist deep to her and chest deep to me, she lifts me and holds me floating on the surface on my back.

"All right, now let your legs go, let your arms go. Let your spine relax. The water wants to bear you up. The water loves you. Feel the love of the water, feel how it wants to bear you, how willing it is to bear you as a mother bears her child."

I feel the comforting pressure of her hands, one on the middle of my back, one on my thighs just below my buttocks, holding me up. Then I begin to feel how the water itself wants to hold me, almost as if there were many hands coming up from the water. Gentle caress of the water spirits, friendly and welcoming as the spirits of the woods. So free and light, this floating. And the pool is depthless no longer; my body sending echoes down through the darkness, mapping the hidden patterns of rock point and crevice, a part of me that can feel how many fish there are moving and darting about, catching smaller fish, tadpoles, dragonfly nymphs. . .

"Open your eyes."

Mina's voice seems far off. I open my eyes and see the sun shining down on me, shining into the pool—turn my head a bit and see that Mina is still at the edge of the pool and I've drifted almost clear to the other side, borne up by the water. Happiness—the water does love me.

She says, "Keep floating and remember the time you were a bairn in your mother's womb."

I close my eyes again and float. The water seems not a bit cold now, warm as if the sun's rays could go all through it rather than just skimming the surface. I remember being embraced in every part of me, and having no real sense of my parts but only of floating and dreaming—voices come dimly—my mother, singing songs—my gran—and the touch of my gran's hand outside the chamber where I floated and dreamed—and the Laird's voice it seems—or am I confusing that familiar voice with the father I do not remember? Another sound, not quite a voice, not a human voice—the voice of the water. The swish and thud of my mother's heart—and more than that, the swish and thud of my heart, and the heart of the water—waterfall pulse echoes through my being as I float, in the closed womb chamber, in the open pool. And again I know myself as a wee bairn about to be born, feeling how the water cares for me and gives me my growth and my birth.

A river otter pokes its sleek head up beside me. No, tis Mina again! I laugh to see her shift shape. She winks and dives back down, popping up again in that playful way otters do.

"Now keeping your head out of water, turn over and begin to paddle—you've seen dogs—there's no reason a bairn cannot swim as easily as a dog providing they're not frightened out of it."

She helps me turn over on my belly—I swallow a bit of water, but not into my lungs. Now I am paddling about—ahh, free to go whither and hither I list! Over to this rock then over to the next, close to the falls and then paddling away. A game of tag with Mina—I have never played so with her—tis like being with Annie, with one of my own age. She splashes me and I splash her back and we go paddling all about. I can near feel my hands and feet becoming flippers.

She says, "All right now, stopper up your breath." I know not quite what she means.

"Here, take the deepest breath that ye can. Now keep your mouth shut and imagine your nose is shut and ye'll not breathe through it a bit." She dunks her head under and comes out again on the other side of me.

"See now? That's good, that's very good. Ye keep holding the breath the whole time yer under the water—when ye come out ye release it and breathe in again."

I take a breath and duck my head under and quickly take it out again, shaking it.

"Now, when you do this, kick with your legs and go down, go down to the heart of M'hira's pool."

I start to feel a little afraid again.

"You will always come back up—you float, girl. There are some that don't. But you have the nature for it and the water will always bring you back up again. You need only to remember to breathe air and not water."

I take another breath and try again and again to dive as she describes, but tis hard—as she says, the river bobs me up again so quickly I cannot go deep. She swims over to the edge.

"You keep trying, I'll dry out my bones a bit. I'm not so young as you. Try opening your eyes under the water—see what you can see."

Next time I take a breath and duck my head under I look all about—there I see a great fish rising towards me, so large that I hurriedly take my head out of the water. The salmon rises up and his back crests in the water right beside me—and then he goes down and I go down too, with my eyes open, following him. Suddenly it is easy, moving down, down through the dark parts of the pool, following him down. He vanishes in the peat-stained depths, but in that instant I become him, my back cresting and thin, my sides smooth and glistening, my feet merging into a tail and my hands into fins—the urge takes me to go up the waterfall, knowing not why but seized with fierce yearning to go up and up, somewhere to go back to, a place that I want to return to so much—as if I could go back farther and deeper than the womb of my mother if only I went up and up the falls. . .

Bursting out of the water I hurl myself up on the falls and begin grabbing for the rocks, pulling myself up against the force of the water. The water battering me back down to pool, pushing myself up and up against it, unable to breathe, current pouring down through me like thunder yet I keep fighting it and move up the cataract.

"I will get back I will get back I will get back I must get back. . ." Then there's not just the water but hands prying me off the rocks and dragging me away.

"No no no! I will get back I will get back!" I cry.

Then I'm out on the grass gasping for air. Yet the air seems not right, as if I wanted to breathe the water, not knowing any more what I can breathe and what I cannot breathe. At length my lungs accept the air, my gasps grow less choked; the trees begin to slide back into focus. Mina beside me, laughing and shaking her head.

"I never saw a bairn take to the water like *that*."

I glare at her.

"I'm not a bairn. I'm a fish."

"Ohhhh—and what sort of a fish do you be?" she asks politely.

"I'm a salmon. A king salmon. And this is my kingdom and I'm going back to it."

She puts her hands over my eyes and says in a very clear bell-like voice, so unlike hers, "Fiona." And I am Fiona again, wondering what sort of dream I have just had about being a fish that was so real to me.

"You have taken a noble ally," Mina says. "The salmon is your power beast of the water. A more powerful ally you could not ask for. You have power with the salmon now, and they have power with you also."

I remember Gran taking me into the woods and telling me the same thing; that all of the woods, every bush and plant and tree, was there willing to be my friend and ally, but there would be one family in particular that of all the plants would aid me more than any other. She asked me not to look for it, but to let it look for me. So I walked along, with her following. At first I was anxious, not knowing what I was expected to do. Her saying, "Do nothing. Allow yourself to be chosen." I continued to walk until there was a group of plants that drew me—when I walked by they began shining with a silver light and I was so drawn by the light that I went over and knelt naked among them all, breathing their scent. My Gran handed me the little sickle she had made for me. At first I was loath to take any of their lives—yet it seemed that by taking their lives I would be giving them some of mine and there would be no loss for anyone. So I cut a portion of them, leaving most to stand. As I sniffed them, Gran knelt beside me and asked, "How do these plants wish to serve you?"

"They want to sleep with me at night. They want to guide my dreams."

She nods.

"Aye. Mugwort. The dream-herb. You have chosen and been chosen well."

Returning to the present, I see Mina, head cocked, watching me attentively, and I realize that her thoughts have journeyed with mine.

"When the mugwort chose me it was to aid my dreams—I sleep with them every night." I do not add that I often have dreams I do not understand.

"What is the salmon for?" I ask.

"Tell me. How is the salmon your friend? What does the salmon have to teach you?"

I think again of my desire to go up the waterfall, feeling powerfully how I would not let anything stop me, that I would attempt it again and again until I reached the upper pool, perhaps beyond that.

"I want to go back. I want to go back."

"You want to go back to..."

"To before I was born. To wherever I came from—really. Before I was in my mother's belly."

Mina nods.

"You have chosen and been chosen well."

I want to go back in the water, but Mina says, "Another day. You're water-logged enough for one day. And besides, I have some fine white-meat and pea bread and a few dried apples—almost the last of the lot but soon we'll have plenty of ripe."

We sit and eat the bread and cheese and dried apples in silence. Again we are surrounded by all the sounds made by frogs and birds, the whispering of bushes, the mice in the grass; the rush of the falls dominating over everything else, sweeping it along. And I hear the fish, too, though they make no sound that my ear can hear, there is some eye in me now that sees below the surface of the pool to the trout and salmon and the smaller fish that are their prey.

Mina says, "Aye, ye have the vision. Clearing vision, Anu has that. You're her child."

I feel so proud to hear her say I'm Gran's child and have the vision that she has, and proud that she can see it in me so soon after I started to see it for myself.

"With Gran—I can see the roots that she digs, too. I can see the earth clear when she's doing it."

"Aye, ye have the art, in plenty. Glad we are to see you again, and to be working these arts with you again."

"What's the next passage?"

"Och so ready you are for all. Ye wish ye could have every bit of knowledge we have, all wrapped up in a ball and given to you. Then you'd swallow it whole, would ye not?" I nod enthusiastically.

"And choke on it too!" she laughs. "Nay, and it comes in bits and pieces not all at once. It comes as you are ready for it. You've done well with the passage of water. That is the first. That is the test that the seven year bairn faces. Tis as I said to you before; you come into this life out of the water, and the young bairn still has a strong memory of it. The next passage will be the passage of fire, but that will not come until you are older. After your first blood and after you have some—" she pauses, "—knowledge of men. Then will come the passage of fire. And it may take seven more years, or twice seven, for you to be ready for the passage of earth. That comes after you have borne your first child. Or, if you're like me and bear no child, then when you are twice the age that you were when you received your blood. I had to wait much longer than your Gran for that reason, for she wasted no time having bairns."

"How many did she have?"

"Three. Three but—your Mother was the only one to come to be fully grown. And there's sad talk there, so let's leave it be." Mina never likes to talk of anything sad.

"The next one must be air."

"Aye, air is the last. Air is the last, and that one, that one comes not until ye've stopped yer blood altogether. And again, as usual, Anu was a bit ahead of me. But she's training me, and soon I'll be floating as well as she."

"Floating? On air?"

As soon as I said it I stopped, remembering a time when I had come to Gran's house and opened the door without knocking. She was kneeling in a circle she had made, bounded with feathers and smoking herbs—floating, perhaps as much as a foot off the ground. I had slammed the door on my memory as quickly as I had on the sight. I look at Mina and see her acknowledging my remembering.

"Aye. We have ways of forgetting what we are not ready to see." She gives me her little scrunched up nose smile that makes me think that she can be only a few years older than I.

"Can you—learn to be like a bird?"

"In the spirit, aye. And long before your blood will stop you may travel as light as any bird—and not only to anywhere on this earth—but *through* the earth." Mina stops and I see her looking at me, trying to judge if I'm ready to hear what she has to say.

"Please. Please tell me."

"We'll do some of that flying—back to before you were born— but that will come later—that's not for a bairn your age. So forget that I said it for now. There are many arts of air. Floating— that is but one and often the latest to come."

"Is it floating that we learn for the earth and the fire as well?" I shake my head. "No, it could not be. . ."

"No, not floating. For all the passages, the art is to become one with the element, however that may be accomplished. The passage of earth must be taken down under the earth, into the earth. Into the barrows. And that is a powerful passage where you learn the mysteries of death and rebirth. And that is why, if your womb is ever to quicken—you must go through that quickening and birth first before you will be ready for that passage. A woman who has borne children," she says, licking her lips and looking away, over the river, "loses many of her terrors."

"Is that true?" I ask, thinking of some of the women in the village who have borne many children, yet carry the scent of a sheep being led to slaughter each time they are again with child.

"I mean not the once-borns," she says. "I mean for a Priestess it is, a path. A path of opening."

"Then why did you have no children?"

"It was not the best choice I could make," she replies simply.

"There are other paths, as many paths as Priestesses, as many paths as the Goddess has faces."

"And what about the passage of fire?"

"Ah—that one—there's no describing it until you're in it. The way to be one with fire is through passion. That will come to you, in its time. And that time is *not* now," she adds firmly.

"Ahhh," she stretches.

We both put on our clothes. She picks up her staff. I place both my hands on her staff and lean my forehead up against it. I look into her eyes.

"Thank you."

She smiles, a halo of light softening her face.

"My privilege. My pleasure."

Chapter 7

This time, I lead. Usually it is Annie who leads, scampering ahead of me. But today we move slowly, as I attempt to recapture the pace at which Mina had led me along the river M'hira to the emerald pool. I stop where I think I remember Mina having stopped, for though it seemed that she stopped along the way only to quiet her heart, it may be that her stopping had another meaning. And so I pause and watch the brilliant dragonflies darting along the stiller edges of the river and hear again the frogs, this time croaking Annie's name:

"Roxanne. Roxannabel. Douglas. Roxanne. Roxannabel. Douglas."

A bee becomes tangled in my hair, and so I stand still for a double purpose, calming my fear that she might sting me, and sending calmness so that she will find a way out of the crimson tangles that she has mistaken, as have other bees, for a flower. She whizzes off without stinging me, and we proceed again, keeping solemn silence. I am astonished again at how much I hear when I am silent. Annie picks up a flat stone and skims it to the other bank. I turn and glare at her, narrowing my nostrils in an expression of disapproval. She looks down, accepting my rebuke.

Suddenly the sky darkens, almost as dark as if I were in a barrow. I see myself holding a standard before me, bearing a hawk with outspread wings—or is it perhaps the head of a strange snake with wings? Serpent or hawk, its metal body becomes animated in the night air, the rustle, very faintly, of feathers, coursing before me. And behind me, a long serpent line of silent humans, no more noise than the occasional scraping of a leather-thonged foot over a stone. And on my brow, the strange snake with swept-back wings. Breath of warm air paints the thin veils I wear against my breasts, the bell of my stomach.

We reach the emerald pool of M'hira and I turn and see that the procession following me is only Annie. She glances at me with something approaching awe, then turns her eyes down to the ground. It is again a sunny day, pierced with an occasional loop of birdsong. My breasts are flat. Yet still the ghost-print of the crown weighs on my brow and I feel as if I should keep my hand cupped to keep the standard aloft, though I know it does not exist in this time. I make a gesture as if I were planting it in the ground. A gust of faint breeze ruffles the wings sweeping up from my temples. The eyes I look through are the eyes of a hawk, the eyes of a hooded snake that I have never seen, and yet know, deep in every part of my body.

Annie comes and kneels before me, places her right hand over my womb, her left on the ground between my feet.

"Priestess," she begins, "I request that you instruct me—" she pauses and I see that she is also gripped by the memory of some deep rite, "—instruct me in these rites—" she looks up at me, "—of knowledge and rebirth which thou hast. I have purified myself in the temple of the nine maidens and there is no blood-guilt on me."

"The wings of the cobra are open to enfold you, daughter of lions."

The ritual phrase slips out of me in another language, yet I know the meaning of it, and I know that she knows also. A gust of dizziness loosens my knees; I kneel beside Annie and take her in my arms, feeling the raith of the Priestess who has been speaking through me towering above us. I feel suddenly unequal to the task of teaching anyone anything. I huddle with Annie, wanting to be one with her, not wanting the separation of me standing and her kneeling, me teaching and her learning. She hugs me fiercely; I feel her nails through the tartan shawl on my back. Daughter of lions. . .

"Tell me about. . . this passage of water," she whispers.

My memory returns to the initiation Mina had performed with me a few days before. I repeat every word that I can remember her speaking to me. Annie draws a long quavering sigh and removes her clothes, preparing to enter the water.

Rather than let her dive in unprepared, I wade out with her and help her to lie on her back, amazed at how effortlessly I can hold her stretched out upon the water. Already the water bears her while I merely guide her to the proper position from which to receive the water's support. Her black hair streams over my wrists and arms. I am not tall enough to guide her very far into the water. I describe how she should move her hands and feet and stretch out on the water beside her to show her how easy it is. At first she lies too rigidly on the water and begins to sink and thrash.

"Stand in the water and watch me."

She runs her hand along my back to see how I am holding it. Then she lies in the water and very cautiously moves her hands and feet enough to buoy herself up and move about a bit. I float beside her. Noticing her clenched jaw I nudge her.

"Look not so serious! Tis fun." She swallows but her expression remains one of rigid concentration. Without Mina's grace, but with determination to be as like her as I can, I turn over onto my belly and dive under Annie, knocking into her as I emerge on the other side. She looks at me, startled. I splash water in her face. She's angry, looking at me as if I had performed sacrilege, as I had glared at her earlier on the path. As she thrashes over to hit me she of course flounders face first into the pool.

She panics as she comes up, kicking; sharp toenails gash my shin. She lurches over and throws her arms around me; then we're both under water. Her panic hammers in my heart as I struggle to unwind her arms from my head. She seems determined to use me as a stepping stone from which to launch herself to land. At length, desperate for air, I punch her midsection and push away. Her head comes up from the water, hair matted over her eyes, blind, desperate look on her face—

"Annie, Annie, relax, remember—" I call, paddling away from her so she cannot grab me again, "—follow me. Just paddle like a dog—think how a dog would do."

She begins a churning dog-paddle towards the sound of my voice.

"That's good, keep paddling, tis but a little way to the shore—you just got scared, it's all right." The crunching of stones under my feet. "There, I'm standing, you'll be able to stand in just a little bit—no, not yet, farther—" She scrambles out onto shore, sinking in a quivering heap in the grass.

"This—is—fun?"

"That happened to me at first, too. It's easy to get scared if you get a little water up your nose. Find a black stone. You can put all your fear into the black stone."

"Why a black stone? she says crossly. "Why not a white stone, why not a gray stone, a brown stone?"

"Mina said a black stone."

"I'll take this one," she says, picking a white stone and looking at me defiantly.

"Mina says black."

"Mina says, Mina says," she mimics. "What does Mina *say* to do with the stone?"

"If you'll not get the proper stone it won't work."

Annie hurls the stone into the pool, scuffs around in the little pebbles, pawing at them like an angry horse until she uncovers a black one. She holds out the small stone on her palm.

"Is this good enough, or must it be a certain size as well? Perhaps shaped like a heart?"

"That will do," I snap. "Now put all your fear into the stone—and all your bad manners as well," I cannot help but add. "And all your ingratitude as well. And put anything that your Mommy or anyone else has ever told you about drowning or fearing the water."

Annie holds the stone in her two cupped hands and then places her hands over her brow, willing all that stands between her and easiness in the water into the stone. I forget my anger as I watch her concentration.

"And now?" she asks.

"Cast it into the water and be free of it."

Where she cast the white stone so roughly, this stone she acknowledges with a nod and slips gently into the pool. She takes some of the water, instinctively wiping her face and her head as if clearing out any such thoughts as have fear in them. She nods.

"Are you ready to try again—to go back in?"

Again she nods, not looking at me, as if she were ashamed of her earlier outburst.

"Try swimming on your stomach like a dog. I think that'll be more comfortable for you. Just keep your head above water. That's the main thing." Beginning cautiously and slowly, ease gradually enters her movements, though she has yet to find any real pleasure in it.

"Now, turn over on your back again."

She turns over obediently.

"What Mina told me was to remember when I was a bairn in my mother's womb."

She turns back over onto her stomach, paddling in place.

"No."

"Well—but that's the way Mina did with me."

"No. I don't want to go back then. That was not a happy time for me. It was different for you. You were wanted. I was not. And am still not." Her face is closed but her sadness is so great that the entire pool fills with it. She starts to cry. We swim back to the edge of the pool and sit in the shallows. She puts her head in her hands and begins to sob.

"Oh," she cries, "I wish we really were sisters. I wish the Laird was my father like he is yours and not some outcast gypsy that no one even knows the name of." She sobs and sobs. How I wish Gran or Mina was here; someone who knew what to do.

Then I remember the Priestess that I felt myself to be as we were walking along. Some part of me does know. I go inside and again remember how it felt to be wearing the headdress.

"*Snake with wings whose name I do not know, speak to me,*" I ask silently. Without thought, the words pour from my mouth.

"Give all your sadness to the pool," I say to Annie, rubbing her back. "Give all your sadness to the pool, and let her take it from you and let you be free of it."

And so she sobs harder and harder and I weep a bit also, holding my hand to the place on her back that curls like a shield over her heart. After she is almost done with her sobs she begins to scream, screaming into her hands to muffle the sound.

"Scream into the water."

She bends her face into the pool and screams into the water, comes up for a gasping breath and then screams into the water again. I see her screams shiver across the pool, radiating out in every direction. At last the screams stop and I see how the air around her looks light and white and shining although her breath still comes shaking into her body.

"Go stand under the waterfall and purify now."

She swims under the falls and stands beneath it until it knocks her down. She stands under it again and again until I begin to fear that she is drowning herself. But then at last she pushes out from the falls and drifts on her back to the middle of the pool. Peace glows out from her now into the pool.

"And now," I say, my arm around her as I tread water, speaking into her ear, "take the pool as your mother. Take the Goddess as your true Mother and feel Her love for you, and know that She wanted you to come and be here and that She brought you forth."

She takes a shaky breath and drifts into trance, into the embrace of the water. Very slowly my arm and shoulder leave contact with her; I swim a little ways off so she may have this experience for herself alone.

After a time she turns on her belly and moves towards me with slow, dreamy strokes, steps out of the water, looks into my eyes. She is smiling.

"It remains to you to find an ally of the water."

She nods and sits on the bank, digging her toes into the mud.

"I know my ally."

"What is it?"

"My ally is the frog. I've thought on that before. They are famous shape-shifters. I will take the frog as my ally and I will learn her secrets of how to transform myself from the tadpole that I am now into a fine jumper and a hunter."

"And a catcher of flies?" I giggle.

She elbows me.

"Into a catcher of—what I want to catch."

"You have chosen and been chosen well," I say, echoing Mina.

"You'd better not eat me," she says. "I don't know as I trust my life around one of the salmon people."

"I'll not eat you," I say, snuggling closer to her. "We're allies too."

"Glad I am for that," she says, giving me another of her fierce hugs. She looks in my eyes. "Thank you for teaching me." She continues in a voice so intense it is almost hypnotic.

"I want to learn everything that they teach you. I want to *be* you. But if I can't be you I can at least be like you."

"Sometimes I feel like I want to be you, too."

She shakes her head. "You don't know what you're talking about."

"No, I don't know—but sometimes I feel like I *am* you or like we are the same person, sometimes—"

"You don't know what you're talking about," she repeats. "No one would like to be like me. What was that thing that happened to us at the beginning—when you were leading me here?"

"I don't know. That didn't happen when I was with Mina."

"It didn't? That was just for us?"

"Well—it didn't happen with Mina. I don't know what it was. I felt. . ." I tell her what my sensations had been.

She nods, "I saw that crown on you. I did see it. I saw you like you were a grown woman. And I was grown too, but I still had something to learn from you."

"We have many different lives. As many as stars in the sky I heard John say once. Perhaps it was a spirit dance. It must have been so."

Annie nods and looks at me.

Our gazes lock. Heat. For a moment the heat is so intense every-thing in my vision goes white. It is so hot there is sweat running down our arms. And my arms are as brown as hers. Her face is different, and I know mine must be more different still. We are struggling with an urn of oil, pouring it into two large offering bowls, staggering it back upright with exclamations of relief that it has not broken or spilled. We each pick up one of the bowls inlaid with beautiful polished stones and join a procession of other girls walking into a tem-ple. Each girl in turn pours her oil over the body of the strangest beast-god I have ever seen. His face twists into a serpent nose, two teeth curl out of his mouth in crescents, like boar's teeth. His ears are huge. He sprawls in an attitude of bliss. We pour the oil over his body and he shines. We sprinkle yellow powder and strong smelling brown powders over him and then we pour baskets of flowers over him so that only his head shows above a sea of blossoms.

"Ganeesha," we whisper.

With that name, colors ripple in front of my eyes as if I were rapidly passing through water.

Annie's face shivers back into focus before me.

"Ganeesha," she murmurs, smiles. "We have been together many times," she says to me. I nod.

"We have served the Goddess together many times. And the gentle Gods. Perhaps some ungentle ones—I—" she starts to speak in a language we do not know, moving into the trance state, eyelids fluttering. Lightly I place my hand on her throat, and for a moment I see her grown, extraordinarily beautiful. A surge of indescribable feeling courses through my body from my thighs up to my heart, rolling like purple clouds in my head. She looks at me, and again we are children, seven and eight years of age.

"I have magic blood too. My father was a Gypsy. Will the coven ever—keep and train me? If you tell them perhaps, that we have been Priestesses together before, and I know that is what I came into this life to be?"

"I know not. Everyone else in the coven—has the blood from somewhere—"

"As do I!" she cries, "As do I! I know not my father but he left his blood in me. I have the sight as much as you. If you teach me what they teach you, and I grow in power and we practice our arts together then surely they will take me, they will have to take me. It's all up to you, Fiona."

"Well, I will teach you everything that I remember, but— sometimes, sometimes, I know that I've done magic with them but I cannot remember it. Sometimes I feel like I have been dreaming when I've been to see Gran—it is like when you wake up and you cannot remember your dreams."

"They must lay enchantments on you to make you forget," she says. "Perhaps they do not want you to share what you have learned." She thinks for a moment. "Well, if there are enchantments to make you forget there must also be enchantments for remembering. We will have to get a charm for remembering."

"But why would they give it to us, if they want me to forget?"

"We won't tell them it's for you," she says, amazed at my lack of guile. "We'll tell them it's for my mother."

"Your mother?"

"Ssh. Never mind. I'll think of something. I have a plan. I will think of a way to get a charm for remembering, and then you must remember to take it whenever you go to see them. And then you can tell me everything. Do you promise to tell me everything?" she pleads, holding my hands.

"I promise."

She takes a little black arrowhead from the pouch at her side. I exclaim with delight at it.

"Ohh—an elf-bolt!"

"Aye I found it the very day that you were off with Mina. Och, I was so jealous that day Fiona, I almost hated you. I wanted so much—" she stops, unable to express her feeling. "Look how sharp it is," she says. "If we cut each other and bind our palms together for a moment then our blood will mingle and we will be sisters. So it will be no betrayal for you to tell me aught and ever for we will share the same blood."

I am afraid of the pain, but allow her to take my palm and cut the heel of it.

"Here, you do me," she asks, but I cannot.

"I am afraid to hurt you."

"I'll do it myself then." Pressing her lips together she tries to pierce herself but fails.

"My blood is stopping," I warn, seeing the edges of the tiny wound pull together. Annie wedges the arrowhead in the ground and slaps her hand on it. She cries out, wipes her hand on her hip then presses it to mine.

"What shall we bind it with?" I ask.

"A cloth. . . in my bag. . ."

I pull a strip of white muslin from her rucksack and together we make an awkward binding.

"We promise to always tell each other the truth."

"Our blood and our hearts are one," I agree.

"In the name of the Goddess "

"So mote it be."

We slowly unwrap the binding and tear it in half so that each has half of the blood-stained wrapper. "I had to cut up my mother's best petticoat to get this," Annie sighs. "I can feel the blows already."

I wince. The mottling of bruises on her back from the last beating has not yet faded.

"Oh Annie. . . if you would only be kinder to your mother. . ."

"Then she would have no excuse for beating me and that would truly drive her mad." She stands, shoulders drooping. She straightens and lifts her chin.

"Well, tis M'hira is really my mother. The water loves me. And someday," she adds, "I will grow to be a frog and hop away."

Chapter 8

Gray and drizzly and wet outside. I'm glad it's still early.
Glad I need not yet rise. Our cat, Mist, gray as a piece of the winter morning, has crawled under the bedclothes to join me. The
other children are still asleep, sounds of their breathing muffled
under the layers of blankets we need to keep warm in March. The
lump beside me snores gently; only a few blonde ringlets emerging from the heap betray it as my sister Eostre.

Mairead has been keeping Annie home at night, so I am glad
of Mist's company. She refuses to settle and sleep, though,
squirming and scrapping about as if she could not find a comfortable spot anywhere. She's usually so calm even the littlest tail-
grabbing bairns don't bother her. Finally she gets half on, half off
my body, kneading my ribs and purring loudly. Petting her, I feel
her belly contracting under my palm, and realize she's getting
ready to have her kittens.

"D'you think you'll be needing a poultice or a bit of tea?" At
eight, I know that there are special herbal preparations for laboring women. I am ready to hop right out of bed to boil a toddy of

water, but Mist digs her claws in and purrs louder as if to say,
"Be still and stay where you are." She twists around again, pushing her spine up against my stomach. I rub her belly, letting her
purr guide the movements of my hands.

She jumps up and arches her back, making a hissing sound.
Bends double, biting at herself—no, not at herself, at the cord
binding her to a small wet lump of fur. She grabs the kitten by
the scruff and puts it beside my face. Makes a low growling,
'Wow-ow' noise and another kitten plops out. A neat snap severs
the cord. She begins licking them, stops, hunches over and
squeezes out a third. The two beside me are shivering, making
tiny noises. I nuzzle them with my chin, petting them and licking their faces. All silk and salt they are; I wish passionately to
be Mist, to be the mother cat and suckle them.

Mist's agitation calls back my human form. The third kitten
is as big as the other two together, but it lies limp, unresponsive
to its mother's lickings and nudgings. I reach down and bring
him up to where I can see, shake him, press his ribs gently, in
and out, coaxing air into his lungs. All the while I call to his
spirit, saying, "Tis well. Tis safe. See what a fine body has been
prepared for you. Come, come and dwell here." So many kittens
are drowned at birth, perhaps he is afraid. But my mother is
kindhearted; she never slaps a child or drowns a kitten.

"You'll be safe, I promise. You'll be my special cat if you'll
come in and breathe—"

Mina's voice in my head, telling the story of how humans
and animals alike were dumb and dark as earth until the Goddess breathed life into them. I purse my mouth around the kitten's muzzle, pushing the ribs out with my breath, stroking his
body with my hands. A blue spark flashes from my forehead, arcing out of the place between my eyes into the space between his.
A surge goes through the little body. I stop and hold my breath,
watching. One by one the breaths come through him, faltering at
first, then stronger, each breath bigger than the last. Plainly
now I see the life-fire ringing his body. The joy and magic of the
moment has pushed my own soul-fire out so it seems the room
can scarce contain it.

"Get yourself a bit of breakfast, bairn." Once attached to
Mist's nipple, he sucks greedily, pushing strongly against her

belly with his forepaws. I will call this kitten Oberon, minding the tale of the King of the Fay who was put under a spell and held there until the Queen of the Fay wakened him with a kiss, as I have wakened this kitten with the kiss of my breath.

*   *   *   *

Soon after they had been weaned, Peat Moss and Grizelda Greediguts were exiled to the outdoors for their habit of stealing food. Mist was such an efficient mouser that we really had no need of another croft cat. Oberon betrayed his parentage, not only by his great size and his markings, which were clearly that of a lynx, but by his hunting prowess. Every morning he would sally forth to the woods, returning shortly with a squirrel or a cony or a bird for our cooking pot, and in this way he earned a place by the hearth nearly as warm as his place in my heart. His morning duties completed, he would melt as much as his structure of fur and bones would permit, allowing his female admirers to bring him mice and rats for his own sustenance.

Mina taught me the charm to make Obie my familiar spirit. She thought Obie a very fine choice, for since he was half-lynx he could teach me about power beasts, as well as serving as my familiar.

Every night from the new moon to the full, I held Obie on my lap, patting him and talking to him of magic, asking if he would willingly blend his spirit with mine so that we might become familiar kindred, each of us opening the other into a broader world. He never jumped off my lap, and always purred his assent loudly when I mentioned magic. When the moon was round, and so bright that she hurt the eyes, I took Obie out to a secret spot overlooking the sea. I pricked the ring finger of my left hand; he obligingly lapped at it. I squeezed a bit more blood into a bowl of milk, which we shared. He licked his chops with evident satisfaction. I grinned.

"Now we are one blood." I put one hand on his head, one at the tip of his tail, and chanted:

"If you will be mine from head to tail,
Then I will be yours from broom to pail."

From broom to pail is another way of saying from birth to death; from the time my parents 'jumped the broom', or first coupled, to the time my survivors bring a pail of water to wash my body. It also means east to west, while head to tail is north to south. In this way we were 'cornered' by the spell, each became a part of the other's balance in a connection that could never be broken. I crawled into a laundry basket and coaxed him to join me. While he purred in my arms, I stared at the moon until my mind whirled and it seemed we were rocking on a tide far from any sight of shore.

"Now we're all in the same boat," I whispered, and concluded the spell with a chant I heard the coven do one night when I had hidden in the bushes eavesdropping on their rites:

"Spun and measured, cut and wound,
One with silence, one with sound,
Earth and sun and moon around,
Likewise now this charm is bound."

Chapter 9

Oberon was very useful from the beginning. He had a trilling little 'purry-up, purry-up' wake-up call that he would utter
close to my ear to let me know when a ritual was happening. Being with him, I learned 'cat-sense'—how to extend my consciousness out like whiskers, to sense danger or to find what I was looking for. I also learned how to move soundlessly through the woods
and how to sit unnoticed near enough to a circle to hear what was
said, though most times I was too proud of having found them to
hide myself. The adults tried to conceal it, but they were proud of
me too, and impressed with Obie.

"Any cat loves a magic circle, but tis a rare beast that will
tromp through the woods for one," noted John. Whenever Gran
started to scold me or threatened to send me away, John would
pull me under his plaidie.

"Naw, this bairn is no danger. Deep as a well, silent as a
tomb, eh lass?" Encircled by his protective arm and the fragrance
of his pipe, I often fell asleep long before the rite was finished.

"Cats all deepen the magic of a circle," Mina said, "but that

Oberon. . ." She shook her head, clicking her tongue in admiration as she bent back over her sewing. When I asked just what sorts of special magic cats performed, Mina said, "Cats are great web fasteners. They're like pegs. They hold the magic down to the Earth. Not that they don't add plenty to the raisin' of the cone* as well."

Obie certainly kept me pegged down. When he draped his full weight across my lap, I had no choice but to sit quiet. After hours of such sitting I would feel the vibration in the earth that was just like Obie's purr.

Even after he was long past kittenhood, Oberon loved milk beyond all things. But it was not an easy task to get milk for Obie. Annie had adopted a she-cat named Tawney as her familiar, so together we had the courage to sneak into some neighbor's byre once or twice a moon and pilfer their milk. Annie would stroke the cow's nose, feeding her bunches of choice flowering grasses, while I squeezed the warm milk into a pail. We were never caught. Our neighbors would always assume a brownie or other fay had done the deed, and the Priest would be called to do an exorcism with his lighted tapers and holy water. Sometimes we'd go for a goat or an ewe if we could get it to hold still, but our respect for William and John as herders most times protected the flocks from our pilferings. Sloshing pail in hand, we'd scuttle off to the woods, Tawney and Oberon loping and leaping beside us in an ecstasy of anticipation. The cats got first honors, standing on their hind legs and leaning their heads down deep into the bucket. Then Annie and I would take turns, tipping the bucket til the last of the cream slid down our throats, making us as giddy and silly as if it had been distilled straight from the moon.

"Mmmm—moon whiskey," I'd say, gulping greedily.

"Ye've got milk all over yer whiskers," Annie would chide, and we'd lick each other's faces until we had giggled ourselves nearly sick while the cats assumed poses of full-bellied satiation on the grass.

One evening, half-dozing as I petted Obie near the hearth, I slipped through the flames' glaze of light and was suddenly in Peter and Sarah's croft. Sarah was cleaning a pot while Peter chopped wood outside, and I could see both places clearly and at once. Then Peter brought the wood in and fed the fire while Sa-

---

*The cone of power is a focused energy raised by Witches working in a circle.

rah nursed her baby, the oldest child running between the two of them, jabbering in the half-human language two-year bairns do.

As soon as Obie got up and stretched, the vision vanished, quick as a stone will shiver a reflection from a pool. But I knew the trick then, and would often practice that distant seeing. Sitting either by the hearth or with a candle, sometimes holding the crystal brought from Faerie, I would pet Obie hand over hand until the tearing in my eyes melted from a liquid gleam to a dance of light. Then I would silently ask what would happen next time the coven met, or what Mina or another person was doing at that moment. The waver of water and fire would clear and I would see, plain as being there, what was happening across the little distance of time or country between me and my wondering. The Laird asleep, snoring with his wine-stained beard beside the great hearth. Sean playing chess with the Priest, practicing his French or Latin. John and William climbing the tors with their sheep, swapping tales. Mina fussing with her sewing as she stitched up herb pillows, for she was growing hard of sight, yet wanted the stitchwork to be as fine as before.

I got cured of my spying early on. Emboldened by my successes, I asked to see what my Gran was doing. In that instant I was within her croft, and much to my amazement she and John Gardener were kissing, and she was slipping off the shoulders of her dress. At eight I had given little thought to passion, but certainly John and my Gran were too old for such things. . .

Gran stopped in mid-kiss and pushed John away, looking straight in my direction with a terrible frown. Without taking her eyes from me, she asked John to fetch her down a dried herb from her ceiling, broke it into a small cauldron and dropped a coal on it. I sat frozen, pinned down by her eyes as a deer will stand mesmerized by a ritual fire. Then the sharp smell of catsbane wafted over us; Obie hissed, 'waugh!', dug in his claws and took off, knocking over the candle, and I was back in my croft, reeling as if I had been thrown by an angry giant.

I put off seeing Gran for as long as possible, quaking every time I thought of what she might say, or worse yet, that she might lay some further charm against me. But finally I saw her, and she said nothing about it, giving me no indication that it was ought but a dream of mine that she did not share. A fortnight after the incident, I took her some stew Mother had made. She showed me how to make the 'superstition packets' she sold to the other villagers. These were small squares of material to be stuffed with herbs and sewn into the clothes. She had combinations to fetch back a failing memory, to rouse a weariness or ease a heartbreak. Mostly she had orders for 'healthy bairn' charms. Our family being many, and healthy, the village women assumed it was charms as made us so, and wanted the same for their children. Gran had given up trying to explain that it took a lot of things to be healthy, not just a charm. She said that land food was fine for building bones, but one needed ocean food to build blood. We ate a lot of fish and tulse, especially in winter, but most of our village had little taste for the seaweed.

Gran also was firm in her belief that one could not be healthy without regular purification of body and thoughts, and came over once a moon to purify our whole house and everyone in it with seawater and burning herbs. We all bathed once a moon as well, even in winter when it took hours to warm the water. But most villagers clung to their protective layers of dirt and woodsmoke as tenaciously as a cat would cling to its fur, and since many were now afraid to be seen drinking aught but whiskey or water, Gran gave them the herbs in ways that could be concealed.

"So will they not work then?" I asked, troubled that Gran could think of deceiving anyone.

"Well, there's the power of the plant, and then there's the power of what people believe," said Gran. "With these, tis more the belief than the thing itself that makes it what it is."

"So tis not real?"

"Every power is a real power. The power of superstition holds more sway with kings and princes than the powers of the spinning world in this day," she shrugged, "you cannot give a person more power than they can use. D'you think you ken which packets go to whom?"

It was my lot to deliver the packets we had sewn. Gran never took a cure to anyone. They had to come to her, but these days many were afraid to be seen doing so, and so the children were re lied upon to bear messages and cures I never saw a man come to Gran's croft seeking help. If a man was ailing or unable to sire children or perform his marital duties, his wife would come, twisting her apron anxiously, hoping her husband would not notice the absence of the few groats or a chicken she had brought Gran in payment.

Just as I was leaving with the packets, Gran said, "Oh, by the way. Go around the house and fetch me some catsbane. I seem to be all out." She gave me a small, triumphant smile.

The message was clear. So while I still occasionally used Oberon to help me see visions, I was careful never again to spy on my own folk while I was doing it.

Chapter 10

Eyes half closed, I let cat sense stretch out of my body, a questioning sweep through the forest, asking the trees where I can find blue flag and cinquefoil, if they know of any mandrake plants that would willingly come home with me. Yes, over that hidden crest, a meadow—plenty of blue flag near the oaks, a little cinquefoil, more across the meadow by the stream. . . I walk in the direction the trees have mapped for me. There is a good bed of blue flag, plenty of cinquefoil near the stream. No mandrake appears to my sense however. Rose has it growing in her garden, but wild plants are required for certain workings. After gathering the plants I cut some dry boughs of pine and oak and lay them on my cloak.

I examine the catch from my day's labors; elfbane, cow-herd, yellow broom, the blue flag and cinquefoil. I hope Gran will not be angry that the mandrake would not show itself today. Mandrake is a trickster, and easily displeased. Only Rose can grow it at will. I arrange the branches on the cloak, hiding the herbs in the center of the bundle. I have walked a long ways, and it will be easier to return to Glen Lochlan by the road. Traffic with any plants save the most common pot-herbs is viewed with suspicion, but no one will think twice about a peasant girl carrying a bundle of faggots for kindling.

As I walk, I spy a large company on horseback approaching. Even one rider is cause for excitement on this road. My heart beats faster as I see men in mail carrying unfamiliar banners. A party of upper class clergy, nuns and monks, riding at a leisurely pace within a protective ring of soldiers.

I stand by the side of the road to let them pass. The nuns are laughing amongst themselves, but one casts a glance my way. My heart sears open as if a flaming arrow had broken open an old wound. Moon round face, black crescent eyes, something in me singing of the love of the willow tree for the cherry. Someone once lost, so beloved, so infinitely dear, riding a white palfrey out of the gates of death. In an instant I dodge between the guards, grasping the pommel of her saddle. Looking into her eyes, I call her by the name I had once known her by:

"Sei!"

The utterance of that foreign name shatters the spell. Cold blue eyes return my stare without seeing me. My heart stops with the immensity of my trespass. I retreat to the side of the road, bowing my head, tugging my forelock in the posture of subservience our differing classes demands. Lips pressed together, holding my breath, I wait for one of the guards to spit me through for my insolence, leaving me gasping my life out in the ditch. The spear thrust does not come. The party moves on without stopping, first their foreign chatter, then the dust, then their hoof-beats dispersing and fading away.

When they are quite out of sight and hearing I walk quickly away, until the force of my sobs pulls me to earth, rocked by a storm of feeling far beyond my nine year old comprehension. Ignorant myself of who I have just seen, I curse her for not knowing me, for thinking herself above me. I pray that if we meet again in another life I will not recognize her.

All the way back to Gran's croft I stumble over my feet, as weak as if ill with gripe or fever. The small bundle of herbs hanging reversed over her door gives plainly the message that she is not to be disturbed. I trudge over to Mina's.

"Ah, poor child, ye look so weary. Sit down bairn, sit down. Such a face! I'll take care of these herb babies here until Ann is finished with her working, concern yerself no more about it. . ." She fixes us both some hot vegetable water, a clump of butter melting gold over the top as reward for my labors. She soon sees that I am in no mood for chatter, so we sit in silence until she fixes us both a second mug. I stare at my cup, so lost in my misery I have no words for it. At last Mina speaks for me.

"So. She did not recognize you." I shake my head, angrily blinking away the tears.

"Do you remember exactly who she was to you?"

I shake my head again, grateful that she can read my mind and speak what I cannot. Mina sighs, taking up the sewing she had been tending to when I came in.

"Well, it seems you have chosen very different paths. You have chosen to be one of those who remember—and it is a Priestess's *duty* to choose to remember. Most who die drink of the waters of forgetfulness. That is why we call those people the 'once-borns' for they live each life as if it were the only one they have ever had, or ever would have." Silence, save for the click of her needle against the buttons of horn she is sewing fast.

"You would do well to forgive her. She has chosen what she has chosen, and no being may choose for another."

I continue to sulk as she gets up to fetch me a bit of short-bread to go with my drink. I take mouse bites of the treat, savouring its buttery richness in spite of my sulking. I am determined to stay angry, seeing over and over the freezing blue eyes staring down an elegant nose, not condescending to speak or even to seem startled by my presumption. They have more than we do so they think they are better—because of them, the people have started to be afraid of us—

Mina interrupts my angry reverie.

"You are young to begin having such memories. Has this happened often?"

"No. Not often."

She places her hand over her belly. "We carry our memories here. When your womb opens—as you have been told before—a part of your mind opens. Memories will flow with your blood. It is well to seek to remember during the time of your blood *only*. For you must be well rooted in this life before the things you remember will make sense to you."

I am so tired of being told I must wait and wait for knowledge, I can only sigh with impatience.

"No, my dear. Your hold on life is still not strong, as the roots of a young tree have not had time to dig deep. It is a danger to you to be so close to death, and memories of other lives will bring you closer to that gate. We will soon teach you to enter other lifetimes at will. But for now, concentrate on being Fiona."

"What happens after you die?" I ask. "Do you take a new form right away?"

"Never was there such a bairn for questions!" Mina exclaims. "Well, there's—some take a new form right away, but this is foolish. There is much to do in the land of the dead. It is well to learn as much as you can there, so as to be wiser when you choose your next form."

"Why does Gran say we must never speak of the dead, or contact them?"

"It makes it harder for them. They must sever their bonds with the earth. If we will not let go of them, then our love can become a burden to them. That is why we do the ritual of cord-cutting when someone has died, so they may be free for their journey."

"Are you doing one for Mari on Samhain*?"

"Aye." Mina suddenly looks very old. When Mari died birthing her fourth baby a moon-span ago, everyone had been stunned. I was shocked to realize that there were limits to the coven's power, that all the herbs and all the chants and magic that Rose and Gran and Mina and Sarah knew had not been enough.

"Will Mari and her baby be there?"

"If they wish."

"Could I come? Please? I need to say good-bye to Mari too."
Mina looks uncomfortable.

"I will ask the others."

"Winter talks of choosing to die. Did Mari choose to die?"
Mina gets up and puts her sewing away.

"I think perhaps you'll be needing a wiser teacher than I. No one expected Mari to die. You will soon discover that being an elder does not give you the key to every lock. You are so young to

---

*Samhain—Halloween, Celtic festival of the dead.

be asking all these questions—" She gets some mint salve and smoothes it between my eyebrows and over my forehead.

"So much frowning will make you look like an elder ere you are twenty. Be a good lass and run out and play."

Chapter 11

It seems reassuring that the day is bright, with only occasional clouds to block the sun. Birds chitter from the branches of the trees and bushes, hopping along and eating the last of the berries and seeds. The oaks have not lost all their leaves yet, though they hang dry and crumpled and witherd; the first storm will take them all down. Most of the trees around the clearing are a pale gold that today seems melancholy. After today we will not be able to gather any more of the wild fruits for ourselves. After Samhain they are the province of the forest folk and of the spirit world, and for humans to touch them is to court the illest of fortune.

Thinking of how hungry some of the animals get in the winter turns my thoughts to Mari's three surviving children, wondering how they may fare. Their father, Galen, will not have to go to the fields again until Spring, but surely by spring he will have to find another wife to care for them.

At Mina's signal, Annie and I put down the basket we have carried between us. Because Annie had grown close to Mari, often playing with her babies and keeping them away from the hearth while she baked, and, because I would not stop pleading and arguing about it, Mina has agreed to do a ritual with both of us releasing Mari's spirit. She takes the top off the basket and we see all the multi-colored yarns of varying thicknesses. A sharp metal shears lies on top, a sheep-shearing instrument rather than the hand scissors carved of bone Mina uses for her sewing.

"Cast the circle with me," Mina says. We stand in front of her; she puts a hand on each of our heads. A current of energy flows from her hands through our bodies, into the ground. Eyes closed, I feel myself become a vibrating reed.

"Air," she breathes.

With that one word the trees rustle, leaves skitter over our faces, into our hair and our cloaks, bent grasses tickle our feet. I shudder, as if I myself were a tree being stripped of my former glory, and for a moment I feel as if the wind has whipped the color out of my hair, leaving it white, and sapped the juices from my flesh, leaving it wrinkled. I keep my eyes closed, not daring to open them, as Mina guides us about the circle to the south.

"Fire."

The roar and crackle that seem to gust upwards from beneath my feet makes me jump; only the pressure of Mina's hand on top of my head keeps me from fleeing. For a moment the sound and heat of a Samhain bonfire seems to surround me; within that light I dim and flicker. . .

"Feet on the ground, Fiona," Mina says, "We are casting a circle."

With her reminding I put my awareness into my feet, feeling the earth supporting my feet as lovingly and firmly as Mina clasps my head as we move about the circle to the western quarter. I open my eyes for a blink, relieved to see that Annie has neither been withered by the east wind nor charred by the south fire, so that I too have hope of surviving Mina's invoking. I close my eyes again, allowing myself to be in the darkness, not fixed to the point of the earth on which we stand, but open to the other world which has come down around us as if it were a cloak over our heads, the other world where the guardians of the elements dwell

"Water."

The water is soothing and serene, arms of the foam embrace us, hissing like friendly serpents. It is comforting to lose form and be one with the water; when the waves withdraw, two tears trickle down my cheeks, as if they would follow. Feet bare upon the earth, we move about the circle to the north.

"Earth."

The earth is flesh beneath my feet, her body is the same substance as mine, mine the same substance as hers. Bone and stone, skin and soil, water and blood. How easy it would be for my body to yield its form into the earth, crumbling back into the dirt, feeding the trees and the plant people, who kill nothing and yet live on the dead. . .

Walking sideways, we return to the east, and from there Mina turns us about and brings us back to the center of the circle.

"Kneel now."

Our eyes still closed, we put our hands on the earth, feeling Her breathe, feeling Her present with us. I feel how She is holding Mari and her baby, allowing them to relax into Her, losing their form. Gentle as the earth's embrace is, I find myself weeping, not perhaps so much for Mari and her child as for myself and for us all, that we must die, wanting to think that I will always have this form, mourning now the many deaths before me. I must endure the shift from child to woman, from my maiden body to the vessel carrier of another, and from that to the old woman's flesh, wrinkled and potent as a dried fruit, and then lose even that, shedding the body altogether and giving it back to the earth while my soul finds a new nest.

Smell of the earth, and the birds still chittering in the trees. I don't want to die. Not ever. Even though I can be born again. I want only to be born again if I can be born again as myself. I sense Mina's withdrawal, turn and look up at her. She is now standing, arms in the wide open crescent of invoking. Sun glints a fierce silver nimbus over her brow; her gray eyes gleam silver as a storm-wracked sea. She raises the shears above her head; the open blades glitter with deadly light. A wave of blackness rises behind her, blotting the sun; a deep unhuman voice resonates up from the ground:

"I am the scythe that strips the field.
I am the wound that cannot heal.
I am the sheath that rusts the blade.
Of open earth my bed is made.
I am the fire that fills the head with smoke.
I am the tomb for every hope.

I am the perilous groan of the sea.
The ruthless boar, the hawk that stoops and strikes.
I am the lightning blasted oak.
I am the unhewn, all-devouring dolmen.

I am the cord-cutter, cunning beyond kenning.
Who cannot be trusted.
And Who must be."

Annie and I cower, not daring to rise. After a long space where sky and sun hang motionless and birds and air are silent, the fierce arms relax and the color of a sharp blade leaves her eyes and they come back to us with Mina behind them once again. She sits down with us, sets the basket in the center of our circle.

"It is our purpose today to release Mari from all earthly connections, to allow her to slip the bonds and reins of this life, passing into the Summerland and thence beyond. Each of these strands represents a cord binding her to us. As you choose, choose a piece of yarn that feels thick if the binding cord seems a very powerful one, and thin for the more minor ways in which you would bind her to the earth."

She takes a stout strand of white yarn, almost as thick as a piece of rope and holds it between her hands tautly. "When I tell you to cut it, then cut it quickly and I'll be done with it."

For a moment she sits silently, letting the tears run down her face. "Mari," she says at last, "this is the cord that bound us as coven sisters. Together we were one womb of the Mother, birthing magic into this world. And this is the cord of my vision of you as one of our successors, one of the young women who would take up the leadership of the coven as our strength waned and the wand passed. But it is you who have gone on beyond us now.

Bereaved as I am, I honor your choice to do so. Farewell." She nods, "Cut it."

Annie and I lift the shears and cut the bond. The cord pulses with a raith-light so strong that when we sever it we flinch, half expecting it to spout blood.

Flaccid and bloodless, the two ends droop in Mina's hands. She drops the ends and sighs. "There. Now each of you, choose as many cords as you have ropes binding to Mari, or to her child, if you have any connection with him, who did not survive his arrival onto this earth."

One at a time, Annie and I take cords, holding them taut between our hands as Mina had showed us, naming our connection to Mari, feeling it become embodied in the cord, then nodding a signal for one of the others to cut it for us, putting the limp ends aside to be buried later. A slender brown cord to signify how much we will miss Mari's baking; she was one of the best cooks, if not the very best, in the shire. A thick white one for the grief that I feel that she will not be one of the ones to initiate me into the coven. A smaller pink one at the grief that my mother must feel at the loss of her best friend, red for the fear I now have that I or another one I love might die in childbirth. A black cord for my anger at her for choosing to let her soul leave her body. Mina encourages us to go as deep within as we may, to find any bonds that might hold Mari back from her journey, and to release them. When at last we have a small pile of wool beside each of us and feel as complete as the ache in our hearts will allow, we each take the aged silver antler which Mina has loosed from the cingulum around her waist, using that and our hands to dig a hole. We bury the strands as if they were Mari's body, mounding the earth above the little graves and ringing them with stones. We take the last of the autumn blooms we had found, and some brightly colored leaves in our aprons, and scatter them on the graves.

"Farewell to Mari, who was Summer," says Mina, unshed tears still thick in her voice.

"May spring rebirth soon come upon her.
Return to Earth and to the hearts that love you
In the form and fashion that are most fit for you.

You who are joy and love and light
Illumine the lovely caverns of the night.
And as the moon gives love after the sun has fled,
Let your love shine forth in the Queendom of the dead.
Farewell to Mari, who was Summer.
May spring rebirth soon be upon her.

We now release each of the ties that bind
Look for these ties and nought but love you'll find.
Love is the cord that never forms a noose.
Hail and farewell dear Mari. Thou art loose'd."

That Samhain eve was blacker than any night I can remember. The laughter at the Samhain games we play with the other children and young people of the village never hovers more than a breath above a sob of terror. Even the ducking for apples which admits us to the ritual field is more harsh than merry; the water in the trough sloshing up our noses, the apples of Avalon spinning away from our lunging mouths as if they scorned our hopes of immortality. The older boys dressed as guisards, horrible in their painted faces, false beards and noses, smear soot on our faces and chase the younger bairns about the field until they escape by running to the Gates of Death, where Mina and Gran push them gently through the black veil. We older and more daring join the game of snap-the-serpent played by the young men and women, but being small are quickly tumbled off the end of the shrieking line. Our oldest, most tattered clothes are shed, to be placed in the Samhain bonfire, before we pass through the black curtain into an adjacent field where we are dressed in black and given a turnip lantern. The scorched smell of the stalks burnt in the fields, the death smell of the tallow fresh from this year's culling of the herds, makes me feel ill.

Thick clouds roll in at dusk, obscuring the tiniest sliver of light the stars might have offered. Annie and I and the other children from our croft huddle together as we make our way back home with our trembling flames. Half way there, drops of rain start to patter. A gust of icy wind blows one of the turnips out; we all shriek as if the goblins would take us on that instant, and run the rest of the way home.

*   *   *   *   *

All of us got sick in the days that were to follow, and were sick often that winter. The winter was black and long as the night that began it; I started to think that perhaps Mari had truly been summer, and we should never see sun or flower or fruit again. May of that year was stormy; even the magic of Beltane did not seem to conjure the summer in as swiftly as it usually did, but my mother bore twins in that month, and we thought and hoped and prayed that meant that all of our luck had changed and that now we would all be happy again.

But how wrong we were.

Chapter 12

My heart beats much faster than it should, considering the leisurely pace of our gallop. It beats so hard I imagine I know how Mina feels when her heart threatens to leave her body after she has walked but a short way.

Knot in my stomach, great ball of unshed tears in my throat. A growing pain in the space between my eyes. The feet touching the ground beneath me feel like they belong to someone else. I follow Annie, cantering when she canters, trotting when she trots, moving in blank imitation.

My mind goes back to the terrible scene last night; the Laird picking up the twins, looking at them in the light cast by the fire, examining first one and then the other as if he had never really looked at them before. His chest moving as if he had been running, though he had been sitting quietly having dinner with us.

"Where do they get their brown eyes?" he asks. My mother comes over, moving a little slowly because of the babe lying in her belly.

"Who gave them—such bonny brown eyes?" He makes a smile that is not a smile.

"Not from me." He takes my mother's chin in his hand and looks at her eyes, which are the purest blue.

"Not from you."

My mother says nothing. For a moment she looks as frightened as a small rabbit crouching under a thicket of gorse.

"Is it possible so many have passed through here that you do not know?"

"Of course I know," says mother at last. "They must be—Galen McClinnock's blood. I comforted him after Mari's death. You never saw a man in more grief. Tis the old custom—if a woman dies her best friend takes it upon herself to comfort the goodman until he finds another wife for him. Now he be married to Jessica Hartch and a good match it be. She is so good to his children. Mari would have been pleased, I know."

"And that's all it was? Old custom?"

"Galen and I have been friends since we played together as bairns. To deny him in his time of need—would have been churlish."

"What of me?"

Mother stares at him, bewildered.

"Why—I have never denied thee, Robbie."

He gets up abruptly, knocking over the stool, looking about at the children all staring silently at them.

"Get out!"

"Robbie, tis night, they cannot. . ."

"Get out! Go!" he shouts. He takes the twins and tosses one into my arms, one into Eostre's.

"Take them to their *father*—take them *now* over to Galen McClinnock's house! Now go, all of you. You too, lad—" he says to Sean, "No—you go back home lad—I'll be seein' you there later. The rest of you—get out *now*."

"Tis dark moon. . . I want them not out. . ." pleads Mother.

"Out!" screams the Laird.

I guide Malcolm with my free hand, pulling the toddler along beside me. Colin huddles close to Eostre as we stumble out the door. Elana is sobbing.

McClinnock lives quite a long ways from where we do. I think of stopping at Peter McIntyre's—he and Galen are often called the twins, so close they are in looks and manner. Peter and Sarah are in the coven and would have more idea what to do than McClinnock who is also descended from Rose, but not versed in the art. But I feel afraid to disobey the Laird and go there, or to Mina's or Gran's that would be so much closer.

So we take the path to the village. By the time we reach the McClinnock cottage my back is crying out under the weight of young Peter and I see Eostre has bitten her lip with the strain of carrying little Sarah.

Galen gets up to let us in.

"What—is your mother in labor?" he asks, seeing us all gathered at his doorstep.

"The Laird told us to come," says Eostre. "He told us to come and bring you your children." She plops Sarah down at his feet as if she were mightily relieved not to be carrying her any longer. Sarah bursts into tears. Young Jessica comes over. She's but fifteen, yet round and merry and as easy with the children as if she had half a dozen of her own. Like me, she is an eldest child.

"Oh now, there's nothing to fuss about. We'll get them a little sugar milk," she says, and starts heating some over the fire so she can give the twins each a cloth teat to suckle on.

Elana buries her head in Galen's thick midriff. Galen nods for me to sit beside him. He's a large man and his benches are higher than most. My legs swing freely under it.

"Is the Laird truly angry?"

I nod, looking at the floor.

"Perhaps. . . perhaps I should go there."

"Nay," says Jessica frowning. "You should not. What is between Anna and the Laird must be between them. You would be the last person he would wish to see."

"Oh. . . Bhari," he sighs, using her pet name. "Twas naught but a kindness—if 'twere not for her—and Sarah taking care of the children—and my brother Peter—I know not how I would have survived—and glad I am that I did now that you're here in my house. Och, it does not well to be jealous of a charity. Tis not like I was courtin' her for myself. I never had any such mind for that."

Jessica pats him on the back.

"There now. It's nothing. It will pass. People fight. My mother and father fought, as doubtless did yours. As doubtless will we when we've lived together a bit longer. If you go siring any other children on anyone else, now that *I'm* here, you may see a bit of a fight yet!"

"I want no one else now that you're here, my sister. Ye know that. Och, tis sorry I am to be causin' this trouble to your mother," he says to me. "Sorry and sorry and sad.

"Bhari—if the twins are causing so much trouble over at Anna's—could we—would you consider—?"

"Well," says Bhari, sitting down on the bench, one twin gathered in her lap, her arm around the one in Galen's.

"Here—give her this bit of a sugar tit." She hands Galen the soaked cloth and puts the other in small Peter's mouth. Their whimpers stop as they suck.

"Well, after they're weaned, perhaps. I have no milk to give them. I've no mind to feed them like this, not when Anna's got what they need. She'll be having her new babe in another three moons is it not? Three or four—so they'd be weaned by then. Tis not thrilled I am Peter, for I would like to have a couple of my own you know. How many can we feed? But of course," she sighs, "I will do whatever is best for all."

Twins asleep, Malcolm nodding off in my lap, I help bed the children down on a pile of blankets by the hearth.

"Please," I say to Galen, "Will you take care of the others? I need to go back and make sure my mother is all right."

He nods.

"Aye lass. Tis a good plan. If there's any problem—perhaps my brother can talk some sense into the Lairdie—he favors Peter. Or John, talk to John, John has his ear. He grew up with John workin' in the house—talk to John."

"I will."

*   *   *   *

Memories more bright than the moment, eyes focussed in rather than out, I trip over a tree-root and sprawl headlong. For a moment, no sound but the echo of my fall. Then I begin to sob.

Annie is beside me in a flash.

"Fiona, are ye much hurt? Where are ye hurt now—is't yer knee? Tis naught but a scrape, does not look so bad—is't yer foot? Fiona, what hurts?"

Tis not so much the fall as is making me cry as remembering the terrible names the Laird hurled at my mother as he slammed out of the croft, tears rolling down his face.

My mother sprawled face down beside the hearth, sobbing as I had never heard anyone sob. Sobbing so hard she did not know I was there, did not feel me patting her back and smoothing her hair. I not knowing what to do, wanting to get help but afraid to leave. My mother seeming not to tire as a person should when they're sobbing so hard but sobbing on and on. Finally clutching her belly and not just sobbing but screaming, and with that I finally got up and ran to Peter and Sarah's. Sarah quickly rubbed the weariness out of her eyes and came. She bade me fetch Mina and Gran. I helped carry the herbs and Gran's largest herb pot to the croft and fetched the buckets of water they required. Then they told me to get out. By that time it was nearly light so I went to wake Annie.

Annie bends over me.

"Fiona are you hurt or are you just cryin' about your mother?"

"My mother." I pull my knees up to my belly, rocking. "What if she dies?" I sob.

"She'll not. She'll not die. Nay, really Fiona, she'll not. I know she'll not."

"No one thought that Mari would either," I snuffle, "and my mother's so sad I think she might just die." For whatever Jessica said, I know this is no ordinary quarrel between lovers. The Laird cursed her when he left, charging her to find another fool to feed the mouths that came from her whoring about.

"And leave her children? No. No, she's not like that, Fiona, she'll not. She'll not leave her babies. Look, we'll go over to the standin' stones and we'll do a spell to help her, all right? You have to think like a Priestess. You have to think like you have some power in it, Fiona."

I sit up, wiping my face with my hair and my sleeve. She helps me up and we gallop off towards the standing stones. As we run, I think about the Great Mare, Anna, Mother aspect of the trinity of Anu, and call on Her to help my mother to bear this child and bear this loss.

We gallop around the standing stones three times, then stand within and call the four directions, asking each of them to help my mother. Eostre the dawn Goddess is rising, robed in pale gold, as we ask the soft feathery touch of the east wind to lighten the load and make it easy. At the south we envision Bridget at her forge, calling on the fire for courage, strength and transformation. The west waters are the powers of the womb—we call to the sea Goddess Marianna for peace and healing. Powers of the north, we call on Anu, strong mother, the earth, the animals which birth easily. And back to the east again, asking the Goddess of the rainbow, Ura, also the Goddess of the resilient heather, to bring us a happy change after this storm.

We mime the rite of the blade and chalice, she holding her hands to make a chalice, I bringing a stone for the sacred blade down into the center, between her palms, imagining the earth and the sky, the fire and the water, meeting as one. We put our palms together, kneeling beside the altar stone and breathing. The knots in my body have loosened, though I still feel a bit queasy. Power of the earth breathing up into our bodies. Power of the air breathing itself into our lungs. Strong breath, ebbing and flowing like the tide.

"Air and Water
Earth and Fire
Bring to us
What we desire," whispers Annie.

"Fire and Water
Air and Earth
Bring what we do will
To birth," I reply fervently.

Together we chant:

"By the Lady
By the Lord
By the chalice
By the sword

By the heart
And by the will
All our wishes
Be fulfilled."

"We conjure safety, we conjure health. We conjure ease, we conjure birth."

"We conjure that my mother be alive," I say.

"We conjure that she be alive and well," echoes Annie.

We take a deep breath. The web of stones around us glistens. The pulse of the earth throbs beneath us, strong as a drum.

"My mother will survive."

"So be it," Annie affirms.

"The child will not survive," I say. "It's too early."

"I came early," says Annie. She makes a face. "A great deal too early, by my mother's reckoning."

We hold hands, not in the palms together pose of conjuring, but loosely.

"Men are so strange," muses Annie. "They want you all to themselves, never to look at any other man. But then they want to be free to have as many women as they like. How do they think that can work?"

"Most men are not like that, I think."

"Aye, they are. Ian McTavish broke off with my mother naught but a day before their wedding when he found she was with child by another. . ."

"How did he know it wasn't his?"

"I guess—others had told him that she was sneaking off to see the gypsy. Maybe he'd not bedded her yet. I know not. He broke it off with her."

"Just as well for her," I say. "He seems like a cold man."

"Aye, just as well for him too." She shakes her head, "My mother's never forgiven me for it. Like it was all my fault, and if I'd not come she'd be married to the wealthy McTavish and have everything she wants instead of having to rely on her father, who beat her every day until I was born, for losing the match. He left her the croft though. Even without a man she has more than some." She looks at our two hands together, hers brown, mine white.

"She said once that the men used to say that a woman who'd let a gypsy go up on her would let a ram do the same."

"We should not talk like this here," I say, looking around at the sacred stones. "I want to go back and see if my mother's delivered."

She nods.

"May it be so."

We close the circle.

"We should leave gifts," says Annie. Quickly we pick up a few wildflowers for the four corners and the altar. Then we run, too anxious to get back to gallop and do our shape-shift into horses. Down and down the hills we hurtle until we get to the croft, panting and out of breath.

Mina greets us at the door as if she knew we would arrive just then.

"You may as well come in and see your brother," she says. "He'll not be here long." She lets us come into the room where my mother is lying on her bed. She is still sobbing, albeit weakly, trying to get the tiny nestling in her arms to latch onto her breast. He's so small, all crimson, bundled except for his face and one frail stick of an arm that seems to be all blue veins covered with the slenderest powder of skin. His eyes are not open—he flails, making sad croaking sounds. As we watch, he stops moving, and my mother cries out and hugs him to her and begins sobbing hard again.

"Get the children out," says Gran, tears in her eyes. Mina takes us to the door, digs in her pocket and gives us each a groat.

"There now—run into the village and buy yerselves a treat from some woman who's doing a baking today—there'll not be treats enough around here for awhile."

Neither of us has any appetite for a treat. Instead we gallop off beside the river, both of us crying as horses do not. We go up to the secret little black pool in the woods, the scrying pool.

"I never want to have children," I say to Annie as we sit beside the pool. "It's too sad if they die and if they live tis so much trouble—either way. Gran says there's ways that you do not have to have children—I'll tell you how after I find out from her and then we'll neither of us ever have any."

She nods, blowing her nose between her fingers and wiping it on the grass.

"Aye, let's never have aught to do with men or babies either. Men are too strange. Let's just be horses when we grow up."

I nod agreement.

"The mares of Scotia Cailleach can never be broke by any man," she declares, "and nor shall we."

A wind through the trees sends a handful of golden leaves sailing across the face of the scrying pool.

Chapter 13

The snow gusts and blows in such thick swirls and eddys I could find my way into the woods as easily with my eyes closed. The Laird's men chopped down several trees for his hearth yesterday, but today the blizzard is so bad that they will not be finishing their work. Well, foul weather shall not stop me from taking my share, I think defiantly. Ice rime clots on my eyelashes; the heavy axe chafes against my shoulder. I struggle on, trying to extend my senses as do the cat and flittermouse, to find the cut trees.

Our fire is near dead, a pile of sticks I could hold in one hand all that remains to coax the embers back to life. Peter and Galen have been trying to provide for us, but they have their own families to care for. Now that John is sheepherding with William he has little enough time to travel to the peat bogs for his own needs. The little ones had complained so of the cold, and mother looked so gray that I burned more of the precious fuel than we could spare. Before the heavy snows we had gathered downed wood, but now...

Rearing branches into the air like icicles, one of the fresh killed trees finally appears. An ash tree, beautiful pale wood almost obscured by the clinging snow. I kneel and lean my forehead against the tree, thanking it for dying for us. I can sense that it was sick. That's why the Laird had it cut. He believes one ill tree affects another, even as sheep or humans may pass on contagion. Of course, Gran says no illness begins that does not begin in the heart. . .

I start chopping off branches. The axe is made for a man, and I am small for nine years. I keep slipping and hitting it sideways, bits of pale wood flying off in the snow. With the ground so slippery beneath me and the snow blinding my eyes tis hard to see what I'm doing. I try not to let my frustration blind me more. What is that clearing chant Rose did at a Sabbat? "Fair is foul and foul is fair—vanish—something something—into air—" Ah, I cannot remember. . .

I remember Peter putting his foot up on a branch to steady it. I hack off a few of the frozen limbs and set them in a pile. Seems like I've done a lot of work for such a pitiful little heap as that. I set my teeth, try to steady my shivering, and start on a bigger branch.

My hands are so numb I can hardly feel the helve of the axe beneath them, and the snow is whirling up in my face like smoke. Either my foot slipped, or the axe did. Sharp thunk of the blade as it bites through my left foot and into the wood beneath it. I stare, stunned, at the dark red blood welling up around the axe, cascading to the ground. Try to jerk my foot away—sharp hot pain up my calf—I'm caught, pinned down. I push up on the helve of the axe—groan of metal leaving the wood. Fire sweeps up my leg. I faint.

Infinite gray space, swirling with flakes of snow. It is so beautiful. I stare for a long time until the throb in my leg distracts me. I hitch myself up on my elbows. Why am I lying in the snow? Then I see the axe, the dark pool around my leg where the snow has melted, and faint again.

Someone is calling me, trying to whisper me out of sleep. Many voices, each one but a bare breath, a feather of sound. As if the white flakes could swarm purposeful as bees, calling to me with the soft voice of the snow. . .

"Kyairthwen, Kyairthwen."

It's not a name I've been called before, yet I instantly recognize it as mine.

"Kyairthwen. . ." hands pushing against my shoulders, gentle but insistent.

"Kyairthwen, you have to get up. Kyairthwen, you have to go home."

Who is calling me? I open my eyes into the dizzying dance of snow. Struggle to sit, narrow my eyes, straining to see through the fog of sleepiness and swirling motes of white. The pain comes in rhythmic bursts up a leg that does not seem like mine. Everything is so numb I can hardly move.

"Take my hand." The voice is so musical, so clear. Though I see no one I reach out; the hand grasping mine is solid, pulls me to my feet.

"'Tis not that far to your croft. Come now."

As I take a step the fire sweeps up my body and I begin to topple. Hands under my arms catch and steady me. The trees seem to sway as if buffetted by great gusts of wind. Gradually they steady. I make a gesture as if to pick up the axe.

"No. Leave it," the voice commands.

The air wavers in front of me and then goes solid, as if the snow were coalescing into form. Faintly through the shifting veils of snow a tall woman appears, hooded in white fur. A strand of black hair blows out from the cowl of her hood. One bare hand rests upon a birch, the other beckons to me.

"Come. Come now."

I shuffle through the drifts towards her. My face is so stiff, it feels as if it would shatter under the slightest touch. I shuffle along slowly, feeling her pulling at me when I stop or falter. My vision is so blurred that I give up trying to see, and move with my eyes closed.

The next time I open my eyes, she is at the door of my croft. She raps sharply. I crumple to the ground.

*   *   *   *

Sensation of heat. Hot cloths, hot water scouring my body. Small quavery voice, "Is Fiona going to die? Is Fiona going to die?"

My Gran's voice snapping sharply, "Go away!" A burst of sobs, small feet running across the room.

*   *   *   *

"Here Fiona." I open my eyes into Elana's gray ones. I'm lying on a pallet near the hearth. She nudges her cloth dolly under my chin.

"Here, 'manda will take care of you, dinna be afeared. . ."
The heat from the fire rolls me back into sleep.

*   *   *   *

Gran's voice sounding clipped, tight. "It cannot be saved. There's nothing for it." Open my eyes—a wavery knot of people clustered around my feet.

My mother saying, "Oh, Mother, surely—"
"We'll be lucky if this is the only one she loses," Gran mutters.
"She's awake," Mina cautions.
"Put the cloth over her face, we'll do it before she wakes further," says Gran.

Damp cloth over my face, strong dizzying smell, suffocating. John's strong hands grasping my arms, holding me down. Sharp pain in my foot—I cannot struggle or cry out—cloth pulled away, whiskey held to my lips, pouring liquid fire down my throat. I gag, try to say no, but they keep pouring.

Wave of fire radiating out from my foot, whiskey throbbing circles of burning outwards from chest and throat. The circles of fire touch and pulse like wings in this heat. Annie is holding my hand. I cling to her, the one solid thing in this waver of fire.

"Everything's going to be all right, Fiona. We're all here to take care of you."
The twins are howling.
"Can you not keep those brats quiet?" Gran snaps.
Sound of my mother's sobs growing more distant as she takes the children into the other room.
"If you'd but taken the medicine none of us would be in this

fix now!" Gran snarls.

Gran should not be hard on Mother, she's so sad. I want to tell her not to be unkind, but I cannot remember how to make my tongue move.

Her hand lifting my head, "Open now, chicken soup." As I drink and become more awake, my foot hurts all the way up to my hip. Why does everything hurt so much? Like Rose trying to do knitting with her swollen old hands, fumbling and dropping stitch after stich, I cannot hold onto my thoughts or weave one to another. Sleep, sleep is better, back to sleep. . .

*   *   *   *

"I'm hot, I'm hot, I'm burning!"

They have me near the fire. I can't stand it. Thrashing, Mina sponging me off—

"I'm hot! Leave me alone! I want my Gran, I want my Gran!"

"Eostre! Bring her here!" Mina commands.

At last Gran comes, puts a cool pastille in my mouth, lays cool minty cloths on my throat and forehead. But my leg is so hot—

"Take me out in the snow, put me in the snow please, it was nice there—" I keep raving, begging them to put me in the snow.

"Where's that Lady?" I demand.

"What lady?" replies Mina.

"The Lady who brought me back, where is she?"

"You brought yourself back," says Mina.

*   *   *   *

When I wake next I feel peaceful, rested. Sara, midwife and healer, is dozing by the fire, full moon belly resting on her lap. She wakes quickly, as if my look had been a touch. Her hand on my forehead.

"There. You're feeling better now."

Her eyes are so kind, her smile is so beautiful. She says when she was little the other bairns called her muckle-mouthed and rabbit faced. It seems to me that her buckling teeth just make her smile that much bigger.

"The fever's broke," she says, smiling her wonderful smile. She gives me a big hug and gets me some broth. I thought it was morning, but it must yet be night. No one else is awake.

I try to sit, but cannot get farther than leaning on my elbows. My foot is swaddled in cloth, wrapped up to the knee.

"I hurt my foot."

"Aye."

"The axe slipped."

Sara nods.

"Will it stop hurting soon?"

"We hope so."

"How long since I hurt it?"

"Five days."

It seems but yesterday. I give up trying to figure how so much time could have passed.

"Your friend Annie is powerful," says Sara. "Twas Annie stopped the bleeding. Before your Mother had time to summons anyone else, she burst in asking for you, as if she knew you were hurt. Your mother sent Eostre to get your Gran. But before she got here, Annie did a charm that stopped the bleeding."

"I never saw her do that."

"She said she needed to do it, so she did it," says Sara. "If she can heal her anger, she'll be a fine healer. I'd be happy to train her in all that I know. And she can teach me what she knows," she adds with a smile.

Sara understands, Sara knows how special Annie is—it's so easy to fall asleep smiling, with Sara stroking my hair.

*　　　*　　　*　　　*

It looks so ugly I want to cry. They had cut off the next to smallest toe. The two that had flanked it are purple and twisted. Black and red streaks mottle the foot and have already crept past the ankle. Gran hands the stinking bandages to my mother. Her face is grim.

"That's the frostbite on top of it all!" She looks at me. "Well, Fiona, you may lose these other two toes. I don't know that we can save them."

I'm crying, "No, no!" shaking my head.

"Better the toes now than the foot later," she says.

I try to sit, reaching a protective hand towards my foot, the adults' worried faces blurring beyond my sobs. Annie appears beside Gran, puts her hand on my foot.

"No, it'll heal," she says quietly.

I see Gran stop herself on the brink of a sharp retort, narrowing her eyes and studying the child.

"How much is wish and how much is seeing?"

Annie juts her chin out.

"You think I'd risk her foot? I'll do magic! It'll heal!"

Gran looks torn, wanting to believe.

"Three days," she says finally, "If there's improvement in three days—then—we'll try three more—" She looks at me in an apologetic way.

"If there's any hope—I just have to keep you alive—"

My stomach twists into a knot. That it could be so serious as that—that my Gran can look frightened—

*   *   *   *

Annie made up a bed beside mine and for a fortnight she would not leave. Every night, and during the days before I slept, she would take me on 'a wee journey.'

"Now you are going into a beautiful garden—and you're walking—and as you step you feel no pain, only the strength of the earth flowing into your feet...take the petals of the most beautiful flowers—and rub them on your foot and wish it to be well. . ."

She bathed my foot in imaginary tidepools, rainbows, bowls of beautiful cream. She would describe the entrance of an ancient temple, I would recall its smell; together we would imagine Priestesses with crescents and eyes painted on their brows, power warm as sunlight radiating from their palms...

When I was wakeful she bathed my foot in warm salt water mixed with the herbs the older women gave her. She would put my mangled foot against her heart and hold it there, and soon the love thudding from beneath her bones into mine would pulse stronger than the throb of spreading poison, and the burning would ease into a glow of green and golden light.

Moments when we were alone she would massage my other foot, sucking and nibbling on the toes, convincing my hurt foot of all the pleasures in store for it when it got better, tickling me until I giggled so hard at her wickedness that my ribs ached worse than my wounds.

The next time Gran unwrapped my foot, the evil smell was gone, the black and red streaks fading. She sucked in her breath; for one precarious moment I thought she might weep.

"Bless the Goddess!" she said, and gave Annie a fierce tight hug. "Bless this Roxannabel Douglas!"

Three days later, when she looked again, my foot was so much better that she could only stare. At last she turned her gaze to Annie.

"If you ever have cause to ask a boon of me, you have it."

Annie met her gaze, level and strong.

"You know what boon I'll ask."

Gran nods, searching Annie with the same piercing gaze she uses to make the earth transparent, to see the roots within. At last she smiles, a wry, half-smile which contains both wariness and respect.

"As you wish."

After she left, Annie clutched my hand, shaking with excitement.

"This means we'll be in the coven together!" she whispers.

*   *   *   *

Once it was clear that I would not lose the foot, the boredom of lying flat soon became worse than the pain. At first it was fun to sleep by the fire every night, and have a chamber pot under my bench like the fine ladies. But soon I'd have traded anything for a chance to get out and away from the smells and noises of the croft. The twins were as mewling and querulous as if they knew they were the cause of our misfortune. Malcolm was not yet two, and as jealous of the babies as any new-weaned bairn. He was not above stuffing his soiled pants in a shrieking mouth, or whacking one with a ladle if he thought no one was looking. Colin and Elana were not so demanding, but not old enough to be much help either. They would promise to keep the twins from crawling into the fire and then forget, until a howl of pain and a flurry of cinders brought Mother's skirl of wrath. Mother was still weak from birthing and losing the last child. At least once a day she would sink to the floor with her hands over her face and sob until the little ones were so frightened that they would wail with her and the whole house rang with the din of despair.

Gran fell ill with a lung sickness which she was hard put to shed, and Sara had her baby and so was confined to her house until spring. It fell to seven-year-old Eostre to manage the household. She bore it staunchly, and despite the burdens was more cheerful and kind than I had ever known her to be. We had had a bitter quarrel the morning I hurt myself, and she feared that somehow it was her fault the axe had slipped. I remember coming out of my delirium at one point to hear her sobbing that she would never say another cross word to me if I would only get well.

Annie stayed on and did much of what I had done before, fetching water, chopping wood, gathering tulse and cockles and crabs from Loch Inbhir. Once or twice a week she would appear with a piece of smoked fish or deer flesh or a fresh killed rabbit. When asked how she came by such she would shrug and say, "I had a bit of luck," or, "I found it." Not until spring when we began to hear villagers complaining of mysterious thefts and pilferings did we realize she had come by her luck in other people's smokehouses.

Mina always said she had no bairns because neither her ears nor her heart could abide the racket, but more often than not, supper time found her stirring a haddie broth or a mess of pottage and kale over our fire. I could do little but tell stories to the wee ones. I helped as much as I could with the sewing, but stuck myself so often I swore the needle was more danger to me than the axe.

The sheep were now penned, there was so little forage for them, so John came over almost every day, bringing wood and peat and trinkets to amuse the little ones. He brought me my first little bone-handled biolline and taught me whittling and wood carving. He brought bird whistles which made the most marvelous gurgling tweeting noises when filled with water, and showed me how to make them, as well as the pan pipes from reeds. Some days he brought a sack of colored yarn and told stories which he illustrated with a game of cat's cradle.

"Here's the castle—made of ice—" he'd say, slipping a web of white wool over Eostre's fingers, "—at the end of the world. And in it, is a sack—" and here he deftly changed the shape of the web to a gunny, "—and in that sack is kept the four winds. And who should be the keeper of the winds but the Queen—" and here he slipped an indigo weft over my fingers, "—of Air and Darkness. When the Queen was content, all was well, but when she was angry she would loose the sack—" here he changed the white wool pattern once more, "—and unleash a bitter violent wind to wreck havoc on the crops and fishermen. But one day, a red-haired boy—" slipping a scarlet strand over Colin's fingers, "—named Gwion came to the castle. . ." And so he would hold us spellbound for hours, forgetting hunger and boredom and cold.

At last the pain subsided enough so that Annie encouraged me to begin trying to walk. My first attempts were the stuff of jest, but for the pain. Instead of a foot I might have a block of wood, so heavy and stiff it was. The place where the bone had been severed hurt the worst, and yet at the same time I could feel the missing toe as plain as ever. Every night I imagined my foot being just as it had been, willing the toe to appear to sight as clear as it appeared to sense. Every morning I would wake and find it still gone. It made me feel downhearted about my magic, that I could feel it there so clear, yet fail to conjure it.

John carved me a staff graved with serpent and flowers and birds. The first time Gran saw me use it she wrenched it out of my hands and threw it in the fire. I tried to snatch it from the flames but she pushed me back.

"I'll not have my granddaughter turned to a cripple!"

"Staghorn gave it to me!" I cried, knowing it was forbidden to speak his true name outside of circle, but not caring.

"Twas well-intentioned but ill-conceived," she replied. She grew very tall, her black cloak sweeping down from her shoulders like folded wings. Even the littlest bairns hushed.

"Walk across the room," she commanded.

Casting a look of longing and resentment at my precious staff I hobbled across the room, hoping she would see how much I needed it.

"Put equal weight on both legs."

I protested that I could not. Gran folded her arms.

I kept trying to put more weight on the injured foot, but it hurt so much that I was soon in tears, humiliated that Annie and the whole family were watching. Finally I faced her, weeping and shaking my head. She bent down from her great height, took my chin in her fingers, tipping my gaze into hers. Her black eyes were kind but unyielding.

"A Priestess stands on her own two feet," she said quietly. She walked to the door and turned.

"The grace of the Goddess saved your foot, but only your will can make use of it."

She came every day after that to watch me practice. Though I saw little progress in the next few days, she said, "In three moons time, you'll be walking as well as ever."

I began whimpering and whining. She gave me a withering glance.

"If you have not the will for so simple a thing as this, how can you expect to summons the powers that dwell between the worlds? Consider this one of your trials. How you handle this trial will tell me much as to whether you may survive the rigors of initiation."

So I knew there was no hope for it. I had to learn to put my weight on both feet. For awhile I would just sob everywhere I walked, especially when fetching water from the well, or walking uphill. It hurt all through that spring, and all through the summer that followed. I learned not to cry when I walked; learned how to put my attention elsewhere. Just when I became resigned to the everness of the pain, I realized it had eased, and by the following autumn I was truly well.

Chapter 14

Impossible to walk silent in the woods today. Dried brown leaves crunching to powder beneath my feet. Damp earth still chill from the first heavy rain. John is stitching up new brogans for me; soon it will be too cold to go without them. I tuck the stalks of cinquefoil and hensbane beneath the napkin covering my basket. A few eggs nestled on top of the bundle make excuse for the bed of herbs beneath, should excuse be needed.

The best cinquefoil grows in the marshy spot between the branches of the forked stream that runs near the castle. Already today I have fetched tansy and willow. Gran has many potions to brew before this season's gathering is over. Ah, a clump of rue, she said there was one here. A pungent lining for an egg basket.

Little grass snake, looped over himself, basking in the sun. I very quickly set my basket down and sit beside him, making a slight beckoning motion with my fingers, as if I were stroking under his jaw, not quite touching him. I stroke him with my raith energy, warm air wafting off my fingertips. He comes closer, seeking the warmth of my fingers, slides his head into my hand, slides his body along very slowly, still drowsy or perhaps even still asleep, until his neck and head are laying down my wrist and his tail is looped around the three middle fingers of my hand. He rests there very quietly. Very slowly, so it feels like no motion at all, I bring my arm across my chest so the snake is cupped under my left ear, in case he should want to whisper any secrets to me. One must be very quiet to hear the secrets of snakes. That's what Mina says, and she should know. She has a large snake who dwells behind her hearth as her familiar. She relies on him for nearly all of her beastly workings now, for her cat Moppet is getting old, more interested in sleep and cream than in magic anymore.

As I lie with the snake close to my ear, my breath moves very slowly and I doze also, the snake curled in my hand. Snakes are such a comfort.

I seem to hear the snake whispering, "Sssisters. . sssisters. ." and something about danger—I begin dreaming about what it would be like to be able to peel off my skin and step out anew. Mina says it is like that when we die, that we shed one body and find that we have grown another. Snakes are sacred to Cerridwen for they have the art of being born again, of letting go of who they were to become something new. And they say that when my womb sheds its first lining of blood, that I will shed my little girl's body, my girl-child self, and become a woman, and that is also the serpent's art.

Again I muse on Cerridwen, Kyairthwen, Hag of the waters. Of all the forms of the Goddess, it is she who draws my mind again and again. She is the Goddess of transformations; soup is also her craft, putting together many ingredients, each of which surrenders its being for the benefit of the whole. The fire of Cerridwen causes us to forget who we were and become something new in her cauldron of change. But she is not the shape-shifter. That is the Horned One's gift. It is he who is at once animal and human, who confers the art of being able to enter into the being of another, as I merge with Oberon or a salmon or some creature of the woods. It must be as Gran says, that we are more water than earth, so easy it is to flow out of that part of me that seems bounded by my bones and skin and into another being. The boundaries of the skin are no walls to me.

I lie there, one with the snake, riding the pulse of my wrist, feeling the body of the baby mouse eaten earlier in the day decomposing inside, giving up its sweet juices to become bands of rippling muscle and shiny scales. My tongue forks, tasting the air, flavor of pine and bayberry, warm earth and warm girl-flesh—and an acrid odor suddenly overpowering all the rest—

A wash of fear through the woods. I stir awake to the bright peal of a hound, echoed by the chiming of another and another and another. . .

The snake slips quickly from my hand, the scent of fear and blood-thirst on the wind so strong, we forget to say good-bye.

Hounds skirling closer and closer—men's shouts, still so far away as to sound like murmurs—rumble of hooves tearing ragged crescents in the earth. The hounds are still far but the fear comes close and close—and I see with my inner eye rather than my outer, the blur of russet and white—the fox scurrying for her life, dashing through the underbrush. I send out a call, "Here—here—come—safety—sister." She bursts out of the bushes and into my lap with such force that I am almost knocked over—panting, sobs in her breath—a very little fox, one of last spring's litter, shivering in my lap—smell of fear bristling from her fur—there's not time to waste—I stand quickly, before I have a plan, carrying her in my arms. She's so frightened she pees on my skirt, but then the idea comes.

"All right, quickly now." I point her in another direction. "Off with you, now! I will take the hounds."

She scurries off, running as fast as she may. I see her limp but have no time to help with that. Quickly I tear some skunk cabbage, and with the rue already gathered, sweep over her tracks, scattering bits of torn herbs along the path where she has gone. I push my herb basket under a thick family of ferns. Then I take off my apron that she has soiled and drag it in the opposite direction, over to the stream. I drag the apron all along the banks, cross over to the other side and rub it in the dirt there. Soon it is filthy but I care not for that, but keep rubbing it in the dirt, dragging it along the bank behind me, slapping it into each tree that I pass.

The hounds are close now. I look around quickly and see a tree that still has some leaves, one of the Laird's apples planted alongside the stream—quick as a squirrel I clamber up the branches, bearing my soiled apron. I huddle on a branch where the foliage is the densest—prop myself back against the trunk, heart pounding almost as hard as the fox's.

The hounds are at the stream now, baying and crying out with their sharp voices—jumping over to the other side of the stream and back again, whuffling in the dirt, looking all around in confusion. One starts off in the direction the fox has actually gone, but soon comes back to join the others who are baying about the tree in which I hide. The din of their baying shakes the branches; they rear on their hind legs, scrabbling to obtain a purchase on the trunk with their claws—leaping up, jaws snapping with excitement and frustration, the eerie whistle of their call never ceasing.

Excited voices of the men—I recognize Lochlan, the Laird of Ross, Laird Lindsay, Lindsay's oldest boys and Sean's excited voice pealing, "We have him, we have him!"

It's not a him, I think, tis a her.

"Get your arrows at the ready," Laird Lochlan calls out. My heart leaps up in my throat. Shall they shoot into the tree without seeing what's there? I begin to climb down. The Laird with his riding crop beating the dogs away from the tree.

"All right. All right you curs, well done! Well done! He's ours now! Back off, now!"

I swing down out of the tree, dropping from the lowest branch into the space Lochlan has cleared.

Look of shock on his face, almost bordering on fear. His eyes flick to the soiled apron still clutched in my hand—oh, foolish of me not to have left it in the tree!

"Aye now Robbie," cries Laird Linsay, "If I get one of your bitches to whelp me a litter, will they tree me such pretty foxes?"

Ross laughs in his deep velvet voice that reminds me of Peter's.

"Tis the red hair has confused them, I'll wager. These hounds hunt by the eye rather than the nose!" The younger lads snigger.

But the Laird does not laugh. He snatches the apron out of my hands and throws it aside. The hounds leap on it, ripping it to shreds, shrieking and snarling. The rank smell of fox piss is obvious—my skirt wet with it also—

Lochlan grabs my arm so hard it is all I can do not to cry out.

"Are these my woods or yours?" he hisses between clenched teeth.

"The woods belong to themselves, m'lord!"

He wrenches me around and lays a dozen stinging blows from his riding crop on my back and legs. I make one cry, then set my teeth in my lip, my toes splay and curl, gripping the earth. He yanks me around again, hisses close to my ear so the others will not hear, "Keep thy witchery to thyself or thou wilt be the sorrier for it!" and shoves me away.

I stumble over the stream, holding my arm, sure it is broken. Stagger back through the bushes; remember the basket but leave it, needing my good hand to cradle the arm that goes from numbness to fire with every step.

The welts on my back and hips ease readily with one of Mina's poultices, but the ring of black bruise girdling my arm did not fade so easily. And the blackness circling my heart stayed, long after my flesh was clear.

Chapter 15

The cold ground seeps icy shadows into my feet, making the left one ache. Dusk is coming down fast; I must work quickly if I do not wish to work blind. The herbs grow so densely in Rose's garden, everywhere I step a bruised plant exhales its pungent fragrance. Rosemary, marjoram, chives; I take the cooking herbs first, careful to wipe the juice from the little sickle's crescent blade after each cutting. I set the cooking basket aside and take up the basket woven with a spiral of black and white fibers that is the magic basket. I take the woodruff first, the May herb always included in love charms, then make my way to the voracious looking sundews lining part of a garden wall. I fear these animal plants, with their sticky, devouring mouths. My offering of dried sage and heather does not seem to appease them. The truculent set of their jaws makes me think they are still unwilling to be cut.

"Never take a plant unwilling," says Gran.

"Bring me the three largest sundews," Rose had ordered. Rose frightens me more than Gran and the sundews together, so

I sever the three largest quickly, half-expecting the remaining stalks to lunge forward and bite me in revenge.

What most of the villagers call Morning Glory, we know as Snake Star, the twisting vine competing with the rambling rose hugging the garden walls. I need a long strand, as long as would wrap around a man nine times, Rose said. Wrestling with the recalcitrant serpent plant, I unravel it from the other plants and loop it around myself, trying to imagine how much bigger a grown man would be. I'm skinny from having been sick all winter; Mina says I'm no bigger than a seven year bairn. Finally I have it measured, cut free and piled in the basket, writhing loops of green spilling over the edges.

Blinking, willing my eyes to adjust, I carry the baskets into Rose's croft. The trouble is, it is not a darkness the eye can adjust to. The house has no windows, and the walls are black with hearthsmoke. Like most of the villagers, Rose disdains our chimney, believing that the smoke of different woods keeps one healthy in winter. Gran says smoking preserves dead animals, not live ones.

Whatever the truth of that, no amount of smoke-stains could create the illusion that confronts me now; a tunnel carved in rock, leading down into a great cavern. Sometimes when I am here I see a huge house with hundreds of rooms, staircases leading off in every direction. Or a blasted plain, bristling with thorns under a hot sun, without a sheltering tree in sight. And the illusions do not stay still, but shift and rearrange themselves like shapes in clouds.

Gran says that Rose has gone behind the veil and lives with that special murkiness that comes with dwelling between the worlds. Mina says that Rose has gotten confused as she has grown older and that's why things are so confusing at her house.

Knowing that it is an illusion does not make the cavern any less awesome, nor lessen my fear of being lost in it. A bat flies down into my face, skreeking, and turns into Rose. She takes the herbs, pawing through them with her swollen hands. She squints through the haws over her eyes as if she could see, but in spite of their fumbling, I know it is really her hands that she has sight with.

"Your hands must grow eyes," Gran would say. "Healing or

herbcraft, tis all the same." She frequently has me sort herbs blindfolded to get the touch, and scolds me if she catches me cheating by using my sense of smell.

Rose instructs me to make a small ring of stones in the middle of the floor. Relieved to see that we are crouching in a small dark croft rather than a vasty cavern, I light the tinder of wood shavings and dry moss with a flint and set a pot of water on the stones. She adds the woodruff, the sundew and a blue-tinted liquid from a vial, muttering a chant in a language I do not know. Soon my head is swaying with the hypnotic rhythm of the chant, the strong smells simmering in the pot. Rose takes the snake star plant and slowly coils it into the pot, chanting loudly. It seems impossible that the small pot is containing it all—could there be a hole in the bottom leading into the floor?

A quick peek reveals that the pot remains solid, but the fire has gone out. The pot continues shaking and bubbling over the dead fire as if it would explode at any moment. Rose's chanting grows louder and more forceful as she feeds the last loops of snakestar into the mixture until, with a great shout, she releases the cone of power. Gradually the pot stops shaking although the contents still seethe. She says something to me in the other language, and repeats it angrily when I do not respond. I realize she means to give her my hands. She begins pressing my palms toward the pot. A squeak of protest escapes my lips as I brace against a pain that does not come. The pot is cool; under my touch, the contents quiet. Rose gestures for me to leave the pot in a dark corner to steep. She takes the stones from the ring and throws them around the house. I clear away what is left of the moss fire, sweeping half out the front door, half out the back. Meanwhile, Rose lurches stiff-legged about the house, head thrust forward, glaring into the dark corners like an owl stalking a rodent. Are we still doing the spell? It is clear that there will be no reconciliation between the Laird and my mother, so we are doing a working to bind him from doing her harm. I'm afraid to move, lest I disturb the magic in some way—

Rose turns towards me, baleful and fierce as a barn-owl. I shrink down, trying to make myself as small as possible, feeling like a mouse under that stare. She reads my mind.

"You are *not* a mouse," she says firmly.

A few more moments of stalking about, and the energy seems to drain from her. She sways on her feet, looking like a very old woman.

"Get my chair," she commands. The chair is as old and creaky as she is. She sits down slowly. I get a blanket to wrap around her, light the hearthfire and massage her knotty, bruised-looking hands. All the while I am trying to work up the courage to ask her the question throbbing on the back of my tongue.

"Rose, William said you would tell me about the Queen of Air and Darkness."

"Who?" she asks, owl-like.

"The-queen-of-air-and-darkness," I say, running it all together as if it were one word.

"Whooo?"

So I tell her the whole story from the axe hitting my foot to the Lady in white fur and how she rapped at the door of the croft but no one else saw her.

"William said he saw her once and that you knew all about it."

"Oh, La Fay." Rose opens her mouth and smacks her lips in a ruminating way. The yellow nubs of her teeth worn down to the jaw, the drool trickling from the corners of her mouth. How can this ugly old woman possibly know ought of the beautiful lady in white fur?

Rose speaks slowly.

"She has little use for mortals. Ye must be of the blood to have interested her. Mmm. Maybe she likes yer hair. They like bright things."

"Like gold?" I ask.

"Aye, gold and silver and bright-haired bairns."

"Do the fay really steal children then?"

She chuckles.

"Oh, not steal. . . borrow. You want to see her again?"

"Oh yes, very much!"

Rose says nothing else for a long time. Finally she shivers.

"I'm cold," she complains. Quickly I feed the fire and rub her hands, hoping she has not forgotten what we were talking about.

"How might I see her?"

She hunches forward, squinching her eyes to call up the memory.

"Take twenty-seven white pebbles, as round as you can find them—little moons, you know, the ones we call moon-drops. Go out to the mounds at night—the black door—too likely to be seen at the white door—"

"Wait—wait—where are these doors? I've never seen them."

She looks up at me like a horse might look at a particularly annoying fly.

"What doors?" she rasps.

"The black and white doors you just—"

She sighs with exasperation.

"The black door is midnight. The white door is noon. The rose door is dawn, the violet door is twilight." She shakes her head. "Anu's neglecting yer education."

"White. . . Rose. . . Violet. . . wait, is that why your name—"

She dismisses my question with a fluttering motion of her hands.

"No one has but one reason for a name. Quit pesterin' me or I'll forget this charm. Choose any door, providin' ye'll not be seen. Make a circle with the stones—each about two fingers apart—and sit in the middle. Then take some flowers ye've brought and face each direction as we do in circle, blowing upon the flowers as if ye were the very wind herself. Then lay the flowers in a circle outside the stones. Take a bit of milk in a bowl mixed with honey—the creamier the better, never stint them—take sour milk an' ye'll get a goblin, mark my word—and put that out to the North. Mind ye stay inside the circle. Then you wait."

"Will she come then?"

"Something might happen. Might not too. Fay only does what a fay pleases." She mutters to herself for awhile, then yawns and falls asleep.

I tuck the quilt under her chin. Someone has left two squirrels and a rabbit outside the front door. Cut up with turnips and carrots and the potherbs, it makes a quick stew. Four of Rose's eight children are still alive, and they all have children, so though she lives alone, she is well cared for. None of her children inherited her craft, for magic tends to skip a generation in her family as it does in ours. Peter, Sarah, and the youngest member of the coven, Jessica, are the grandchildren that are heirs to her art. It was much disapproved of when Peter and Sarah wed, for they are first cousins, but they say that in olden times even a brother and sister might wed and their children would be none the worse off if the stock was good to begin with. Peter says their children will have the gifts stronger because of the double potency of their blood, and that it is cross-breeding with once-borns that weakens the strain and causes the magic to skip.

Finished with cutting up the meat and vegetables, I add some water and wine to the pot and leave it to simmer over the hearth. It is brighter outside than in, for the moon is just past full. Rather than return home, I race for the beach to find twenty-seven round white stones.

Chapter 16

Carefully I adjust the stones so the circle will be perfectly round. Surely the Queen of Fay would not deign to appear at a ragged circle. I pin one end of my middle-clout in the center of the circle and sweep the other around to get the edges even, wishing I had a real nine-foot cingulum, the ritual sash used to measure magic circles. Turning to the east, facing into a cold, wet wind, I hear a waft of faraway music, flute and drum. At first I think it is coming from over the hill, but then it seems to be coming from under the ground. My legs go all trembly. I weave daisies and roses into the eastern quarter of the protective ring of gorse surrounding the circle of stones. To the south I offer yellow laburnum and lilacs and the bright red poppies. At the western quarter, the buttercups and Mari's cloak, the wild flowers that drape like a robe over the sea cliffs. The buttercups have wilted; I fret over whether they are fine enough to offer. At the north, pointing right to the barrows where the Fay are reputed to dwell, I fashion an altar with dandelions and lily, daisies and larkspur.

Finally I loop the snakestar plant around the circle, calling

on the serpent spirits for protection and wisdom. I lay a white ce-
ramic bowl filched from the Laird's house in the center of the
north flowers and pour the milk and honey from the sheepskin
jug into it. I taste the mixture to be sure it is sweet, minding
what Rose said about goblins. Nervously I finger the biolline
blade John made for me last winter, hoping it would be enough to
fend off any gobbet or grobbet or ghostly thing which might appear.

Tipping my ears to catch any sound of approach, I can dis-
cern nothing but the pounding of my heart. The damp wind soaks
through my clothes, drawing my skin into goose prickles. Mist
rises from the ground, vague white forms undulating and pulsing to the music of my heart. I kneel, shivering, mesmerized by
the shapes. Almost I think beings are approaching, but then they
turn, twist, spiral away, leaving only a slap of wet moor smoke
against my face, my hair.

*   *   *   *

I wake on my side, curled up in the kneeling position as if I
had simply toppled from exhaustion. Sit up stiff and shivering,
the disappointment so sharp it aches like a physical wound.

The cream has vanished. The bowl licked clean.

My right hand is cramped so tight I must use the left to pry
the fingers apart. Inside, a small cylinder of bone, like the middle
section of a finger, with three holes bored into it to make a
whistle. Tipped with a silver mouthpiece marked with tracerie so
fine it seems to have been carved with a hair. The faeries must
have come, they must have given me this gift. Hard as I try, I
can remember nothing; nothing but the sense that I must never
speak of this, not to Gran, not to Rose, not to Annie, not to anyone.

The sun spills early light over the hills. The rose door is wide
open. Hurriedly I pack everything into bundles so as to leave no
trace, and scurry home.

Chapter 17

"Hurry-up," Obie rumbles in my ear. Swimming up from sleep, I hear the sharp neigh of Annie's call. Slither down the ladder, hop and tiptoe over the forms of my sleeping siblings. The door opens me into a sea of mist. I trot out, toss my head and neigh in reply.

Snorting, Annie trots out of the mist, arching her neck to look like a fine charger.

"The Mares of Scotia go galloping up the hill," she says.

My whinney echoes hers as we turn and canter up through the woods. The hair that slaps in my face is the mane of a roan mare. The mist and our wish combined imbue Annie with the flickering appearance of both black horse and gypsy girl.

By the time we have reached the other side of the rise, we are firmly ensorcelled, scudding down the crest under a rain of arrows, slipping and sliding over a field of corpses. We are the mares of Scotia Cailleach, the dark Goddess who causes men to battle whenever she needs enough spilt blood to birth the world anew.

"Watch out for the spearman!" I cry, bucking and dodging a twisted tree in our path.

"Ha!" Annie rears and strikes the tree, cracking off a rotten branch.

"The Mares of Cailleach cannot be killed!"

As we gallop through the woods and mist, no creatures other than the ones we conjure come to view. A straggley elder bush snags my hair ribbon.

"Stop, my bridle is caught!" I call.

"Ye dinna *have* a bridle! The mares of Scotia can never be broke," replies Annie.

"Tis my mane then."

She canters up and bites at the branch until it releases me.

As the fog burns off we begin to get quite warm galloping in the sun. We are far from any villages now. We take our clothes off, hanging them from the limbs of a sprawling oak we will be sure to recognize. We feel more equine than ever with the sun and the wind singing on our skin.

In keeping with our transformation we quiet our hungry bellies by grazing on succulent herbs and grasses. Young dandelions so bitter they make our eyes squinch, purselane, shepherd's share, wild parsnips and carrots and the sweet tops of wheatgrass are satisfying, if not filling.

Sauntering through a large meadow, imaginary tails swishing the backs of our knees, Annie makes a lucky find of some clover blossoms. As we finish inhaling them, something in the shadowy crescent where the meadow melts back into woods catches our gaze. We canter over and then stop in our tracks, giving very unhorsey gasps of surprise. There must be twenty of them, half a foot tall if they're a knuckle, standing in a quiet ring as if they'd only just stopped dancing. Nothing like the meadow mushrooms we are accustomed to, this faery ring is peopled by white-stalked mushrooms bearing caps like conical scarlet hats ruffled with white.

Long exhalation of breath. I find myself kneeling beside one of the largest mushrooms, Annie across the circle from me bending over another. Gran and Mina dry some of these each year; when we ask what they are for, we're told they are for initiates, their purpose secret. We let our vision go soft, the way we have been taught to examine a plant and discover its uses by going inside it and knowing what it knows.

This plant is seductive, hypnotic, as if some sort of slow, swaying dance was going on just beneath the crimson skin. I find myself dropping closer to the cap, breath coming slowly as if the air was water. With effort, I peel my eyes off the mushroom and look across the circle to Annie. Our eyes meet, holding the same question. Then my head bobs down as if jerked by a halter; I find myself biting off the top of the mushroom, chomping it down to the stalk. The flavor is smoky and bitter, the mouthful so huge I can barely chew. Annie has munched hers too; we sit staring at each other, cheeks bulging like greedy groundhogs. The absurdity of our fat cheeks and the boldness of our actions seems funnier and funnier—we dare not guffaw, lest the mushrooms spill, and so the laughter gets in our eyes, streaming salty down our puffy faces making us look funnier yet. . .

At some point I realize that I have swallowed the last bits of musky flesh but am still chomping as if it were a new acquired skill I was loath to leave go of. Annie flashes me a look of merriment and bends down to chomp another; faithful as a shadow, I copy her actions.

But then I'm not seeing her anymore because bright colors like little sprays of fire are going off from between my teeth. Oceans of impossible fragrance and hue froth over my palate and tongue. Finally the colors slide in a sparkling waterfall down to my stomach. My heart is thumping like a big boran drum. Darkness broken by spangles of fluttering color, the swish of blood and the thump of pulse. . .

I realize my eyes are closed, and at that moment, they open. Annie sits motionless as if carved and painted, gazing off to my left with a glassy, unblinking stare. I begin to turn in that direction. . . it's like turning a thousand times before getting there. Meanwhile high-pitched giggles like silver bubbles are pouring into my left ear and bouncing out my right. The thousand variations of my turn finally completed, I fasten my gaze at the glade where Annie has locked hers. At first the trees, ferns, elyssum and meadowsweet all seem to be shivering, as if a wind was blowing, but a giggle wind rather than one of air. Then I see a young man in green leaning against a tree. . . and other faces, half human, half flower, winking in and out of the greenery. They come and go, appear and disappear faster than eyelids can flutter, but the giggling goes on and on until suddenly there is a lull, as if the wind had died down, leaving an ordinary forest in its wake. I have the terrible feeling they are leaving, going away, and cannot bear to have them go. I still have my sheepskin magic pouch around my waist, for I never take that off except at night when it is tucked beneath my pillow. Remember the faery whistle, untouched since first it appeared in my hand, and put it to my lips. Deep resonant sound, deep as a calling shell, then deeper. Deep as the ocean, deep almost below what I can hear. I experience a seam running down the middle of my body, a seam held in place by the sound, as if without it the two halves of my body would crack and fall asunder. Then I no longer make the sound but am made by it, blowing effortlessly through my body. I know now how the elders can sustain that hum they do for raising power in the circle; it has naught to do with holding one's breath, or with holding anything except the open hollowness of a bone whistle or a reed. . .

The wonderful Lady who saved me by guiding me through the snow appears before us. This time she is dressed in ivy, a crown of dripping green and white tendrils through her long black hair, strands of the heart-shaped leaves draping her body, regarding me with her wise smile. And my eyes are open.

Behind me Annie whispers, "Mother of God!"

The same melodious low sound of the whistle rumbles like a laugh in the Fay's throat. She speaks without altering her smile, her voice rippling inside my brain.

"No, I am not the Mother."

She turns and beckons us to follow down a path that seems to make itself under her feet. Following without hesitation, I hear the thump thump of running footsteps.

"Fiona!"

Turning, I see that Annie is dressed in ivy like the Lady. So am I.

She whispers, "Is it best?"

"She's the one who saved my life," I say, taking her hand and pulling her along. Deer and birds appear alongside the path to escort us. We also catch the in and out flicker-quick flashes of the other Fay, and I realize I've seen them before but had not believed my sight. Like leaves flickering green and silver in the wind, or the shape-shifting fog, the images are too quick to hold firmly in the eye. The Lady, however, remains as solid-seeming as we do.

The path slopes down, the earth arches over our heads. Annie holds my hand tightly as we pass beneath an earthen dolmen curtained with ivy. A brief steep passage through darkness opens us into an egg-shaped cave covered with violet crystals. It is so beautiful, Annie relaxes in an instant. Nothing that beautiful could be bad. In the middle of the cave are steps rising to a round dais in its center. We kneel across from the Lady at a low black table. Two more Fay appear, a blond maiden and a youth so like her they must be twins. The Maiden holds a tray of carved vessels, her brother presents them to us with elegant flourishes. They vanish. With a graceful gesture, the Dark Queen indicates that we may take our choice. Annie grabs me under the table.

"Do not touch it to your lips!" she thinks loudly. There are plenty of tales of what may become of mortals who eat or drink what the faeries serve under the hill.

The Queen hears our thoughts as easily as if they were spoken. She smiles, kind, amused, and gives a little shrug as if to say, *"Do as you like."* I see Annie staring into a vessel almost as flat as a dish. The black surface of the water breaks into silver ripples and she moves into trance.

The vessels are to scry with, then, not to drink. I pull one over. As I look into it, the water shifts and starts to spin into a bubble of glass, a crystal ball dancing with bright fire at its center. The spinning stops. The crystal ball sparkles, alive with bits of broken rainbow. Then I see the pictures, not as if they were just appearing, but as if they had always been there and I was just now able to see them. Life after life of mine, strung together like a strand of pearls, receding into the future, advancing into the past. And in each one there are crystals, held in the hand to heal illness, to divine for truth or water. Crystals carved into balls like pearls of air through which the visions float. Crystals soaked in water to make a fluid potent for protection and healing; crystals held in the hand for leaving the body; geodes cupped to the ear to hear what is spoken at a distance; crystals cast on a sacred cloth and read as rune stones. And at the point where past and future curve and meet and become one, a magnificent city appears where whole towers seem to be made of crystal, dazzling as ice under the moon, sparkling like frozen fire under the sun. A city where I have so much power with the crystals that I vision the pictures as I want them to be, bring them into the crystal and thence project them, small and potent as the sun concentrated through a glass, into the world.

I see times when the power moves through me as easily as the sound of the magic whistle, when the crystals grow hot in my hands and the sick are healed. Times when I help others choose a better fate for themselves by seeing where their choices shall lead them. And I see times when I misuse the crystal; when I lie about what I see to make people blind or afraid, when I refuse to heal without money. Times when I am afraid to look, times when I look and do not allow myself to understand. Lives where I am cherished for my gifts, lives where I am murdered for them. . .

*   *   *   *

Something hot in my left hand. Coolness in the right. I'm lying curled beside two battered-looking stalks of mushroom. On the other side of the faery ring, Annie stirs and moans. In my left hand, a small ball of quartz, perfectly round and clear. In my right, the bone and silver whistle. We crawl towards each other, heads throbbing as if they could not recall their proper size. Annie shows me her gift; a small flat piece of polished rock, black and glossy as the elf-bolts we occasionally find. We speak little of our visions, sensing more than can be said. The gifts safely stashed in our pouches, we walk with wobbly legs through the meadow, down the slope to the stream. Almost to the water, we collapse to our hands and knees, vomiting. We crawl moaning to the water, dunk our heads and drink.

"If we purify we'll feel better," I suggest.

Annie nods assent. We immerse ourselves in the stream, willing it to wash our sickness away. Hauling ourselves back up to the bank, we lie on our backs with our knees up, trembling and weak for a long time.

"I'll tell you one thing. I'll never eat those mushrooms again!" Annie says.

Strange. I was just thinking 'twas not such a dreadful price to pay, and I would eat them again whenever I got the chance. I pat her hand and say, "You'll feel better in a bit. And anyway, 'twas a fine adventure."

She groans and turns on her side, holding her belly.

"My lights are of another opinion."

It is a long walk back, as even when we can finally rise we are in no mood for a gallop. We are silent until we approach the village.

Then Annie says, "Fiona, let's keep this a secret, not even tell your Gran or Mina."

"Tis secret," I agree. "Secret as the caves of Annuven."

Hands clasped and eyes locked, the moment of silence broken at last by birdsong seals it.

Chapter 18

Barley, Rye and Flax. Barley, Rye and Flax. Twisting triple braids of the long grains, forming them into charms to protect our animals. These will be woven into the double looped sigils that signify unending life and placed about the horns of our goats and cattle as protection from illness. Any weakness within them goes into the grain; when they toss it off we gather and burn it in the Beltane fires. Annie and I work quickly and silently, feeling graced that Gran and Mina have called on us to work the life loops with them. We want so much for them to think well of us. I am glad that Annie's fingers are so deft and her work is so fine. Anyone can see what a value she will add to the coven.

"Fiona. Roxanne."

We look up.

"You may keep weaving," Gran says. "Do you still believe in Faeries?"

We look at each other, wondering if she knows about our eating of the mushrooms and our journey.

"Well, of course we believe in them," replies Annie. I nod, feeling as if she had asked if we believed in trees.

"Ah, well, you know," she says, "there are those who doubt that they are real."

I shrug. What of those people? Gran is always saying how foolish the once-borns are.

We hear barking outside.

"Mina, to the door," says Gran softly. "Girls, be ready to put things under my bed in a moment." She rises. We quickly gather the rushes and prepare to hide them.

Mina peeks out. The Laird and his minions, going hunting.

"Ah, well," comments Gran, "I knew there was a reason I chose to do this weaving on such a sunny day, leaving the herb-gathering to another time." She makes a motion with her hand; "Pass-by, pass-by, no flickering fly of thought turn thee from thy purpose." We bring the weavings out again.

"The Laird likes our weavings," I say, "why are you worried about—"

"I'm not *worried* about anything," corrects Gran. She takes a breath. "Ah, well then. Your sense should tell you that is not quite true. Very well then. I have some concern. Ummm—the sight has brought me some visions which—please me not. And it has occurred to me that it might be well for—someone—to go under the hill and speak with the Fay. To tell them of our concerns and ask for their—" I know she wishes to say help, but the word that comes from her is, "—advice. Now I am too old and have been on this world too long to make this journey myself. As is Mina. And Rose is too old to even walk out to the mounds with any degree of comfort. So—my request is that—you two girls—wrapped round with every spell of protection that you could possibly need—make this journey to our kin under the hill and ask for their help."

She looks at Annie.

"Art thou afraid?"

"Well I—I certainly do as you ask. I will certainly do as you ask."

"But you have some reservation, I see it in your shoulders—so tell me what your fear is. If not, I will not send you on such a task, burdened by fear."

"It seems strange to me—Mother—they are like people and not people and real and not real—they seem strange to me."

"So you have seen them then?"

Annie looks at the floor. We agreed, after all, not to speak of our journey.

"I believe these girls know more than they are saying," remarks Mina, pulling up a stool to sit next to Gran, who is scrutinizing us closely.

"Well, we never meant it to be a secret," I say, though of course that is exactly what we meant it to be. I take the whistle and the crystal ball out of my pouch and show them.

"I got these from the fay."

Much as they try not to show it, I see that Mina and Gran are both startled and impressed.

"Well," Mina smiles, "we're certainly asking the right people for the quest."

Annie reveals the black polished stone she brought back.

"Ah, these are power gifts indeed!" exclaims Mina. "You girls are favored by the gentry. Tis well, tis very well."

Gran frowns.

"Did you find these things? Tell me the truth now. Did you find these things and make a story about it?"

"No. Rose told me how to call La Reine. . ." Quickly I tell her the story of our adventures.

"Well." Surprise makes Gran look younger.

"Well." She looks at Mina.

"Well then, we'll bring you—to our coven meeting tonight. The veil between our world and the realm of faery is thinnest now—we will meet here and from here go out into the woods. And from there we will send you—if you are willing—under the hill—and, provided that you do everything that we tell you, you should have no difficulty in coming back, and we see that they have already once let you in, which is well. It is actually harder for mortals to gain entrance than to be released from that place, whatever the legends may say."

*   *   *   *

That night in the clearing, around a small fire, John beats

his boran drum.

"I'll drum you into the hill and I'll keep druming. When it is time for you to leave, just listen for the sound of the drum and come towards it. And if for some reason you should stop hearing it, listen to your own heartbeat and follow the sound of your heartbeat. It will lead you back to the sound of my drum. Understand that you shall not be alone; my drum will follow you down and my drum shall bring you back up."

As we sit and talk, Jesse works the piece of embroidery she has, which is a spell she has just started for a mate and a safe place to raise her children in the old ways. She is newly brought into the coven, the youngest of Rose's grandchildren who has the art. How I envy her status now. Mina also works an embroidery. Gran rolls a sacred stone about in her hands.

"Our concern is that the fires are spreading. First I have seen, and then, scrying in flames and in the vision pool, we have all seen that the fires burning in Europe are spreading here. Our king is all too heavily influenced by his French blood and his ties to those lands across the seas. The accusations that happen now, which the bitter bring upon themselves, are only the presagers of a dreadful time. We will do all we can to avert such a time; at the same time it would be foolish to deny its coming, for this wave is vast; all our magic cannot unmake it. The fay have protected themselves by going under the hill, living amongst the crystal caves. We need to know how to best protect ourselves in the times that are to come, to ask for their alliance and succor."

"So," she says, "here is a gift." She hands us a large bundle.

"And—ah—here's a potion for you to drink." She hands us each an oxhorn chalice. The top is blue and frothy. I recognize by the stink it is largely composed of the mushrooms. A swallow tells me I am correct; curious taste of mushrooms mixed with mead—faint flavors of woodruff, mugwort. . .

My mind ceases to separate one flavor from another. The blue smoke rises from my belly, then spreads out from my center, swirling, and I feel how my flesh is not really solid, how the smoke moves and dances among the tiniest particles of myself, that even these particles are not solid, that all that keeps me together is a dance; a dance of swirling light. I set the horn down. My Grandmother's eyes looking through me, black as jet, black as the handle of her athamé. She also

*is moving and vibrating, also not solid. The world is not solid. Fire,
air, water, earth; it is illusion that makes some elements seem more
solid than others. It is all a dance.*

*Swishing his beater against the drum, circles and circles and cir-
cles of sound. . . Staghorn enters the dance going on inside me and directs it, directs me to rise. My rising and following him becomes part
of the dance.*

I carry the sack of gifts. Annie stumbles along behind me, my
reluctant shadow.

*Nothing is solid. Doors are possible everywhere. Stars above me,
their light coming down, moving into my body. . . nothing is solid.
Walking up the hill to the barrows, drums of excitement vibrating in
my bones. . . nothing is solid.*

Annie raps at the door with the wand that William Winter
has lent her. I fumble in my pouch for my whistle; before I can
find it, a whistle comes up from under the earth and the stone is
gone—not as if it had opened like a door, but simply as if it had
not been there at all. I go first; the opening is small, but Annie is
right behind me, holding my arm. I slip and roll, scudding down
the narrow passage and drop into a large room. Black. Black.
Black. My throbbing pupils open wider and wider. Black. I am
glad Annie is sitting here close beside me. Breath catches in her
throat with almost a moan.

A spire of crystal, capping a dim wand, wielded by a figure I
cannot see. The wand describes slow arcs across the ceiling of the
cave. White torch of the crystal wand strikes fire into each crystal it passes until the entire ceiling glows. The wand whirls in
circles, and like fireflies responding to the call of lightning, crystals ignite all along the sides and floor of the cave, their dim
glow reveals that we are in a small, egg-shaped room lined with
quartz. The figure wielding the wand at the center of the room
remains dark. It looks like the same room we were in before, when
the Fay taught us scrying, yet it cannot be; we are nowhere near
the part of the woods where we ate the mushrooms and followed
the Fay before.

I rise and slowly approach La Reine and open the sack of gifts
for her. She takes black flint stones from the pack; strikes them
together, smiling at the spark. Casually she rolls the wick of a
long taper between her two fingers, lighting it with blue fire. Her

face does not look as it has looked before, but seems dark, foreboding. Awareness flickers like the lighting of the crystals; Annie's fear has entered my body and is distorting my vision. Consciously I clear my sight, calling on the crystals of the cave to help me. Then I see her true, her loving and serene face white as the moon, her eyes deep and sparkling. She examines the other gifts. I gasp at the beauty of one of Jesse's embroiderings. It shows a crystal cave lined with glittering stars, above it a circle of humans weaving a dance of sparkling light about their heads and upraised arms; above that, a circle of stars in the sky. The embroidery is small and delicate; the whole of it would fit on the palm of my hand.

Gran has sent some of her most uncommon shells; the Fay takes each one out, gazes at it and listens to it intently as if each had a particular message she alone could hear. The whitewashed rocks found by the sea called moonstones; herbs from Rose's garden; a fine mandrake with arms poised in the invocation of 'as above so below'; a small carved object of Staghorn's creation. Each gift she receives as a personage of importance, a presence to be accorded with sober concentration.

A young blonde woman appears at one of La Reine's elbows, a young blonde man at the other. She nods to them, indicating the gifts.

"Take these where they belong."

They nod and without walking out, simply vanish.

Nothing is solid, I remind myself. An old woman appears with another bundle. She and La Reine bow towards each other. When she comes up from her bow, the bundle falls open and she becomes a very young girl, perhaps thirteen or fourteen. Her gray eyes twinkle mischievously at us as she disappears. Within the bundle are nine wands, graven with beautiful sigils. So smooth they gleam, they have an air of being as old as the broken stone circles which crown the barrows. I cannot resist; reach out a hand, run it along the smooth surfaces and graved words. Each wand is from one of the nine sacred trees. . . as I touch one the power of that tree surges through me, as if the essence of all rowans or all alders or all birches flourished in that branch.

"These are the nine sacred wands of the nine sacred trees," she says. "We have taken them into our keeping. If they will help you to survive, to play the part that is yours to play in this dance of light—" she indicates here the embroidery Jesse sent which has woven itself miraculously to her sleeve, "—if these will help you then we send them back into mortal care.

"Be comforted. Time is not time. It may be that this long dying is but a sleep. There will be a waking on the other side of it, as there always is.

"The trees from which these wands are cut are dead, more than a thousand years ago. And yet the power of the tree moves here, in this, its bone. Where the power of the sun moved through these veins in green life, now the power of all the stars moves through in healing." She curls my hands around one of the wands. At her touch, thousands of tiny particles flare to life inside me, bright as the crystals she had ignited in the darkened room.

"There is no death," she says. "And we who choose not to die live here, but we are not separate from the world. Rather we have chosen to be deeper within it. For here in the caves of crystal, time and death and all manner of transformation and change are different, for here we are choosing what we truly desire. When humans remember their heart's desire, then again will there be no difference between the crystal caves and the world above ground. As indeed, no difference exists now."

She smiles at me. She reaches a hand to Annie but stops short of touching her.

"All must come and go within their own place and in their own time. If you do not wish to be here, attach no regret to your wishing. Be where you choose. It is all right to leave and to return. There are so many circles, so many ways of coming full and empty, ebbing and flowing. There are circles and circles, and some are large and some are very small. No matter what the size, the circles are the same.

"Tell them," she brushes her hand gently over the wands, "that even if there is not so much left of the Craft as this, if it goes to bone and ash, that within that bone and ash will be all the power of it that ever was. The power leaves not. It changes shape only. Every power that has ever been here, remains here. And the only powers that will leave this earth are the powers that did not grow here, the powers that were not natural to be here, and while these powers may seem to be great and overwhelming in this day, I will tell you that they are soon to leave. And only those powers that believe in death and end shall experience it. The mystery and the power of the circles that you practice shall remain. This I promise. Sit with our sisters the mushrooms and learn their ways. It is their web underground which sustains and renews them. The fruiting body of them comes and goes. The body is a gift to the world."

She hands us the wands.

"Follow the drum," she says. "The heartbeat's drum will tell you where you want to go. It will lead you in and out of deeps—caves of crystal and barrows of darkness alike. And know that every choice is yours, regardless of what others choose, even the choice to be human was your choice and yours alone, and subject to your change.

"Go now. To the heartbeat's drum."

We turn from her and again are in blackness. But not in the narrow hole that brought us here. We walk as if we walked in a space where no stars hung. Is there ceiling above our heads? Is there floor beneath our feet? The blackness has no texture. But we follow the sound of Staghorn's drum. When it seems we can walk no further, we wake to find him washing our faces with cold water.

Annie carries her end of the wands. Mina hurries to meet us at the foot of the hills, casts her spell of invisibility over us and leads us back to her croft. There we find the coven waiting for us. Fresh flowers decorate the house; eggs and scones are prepared for our breakfast.

I tell our story. As I speak my hands dance like happy birds. My heart beats in a cave shiny with crystal; its soft music pushes light through my veins. Annie sits beside me brooding. Though almost as beautiful as the dark queen herself, she seems to have absorbed none of her light.

Gran and the others receive the wands with reverence and awe, listening quietly and carefully to all that I report. Gran fills our cups again with steaming mint and chamomile.

"You have served us well. It will be to our good fortune to have you in the coven. When we are nine, and with these nine wands, our place will be assured, even in the harsh times that are to come."

Chapter 19

Salt sting in the air makes my eyes tear a bit. I breathe deep—the freshness of it makes me feel light, hollow-boned like a bird. And this is fitting, for it is the day for me to contact my ally of the air, the day that marks the beginning of my eleventh winter. Mina had asked me to walk through the woods, and then by the marsh, and then by the sea, so that whatever type of bird it was, pheasant or songbird, gull or hawk, I should be sure to attract it to me. Climbing this cliff beside the sea, I know that this is where my ally will appear, and the knowing fills me with wild excitement.

The day is gray and overcast, as is usual for November. I am walking and calling at the time of day my mother was in labor with me. This is a powerful time to attract to me anything that is mine to keep and find, and the moon is new and also right for quests and beginnings, a doubly propitious sign. I am hungry from fasting, but it is a hunger that makes me feel light and powerful as a bird, and I know that it is impossible for my quest to fail.

Annie's bird is the thieving and all-knowing raven, which came as no surprise to anyone. It was her task last spring to walk in the woods at the dead of night, for that is when her mother had labored with her. The raven had first knocked a stick down from a tree, blocking her way, and then actually landed upon her left shoulder and cawed loudly in her ear. She said she was frightened almost to death by the suddenness of it and fell to her knees, then realized that the alderwood branch that the raven had knocked down was a gift intended to be her wand. She carved a sigil of a raven flying under a waning moon on it and vowed she would use it as her wand for the rest of her life. I felt that the elders respected her in a new way when she told her story of the raven. It has been hard for me to wait all these months since for the time of my birth and the seeking of my own ally of air.

The sea below is tumultuous and gray; she embraces the rocks noisily, leaving rings of white foam as evidence of her wild love for the land. I am climbing higher now, and the salt spray no longer dampens me, though the scent of it is still clear.

"It is the task of the earth ally to teach you the ways of being fully alive and aware, like the animals of the earth. The water ally teaches you to let your mind go absent, to move with the flow of the water, surrendering to the instinct to be guided purely by that force we call the Goddess," my Grandmother had said.

"That we *call* the Goddess? But is it not the Goddess?" Annie had asked.

"Of course it is the Goddess," Gran smiled with a wryness I did not understand. "That is why we *call* it that." For some reason she seemed amused by this interruption rather than angered as is more often her wont.

"I did not mean to interrupt," Annie said, regretting her hasty speaking. "Please tell us—how does the ally of air serve us?"

"It is with the ally of air that you will learn—how to move beyond—your skin," Gran responds. "The ally of air gives you vision. As you enter the ally of the air you will see how small your own life is—and how vast the world is. And that—" she concluded, "—will change you."

I pause, summons my water ally, the salmon, allowing the presence of the fish to empty me, empty my thoughts, so that I am movement only; then I become the lynx, my earth ally, stalking, moving now on all fours up the craggy cliff. The moss and lichen on the rocks are slippery. Most of the rocks are bare even of that. A gust of wind blows across my face, moistening me with a few pattering drops of rain.

A dangerous place to seek an air ally, I think with exhilaration! I lose my footing on one rock and bang my knee slightly. Take a deep breath, again will myself to cat awareness. Oh—what if being a cat should frighten off the bird I seek? Safer to go as a fish, I think, though it is hard to imagine a fish doing the hard work of crawling up these rocks which I must do now. Well, salmon go up waterfalls; a salmon I will be!

I reach the top of the tor overlooking the sea, crowned by a great round knob of stone. Suddenly I am seized with the bold idea to tie one end of my middle-clout around this knob and lower myself from the other so I will be suspended in mid-air, to call out to my air ally to come to me.

Too drunk on the salt wind to be frightened, I tie one end of the clout around the narrow neck of the stone; the other I loop about my waist as I have seen egg reivers do when they lower themselves to rob the sea-birds of their eggs.

Before I have time to think, I lower myself over the edge and find myself swaying in space. My middle-clout is nine feet long, in imitation of the real Witch's cingulum I shall have when I am grown, so I hang some several feet over the cliff, swaying like a spider on the end of a thread. How far the ocean is below! The rocks—

I feel like a bird and long to stretch both my wings out but caution keeps me holding one hand tightly to the rope that wraps my middle and one foot against the wall while I lean out and test the air with the fingers on my left hand—

Loud, ear-splitting cry—a black shape hurtles past me, plummets down and down. I am overwhelmed with terror—it is me that is falling, the black shape my shadow—

Green water closes over me—something squirming in my feet, my claws—strong wings beating, lifting me out of the surf, up and up, scaling the cliff as easily as a horse skims over a meadow, wings pushing the air down, compelling it to bear me—and then I am looking at an extraordinary sight; a white-faced, red-haired girl, hanging by a thread—I pause, letting the wind bear me, fish squirming in my talons—and then I am Fiona, the sea-hawk's golden eyes burning behind my green ones, my hands clenched like claws as if I were holding the fish I see gripped in the osprey's talons as she rocks on the wind, staring at me—and then her great wings beat—up and away.

I find myself merged with her again, hurtling over the cliffs into the tall pines to where her nest stands like a great solstice wheel on top of the tallest pine. Softly the air floats her down to the twin young in her nest. She tears off pieces of the fish to feed them. Smell of the salt, taste of raw fish—and the feeling like a fierce sea wind that flows through her body when her great-winged mate soars to the nest with his gift of fish and nurtures their brood with her.

Dizzy swirl of rocks and ocean below. Clutching the middle-clout with my right hand, my other arm hanging—sweet Lady! What in the name of God possessed me to dangle myself over the precipice like this? My skin is clammy with sweat and mist.

I sway myself over to the cliff and start scrabbling with one hand and both feet, trying to pull myself up the slippery sides. Tis one thing to get down, quite another to get up! Again and again my fingers grip some tiny crack in the rock, only to slip and sway me out over the abyss once again. I call for help and then realize that there is no possibility at all that anyone will hear me.

The sky buckles with thunder. A fierce, sudden wind whirls over me; slashing rain drenches my hair and my skirts. The rock face before me has become impossibly slippery.

No good to think of myself being a fish or a lynx; neither would ever be in such a predicament. *"How do the egg reivers do it?"* I think, quieting my panic. That's right, hand over hand on the rope. They cannot always rely on help from the cliff face either. I struggle up, my clammy hands slide some on the linen sash but inch by inch I gain. As my eyes become level with the ledge I see that I had carelessly draped my sash over a rough rock protrusion and the material is nearly sawed in half. For a moment I am paralyzed. Then the shrill shriek of the osprey as she hurtles down behind me. As she rises, coming up from the sea, I remember how it felt to sense that the air was solid under my wings, and I will the air to push me, as it pushes her. I heave myself over the edge and roll to the other side of the knob, panting and shivering. The osprey shrieks overhead and then something slops down beside me, flops a few times on the rocks and lies still.

A fish! The osprey left me a fish! I look up but she is winging far off in the direction of her nest.

I crawl up on my knees and take a shaky breath. I untie the end of my sash from around the rock and touch the part that had frayed with trembling fingers. Only a third of the linen remains unshredded. I have heard William Shepherd say that I nearly died of the fever I had when I hurt my foot, but this is the first time that I have ever consciously felt myself to be close to death.

I pick up the dead fish and roll it up in my apron, tucking the ends into the sash around my waist. It forms a wet bundle that flops about my knees as I walk.

Mina said she would meet me on a medium sized hill in Glen Lochlan, 'not in the mountains, not in the valley, not the forest, not the seashore—betwixt and between,' a meeting place which would not bias the direction in which I went to find my air companion.

I walk the miles between the cliff and our meeting place as exhausted as I was exhilarated before. The fish in my apron feels as heavy as the smith's hammer. By the time I finally drag myself to the foot of the hill I am reduced to crawling the rest of the way up to where Mina stands, regal in her long tartan cloak, waiting for me.

"About time!" she comments as I haul myself over the crest of the hill. "Taking your own time about it, and me waiting here catching deadly chill in this dreary rain."

Then she sees the look on my face. "Was it a complete failure then?" she asks in a tone indicating she can hardly believe that should be the case.

I shake my head, raising to my knees. "No. It was a great success." I unroll my apron, letting the dead fish flop out at her feet. "My ally of the air—is the sea hawk—the osprey."

"Did you shift and dive into the sea and fetch that fish yourself then?" she asks in a tone that implies that she is half-ready to believe it. "Dear Lord MacLir, you look soaked enough for that to be the case indeed!"

"I became the osprey but—the sea-hawk—she gave me this present—after."

Mina picks the fish up by the tail, examining it. "Not bad," she says, trying not to appear too impressed. "Not bad. Your grandmother has high hopes for you, but I do not think she will be disappointed."

She gives me some sun root to chew on. "Save your story then, lass," she suggests, "until we can all gather tonight and hear ye out."

I inch myself up to my feet and stumble down the hill with her. All I can muster the wind to say, all the way home, is, "If I've truly a bird ally now, why can't we just fly back?"

*   *   *   *

Gran is furious when she hears how I risked myself with my middle-clout, but old Winter stops her in the middle of her diatribe.

"The girl must do as she's led to do! She did no more than was asked of her, and what was right and proper for her. And she came through it all right! So leave her be! You've got a sea eagle on your hands and they don't take well to criticism!"

Peter laughs and slaps his knee and soon all, even my Gran, are laughing. I hug Winter gratefully, thinking this is the first time I have ever heard him say anything that did not concern the sheep that I thought was truly wise.

That night was full of glory. The next day I walked all the way back. I left an offering of herbs beside the rock that had held me so faithfully. Then I walked into the pines, guided to the tree where the osprey lived as true and straight as if I had been shot from a bow, and there I left her a fish that I had caught in the river M'hira in exchange for that with which she had gifted me. I found three feathers at the base of the tree and put them into my magic pouch. Now I have my ally of air.

The sky is a boundary, but not a limit.

Chapter 20

We brush out Bonny's tail and mane and weave the tiny faery daisies we have found throughout the dark strands. She whickers happily through her nose, enjoying our attentions. We've gotten so tall, our legs and feet drag on the ground when we ride her now. Most times she will not so much as break into a trot if we are both on her, turning her head and puffing to show us that such a small pony as herself is not equipped to carry two lasses of twelve and thirteen who are growing so quickly.

Three years have passed since Annie bought the pony for a groat from a man she saw passing through on the main road. He had a thin little horse, and a pony that was so sick that it stumbled and fell as she watched. She saw him beating it and ran down the hill, asking him to spare it. Taking a coin that Mina had given her she persuaded him to sell it, seeing as how it would surely not live.

She kept it in her mother's orchard, feeding it on apples and pears, grasses and herbs, bushels and bushels of comfrey scoured from every marsh and field in the district. And we did magic with her, Annie singing to her, "Oh, you're a fine bonny horse. You're a bonny horse, you are," over and over so that 'Bonny Horse' became her name and she turned from that starved and dying pony into a fat and sleek one whose sides bulged out so that she was nearly as wide across the middle as she was long.

She was no more of a galloping charger than we were, and it took all of our imaginative faculties to make her seem so, but occasionally she could be persuaded to race with us about the orchard, as all three of us became the mares of Scotia Cailleach.

Today she merely drowses in the sun, passively becoming as beautiful as our flowers, swift fingers and affection can make her. Bored, I suggest, "Let's go see the kittens."

"Very well," Annie replies. "Now you guard the gates," she charges Bonny, "and sound the alarm should any of the foe approach." Bonny nods accomodatingly and bobs her head to crop some more of the lush May grass.

After my foot was hurt, Mother urged me to spend more time outdoors, running and playing, to strengthen it. It has been well a long time now, but both Annie and I have gotten into the habit of spending far more time away from the croft than we spend helping maintain it. We go over to the old and falling down barn which once belonged to Annie's Grandfather, but which the Laird now uses in the deeps of winter for the sheep. This time of year the sheep are all up on the tors, and no one comes there.

We climb a ladder up to the loft; breathing the comforting and familiar perfume of old hay and droppings sweetening into earth, rising warm into the eaves. The she-cat, Tawney, Annie's familiar, is curled in a corner of the loft in a nest that Annie had made for her when the labor pains came upon her. She knew that Mairead would not tolerate a passle of kittens anywhere on her land, much less in her house.

There are six, still little and ratlike, eyes not yet open, all squirming and kneading Tawney's belly. We touch their tails, try to guess what their markings will be from the blotchy grays and blacks and yellows their bodies bear now. Tawney purrs, soaking in our admiration and the warmth of our hands stroking her back. I give her a tiny clumpet of smoked fish that I saved for her. She sucks it up on the instant and purrs louder.

"We'll bring some milk tonight," says Annie, "we'll go on another run. I know you need milk to make milk." Tawney purrs her assent. "Oberon will go with us and we'll see to it that we get the creamiest in the whole shire and bring it back to you. What a fine strong mother cat you are."

It grows hot inside the barn as the day begins to warm. I take off my plaidie and lay it down on the prickly hay. Annie throws hers off too, laying it beside mine to make a blanket, and then dives for my belly. Tickling each other into hysteria, rolling off the blanket into the hay, yellow prickles in our hair; "Ow! Stop your silliness!" giggles snickers snorts horsey smells in our noses.

"You be the kitten and I'll be Tawney," she says.

"If you're the mumcat, where are your teats?" Russet kitten I become, pawing through her clothes in search of milk. I find her slight round breast and latch on. She cries out and cuffs me, "Ow, damn kitten, I think your father was a robber lynx! Settle down bairn, tis time for your bath."

I make no protest as she undresses me. We've slept and played naked together before, to both our mothers' distress. My mother would only say that it was not seemly. Her mother would screech, "Gypsy brat!" and worse things. Everyone expected Annie to be bad since her father was a bad thieving gypsy. Bad she was.

But what a sweet tongue she has. Not rough like Tawney's; so smooth and warm. My skin rumples into goose-prickles along the paths her tongue leaves wet to the air. But who would complain? This shivering is different from any I've ever known, quivering in such a strange way that even as my skin prickles I get warmer and warmer. The between-my-legs-part feels the most shivery of all. As she moves from my breast to my ribs across my belly, I become aware that I want her to put her mouth there. Instead she goes down my leg—oh!—under the knees nipping my toes teeth sharp as a cat's, tongue flickering wet flame back up my thighs my belly my flat nipples sore with their first swelling her tongue sharp on my nipples, heat flooding my chest. The between-my-legs-part is burning aching hot but it feels good—how can anything that sharp feel good?

Under my arms and down my arms, "You're supposed to purr," she says. I have been holding my breath. Obediently I purr between short gasps, wanting her to touch between my legs more than ever and wondering at my wish.

She turns me over, licking and biting along my shoulders and neck purring or growling at me occasionally; is this still a game? Oh I cannot bear it and I want her never to stop, her licking at the lower curve of my ass I biting my lip and holding my breath again feeling like I'm about to turn into air or steam.

Turning over; "Annie. . ." She shushes me kissing my thighs again—she is kissing not licking then she is cautiously pushing my legs apart looking up into my eyes; "*D'ye want to play?*" her eyes question, see the answer in mine, then her tongue touching me, caressing that wrinkle of flesh at the center of my cleft. It hurts—I feel some deep opening, some emptiness that never felt empty before. Then something happens and I explode in wetness, tears flowing out of my eyes.

I come back to myself clutching her shoulders, she lying on top of me propped up on her forearms, looking searchingly into my damp gaze.

"Are you all right?"

I'm not sure what I am but I nod and smile. Something is changing inside me that is forever.

"Good." Annie huffs down beside me. "Then tis my turn to be the kitten and you be the mumcat!"

Moving slowly as if I were in a dream where the air is as bodied as water. . . where are my feet now, my hands? I move carefully as if I were underhill with the fay in their hall of harpsong and crystal, aware how thin the veils are that keep me here.

Annie purrs. I try to think of myself as a mother cat licking her kit, but in truth, I do not feel that way. I do not know how I feel. There's a light shining through the top of my head, brimming over into my body, squeezing out all possibility of thought.

Follow my tongue on a journey from her shoulder along the inside of her arm, around each finger and back again. Pulse along the inside of her elbow, beneath her jaw, under her breasts. Familiar music, elusive as the drums under the hills of faery, and as beckoning.

One palm buried in the straw, every stalk of hay grows sharp and separate and distinct, my hands more awake than they have ever been—the other palm circling her left nipple, cloud stroking the peak of a new mountain. My tongue licking her nipple, her nipple licking my tongue.

*Breathing tides of water and flame surging beneath her skin. . . I
am in another country touching with my mouth a body I have never
truly seen. It is not only the new breasts, the narrowing waist, the
curve of her hips that are different; the shape of her hands, blue harmony of her veins, white lace of old bramble scars on her ankles, all
new territory, mysterious and vast as the land of spice over the western sea.*

*Scattered curling hairs on her mound she showed me so proudly a
few days ago. . . massaging her thighs, I open her as she opened me.
Breathe in the unfamiliar smell. . . ringing in my ears as if the full
moon had entered my skull. I begin licking, finding that wonderful
rumple of skin at the heart of her flower, losing it and finding it again.
Her body grows very tense as I lick her and for awhile I fear she is
wroth with me; when I remind her to keep purring she says, "Not
now!" in a harsh voice. But then she grabs my hair and presses my
face deeper into her cleft and cries out; I taste smoke salt flowers and
again dissolve.*

I don't remember how again we came to be lying together side
by side. This dying and being born again so soon after is very new
to me. Looking into her eyes I feel we are no more the children
who had raced into the barn together.

"It's like we have wings now," I say.

She nods and adds, "I think we'd best keep this a secret too."

"Aye." Hard to imagine who we could tell. Think of Mina
and Gran who've started teaching us the Craft in earnest now,
preparing us for the time when our blood will come and we will be
initiated. Is this part of what we are learning? Surely this is the
most magical shape-shift I have yet experienced.

"Remember when they were teaching us how to go down the
stone stair to the center of the earth and from there out to different lives—and we each went to another lifetime—and they told
us—to keep solemn silence about whatever we had seen? To gather it into us as a part of our power?" asks Annie.

"Of course."

"We were together in that old time that I went to. I think it
no harm to share it just between the two of us, close as we are."

I snuggle closer, twining my legs through hers.

"We were together, and we touched each other like this."

Suddenly realizing, yes, there is a part of this that is so familiar, so easy, at the same time that there is a part that seems so unsettlingly new.

"What did you remember?" she asks.

"I remembered being in a great building shaped like this," I say, holding my hands together to make a point at the top. "We were making sounds—or the sounds were making themselves with us. You know the crystals that they have showed us, how they can hold and transmit a picture?"

She nods.

"We were like that, like the crystals, in our bodies. We were holding and transmitting the sound as if the sound was always there, in the air, and we pulled it out of the air and just opened our mouths and it came out and bounced off the walls of the temple. And the way the air moved was like it was made out of wings, beating very fast, like a hummingbird. And the sick could be healed in that way. And the crystals were charged to be more potent, I think, than even what Gran and Mina have. Though perhaps they have not showed us the strongest of what they have. Probably not."

Annie's eyes flicker. I feel her entering my memory.

"And new ideas could come forth as well—like how to heal the sick, what medicines to use and how to build the temples that we built then—how to call the river so it would bring fertility to the land—many things."

We stop talking and kiss. We have kissed so often before. This time we kiss with our mouths open; our tongues explore each other. We smile, eyes not more than an inch apart. We have reached the secret-keeping time, but we will not be keeping them from each other.

We go over to Mina's that afternoon, bringing wood for her hearth as well as the flowers and herbs she had asked for. She looks up and gives us a big beaming smile.

"Ye've got yer blood!"

We laugh, hastily shielding our minds so that she will not read them.

"Nay, nay, we have not."

She looks at us, puzzled.

"Ye must tell the truth about this," she admonishes, "there's nothing more important—yer blood signals the time of initiation, ye know that."

We nod, trying to suppress our laughter.

"Tis not our time yet."

We put the baskets down and run off giggling. She sees the change in us. And we feel not but a little proud at having done this magical thing without anyone instructing us on how to do it.

Every day after that we galloped to a far place or a hidden place and lay down among the flowers and practiced this new art. The sky was the most beautiful blue it had ever been, and there were more flowers than I ever remembered seeing in a May before. Not one of them could compare with the dusky petals that she opened to me; no bee was more drunk than I on the raw nectars of that spring.

Chapter 21

Birds singing in a circle around us. The circular loom of trees surrounding our small clearing vibrating with interwoven melodies as we roll over and over with each other on the damp ground. Our sound mingles with the birds's songs, heat from our bodies enters the earth, warming her, conjuring the spring. Taut clouds of our breasts rubbing together. Lips, teeth, tongues, merging, melting; fingers sliding in and out of each other's wetness. Eyes closed, boundaries between us vanish. A pair of candles, two flames may be said to be separate. In a bonfire, they are not. We leap and twist, arch, flames leaping together, fishes in each other's rivers, flashes of light—water and fire, water and fire.

We scream in orgasm, holding our mouths tight over each other's bodies to muffle the sound, well aware that what we are doing is magic, therefore forbidden; therefore dangerous.

We are becoming solid again. Her body. My body. Deep panting breaths flowing in and out of each other's lungs. Earth and air. Earth beneath us, earth that is our bodies. Air of our exchanged, fragrant breath.

Pulse in her vagina thudding against my two fingers which would take root and grow there if they could. Slowly she withdraws her fingers from me, my vagina squeezing them as they leave, reluctant to let them go. I withdraw my fingers a little at a time, slowly as I can so as to not seem such a hardship. Looking into each other's eyes, the space between our eyes almost touching. We have discovered that when we put our brows together, the dark space between our eyes merges and becomes one, dropping us into the starless place, the dark place of all possibilities.

Gran said that place would open when I got my blood, but we have found another door. Now we often start our lovemaking by putting our foreheads together, looking into each other's eyes until they blur and merge into one eye, then into the magical darkness in which anything may occur.

We receive each other as Goddess, mirror each other. This is ancient magic. Time after time we go to different lives where we practice this same magic, where it is held sacred. In this time, of all the bawdy, laughing songs of love sung in our village, there is not one of the magic mirror one woman can hold to another. When we go to other times, there such songs are sung and our hands hold instruments unlike any in our current day. And it seems to us that the colors we wore were more bright, the earth herself more like a young maiden than a worried mother with too many children to feed. There have been times when no man looked at us, or at any other woman, with disrespect. We know this now, not only from the tales of Mina and Gran, but from our own journeying.

This afternoon we had gone to a place where we both had dark hair and wore white. We were weaving on a large loom, stopped to make love, and in the making love, discovered a new pattern, a motion of light which we wove then into our tapestry.

Yet that was just the beginning of our lovemaking. Hours have passed since then, and as is always so, most of what we experience together comes not in pictures or in words but only in feeling. Most of it I cannot remember after.

Slowly we move apart, stretching. To my dismay, I see blood on my fingers.

"By the Lady!" I cry, "I've hurt you Annie!"

She feels between her legs; a few dark drops speckle her fingers.

"Doesn't hurt," she says.

"Perhaps I've injured your maidenhead."

She kneels, putting a hand over her belly, closing her eyes. Two small tears pearl at the corners of her eyes—she opens them with excitement.

"Fiona—it's my moonblood!"

I sit up. "Are you sure?"

"Yes. I feel it. I feel the moon moving in my belly."

I put my hand on her belly to see if I can sense the moon within her, and gasp.

"It feels like snakes. It feels like serpent energy!"

"Aye, of course!" She lies down elated, stretches her arms up to the sky and hugs herself, hugs the earth.

"Oh, thank you Mother, thank you! Oh, Fiona, I can have a baby now! I can be initiated. I'm a woman now, truly." I cover her belly with kisses. Slight seep of blood at her cleft beckons.

"May I taste?"

"Oh yes."

Reverently I press my forehead against the top of her pubic arch. Another opening, another mystery we have discovered, this correspondence between the space between the eyes and the womb space in the belly. We open blackness to each other and enfold ourselves in it. I run my tongue along the soft wrinkles of flesh. Salty. Sacred. Out of the darkness, light streams into my face; the moon glows in my skull. Raw power. Suns of light. Moons of light. Power to bring forth, power to grow. Raw flowing fire deep in the cauldron beneath earth and sea. Power of renewal. Power of change.

The light lifts me to kneeling, looking in Annie's eyes. She has changed. She is a woman now. I am as much in awe as if the Goddess of All Things was before me. A knot of pain tightens in my own belly.

"Och. . ." I bite my lip, tears starting to come. "Oh, I want to have it too!"

She pats the ground for me to lie next to her. Tears are running down my face in earnest now.

"Well, let's magic it so," she says. "I've all the magic in the world."

She reaches inside herself, dying her fingers, presses a circle of blood upon my brow. Dips her fingers again and paints it on my lips, and dips again, placing some of her blood inside my vagina, fingers stretching to touch the tight rosebud opening of my womb, rubbing, coaxing.

"Open now," she whispers, presses her forehead to mine, her blood glueing us together, stickiness of her blood like berry juice on our lips. She paints her blood on my body, reaches her long fingers inside me, her longest finger touching my womb, moving it back and forth and around in circles.

Deep trembling inside me. My body, not quite as ripe as hers, resisting the power, then yielding to it, like a fruit tree flowering at Bride, seduced by an uncanny spell of sun.

She sings a bleeding song into my mouth, "Oh, you pinks and posies come down—you red red roses—come down—"

The shadows are creeping over us. It is not long from the spring equinox. Days are lengthening, but they are not summer days yet.

"Aye, tis cold," she says, reading my thoughts, sliding her hands out of my body. "Let's go tell your mother that we're going to sleep out tonight. We'll get blankets and bring them back here. We'll sleep together and do magic together and your blood will come. I want us to bleed together."

I nod. We wash the blood off our faces at the river M'hira and gather some moss for Annie to bind between her legs.

We burst into the croft.

"Annie's got her blood!" I call to my mother. "We're going to sleep out tonight and do magic for me to get mine." Mother exclaims with delight, hugs and kisses Annie all about her face. We tarry not, but gather up our blankets and hurry back to the clearing. First blood and initiations are times of fasting, so we need not bother with food.

We arrange our blankets in the small meadow, chasing off a few sheep, then follow the river M'hira down to the beach to watch the sunset. Dip our fingers in the ocean and taste. It is not unlike the taste of her blood. Annie sings a woman's hymn to the ocean:

"I am the earth
I am the sea
Power of making
Flows within me.
I am the weaver
Red blood is my threading
Loom of bone weaving
Spinning and shedding.

I am the earth
I am the sea
Power of making
Flows within me

I am the ocean
And the tides are in me
I am the earth
And the moon dreams with me.

I am the earth
I am the sea
Power of making
Flows within me."

I have been humming in the background as she sings.
"Now you sing it," she commands.
"That is a song for women who have their blood."
"Sing it, and your blood will come."
I kneel, letting the gentle tide lap my knees, and sing the song.
"Put some of the water inside you," she whispers.
I obey, feeling a tug of pain within.
"It hurts?"
"Aye."
"Tis a good sign."
"Yours doesn't."
"We're different."
We walk back up the hill.
"My mother says gypsies are more like animals," reflects

Annie. "They have an easier time with bleedings and babies and so forth. My mother lays three days sick in bed when her blood is on her."

"I'm every bit as much an animal as you!" I snap. "I have no intentions of laying in bed!"

We're at the top of the hill. Ignoring my crossness, she clasps me in her arms.

"I hope I can change your mind about *that*," she says. I giggle as we crawl under the covers.

"I don't mind laying in bed as long as I've you to lay with."

"I feel a bit achy myself," she confesses. "Not in my belly but my back "

"Let me see if I can ease it with my hands "

"We used to heal with hands," she says, remembering a life we glimpsed together. "Why do you suppose the coven does it not now?"

"Probably because our hands are cold most of the year. That was in a warm place we did the healing with our hands."

"Ohhh. Your hands are warm enough now. Keep rubbing me like that."

Soon she coaxes me to put my head between her legs again At last, dizzy with pleasure, drunk on her blood, we sleep.

I wake up while it is still early. Squatting to relieve myself, the cloak of dream still soft around me, I take my time digging the hole with a rock, wiping myself with soft leaves. Touch my vulva—my hand comes away dappled, wet. Smell it, taste it. A smile spreads across my face.

Annie murmurs and stretches when I get back into bed with her.

"Annie, wake up, wake up. Look at this."

I put my fingers inside my vagina, show her the stain.

"Mine or yours?" she whispers.

"Mine."

"Oh! Ooooh!" she exults. She squeezes me, laughing, gig gling, we roll over and over into a rock, don't care, roll back off, giggling and ooohing in excitement

"We did it! We did it! We did it at once!"

Giggling and hooting we get up, running naked in the mead-ow and the woods, laughing with delight. Women we may be, but it is the girls in us who stoop to capture snails and dye their shells red before releasing them. We adorn trees and mushrooms with bloody fingerprints, sit on large smooth stones, making prints of our vulvas. When we have worn ourselves out with our gleeful cavorting, we stop and bathe briefly in M'hira, dress each other and brush our hair.

Our lunacy over, the moon pulses quietly in our bellies as we hold hands and walk silently and decorously to Mina's house to tell Mina and Gran of our transformation.

Chapter 22

At twilight I walk alone to the stone circle. I circle around
the stones three times, calling the guardians of the four corners
to be with me, calling upon the Old Ones to witness and guard
and give guidance. As I move in circles around the bigger circle I
walk widdershins* to wind back time; the broken stones right
themselves into pillars and lintels and the old circle stands
whole again. I enter through the Gateway of the North, making
the sign of the crossroads to assert my balance and invoke the
Dark One, the Crone who is death and rebirth, the Goddess who
rules the waning moon, the power of women's blood, and Initiation.

I lie down in the center of the circle, holding pungent herbs
over my heart; heather for courage, rosemary for memory, sage
for purification, Witch's rue and henbane for calling the dark,
mugwort to open the door. Periodically I crush some of the leaves
between my fingers to stay surrounded by the scent.

*"You must go to the Well of Connaught. That well sinks deep to
the center of the earth. It is a gateway to the land of the dead,"* Gran

---

*Widdershins—counterclockwise, opposite direction to sun and moon.

had instructed me, reminding me of the trances she had guided me on throughout my training. So I lie, breathing deeply, inhaling the herbs, letting the late afternoon sun fade and the darkness envelope me.

The ground under my back softens as I imagine myself floating on the surface of the ancient well. Dark as the starless place, yet I imagine stars shining in the sky, reflecting down into the well. As I float, time shifts like a boat cut loose from its mooring, and I move across seas into other times and places back beyond Fiona. I am in a long ago time, floating across a lake in a dragon-prowed ship, invisible oars steering me to the land of poppies and apples. My child self dies, my deep self opens.

I feel myself bleeding, the red fist in my belly opening and closing. Never aware of it until my blood started three moons ago; now I feel the tides sucking and sighing inside me, my own dark red inner ocean. On that sea, drifting sails billowing and bleeding with the waning breath of the moon. All this power here, inside my body. I move into this center of power, at once the cave and the boat drawn into it.

Both Annie and I started bleeding at the dark of the moon, a sign that we were consecrated to the Dark One. Now I enter Her domain.

The cave is like the inside of a fruit. The name of the fruit comes to me in another language. It is nothing I have seen in this life. Round as the belly of a pregnant woman, inside, each seed nestles in a bright bubble of blood. The water churns dark red, sucking and sighing sounds echo all around me. I feel no fear, only excitement and a sense of return, return to an ancient place of knowing.

The boat stops, bobs to a rest. I get out and walk up a twisting stone path. I come to a throne where a woman is seated. She is ancient, but old as rocks are old, not withered, but weathered, awesome in Her power to endure. Her red hair hangs braided to her knees, her eyes are gray, full of light and depth. She hands me two pomegranates, the ancient womb-fruits. As I hold them before me they break open and bleed, dark red blood dripping down over my hands and wrists. Little flames spiral out of the center of the fruits, dancing and rising higher, a bright colored bird rises up out of each blood fruit fire circling up and up, a rush of wings passes my ears as a third bird rises out of my head to join them in a cone of power. My body wavers like the flames, the woman's words drift through me like a haze of smoke. She says that my path is a passage of blood and fire, that the fruit must be broken for the seeds to be scattered. I understand, yet do not understand.

She asks, "Art thou willing to suffer to learn?" I say aye.

Then I am again floating, up through layers of black water to the top of the well. The water grows solid again into ground under my back. The coven is chanting to draw me back:

"Back along wells
Back along stars
Back along midnight
Back along passageways

Back from darkness
Back from moonlight
Back from the earth
Back from the grave

Back to the leaving place
Back to this body
Back to Fiona
Back to the circle."

I open my eyes. It is night now, the stars are as I had envisioned them when I first entered trance. I am surrounded by black hooded figures gently shaking me. They fall silent and begin removing my clothes. I know that I must not speak until spoken to, though I long to share my vision and receive their words of comfort and wisdom.

When I am naked they begin rubbing my body with my moonblood mixed with mud. It is so cold I shiver, feeling as if I am truly dead and turning into earth. They pull me up and throw a freshly butchered sheepskin blanket over my head. The skins are still bloody and raw smelling. After a long pause in which I wonder if they are still here or if I have been left alone, the silence is broken with terrifying shrieks and howls. Banshees grab me by the shoulders and start to run with me, hooting and howling to wake the dead. Running blind, I know we are in the woods because we are crashing through the underbrush; my bare feet must be bleeding but I feel no pain, only a sense of panic—this cannot be my coven, the old people could never run this fast—wondering if I have been kidnapped by faerie folk or goblins and certain that any moment I will be slammed into a tree. The mad pell-mell race ends abruptly; my feet are kicked out from under me and I land hard on my back, gasping to recover my punched out breath.

A fast drum beat begins, meshing with the crashing rhythm of my heart. Animal noises—owls, ravens, cats, bulls—mingle in a staccato pattern with hands patting the ground and clapping. My heart slows gradually, still fast but not so fast that I fear it will fly out of my body. This is my coven indeed, the sounds are familiar now.

They raise me up, we begin dancing in a circle. They chant my name and its meanings along with the names of my companion animals.

"Fiona McNair
Pale One
Child of the Stranger
Winter Born

Winter Pool Salmon
Gray Feathered Osprey
Cat-eyed Lynx Woman."

The chanting stops. I hear them lighting two fires, one to either side of me.

Someone is gripping me by the shoulders. Blinded by the sheepskin, I see nothing but blackness.

"Do you have the courage to enter the realm of the dark one and learn of Her secrets?"

"Aye."

"Remember your gifts from the land of the dead. They are a charm of protection."

I remember the pomegranates and imagine holding them in my hands.

The voice hisses, "Between the fires to the heart of the darkness."

Walking between the two fires I cannot see terrifies me but I swallow hard and pass through their threatening heat. I walk into a sharp knife poised at my breastbone. Then a dry voice like the wind cracking the spine of an autumn leaf, "Who dares to enter the realm of the Dark One?"

I know the answer I must give.

"I came into this world as Fiona McNair. As I move between the worlds I will move as Kyairthwen."

"And how will you leave this world?"

The question slaps me like a cold wind. I have not been prepared for it in advance. But the answer flows from the fruits in my hands up through my chest and throat.

"As a bird flying up from a fire."

Long pause.

"What is your purpose in entering this realm, Kyairthwen?"

"It is my purpose to be made Priestess and Witch and to return to the freedom of the Mother."

"Who vouches for thee?"

I hear Mina Wind Mare's voice saying, "I vouch for her power."

John Staghorn adds, "I vouch for her courage."

Sarah Snow Flower whispers, "I vouch for the love in her heart."

Another long pause. My heart leaping against the point of the athame as if it would be married to it.

"Know you that it is better to fall upon this blade than to enter with fear in your heart?"

"Aye."

"And do you fear?"

"Aye."

"Give me the words that free you from fear and open the door to this realm."

"Perfect love and perfect trust."

The sheepskin is yanked off my head.

"Never enter blindly. Enter with true sight," my Gran says.

I am surrounded then, my now unhooded coveners greeting me with hugs and kisses.

"Welcome home, Kyairthwen. Welcome to the realm of the dark." They put me in the center of the circle cast in a clearing. All of us face the east.

Gran calls out, "Great eternal powers of the East! From the land of sunrise, bring us your birdsong and flight. Power of the mind to move beyond time and space, enter the body of thy child, Fiona, accept the service of thy Priestess, Kyairthwen." They bring a feathered headdress and crown me with it. We face the south.

"Great eternal powers of the South! From the blazing King-dom of the mid-day sun, bring us your courage and will. Power of the spirit to burn as the torch of immortality, enter the body of thy child Fiona, accept the service of thy Priestess, Kyairthwen." They place a lighted torch in my right hand. We turn and face the west.

"Great eternal powers of the West! From the land of twi-light, bring us your water's teachings of healing and change. Power of the heart to shape-shift and flow, growing deeper in love's wisdom, enter the body of thy child Fiona, accept the ser-vice of thy Priestess, Kyairthwen." They bring me a chalice brimming with whiskey and water and place it in my left hand. We turn and face the north.

"Great eternal powers of the North! From the cold Queen-dom of midnight, bring us the patience of stones and the secrets of caves. Power of the body to birth and die and be reborn in an-other form, enter the body of thy child Fiona, accept the service of thy Priestess Kyairthwen." They place round white stones be-tween my toes.

The chalice and the torch are taken from me, placed one on each side of the dirt mound altar which is adorned with shells, holy stones, feathers and candles. Cauldrons of water have been warming near the fire. They pour the cleansing liquid over me.

Staghorn cries, "Out of mud and blood and chaos, the body of the Goddess stands revealed!"

Everyone kneels now and adores me as the living Goddess. I feel radiant, light-headed, so overwhelmed I can only giggle with delight as each of them gives me the five-fold kiss—pressing their lips to my feet, sex, belly, heart, and mouth.

Jessica, Snow Flower and Wind Mare surround me. Jessica

holds a coarse woolen cord between my legs to stain it with menstrual blood. Snow Flower measures me with the cord and Wind Mare cuts it.

Gran asks, "Are you willing to suffer to learn?"

I answer aye. She cuts into the heel of my palm at the part known as the moon's quarter with her athamé and places the cord over the wound.

"Know that all learning comes in the form of an opening. While the learning may feel like a wound or a suffering, know that every time you open, you deepen, and all that is hurt is healed again by the love of the Goddess. Know that the hand that has wounded you is the hand of love." She makes a matching cut in her own palm.

"And know that we who love you never ask anything of you which we would not willingly give ourselves." She places her hand over mine; our blood mixes in a scarlet dye for the cord.

"Now make the blood bond with each one of this living circle, that we may be family of blood and spirit. And make the oath of secrecy as you do so," instructs Gran.

I move slowly around the circle. Each person in turn cuts their palm and clasps it with mine over the cord. We look in each other's eyes.

Each one says to me, "I swear never to betray thee, nor these secret arts we practice. Thy life shall be more precious than mine. Though our enemies are great and in power, I fear them not. Our bond is eternal and we shall know each other again in another life."

I tremble and my eyes spill over with tears as I repeat the vow to each one, gray eyes, green eyes, eyes of brown and cloudy blue. I feel my heart opening, more painful than the palm's flesh yielding to the knife, but sweet and rich and deep. The faces blur; I see them melt and congeal into other forms holding the same spirit. Awe and certainty, aye I have known you before, and will know you again. Our bond is eternal.

When we finish, Wind Mare passes out wefts of cobweb to stanch the bleeding. We tie the cord in a circle and stand shoulder to shoulder, holding it. Gran moves me into the center, tells me to kneel. She admonishes me to be faithful to my vows.

"Place one hand on your head, the other on your heel, and

say, 'All between my two hands belongs to the Goddess.'"

"All between my two hands belongs to the Goddess." As I speak I have the sensation of door after door opening onto vistas of space. Sound of a high pitched bell wings like a cormorant through each opening, and the universe curls into an ear, harkening.

They scrape the two fires together into one, signifying that we are joined. We all drop the cord on the fire. The blood sizzles as the cord turns black and shrivels into threads of dark smoke.

"The power of that which has been spoken rises with the smoke of this blood and this cord. They become one spirit, one messenger to the heavens that what has been done here is eternal and now lives among the Gods."

We sit around the fire; I realize how hard my knees have been shaking once I am seated on firm ground. The torch and chalice are handed back to me. I consign the torch to the fire and pour the whiskey over it. The flames rise in a blue rush.

"May I never be separated from the powers of light and the spirit of life," I say. John refills the chalice and I pass it to the left. Before each person drinks they give me a blessing and offer some whiskey to dance like blue angels in the flames.

We do not feast, for my ritual fast must continue throughout the three days of my dream seeking. Friendly spirits are charged to accompany me and protect me from danger. Staghorn, wearing the horns and his cloak of seven skins leads me through the forest to the rolling hills. He took me to the vision caves earlier in the week to show me where I must go.

"D'ye remember the way?" he asks. I nod. It is a long way but not hard when you know it. He gives me a sheepskin pouch to carry water, though there is no shortage of streams along the way. He asks if I am willing to be alone, to confront my own wilderness. He reminds me that I will encounter no danger to myself greater than myself.

"So it is, and so it should be. And may it ever be so," he says solemnly.

"So mote it be," I laugh, kiss him on the nose, and start out for the dream caves that lie in the east.

Chapter 23

I begin to walk. The hunger I feel only serves to make my steps seem to float without effort. I am an adult now, a Priestess. All my life has been shaped to this point, and now the arrow flies! I walk through the gray shifting mists, through the waking songs of birds. I rest only briefly, though enchanting crooks in the stream tempt me to linger. I pause to gather some herbs, aware that everything I do for the next moon will carry special potency. I will make a dream pillow with these. The stream branches many times. Near dusk I follow one of the streams between the breasts of two hills. The caves are half-way up one of the hills. I choose the largest of the three and hurry to gather firewood while it is still light.

I build my fire and watch it move yellow and white against the sudden blackness of the air. The tiredness comes upon me as suddenly as the dark, but I fight to stay awake, thinking the time too valuable to be lost in sleep. I watch the fire people swirl and pivot from branch to branch, the wood cracking like old bones under the heat. I fear the fire people. Their beauty is no less than the sylphs of the misty air or the graceful undines, but they have a ruthlessness to them, for they need to consume other beings in order to survive and they will devour whatever is in their path without hesitation or conscience.

"Very like ourselves," Gran said when I told her why I mistrusted the fire elementals. "And how we hate that which mirrors us."

I look to see if it is myself dancing in the flames with ruthless passion, but I do not see it. Sleep eddies seductively around me like water and I sink with gratitude into the gentler rhythms of that element.

I wake only once, having the keen sense of being watched. I am still propped up against the cave wall. The fire is out. For a moment I am not certain who I am, far less where. Then I see her, crouched silent and still on the cliff ledge not an arm's span from the circle of ashes.

Mother lynx, cool green eyes looking steadily into mine. My heart jumps to see her, my earth companion, welcoming me so plainly. An eyelashes' involuntary flutter and she is gone, melted into the mist, leaving the print of her paw in the charcoal ash as a sign of protection.

I pray to the Goddess of cats to grant her good hunting, pull myself to the back of the cave and fall once more into the dim country of dream.

I wake the next morning to clouds and rain. It seems so odd to be alone, no babies crying, no chores to do. I walk down to the stream, drink, splash water on my face and wash the blood from my thighs. Small fish flicker among the weedy rocks. I assume my lynx aspect and crouch down, the patient huntress, to observe them. As I watch, I move closer and closer to them with my mind until I enter into one of them, waving my fins in the current that is as natural to me as air, darting sideways without thought at every shifting pattern of light and shadow. The salmon is my water companion, and I am a great huntress of salmon and trout so I know their thoughts and movements well.

From the fish I slow my thoughts further and enter the body of a green bearded rock, feeling the sluice of the water polishing my skin. After a calm time of being the stone I return to my own damp skin. I thank the fish, stone and stream for our merging and return to the cave. The day crawls by. I have never considered what life would be like with no chores, no meals, no one to talk to.

The sky clears for a bit near sundown. Seven ravens come and circle above me as I am starting my fire. I am glad of their brief presence but soon I am alone again, feeling hungry, bored and lonely. Annie and I together spend long hours away from the village but I have never been alone for so long. I wish for something special to happen, yet at the same time I fear it. My new feeling of adulthood is slipping away. As it gets darker I begin thinking about bears. I have never actually seen a bear, they are terribly scarce and shy, yet I have heard about them often and know that they must have lairs somewhere. Suppose a bear wants to use this cave and finds me in it?

Full of misery, I crawl to the back of the cave and fall asleep. While asleep I dream that a creature that is like a bear only with a man's head, baring horrible large fangs crawls into the cave and begins pawing at me with sharp claws. The fire is no more than half-way down when I shudder upright yet I am too frightened to see it as an ally, thinking its hiss malevolent as it eats the wet wood and throws shadow-demons on the cave walls. After a few moments of paralyzed panic I realize that I *am* alone and that no one will come to save me but myself. I remember that I am supposed to be a Priestess now, the Goddess on Earth, and that there are powers I can summons to help me.

I bank the fire higher and take a burning brand from it. I draw a circle of protection around myself and the cave, making the signs for banishing and bidding all nightmare images to be gone. A strong voice sounding surprisingly like my Gran's rises from the soles of my feet as I call upon the four corners for protection. I feel the presence of the Mother lynx and call on her power to shine through my eyes. I call to my companion of the water and my companion of the air, the salmon and the osprey, to bring me their strength. As I call I feel the courage of the salmon fighting upstream in my blood and the calm of the eagle in flight settle in my bones.

"Power of the rock
Power of the sea

Standing stone
And twisted tree
All that swims
And all that flees
All this power
Moves through me."

I chant over and over until I feel myself in the center of a great shining web, where every creature chants in its own language to the same rhythm. I am not alone at all.

I remember Mina at her loom saying, "*The Goddess is the weaver, and each one of us is but a thread in the weft. Every thread depends on every other thread, none can do without the others. Our task is to fit into the Lady's pattern so the whole is kept in harmony. Dinna be a snarly thread—a snarly thread will not lie wi' the others, it fancies itself to be alone and apart. When we forget we are part of the pattern we act like the snarly thread that will not do its part.*"

I lie down, drowsy and comforted, watching the firelight weave beautiful patterns across the ceiling of the cave, willing myself to be the strongest, finest thread on the Lady's loom. As the click and slide of the shuttle weaves me into sleep I hear a voice saying, "*Never alone. Never alone. Everything is alive and with us all the time.*"

I wake long before dawn, having dreamed that I was at home and needing to get up to milk the goats. I close my eyes to try to call back the other dreams I must have had, important dreams, but they dance away laughing back to the shadowy realms from where they came. So dark and cold, it feels like autumn perched on the banks of winter, not like spring with any hope of summer. It will be awhile before dawn yet so I attempt to build another fire. The wood is damp and my flint indifferent. I am not the best fire builder; the fire folk sense my fear of them and scorn to come when I call. The sparks die and I grow bored of trying to coax them. I put the wood inside the cave to dry out and walk back to the stream. I'm wavy on my feet, all I can think about is all the things I wish I had for breakfast.

As the dawn light brings a glimmer to the rocks I wonder where the mounds which are the doors to faery lie in this area. I know the places to go near to home to find the doors to faery, but I have not wandered so far in this direction before and know not the secret places here. I feel the faery-folk's presence though, can almost catch sight of their gleaming eyes in the wind-stirred rushes.

I've been told not to leave sight of the caves; feeling as weak as I do this seems a wisdom. Crouched down in the heather and moss I make myself small so I can wander through towering forests of fern, finding tiny blue starbursts and yellow bells growing from crevices in the dark-ridged rocks. Trundling along ant-size, I crawl up on a polished surface like a black table. Snapping back to Fiona size I unwedge the shiny thing from its mossy hiding place. An elf-bolt!

Tiny glossy arrowhead, sharp and perfect as the day it sang from the bow. The faery folk are here, watching, shrewd and kind enough to send me a gift signifying their acceptance of my presence. I kiss it in thanks and put it in my magic pouch to tumble with my faery whistle, a snippet of lynx fur, an osprey feather, salmon teeth, herbs and magic stones.

I wash again in the stream, rinsing the sticky blood between my thighs. My fingers prod the stream stones, roll them about and pick out the roundest and smoothest to take back to the cave. I feel weak and tired, wishing that something magical would happen. Gran said she could not say what would happen. Some people find a guide, she said. Some people meet their death. Some see who they have been in other lives and who they are to be. They all sound frightening. But what if nothing happens at all?

I'm leaning up against the cave wall, sucking on three stones, rolling them around on the roof of my mouth. I doze off sitting up and dream that the lynx returns. She walks over my lap, calm as a house cat, her three kittens pouncing and bounding behind her. They promenade in this fashion to the back of the cave where they disappear. Wide awake, eager, I crawl to the back of the cave to look for them. Vanished. Could there be a magic door here? I say all the door opening incantations I know, knocking on the cave walls. Nothing. It was just a dream. I crawl back out to the cave's mouth. Rain. Big drops of it. How will I make a fire in this rain? I watch the lynx tracks on the ledge fill with water, wrap myself in a tight ball under my wool. Can't seem to get warm anymore. I'm not supposed to tell anyone what I see during my alone time, but I feel sure that if I do not see something splendid everyone will know that I have failed. Gran will certainly know. She will take one look through me and she will know. I found an elf-bolt and saw the lynx, but these are signs one might receive on any smiling day. I cannot remember ever feeling so sad. I stick my feet out and wriggle my toes, lamenting how ugly they are on my left foot, the one toe missing, the littlest one twisted and purple. Well, as Gran says, nobody courts feet. They carry me where I need to go, that is what feet are for.

I shift my body around in different positions, muscles aching from two nights on a cold stone bed. The cave floats in a cloud of mist and rain. Apparitions of the mist people blossom and fade, animal shapes, faces, seen for a moment, changing, then gone. What food will Staghorn bring me for my first meal tomorrow? Och, thinking of food again! How can I have a vision when my stomach talks louder than my eyes? I doze on and off, but no dreams come. Sometimes I wake thinking I'll find myself at home. Sometimes I dream there's someone in the cave with me. But when I open my eyes, no one is there.

The mist clears slightly. The sun is still veiled however, so I have no way of judging the time. Whatever time it is, this empty waiting is tedious. I chew on a little heather and spit out the bitter bark. Return to the stream for more water, decide to try to start a fire again. The wood I have kept inside is dry and catches easily. I welcome the flames, warm company on such a dreary drizzly day. Once the dry wood is well alight I add the damper bits. I want a big fire tonight, big enough to withstand the rain. The flames hiss as steam rises from the wood to mingle with the smoke. I imagine red-gold snakes twining among the logs. I like the snake people; I wish I had one here now for company. They are so wise in the ways of change; if one were coiled about my wrist now it could teach me what I need to know about shedding this child skin as easily as my new womb sheds blood. I am a woman now, I must trust to my own body's wisdom and not lean so much on the counsel of others.

As I watch, the mist dissipates so that I catch glimpses of stars. The last night of the moon's dark; the stars will be splendid if the fog clears. I drop off to sleep, waking to find that I have my wish; the sky is clear, the white fire of stars glittering cold and bright as moonlight. Yet while the sky is all indigo and sparkle, thick webs of mist like the gauzy traps of ground spiders shroud the cave entrance and all the earth beneath the cliff is like a sea of wool. The fire seems even larger than when I dozed off.

As I watch, all the ragged edges of the flames smooth themselves out and begin forming themselves into a shape like a bell. No, not a bell, it is a long flowing skirt, the flames rounding into a woman's figure. Then I am staring at a woman about two feet tall, the exact hue of the flames' blue heart, outlined in yellow fire. Transfixed by the wonderful indigo depth of her gaze I sit motionless until she alters the trance by saying my name.

"Kyairthwen."

With her breath the blue glow coils out of the fire and weaves in slow spinning arcs through the cave, everything drenched in blue. The blue fills me, sending its comforting warmth deep through my bones, deep into spaces between sinew and spirit which I had never known were empty. I recognize this being as the Goddess. Small as She is, She is the universe; stars bloom and die in the creases of her robe. Her eyes like no color I know, only the color of infinite deepness. She asks if I love Her; how could I not? At home and at peace, everything I want lives in this blue healing light. She asks what I would have from Her. It is hard to find words, to say that everything I could wish for is here, that I only want to be able to stay. I stumble through some words that all I want is to be a part of Her light, that if I might be a Priestess of that light I would wish for no more.

"Would you be one with the light, then?" She asks.

Aye, that is it, that is what I wish.

Whoosh of wind and crackle of thunder She shoots up—three times as tall, five times as tall, towering over me. The flames flow in a rush, almost concealing her form, driving me back with the heat. She asks if I will follow Her into the fire. Tears run down my face from terror and the sheer power of the heat. Ah Lady, how can you ask me for what I fear most? I stare silently into the inferno where I can no longer distinguish Her.

"Wilt thou follow me into the fire?" Her voice again, or perhaps an echo in my skull. I shudder.

"Aye, if thou wish it," I whisper.

A tunnel opens in the fire. She shimmers blue and beckoning, small again, and very far away. The heat blurs my vision and I step into the tunnel, into the flames, into unspeakable agony.

Anguish. All I have loved has betrayed me. Destroyed. I am nothing. Gray powder at the black base of the fire. Form and memory of form scatters, beyond suffering. Her voice:

"Remember the bird."

My ashes pull together in the shape of a bird and I fly through the flames as if my feathers were made of fire.

I move up into the cool night, fire and caves growing smaller and fading out of sight as I spiral up into the still blue light at the center of the sky.

*   *   *   *

Brilliant light shimmers through my closed eyelids. I open my eyes and shut them quickly. Sun streaming down, cool but bright. I am lying half in and half out of the cave.

I've had my vision. I should feel happy. Yet I feel cold all through to my bones, all cold except for the liquid fire stinging my eyes.

"*Some meet a guide. Some meet their death.*" Witches are burning. The fires move farther north each year. I shake my head. A vision can mean many things, not just the first thing you think of. I do not know what it means. I'm too young to know what it means. When I'm old like Gran I'll understand these things. My mind shifts back and forth from the vision at the cave to the vision I had in the stone circle. The fire. The firebirds. Gran or Mina would know what they mean but I cannot tell them. No one can help me.

I hear a low melodious whistle, turn my head to see Staghorn walking up the stream, sure footed with his walking stick, sack slung over his shoulder. As he comes up the hill he sees me lying down and laughs at me, pointing out that my hair is full of ashes.

"Is it so cold ye were sleepin' on yer fire then?" he teases.

I sit up, brushing the gray film from my hair and skin. He gives me cheese scones and smoked trout and dried apples from his haversack. I bolt everything; he keeps cautioning me not to choke on the bones. He says not a word of my visioning. My mother has not yet been delivered of her latest bairn but she's throwin' fits about my absence. Gran says I'm runnin' a special errand for her.

"So yer mother fumes because she knows where ye be, and does not wish to know it—well, ye know how things stand between yer mother and Ann. We'd best get back as soon as the food takes hold in your belly."

He leaves me alone to bathe and say my farewells to the vision caves. I thank my vision, salute the four directions. As I bid farewell to the East I see a bloody cardinal feather by the cave entrance. A gift from the lynx, yet it sickens me. I put it quickly in my pouch. When I have finished thanking the spirits I leave a bit of trout with a special blessing for the Mother cat. I scatter the ashes and bits of blackened wood from the fire, use a swatch of heather to sweep the cliffside clean.

When he sees me coming downstream, Staghorn tucks his flute in his sack. We start back in silence, him light and quick with the step of a man forty years younger, me heavy with the burden of the vision I cannot share.

Chapter 24

The steam makes a film of moisture on my face. I shut out the image of my mother's face, glazed with perspiration, deafen to the sound of her groans. I gulp the steam in quick breaths, hearing the fear in the rapid knocking of my heart. A small cauldron of the heavy relaxing syrup used at the beginning of labor bubbles sullenly.

The labor has gone so quickly there has been no need of it. Gran says Mother's womb is already nearly open. Mina sent me into the other room to fetch the Mother's-ease tea, a mixture of herbs that both relax the laboring woman and help her womb to contract. I breath the soothing scents of chamomile and poppy, black cohosh and coltsfoot, lemon verbena and rosemary.

Sarah says the most important thing is to never bring fear into the room of a laboring woman.

"A woman must be completely open to birth the child," she says, "and so she is unable to defend herself from the thoughts of those around her." But Mother lost the last child she bore, in that same awful year that Mari died birthing her fourth child.

No sooner do I shut the image of Mari's gray, slack face from my mind than I see my brother, all red and spindly like a featherless nestling, his hoarse little voice croaking fainter and fainter until he stiffened and died. . .

A tear plops into the seething cauldron. I shake my head angrily, then remember Sarah saying comfort heals a fear while anger feeds it. I imagine wrapping myself in white wings, center and breathe into the steam, willing myself to a calm place of vision. A sparkling amethyst slowly swims up from the bottom of the cauldron; all the colors of a clear dawn blend and move about it, clouds moving up and away. . .

Mina's mind speaks into mine, *"Bring the tea."*

I ladle the brew into an earthenware cup and add a dash of well-water to cool it. I return to Mother's room. She's panting hard, holding onto the edge of her pallet, squatting. Tremors run through her body, giving off palpable light and heat. I hold the cup to her lips, but not until Gran says, "Take the tea, Anna," does she notice it and sip. Then she forgets it again, her being consumed in the gulping of air and releasing of deep agonized sounds, noises that sound as if they issued from the deepest cracks of the earth rather than my slender, mortal mother. She is shaking like a grove of birch in a howl of north-west wind. Mina and Gran support her legs and press against her lower back, panting with her and offering bits of encouragement.

"Close, you're close Anna. No, don't push yet, pant through it, just pant—soon now—"

Hair dark with dampness on the nape of her neck, trickle of sweat down her back. I hold the tea to her open mouth but she doesn't see it, doesn't hear the sounds rumbling out of her body. I wonder where she is now, wonder if the Goddess takes women away somewhere so the pain shaking through them does not tear them to pieces. . .

I watch her huge belly rise and harden, rise and harden again with the rhythm of the breath. We are all breathing together now, the whole room seems to be panting with us, the fire panting in the next room, the flurry of wind outside gasping in regular intervals with our breath.

There is a moment when everything shifts and seems to open; for the first time I sense a fifth presence in the room with us. Mina reaches inside my mother.

"Good. You're open. I'll break the waters."

There's a rush of water down to the ground. The next pain makes Mother's face go scarlet, then white.

"Push?" she grunts.

"Yes. Go ahead," urges Mina.

"Fiona, get the cloth," says Gran.

I lay the baby-catching cloth under Mother's straining thighs. Her face scrunches up, turns deep red, then purple. The muscles in her arms stand out; her body vibrates with effort. She gasps in more air, and then again holds it for a long push. Awed, I watch her control the energy, riding it, using it. It seems impossible; like watching someone harness a bolt of lightening to a plow, but she is doing it.

Then I see the purplish wad of the baby's head peeping out, and retreating, crowning and dipping back again.

"Not too hard, give it time," cautions Mina, rubbing salve over Mother's genitals to help them stretch. She pulls the distended labia, working the opening wider and wider apart, coaxing the head to emerge. Another push and the head bulges out. Bracing herself with one hand, Mother reaches out to touch the child with the other. A final push and a gasp and the baby slides out— powdery, purple, wrapped in a bluish cord.

Mother collapses back on her haunches so quickly it is all we can do to catch her. She scoops up the baby, laughing with happiness and relief. The baby moans and wriggles, paddling with its feet as if it sought for the safe boundaries of the small chamber it has left forever. The little scrunched up face rapidly goes from purple to red. I'm so excited I didn't notice if it was a lad or a lass. I want to touch it, but it is so fragile and slippery looking I hold back.

"Hello, my wee lassie," Mother croons, patting her on the back. "Hello, my small queen."

What a laughably ugly little being she is. Surely the rest of us were not so ugly at first. I feel proud of my mother for loving her so much and not minding that she is ugly. Well, I don't mind either, I think with a surge of warmth. She's my sister. If she's not pretty, she'll be smart then, that's better. . .

"Will she suck?" asks Mina. The baby nuzzles awhile as if-confused, making squeaking noises like a rat. Then she latches on and sucks fiercely.

"There. There now, that's good," says Mother, patting the baby. "Aye, you'll have milk soon enough if ye keep after it."

Mina nods. "She's a good strong will in her. Well, she's a spring child for sure, full of the new fire."

Meanwhile, Gran sits patiently, feeling the cord pulse, waiting for the proper time to sever it. Finally she nods towards the scissors, indicating I should cut it. Though prepared by her description in advance, I am afraid—the cord seems so much like a part of the baby. She does not rebuke me for my fear, but matter-of-factly cuts the cord far away from the child's body, then quickly ties it close to the navel and cuts it again.

She lifts my mother up, puts a bowl underneath her. The big gutty ball of afterbirth plops out. Then we help Mother sit on the edge of the bed and wash off the blood. I'm awed by her distorted, stretched out genitals. It seems like all her insides would fall out. But no one else seems concerned about that, nor about the blood streaming down her legs, soaking the birthing sheets, puddling in the hard dirt floor. I feel slightly sick, and dizzy, remembering that in the excitement I had eaten no lunch.

The other three women are laughing and chattering away. Is it all over then, the pain gone so quickly? I look at my mother with new eyes. Nine times has she made this journey to the land of apples to bring back a soul, and she has eight living children to show for it. To survive such a thing once seems extraordinary to me. And here she is, laughing, throwing her hair back like a young girl. . .

The older women put clean cloths spread with a blood-stopping ungent against her vulva, and wrap her hips and thighs to keep her legs together. It looks uncomfortable. Mother seems to think so too.

"No need, I'm fine," she protests.

"Wait til Sarah can get here and make sure," says Mina.

Mother lies down, still stroking the baby and cooing to it. I have a flash of memory, what it was like to lie face down, happily lost in the nuzzling of her soft breasts, and again warmth flushes through me, making my own breasts hot.

"Who have you brought through this time?" asks Gran,

stroking Mother's hair.

"This is Myrrhiana. Born from the sea."

Peter must be the father then, I think, remembering the times he took Mother fishing with him last summer. Just north of here there are fisher-folk, but Peter is the only one in our village who goes out past the cove in his boat. He also eats lobsters and spiny crabs, things the other villagers think he is daft to touch. He taught us to eat them too; and while their flesh is not so fine as salmon, it is far too good to scorn. Well, perhaps Myrrhiana will be like those shellfish; not so lovely without, but sweet within.

"Inches to ells I'll wager you have another redhead," Mina says.

Mother makes no reply. She has dozed off. The baby also sleeps, riding the gentle swell of Mother's breath. We clean up quietly and go in the other room.

"Small use for this," Mina says, taking the relaxing syrup from the fire. Gran shrugs.

"Tis well to be prepared." She fixes us another herbal brew and we sit at the table drinking in quiet satisfaction. It feels good to be accepted as an equal, as if I had done this many times before. I try not to think about the way Mother's vulva looked. I don't like the idea of being pulled apart like that. I cross my legs together tightly. And yet, she was so happy. . .

The latch opens. Annie peeks through the door, looking flushed and excited.

"Did Anna have her baby?" We nod.

"Tis a wee lassie," says Mina.

"Oh, Elsabeth had a lass too!" She's fairly bouncing with excitement. It's unusual to see her so agitated about something. Mina makes a gesture indicating that Mother is asleep. Annie nods and enters quiet as a cat, but still bouncing on the tips of her toes as a grown cat would never do. She clutches my shoulders.

"Tis wonderful!" she whispers. Sarah enters, wearing the same triumphant smile we have been sharing.

"How's Elsabeth?" asks Mina.

"Och, resting easily. Her lass is fine and healthy," says Sarah.

When Elsabeth went into labor yesterday, Sarah had agreed to take Annie to assist at that birth while Gran and Mina and I stayed with my mother, for Mother had predicted that this would be her day and I did not want to risk missing the birth of my sister. It is not uncommon for two women to go into labor on the same day; babies like to be born at the full moon.

Annie is so flushed and sparkling I can scarcely take my eyes off her. Colored sparks seem to fly off her in every direction, though she is sitting still.

"Och, tis so magnificent!" she says, "I cannot wait to have one of my own!" Gran frowns.

"You'd do well to wait. With lasses too young, the outcome is not so happy."

Annie brushes off Gran's remark. Of course not right away, but what a fine thing to look forward to. . .

"Let's get ourselves with child at the same time," she says to me, "when we're *older*," she says, placating Gran. "Then we can help get each other's bairns born and raise them together and all—"

I wind my legs tighter together. "I'm in no great rush for that."

We hear stirring in the other room.

"Do I hear Sarah?" Mother's voice calls. We can barely fit all of us in the small room, clustered about the bed. We all huddle in silence, adoring the new baby. She seems so sleepy, I wonder if all is well with her. Sarah hears my thought, puts a reassuring hand on me.

"Och, they all are at first. Tis a big change." She undoes the bindings, checks Mother's bleeding. "Och, you'll never even know you had one in a few days, but for how hard your breasts will be."

"How does Elsabeth fare?" asks Mother.

"Och, she's made for bearing babies. She was frightened at first, as everyone is at their first bearing. But she could have pushed for a fortnight, she had such a good strong back on her."

Mother smiles at me and Annie.

"What do you think of this business of having bairns?"

Annie ducks her head shyly, tracing her finger across the baby's back.

"It makes me feel a bit more gracious to my mother."

"Och, aye and what you girls saw was nothing like what Mairead went through. Of course, it was her own stubborness gave her the most trouble," says Mina.

I avoid Mother's eyes, petting the blue veined dome of my sister's head.

"She's so pretty," I lie, hoping the question of my feelings will be forgotten.

As if in answer to my wish, a knock comes at the door. Peter enters, leading the other children. Eostre marches in with her lips tight and her shoulders squared, seething with rage that Annie and I got to attend the births while she is yet considered too young. Elana darts to the bed, oohing and ahhing over the new baby. The boys hang back, scuffling their feet in the doorway, looking abashed.

The twins immediately set up a howl, seeing themselves supplanted, and howl louder when we pull their clutching hands away from Mother's feet.

Annie and I walk about in the other room carrying the twins while Peter admires Myrrhiana. Sarah smiles, radiating her warm, contented glow, sharing her husband with my mother as easily and naturally as Mother had shared herself with Mari's husband after Mari died. *Why didn't the Laird understand about friends healing each other's hearts?* Then Peter and Sarah take the twins and the older boys, Malcolm and Colin, back to their croft with their own three bairns, while we girls set to fixing Mother a special supper of fish, and deer liver, and the special cunny cheese made with a bit of mother's milk and blood mixed in with the cream of goat, ewe and cow.

*   *   *   *

Three days later our croft was bulging with well-wishers bearing every kind of fish and meat and cakes imaginable, and kegs and kegs of claret and ale and whiskey. The wave of happy faces began at midday with the women and old people, the menfolk coming in from the fields as soon as they could get away, mud fresh from the plowing still clinging to their clothes. The seining, or blessing, of a new child is always a festive occasion, but the first child of spring seems a special blessing, a good omen for the crops, the sheep, and the babes yet to be born. Mary, Elsabeth's child, was actually born a wee bit before Myrrhiana, but Elsabeth has asked for a seventh day seining, to give herself more time to recover from her labor.

Most people have brought presents of food, but there are also plenty of baby clothes and a few wooden toys. John has brought a marvelous thing that rattles and rolls about on round wheels. Ewan, the young blacksmith, offers a hanging toy he has made with three five-pointed stars soldered from iron and some colored ribbons.

"They like to watch things," he explains. Tis a curious notion; nothing will do but that everyone must take a turn fingering it and exclaiming over the waste or wonder of lavishing so much care on a toy that is only to be looked at. It is hard to tell if Ewan is more mortified or pleased by the attention, but he looks at me shyly and fidgets as if the gift were more for my notice than Myrrhiana's.

I turn, pushing my way through the throng to the hearth, where John cuts me a piece of lamb off the carcass which is dripping fat and charred rosemary onto the flames. The Laird could not come, of course.

"Regrets and regards," his vassal bore us. But at least he sent the lamb.

William's elbow thuds into my side; the old shepherd nods towards Ewan, "He'll make a fine father, eh lass?" Not for any of my bairns, I think rebelliously. Suddenly I am thought a woman, and everyone talks to me of how comely such and such a lad is, or what a hard worker another. I slink away, worrying the lamb to shreds between my teeth, trying to blend unnoticed in the crowd. As well hide a beacon in the dark; my bright hair draws knowing looks, smiles, nods. All my life I had longed for the time when my blood would prove me a woman; but I had not bargained for how differently I would be treated.

Peter pounds his staff on the floor, silencing the revelers before they become completely raucous and out of hand.

"Spring is come
The lambing begun.
Out of the earth, out of the air

Out of the water, out of the fire
A child is born.
Welcome we now
Myrrhiana McNair!"

Cheers, whistles, stomping on the floor greet his announcement. Mina and Gran and Jessica bring a cauldron of warm water, fragrant with herbs, to the center of the room. Peter takes a coal from the fire and passes it quickly through the water. Mother places the naked child in the basin. Admiring hmmms and ahs fill the room. She immerses Myrrhiana quickly and draws her out. Sarah helps her comfort the crying child and wrap her in a man's shirt. They hand her to Gran. Gran smiles fondly at the child, then addresses her seriously.

"Do not forget, what seems the most different from you is not different, but a part of yourself, a mirror to your deepest nature."

Everyone nods. If the child had been a boy he would have been wrapped in a woman's skirt, and the same thing spoken to him.

Mother says, "Today Myrrhiana chose the oak to be her guardian." That means that when she and Gran took Myrrh out to the woods today, they buried her placenta beneath an oak tree.

They say I chose a pine near a pool, though I am not clear on how they can know the choice of such a wee bairn. When I was seven they introduced me to my tree guardian, and I have spent many hours since in the loving shade of its scented boughs. Peter and John and William pass smoldering oak boughs from Myrrh's special tree around her.

They face the east. Peter says:

"Let the air come
That bears the hawk
That brings the clouds
And the life-giving rain.
Let the air come now
To be a friend
And guardian
To Myrrhiana McNair."

Sarah calls to the South:

"Let the fire come
That shines in the sun
That shines in the heart
And opens the womb.
Let the fire come now
To be a friend
And guardian
To Myrrhiana McNair."

John calls to the West:

"Let the water come
That freshens the pool
That moves with the moon
And boils in the cauldron.
Let the water come now
To be a friend
And guardian
To Myrrhiana McNair."

Gran calls to the North:

"Let the earth come
That grows the grain
That is flower and fruit
And the deep hidden caves.
Let the earth come now
To be a friend
And guardian
To Myrrhiana McNair."

They then tuck her in a willow basket lined with the best white linen, never used, and tuck the cloth under her chin.

"Lord of grain," Sarah calls, placing some bread on the linen.

"Mother of milk," invokes Peter, placing a cheese beside it.

"Fire of immortality," whispers Gran, whirling a taper of fir three times over the basket.

Mother stands holding the basket in her arms. Peter holds his hands as high as he can reach over the basket, while Sarah

lays hers upon the earth beneath it. Slowly, with barely percepti-
ble movement, they bring their hands closer together as an expectant warbling hum rises from the gathering. As their hands
meet at the basket, signifying the meeting of heaven and earth,
shrieks and skirls of excitement burst from every mouth. The
seining is complete, the survival of the child as assured as the
community's magic can make it.

The feasting and celebration continues, Mother takes Myrrh
out of the basket and sits holding her in her lap while people
kneel one at a time, placing their hand on the child and making
a happy prophecy. Soon she has acquired so many wishes for "a
good marriage" and "fertility" that I fear her future will hold
nought but an endless round of husbands and bairns. Myrrh
whimpers and fusses, nurses and falls into an exhausted sleep.
Mother looks as though she would be happy to do the same, but
continues to smile bravely at the endless line of well-wishers.

Mina kneels and predicts, "She'll have Fiona's fiery red hair,
and beauty to rival her and Eostre both."

Looking at my sister's pinched head and blotchy skin, I judge
that Mina must be imagining with more wish than sooth. Mina
also gives a small necklace of acorns and seashells.

Gran has an offering of an unusual shell that I have never
seen the like of. Myrrhiana is named for the sea Goddess, so it is
only fitting that she should have it, but I feel an unwelcome
surge of jealousy. I take for granted that I am Gran's favorite;
"My heir of queen and darkness" she would joke, laughing that
wild laugh that is like the wind rushing through the hills and
downs of heather. I bridle at the thought of her liking any of my
siblings as well.

I move to the door, suddenly desperate to be away from the
winks and smiles that suggest I might soon be seining a bairn of
my own. Outside, the bairns of the village are jousting with
stalks of marsh weed, tumbling and fighting over a game of gutty ball, wild with excitement over the unaccustomed pleasure of
moonlit play. The wailing at the center of a tussy-puzzle of small
arms and legs betray the location of the twins. I wipe their noses
and feed them some of the dainties I had palmed on the way out.
They burrow into my skirts, whimpering, and I am sorry I had
not come to comfort them sooner, for of course, they were far from

sharing the general joy of the occasion. The next youngest child, four year old Malcolm, comes over and buries his head on my lap as well. We sit in a heap of forlorn weariness, listening to the loud toasts and boasts and drinking songs pouring from the croft into the chill night air. At last comes the song that signals the party is coming to a close. The women sing the lyrics, while the men follow each line with the booming refrain, "To the child, to the child!"

"Sent from God
Made of gold
Bright as Blouwedd[1]
Happy as the Cloved[2]
Headed 'i the sun
Footed 'i the moon
Child of the Earth
Be welcome home."

A babe on each hip and one clinging to my skirts, I struggle upstream through the flow of departing revelers. I chase a pair of amorous lovers out of the children's room and settle the sobbing twins into their new bed. With Malcolm huddled in my lap, I rub the twins' backs and sing softly until the sobs turn to sighs, and then snores. The older children creep into their beds. The last stragglers bid Mother good-night. I climb up the ladder to the loft to find Annie already asleep in my bed, wrapped in a dishevelment of black hair. She wakes enough to pull my head to her breast, and my heart to a comforting sleep too deep for dream.

---

1. Blouwedd—the Goddess of beauty and flowers.
2. The Cloved refers to the Horned God whose feet were cloven like animal hooves.

Chapter 25

Annie took the name Nimué, the sorceress who had enchanted the Merlin in the wood and taken his power. Our Initiation and
name-taking deepened my awareness that she was no longer merely my dearest sister, but enchantress, beauty, the embodiment of
magic. The innocence of the white and yellow she wore pulled me
into the blackness of her hair and eyes; the light of her smile
caught me like the invisible web a candle casts to snare a moth.
Day after day we escaped from our chores and lay together in the
hidden thickets and secret glens of our childhood, making love and
practicing the arts of ensorcellment. Letting our voices lead us
through the dark, we walked in trance down the long stone stair to
the center of the earth and then up a passage which opened into
the light of a different life, in another time.

In this way we found two temples where we had served together in countries of heat and light beyond imagining. Returning to our own time giggling with excitement, bunching up our
underclothes, trying to hold them so that they fell in folds like
the white dresses we remembered wearing then. It took Annie

only a few days to scrounge enough material to make the dresses
we remembered. We wore them when we were alone together, not
that it was warm enough but two or three months in the year.
We talked about how amazingly warm it had been in that temple
by the sea, and in that other island temple of the river. How cold
and smooth the stone was, how large the temples had been. Had
the Wise Ones truly had such wealth and power then? To serve
the Goddess in the marketplace as well as in the heart was an
extraordinary notion, heady as whiskey.

*   *   *   *

We braid our hair in the 'crescent coil' we remembered wearing, three rows in the back like a downtilting crescent moon. We
lie together shivering in the weak sun in our thin one-shouldered
garments telling each other stories:

"Remember when you knocked over the big urn full of oil?"

"Remember the ritual where we wore the headdresses of
wheat and grapes?"

Mostly just remembering lying down together in a warm
field, drone of bees, heat shimmering in the strange twisted trees
sighing above us, taking each other's clothes off, both of us dark
of hair and skin and eye, white garments gleaming, falling from
our copper smoothness, and the touch, the touch feels the same.

"You still know how to touch me from then," she whispers,
and I marvel that it is so. Her body is changing so fast now, all
curves, her hips flaring more each time we lay together and now
we lay together every day, entering again that ancient world it
seems we have just briefly left.

Giggling behind our hands as we avoided the stern looks of
the older Priestesses as we prepared to dance the Kore, the Dance
of Maidens. The voluptuous self-absorbed Priestess ten years older who we admire so. And mostly just re-enacting over and over,
remember you liked me to kiss you here? Yes, with your tongue,
like that. The feeling is the same; we blend, shimmer, we are
each two and sometimes three and sometimes it seems like an infinite waver of women vibrating through us; smiling through our
smiles, kissing through our kiss as if they lived again in us.
Kiss, hair, eyes, wetness; the dark pool of the eye in which I see

her, my sister, my lover, my Nimué and beyond Nimué; and she enters enchanted portals through this blackstone tunnel to my soul; how far we dive, we lie together and look and look and pass through endearments in several languages and then into a place where no language exists, just pictures and then no pictures, but something like a black river or a river of light.

We shine and gleam; bodies of shadow and smoke play through our flesh, we return to our bodies tangled in the sense that we have been dreaming, each time leaving more and more tracks in the labyrinth of each other.

"The bulls with flowers on them; remember how gentle they were, like big tomcats, sweethearted towards us as we brought flowers to twine around their horns."

"Aye, and their plushy noses snuffling up blossoms from our hands."

"They're not gentle like that anymore," she says sadly, and I am not surprised anymore that we dream the same dreams together as we touch, trance, or sleep.

We don't tell the older women or ask them about it. We have reached the secret-keeping time of youth, and it is sweet to have these secrets between us. How passionate our secrecy, our code-words, our special looks; I can read now every feeling so plain on her from the pulse of her throat to the way she shifts a foot. Gran and Mina and Rose ignore us, we imagine the others don't notice. Occasionally my Gran says something pointed about a Witch's need "to be herself *alone*."

More often than not when we are up to some mischief it is Annie's idea, but I am always an eager second. We race to see who can take her clothes off faster, argue about who moans the loudest, flirt with the men and then giggle and race away. She is the first to try and see what it is like with a lad. She grimaces, scowls, bold and sorry at thirteen.

"It hurt, it was no fun at all!" she insists. But a few months later she confesses that she's been trying it some more and it's not so bad after all. Hiding my jealousy I ask if it's the same as with me.

"Oh no, not at all," she says, "it's nothing special like us," and I am reassured. She tries them one at a time. Each time she wrinkles her nose afterwards with disdain and ignores that par-

ticular man from then on, but a few weeks pass and she tries it
again with another.

I am jealous of her boldness, but the way the men of the village look at me scares me. Like there is a wanting to hurt in
them along with the wanting to love. I'm not so eager to try, especially since Annie keeps saying it's not the same at all and not
nearly so much fun.

We sleep together every night through the winter and for
awhile, lads are forgotten. Late April, at Beltane, we go up north
for a big festival with three other covens. Gran and I use the excuse of visiting relatives and Annie tags along with me as usual.
She's almost never at her mother's now, they just spit at each
other like cats and have scratched each other's faces more than
once. Her mother is so sharp-mouthed and thin, so mean and sly.
But for Annie to strike her mother horrifies me. I cannot bear to
be around Annie and Mairead when the cruel words start.

It is a day's journey to the meeting place for this year's Beltane. It's a rare thing now to meet in a Grove with others. There
have been no burnings in our village, but others have not been so
lucky.

We have a Maypole and the early flowers. It is a warm year
and we wear our brightest clothing. I am in green and Annie
wears her yellow and white. There's a tall blond lad in yellow and
green talking to Annie and it's clear to me where she'll be lying
this night. Beltane is the high night of sex magick and the
young people especially are looking at each other with bright
eyes.

An older man, small and slender and very dark with a dark
beard joins the circle as dusk comes on. I like his looks and his
bright blue tunic and his frank smile of appreciation as he looks
me over, appreciation clear and free of the fear and anger I feel
mixed into the lust of so many of Glen Lochlan's men. I walk
over to him and hand him some chicken; he has come late for the
feasting but there is plenty of food left. He eats with a dainty
savagery that reminds me of a cat. I like the way he tears the
bread. I like the way he licks his fingers. I realize that I have chosen my first consort and smile, it seems so right, this is the sacred time. He sees it in my eyes and smiles back. I cast an indul-
gent eye on Annie and the yellow green lad fawning on each

other; a daffodil marriage, they do indeed look made for each other on this day.

We join the greeting dance.

"Tout, tout a tout tout, throughout and about," we chant as we weave around the Maypole; I seem to realize for the first time how the Maypole is phallus as well as the tree of life. We are kissing each person as the cord of dancers doubles back on itself, laughing, everyone is laughing, moving fast, 'striking the serpent' as the line snakes back and forth. I kiss my bearded one as he laughs by. He is such a Pan, my heart is delighted. The children are screaming with laughter, it makes me think of all the happy rituals I spent playing tag on meadows like this one, the ribbons for May day, the eggs dyed red with onion skins for Ostara, and the glorious food, so rich and different from our daily fare. We eat so well at Sabbats, no one thinks of stinting then, everyone brings their best.

The snake catches its tail, pulling us into a circle, and we whirl in a ring until dizzy, collapse, sprawling on each other, panting and laughing, and out of the panting and laughter the names of the Goddess start bubbling up like a spring from the earth, then a babbling brook of names over names, names colliding and skating over each other and weaving, the pattern starting to show now, the sky turns purple, the stars glitter and several fall as the names keep winding in a spiral up the Maypole and then out into the sparkling mysterious night. Then we face the ground and speak our secret boon we desire from the Goddess into the earth.

Gradually a thumping rhythm trembles through the earth; the Godlink* with the staff starts it, and the other men take it up. The women answer the stomping on the earth with a sharp clap. Thunder and lightning were always honored in this way at Beltane, and many times it rained. But this year the night is uncannily warm and I am fourteen, feeling lightning snap through me as I clap my hands. We dance then for the God, calling to Pan, Mannanon, Cernonus, Robin the Good, the Horned One.

The women sing to the men:

"On the first day of May

---

*Godlink—a man embodying the God for a particular ritual.

The Queen has no sting
Then shall the bold one
Swift on the wing
Heart of the butterfly
He shall be King."

The men sing an answering song to the women about the ivy that clings to the tree of its choosing, the women on one side of the Maypole dancing to the men on the other. Then the men dance a coil around us, there is much screaming and squishing together, more women than men as always. Then we surround them, coil ivy around the men of our choice and bind them with it. The men mime distress so we free them by cutting their bonds with our knives. This is a time when the women make their choice known by who they bind and release.

I bind my bearded one and free him, "On the promise of your kind behaviour, sir!"

"I live to serve my lady," he replies. He has laid his head imploringly in my lap like a unicorn and I brush my breasts lightly along his neck and back as I lean over him to sever his bonds. Then we get up, there is dancing again, more people dancing in pairs now and playing tug of war with strands of ivy. Bawdy songs play faster and faster about unicorns and virgins and loving the whole night through on Beltane Eve to conjure the summer in.

"Tell not the Priests where we've been
They might think 'tis a sin—
We'll be out in the woods all Beltane night
A-conjuring summer in!"

Then a big tug of war, women on one side, men on the other, the thick braid of ivy hot in our hands as we slowly pull them off balance. They gain control and tug us towards them. A shriek from one of the Priestesses and the women let go suddenly, the men sprawl back and all the women old enough to swive* and young enough to run take off shrieking into the woods.

The men follow in hot pursuit. Scrambling up the hillside, I look back to be sure my chosen is following me. He is. I reach the

*Swive—make love

summit and take off like a mare, like Rhiannon[1] leading my
suitor a merry chase. Fleet and giddy as an air sprite though I
feel, when I look back again he is almost on me, and I gasp, then
tumble with him over and over—"Ow!"—over a rock and into a
tangle of panting arms and legs in the wet grass. I am happy as
Epona[2] to be caught, wild with excitement and a little scared, my
heart hammering as fast and as noisily as a deer crashing
through the brush. He's so merry in his eyes, though, my fear
eases swiftly. He pulls me up, and then kneels before me.

"In the name of the Lady of the Summer, and the Lord of
Light who is Her consort, I beg you to accept my services." His
tone is formal, but he is smiling that same mischievous and delightful smile.

"In the name of Litha, Lady of Summer, in the name of Lugh,
Lord of Light, I accept your services," I reply as solemnly as I can
and then kneel, facing him.

He reaches a gentle hand, caresses my touseled hair back
from my forehead.

"You are as beautiful as the Lady of Summer Herself," he
praises me. "What is your name, my lady?"

"In Her circles, I am Kyairthwen."

He looks surprised. "Such a dark aspect for a maiden of such
brightness!" he exclaims. His smile becomes uneasy. "Maiden
Kyairthwen," he says, "in you, I honor Maiden, Mother, Crone. I
surrender my seed, that life may thrive. I will surrender all my
life to that purpose, if need be. Thy will, and not mine, prevail."

I do not feel in myself the sobering vision that has come
across his eyes, and I like not his change from laughter to solemnity.

"And thy name?" I ask, tracing the warm blue pulse in his
throat.

"Ah, my lady," he smiles, his gaeity returned, " in Her circles, I am called Pan."

I giggle. It is so perfect, as if the Lady had known my mind
before I knew it myself. And now indeed I see he has the aspect of
both goat and gentle goat-herd in his dark, alert manner.

He cups his hands around my breasts.

"What is thy will, lady?" he asks huskily.

"To learn of the mysteries of the God," I reply, my voice shak-

---

1. Rhiannon—a Goddess of horses
2. Epona—another mare Goddess

ier than I had hoped it would be.

He brushes his hand over my mouth and then his mouth covers mine. My body enters that wide awake and yet dreamlike state that comes over me when I make love with Annie. His beard and mustache tickle. May all the differences, I think to myself, be so. delightful as this. He pulls my blouse to my shoulders, glides his tongue along my neck and collarbone. I cannot help but giggle as his beard tickles me, but he is so gentle that while I am in no hurry for him to go further, I am not fearing it either. His giggle is as innocent, pure, and full of delight as mine. He licks and nuzzles my ears, calling them little shells, complimenting the whiteness of my throat, the rose of my cheeks, the green of my eyes, and I blush with pleasure at being so worshipped.

He pulls off the leather jerkin that he wears over his chest. I do not think he is any taller than I, his body muscled but slender and lithe like a cat, or a young stag. I touch the dark curling hair on his body. He is much darker than most of the men in these parts; from his size and darkness I guess him to be of faery blood and this makes me feel a kinship with him. He kisses and bites the fleshy base of my thumb, down along my wrists and arms. The whiteness of my arms against his darkness pleases me. A breeze lifts the curls on his head, moves my own hair carressingly over my shoulders. He spends so long kissing and carressing my arms that I am almost bored. But then his mouth is hot against the cloth over my breasts, he pulls the cloth down and the shock of my breasts in his mouth makes me tremble, suddenly afraid again. He stops and steadies his breathing.

"Art thou maiden in truth?" he asks.

I nod.

He pauses. "Thank you for blessing me in this way." He kisses my heart. "I promise you that I shall be gentle and considerate of you in every way. You have but to ask and I will stop at any time. I am here at your service," he emphasizes, "and at the service of Her whose name you bear."

I smile at him gratefully, and show my confidence in him by unlacing my bodice. He helps me unlace it and put it aside.

"You're so young," he says with a sound that must be a laugh but sounds more like a sob. "As fair as Blouwedd you are, my

Lady. Whatever name you go by, you are the maiden of flowers, and I am a mortal caught in the web of your weaving."

"No mortal," I say, "but a God." This time when we kiss he rubs his chest against me. My nipples delight in the unfamiliar sensation of muscle and fur and bone pressed close to my softness. Oh yes, I like this. We are both giggling. I pull off my skirts, thrilling at the expression of delight and desire that flutters over his face.

"Oh, Goddess, thank you," he murmurs, kissing my belly, all the way down my thighs, turning me over on my side. He presses his body up against my back, pushes his pelvis against my buttocks and moans, carressing my breasts with his hands. He slides his hand to my cleft, carressing the most sensitive places with his fingers until I am wet and gasping.

"It will be easier," he gasps to me, "if I take you this way."

"As you like," I gasp in return.

Sensation of pressure, then tightness as he begins to enter.

"Open," he encourages me softly. "Open to me. Open to the God."

I let go of all my muscles and slowly he eases his way through the tightness. We rest quietly for a few moments, and then he moves in me. I relax and consciously breathe, relaxing my flower, relaxing into the strange sensation of being so full and finding it growing more and more pleasant every time he moves and adjusts himself in me. He pulls out and I think it is over, but then he turns me onto my back and penetrates me again. This time I can watch with awe as his member slowly sheathes itself in my vulva. I spread my legs wide, glorying in my power to do this amazing thing.

"Oh, you open so well," he praises me, and I flush with delight. I am a woman now. I am the Goddess embracing the God. It takes longer for the pleasure to come than it would with Annie, but it does come, soft, warm and subtle as April sunlight.

It is everyone's duty to keep vigil on Beltane eve and conjure the summer in by making love all night through, but he collapses across me and I sleep, contented and dreamless beneath his warm body as if he were the grandest blanket I should ever have.

When we wake it is raining a light spring rain and the sky is a pale pearl like the inside of a shell.

"Ah, no dream but the fairest of truths!" Pan exults, waking to find me in his arms. He pulls his tartan over us so that we are in a tent, the raindrops patting over his back like a troupe of elf ponies, the rich smell of the wet earth rising into the mushroom and musk of our mingling. We giggle and chuckle and giggle some more as if our giggling were an entire conversation. Our friendship is a conspiracy woven of giggles. His hardness presses up against my belly and he nudges me more insistently now that he knows I am not frightened of him. I touch his cock.

"Oh, yes, touch me," he urges, clasps my hand so tight around his member I am astonished he does not cry out with pain as I should do if anyone grasped me so. This part of him is strong, the God-part, strong and solid as the Maypole, pulsing with all the life of summer. Trembling, I guide him back into me, responding with excitement this time to the initial tightness of the fit. Moaning, I pull his hips tight against me, wanting to feel him as deep as I can, all the deep, womanly hungers of my body awakening into life. The earth breathes her strong yielding power into my body; unselfconscious as any mare I groan and writhe under him, wanting with the full depth of my being.

"You are the Goddess," he gasps.

Yes. I am the Goddess, and I love the God.

The life force bursts through us in glory. I roll over the edge of some high cliff, fall with him, the sun rises and explodes in us, the hot red sun of summer. I go deep with him into the dawning, so many colors, like a fat, buttery rainbow under the wool, while the gray rain whispers down and turns into green all around us as we conjure the summer in.

Chapter 26

Evening is coming on, bitter cold. We have not had a truly warm night since Beltane. But less than a fortnight has passed; surely the warm summer nights will be on us soon. Annie and I stand wrapped in each other's cloaks, near the forge. Ewan Smith is just finishing his work for the day. The man waiting for the horseshoes stands, combing his horse. Other men from the village stand clustered about, drinking their home-brewed ale. Many prefer to drink here at the smithy, bringing their own ale, rather than paying the prices Bluebelly asks at the Inn. A skin of ale passes in our direction; Annie holds out her cup and we share it.

Sean is here, warming his long fingered hands. In the years since the Laird abandoned my mother we have not spoken, even when standing so close as this. There is another lad here younger than he, but he seems the youngest. He watches Ewan so intently, I wonder if he still dreams on being a smith, as he did when we were children. His hands and arms are not made for such as that. It does not look as though he will grow to be built like his father, who is so broad and bluff and strong. Sean is slender, shy. He tries to hold manly discourses with the men, but where his father can mingle with the men of the village, sit by their hearths and be accepted at once, Sean is too wordish.

A couple of the men pull out flasks of the whiskey I was wishing for.

"Come now," they call to us, "come sit in our laps and share our whiskey, we'll get warm together." Their laughter is hearty, the lewdness of their intent obvious. I'm not insulted, but I'm not tempted either. Annie feels too good to move.

"We're fine as we are," I call back.

"Yer too old to be clinging to each other like snotty-nosed bairns," one joshes.

"And too smart to be clinging to the likes of you," retorts Annie, kissing me full on the mouth in front of them. We toss our hair like wild horses and canter off through the frost, laughing at the looks on their faces. But while we laugh I feel a cold, hard knot in my middle, a fear that someday these men will remember us playing them for fools, and pay us back for it.

*   *   *   *

Later that night Annie and I snuggle in bed.

"Did you see how Sean looked at you today?" she asks.

"No."

"He wants you."

"Well, I don't want him," I say, feeling the old anger at the Laird and his treatment of us.

"Don't be so quick to decide that," she chides. "Which of the lads d'ye like better?"

"Annie, I don't like any of the lads. I just want to be with you."

"Oh? What about Pan?" she teases.

"Och—if he lived in these parts, sure and I'd be sneaking off to the woods as much as you, I expect." I feel a little resentful of the time she spends teasing and swiving with the lads of the village. Besides, many of the village women give us bad looks now, and whisper behind their hands when we go by.

"Well, give it some thought. He's not what you'd call the

spitting image of his father, now is he?"

"No, that's for certain."

Next evening, as Annie and I come back from some herb gathering, she suggests going to the Smithy again. But we meet Crosby outside the entry. Crosby is Jesse's brother, two or three years older than she; at twenty-one, the handsomest man in the village with his green eyes and dark brown hair. His mobile, sharp-featured face is so different from Jesse's round and tranquil one.

"Aye, lasses!" A smile spreads over his face, already lined and weathered from years of work in the fields.

"Coming in to get warm?"

"Mmmm, aye," says Annie, "tis warmth we seek." Annie has just recently bedded Crosby. She says he's the first of the men she's been with who's given her any pleasure. "Perhaps a man needs a bit of Witch-blood in him to be worth anything as a lover," she had guessed.

He stares at Annie with intensity; she gazes cooly over his left shoulder, as if studying something in the distance.

"Tis not this forge that will warm me," he says, "as I would wish to be warmed." Ignoring me, he catches her in his arms.

"Take my iron for your forge," he whispers huskily, "shape me to what you wish."

Too embarrassed and jealous to watch, I duck into the Smithy. The men there nod in acknowledgement, then go on with their laughter and joking. One calls, "Hullo, little fox." The tale of my deceiving the Laird's hounds has enjoyed many retellings in Glen Lochlan. Sean looks at me; clearly I see his longing before he drops his gaze.

"Crosby!" one of the men calls, going to the door. He comes back snickering.

"That gypsy slut is leading Crosby around by the cock again."

"I wish she'd lead *me* around by *mine*," one of the older men complains. "I wouldn't put up any more resistance than he does. Tell yer friend," he calls to me, "there's more cocks for her to play with."

"Aye, enough for you too, Fiona." The man who called me little fox comes up and puts his arm around me. He is married, but neither marriage nor anything the Priest preaches from the pulpit seems to affect how the men look at the younger lasses. I push his hand away.

"Leave her alone!" Ewan commands sharply. "She's a virgin."

I move around to the other side of Ewan, close to Sean, hoping they'll think my blush is a maidenly one.

"Well, that can be cured," the man who put his arm around me persists, "I meant not to frighten ye lass," he says kindly. "Yer friend's so bold—and the two of you so close—" his voice has a question in it my eyes refuse to acknowledge, "—natural for a man to have ideas—and hopes!"

I am surprised when Sean puts a protective arm around my shoulder.

"Leave her alone, Stephen," he says, trying to sound as authoritative as Ewan, "Leave her be."

"Ah, tis just teasin'—ye want her for yerself, my lad—not that I blame ye—"

A few more jokes. Sean whispers, "If you want to go home, I'll take you." I nod. He takes my arm, we walk past the other men.

"Don't these young girls realize an experienced stud is a better stud?" complains one of the married men.

"Don't take offense Fiona. No one meant any harm," counsels Ewan.

"I know," I say, just wanting to get out of there.

"Don't be forgetting that—the lass is yer sister," one of the men calls to Sean. "Treat her like a good brother now."

We walk in silence. Sean has not let go of my arm. His touch is gentle. He doesn't seem so much older than the boy I used to play with. I begin to remember how much I liked him then.

"When the talk is rude like that," he says, "sometimes I feel ashamed to be a man."

I look at him gratefully. Full lips. Laird's bent nose, but set in a narrow face; small, indrawn chin, blue eyes. Hair still so blond as to be almost white. His slightness and awkward protectiveness set me at ease. He looks down and takes a deep breath.

"If any of these men—ever dares—ever dares try to lay a hand on you, you tell me," he looks at me, "and I'll take care of it."

I almost laugh. A fight between him and most any of the

other men would be like putting a sparrow up against a rooster. But then, I think, he need not fight. He is the young laird. The intensity of my relief catches me by surprise.

"Thank you. I do feel frightened sometimes. I wish I was bold like Annie," I shake my head, "but I am not."

"Well, some would say that Annie is too forward. A decent man—wants a girl who's—innocent and shy. Like you."

I look at the ground and say nothing, glad we are almost to the croft. I stop before we reach the end of the fence, knowing that mother would be upset to see him.

"Thank you for walking me home." He does not let go of my arm, but takes my other hand.

"I'm happy to do it Fiona. I—I've wanted to before—I was too afraid to ask. You don't hate me do you?"

"No. No, I don't. I did but it was just because of your father."

"I'm not my father, Fiona. I would never—don't judge me by his acts but—by my own."

"I will."

He still holds my hands.

"Fiona—would you like to go for a ride with me? I have a splendid stallion. His name is Coal."

"Aye. I would like that."

"Tomorrow?"

"Aye. But meet me not here, meet me by the well."

I run into the house, feeling the blood dancing in my cheeks. Sitting and looking in the hearth that night, it seems to me that his hair is as light as the top of the flames, his eyes as blue as the heart of it.

*   *   *   *

After my ride with Sean, Annie quickly pulls me into the woods, eager to hear all that had transpired.

"Well? How was he? Was he any good?"

"He just read poetry. And we ate the most wonderful food—"

"Did what?"

"He read poetry, from books—he brought some wonderful books—in French and Latin and English—he read it as it was and then made the words into words that I could know. I think it would be easy to learn more English. It's not such a hard language, it just sounds harsh—as he was reading it I almost felt like I understood."

"Fiona—did he bed you or not?"

"No I said—he didn't try. He kissed me, that's all." She looks perplexed.

"Must be the gentry have different ways. Must be courting. Crosby does some courting kinds of things but—it doesn't last long."

"Are you in love with him?"

"Crosby? No. No—he is in love with me. I like him well enough. It's not like being with you—someone I can really talk to—not like that. Maybe it never is—with a lad and a lass—maybe you just have to settle for what they have," she concludes.

"Annie, remember we said we would never marry?"

"Oh Fiona—we were children when we said that. And maybe we won't marry—but I want bairns at least. It's hard to raise bairns without a man around. Anyway—dinna fesh yerself—I'm not ready to marry—Crosby or anyone else. And for that matter, nobody's asked me yet. Well—are you going to see him again?"

"I said I'd go riding with him again—but not tomorrow because tomorrow we're doing the herb magic with Mina and Gran. I didn't say *that* of course."

"Aye. So he asked for the day after?"

"Annie—I don't want to spend so much time away from you."

"Oh, we have plenty still. Dinna think of that. It would be well for you to—life could be a lot easier if you were Sean's mistress. A lot easier."

"How?"

"Don't be a goose! He has money. You could ask for anything. That lad is falling in love with you. You'll be able to ask for anything you want and he'll give it to you. If it doesn't last—you don't have to have bairns with him. Take what you can."

"If you're so hot, why don't you bed him yourself?"

"He doesn't look at me like he looks at you. When we're together he doesn't even give me a glance."

I remember what he said about Annie being too bold, and realize he would be afraid to even think of bedding her.

"He's still a lad," she says, "a virgin no doubt—you might have to throw yourself at him. I'll help dress you—make you so pretty that he won't be able to resist." She strokes my cheek.

"And I know just how he feels," she coos, rubbing her nose and lips softly over mine. Our tongues slip deep inside each other's mouths, her hands pull my bodice down, freeing my breasts.

"Sometimes I wish I were a man," she whispers, "I'd marry you in a moment if I were."

Soon we are rolling and twisting in the ferns. One magic in the light of the fire, another in the darkness that cradles it. The sacred silence that follows our loving is sweet as the flame that ignites it. Casting dappled patterns of shadow on our bodies, the ferns breathe gently in response to our breath. A doe steps close to us, stares at us with wide eyes and bounds away.

"I wish it felt as good to lay with Crosby as it does with you," she says. "It's not fair the lasses are so much more beautiful than the lads. It's just not fair."

"No, it's not," I agree. Here with my chin nestled on top of her breasts, my nose in the hollow of her throat, I am feeling neither sad nor deprived. I feel her sadness though.

"Doesn't matter about the lads, Annie—we'll always have each other. We'll live together—we'll be like Gran and Mina—we'll be together always."

She says nothing, but hugs me tight and fierce.

Chapter 27

"Now," says Gran, "when doing green work, a balance must be kept, else your remedies shall lack potency."

Annie and I nod. We have been drilled to the notion of balance for as long as we can remember. Mina and Sarah are as attentive as if they too were new initiates being tutored at the arts of wortcunning. I wonder if Annie feels as proud as I do to at last be one of the women's circle, learning the arts that only women could know.

"So, when we make a death-dealing potion, we stir a life-giving one over the same fire. We make an attraction charm with one for protection."

Gran goes on to show us that some of the same herbs are used for potions to conceive as in the ungents to cast a child forth, and yet again in the teas used to aid in labor. She explains the importance of asking each swatch of herbs which purpose it wishes to serve, so that the plant will lend the full strength of its spirit to the effect desired. She starts us with bunches of the red and purple heather we had gathered, demonstrating how to hold the plant gently in the cupped palm, passing it over the three piles and placing it in the pile that made our hand tingle and glow when we passed over it. As we became more adept, she promised, we would but touch the herb and know in an instant what its choice would be.

Annie quickly gets the hang of it, her fingers sorting the plants as deftly as they wield a needle. For me, the work comes harder. I hold a plant seeking its purpose, and instead see the part of the forest or heath it came from, feel the hooves of browsing deer or sheep, sense the burrowing of roots, the ecstatic indrinking of a deep rain. . . I find it hard to narrow my vision.

I hear my Gran saying in exasperation, "This child's mind is a scattered as a float-about." I look up guiltily, but her exasperation is a vivid memory only. Her eyes closed, she is absorbed in the pounding rhythm of the mortar and pestle and the interweaving chant she and Mina and Sarah are braiding into shining ropes of water and color and fire.

Eventually my mind quiets to the rhythm and I see that there is a light around my hands that changes colors as I handle the plants, as well as the trembling and heat that comes when I hold the plant over the pile where it belongs. The chant quiets to a hum as the women finish grinding. Sarah rises to set the mixtures over the fire. Mina rinses the pestles with salt water. Gran makes us all a tea to aid concentration. Annie and I rest quietly, listening to the rain, keeping our centers steady so we will be ready to start again.

We kneel in a circle, sipping our tea. The women bless the vulval stones by holding them to their bellies, willing the power of the womb to enter the vessels. Just as we are about to resume our work, Annie breaks our concentration.

"Why does Mairead hate you so?" she asks Gran.

"I denied her the herbs that would have ended your life before you began it."

"Why?"

Gran shrugs and begins her work. The other two women join her rhythm.

"Have you—do you often refuse to help a woman who—"

Gran shakes her head. Annie has stopped working, a frown of puzzlement and awe on her face.

"Then why—? Did you know that I would someday save Fiona's life?"

"Nay. Fiona was not even conceived. I knew only that the spirit dwelling in Mairead's belly shone brighter than the one she bore in her heart." Annie looks down at her hands, sorting the herbs quickly.

"Did you say such to her?"

Gran frowns and shakes her head.

"Aye, but ye did, Anu," Mina corrects her. "Ye told Mairead the child she would bear was worth two of her. I was there, I remember!" she said, responding to Gran's withering glance. "Not the most flattering refusal ye could have given a lass whose life was to be ruined by it!"

"Mairead ruined her own life. And our work here shall be ruined if we lay our old bitterness on these herbs!"

"Ya va ba tu saba yanda va tu sieb. . ." Sarah's high voice brushes its wings over us.

"Ya va ba tu saba yanda va tu sieb. . ." Gran's gravelly voice and Mina's resonant one join in.

"Ya va ba tu saba, van tu manya san ta sien, Van tu manya san tu sien."

And the chant and the pounding and the motion of our hands and the steady rain and the cats purring and the fire talking weaves into a song and soon all is so braided I cannot tell one thing from another and nothing exists but the rhythm and all that is not part of it vanishes.

Chapter 28

How quickly the miles go when one is riding. Sean must have plans to ravish me, to take me so far from the village. But perhaps not. Our first time together we ate and talked. He did not touch me, until we were ready to leave. Then as he was helping me mount the horse, he kissed me with his mouth open. I startled at the suddenness of it; he flushed and apologized as if he had offended me gravely. It must be as Annie says; the gentry have different ways.

Soon the jouncing of Coal's long galloping strides shakes my belly hollow and the flutters of anxiety and excitement I have been feeling are replaced by simple hunger for the meal packed in baskets, jouncing behind me.

The meadow he has chosen is pretty, bordered on one side by the cooling presence of a lovely strand of birches. Sean releases Coal to graze in the grass beyond us among the yellow dandelions and the blue star-vetch. He lays out a cloth upon the ground and unpacks the wicker baskets. Och, here are the same beautiful wheat rolls he brought before, and the ham, and smoked pheasant and a lovely yellow cheese, not like the sour milk cheese we make at home. I quiver at the sight of apples and currants, and wonderful sticky buns, covered with chopped nuts and honey and a spice that is unfamiliar to me.

I eat everything with a greed that astonishes him; eat until I must unlace my stomacher to eat more.

"I love to watch you eat," he laughs. "How can such a small lass as you fit it all in?"

"If you like to watch me eat, you may watch any time you like," I mumble through a full mouth. He has brought both a skin of white May wine and one of claret.

"One for the ham and one for the pheasant," he explains. "Besides—I didn't know which one you'd like better."

"I like them both. The May wine tastes like—a maiden—and the claret—like a young man."

Sean raises his eyebrows. "You have interesting thoughts."

He opens one of the books of poetry he has brought and reads me a poem. The poet speaks of how his love's lips are like the reddest wine, how he is drunk on her kisses, and would never be sober again. The fancy language makes me shiver with delight, the pictures the poetry makes shine inside me like the visions that come during trance.

"I like it when he says his love's kisses are like the wine. I like to think about—what's like what—a kiss isn't really like wine, or the summer sun, or like honey, but if you say it is then it somehow makes it so and you taste the wine and the sun and the honey in every kiss after."

Sean shakes his head and looks at me as if I'd said the most amazing thing he'd ever heard.

"You're a poet with no pen," he says. "What a mind you have under that bonny red hair. If only you'd had teachers—though some say tis not well for a woman to be too wise in her brain for she needs her wisdom—for her womb." He swallows and looks away from me uncomfortably.

I laugh. "I daresay there's plenty of wisdom to go around. Tis not as if one had to choose one or the other, is it?"

"Perhaps not."

I am eyeing the rest of the sticky buns longingly, wishing I could take them home to share with Annie and my siblings.

"Sean—could I—could I possibly take these home with me? I've never had anything so lovely."

"Of course. Of course you could." His blue eyes are glowing into mine. How happy I feel that we are friends again. How generous he is to share with me like this.

"Have as many as you like. I'll bring you some every day if you fancy them so. Mary cooks them for me. They're my favorite too. She's been very good to me. She's been like a mother. Anytime I hurt myself as a bairn she'd put me in her lap and bake me a bit of a sweetie to make me feel better."

The castle cook is a stout, dour woman, one of the kirk followers who looks down her nose at mother and would not share the same pew with her when mother started attending kirk after the Laird left. But if she has been kind to Sean then she has a side I know not of and I'll not be so quick to judge her.

A strand of his hair has come out from the ribbon he has tied it with in the back. White-blond, glinting in the sun. I'm wishing to untie his hair altogether and run my fingers through it, but I finger the edge of the cloth broidered with purple thistles on it spread for our feast instead.

"I brought you a present," he says. He fumbles in his bag and brings out a pair of rosewood broaches with roses carved on them, matching brush and comb.

"Ohhh—lovely! Where did you come by them?"

"They were my mother's." The pain cramping his mouth causes me to lean over and kiss it. Our lips barely brush but he ducks his head, looks at the ground, tearing bits of grass and shredding them between his fingers. Ah, I've been too bold.

"I'm sorry—you looked sad—"

"You feel sorry for me?" he asks quickly.

"No—" I stop. Do I feel sorry for him?

"You do seem lonely at times." Worse and worse. Is this any way to talk to a Lord?

"Aye, I am lonely at times. Isn't everyone?" Odd notion.

"No." I try to think of a time when I have felt lonely.

"With a croft full of brothers and sisters tis not easy to feel lonely."

"No, I suppose not," he says shortly. "Well, sometimes I'd leifer be a simple man. I love the woods, the senses—I'm—more

Pagan than Christian I suppose. When I was a lad I used to always wish I could grow up and be a smith, like Ewan. A Laird
doesn't seem to do much. What a smith does is real. Solid. You
can hold it in your hand. And if I was a smith—" he looks at me
wary as if I might bite, "—I could marry who I liked as well."

"And if you were a smith we would not be sitting here eating
ham—and pheasant—and beautiful sticky rolls." I stretch, lying
down in the grass, rubbing my back up against it like a cat greeting a friendly palm.

"Read me some more poetry."

He spreads the books out in a fan as if they were gypsy scrying cards and pulls out yet another flask.

"I brought a special treat—seeing as how much you like honey—I remember you saying last time—you knew not which you
liked best, honey or cream—but together was best of all. I brought
some whiskey with honey and cream mixed in, Atholl Brose they
call it, after the Duke of Atholl."

"Aye, snow broth they called it, long before the Duke of
Atholl. Twas a Witch instructed the Duke how to make it, I'll
wager you that."

The yearly Yule treat drunk under the hot June sun makes
my head float. My ribs expand, inhaling the flower-scented air.

"Please read some more. I liked what you said the other day
about how when you read the poems that—sometimes you
thought of me and wished you had written them yourself. Read
me some of the ones that make you think of me. The ones you
wanted to write yourself."

He reads me a short one, which he says is from the Greek.
Written by a woman, he says. Something about a purple flower,
unnoticed in a meadow, trampled on the ground, leaving a stain.
It makes little sense to me.

"I don't like that one so well." He puts that book aside and
picks up another.

"Perhaps this modern English poetry will suit you better."

"Here in this secret shade-embowered glen,
Wilt thou still claim thou hast no use for men?
Ere forty winters etch themselves upon thy brow
Wilt thou not look back on this day and sigh,

'Ah, would that youth's fair passion be here now. . .' "

The poem could indeed be of the two of us, lying in the sun, although the lady of the poem is dark, and must be protesting great reluctance for the man to needs woo her so. I like the next bard best of all:

"In thin array, after a pleasant guise,
When her loose gown from her shoulders did fall
And she me caught in her arms long and small,
Therewith all sweetly did me kiss
And softly said, 'Dear heart, how like you this?' "[1]

It takes him awhile to translate the poems into Gaelic.

"I'm making a mess of it, I know," he grumbles. "You must learn English. I'll teach you. Then you can ken the poems as they are."

"I almost understand them," I reply. "I do like to hear it both ways. And I will learn it if you keep talking it to me." I do not tell him that as he speaks the Sasanach tongue that I see pictures in my mind before he can translate it for me into the speech that I know. For that 'talking through air', that reading of thought, is a Witch's art, though Gran says that once all creatures and all humans spoke the language of air with each other, most humans have forgot it now. The few who remember it now must conceal their knowing.

He reads a few more poems about maidens and flowers and passion:

"Merry Margaret
As Midsummer flower
Gentle as falcon
Or hawk of the tower. . ."[2]

There's one that makes me blush, about a Witch,

". . . her self solacing
With a new lover who through sorcery
And Witchcraft she from far did thither bring,

---

1. *They Flee From Me* by Thomas Wyatt
2. *To Mistress Margaret Hussey* by John Skelton

There she had him to lay slumbering,
In secret shade, after long wanton joys. . ."

It ends sadly, speaking of how quickly roses and all of life
withers—

"So passeth, in the passing of a day,
Of mortal life the leaf, the bud, the flower
No more doth flourish after first decay,
That earst was sought to deck both bed and bower,
Of many a Lady and many a Paramour;
Gather therefore the Rose, whilest yet is prime,
For soon comes age, that will her pride deflower.
Gather the Rose of love, whilest yet is time. . ."*

How do the once-borns see time, I wonder. How frightening it
must be to think that one's time is so short, that death would be
the end of all time that one had on earth. Hard enough to let go
of a body knowing that one should have another. Imagine thinking that you had one chance, and one only.

He tosses the book aside, suddenly sulky. What is wrong? We
had been so happy at lunch. I take the brush he gave me and
brush out my hair. The bristles feel so good against my scalp, I
almost purr.

"Look," I coax, showing him how the combs look on my head.
He looks and then drops his eyes to the ground again, as if the
tiny flowers growing there in the grass were of far more interest
than me or his gift. I take my hair down and brush it over my
face, looking at him through that auburn screen, glinting gold
and red in the sun. The grim look on his face does not seem promising. What can be bothering him so? Perhaps it is that notion
that he has so little time. Or perhaps his mother? His wishing to
be a smith? He seems so complicated, his books and his high language, his sudden moods. I feel very simple beside him.

Coal whuffles happily, grazing in the rich sorrel grass beyond
us; small butterflies weave wreaths of yellow and blue over his
withers. I brush my hair down my back and sigh, stretching out
in the sun. Between the fire in the sky and the fire in the flask I
feel like meltings of honey and wax.

---

*The Faerie Queen by Spenser

Behind orange eyelids my mind is wandering. Maybe he does not want me? Nay, he wants me. He's shy, just. A gentleman, after all. I breathe steadily, near the edge of dozing off.

His hand on my hair, then my breast.

"God forgive me," he chokes, kissing me hard and deep. Rolling on me, pulling my clothes apart, his roughness frightens me; where are his gentle manners now? I twist my head away, tell him to stop.

"Do not deny me, do not deny me," he begs. He pleads with me to have mercy on him, tearing my underclothes to pieces all the while.

"Go easy. Be gentle. I'll not run from you if you be gentle with me," I admonish. He is a bit less rough but still frantic and hasty. Both of us still have most of our clothes on when he penetrates me and it is over before I have time to really feel him inside me. I am too dazed to be disappointed. Neither of us knows much about this, I reason. We are lovers, that much has been accomplished. Next time we will tarry and it will be as it had been with Pan.

He rolls off me over onto his back, eyes shut tight, mouth a thin line. He looks the very picture of misery. Christ! There's no understanding the lad.

"I've done you wrong," he says, despondent.

"You did me fine."

"I might get you with child."

"'Tis not my time. I'll have bairns when I choose them." What a startled look he has.

"'Tis Witchery—"

"What of it. Be not so serious." I hug him. He remains steeped in remorse. I'm so brave, he says. Did it hurt much? Am I bleeding? I have a feeling he is going to be disappointed that he was not my first. I tell him anyway. As I thought, he sits up and turns his back on me.

"How many?"

Should I count Annie or not? Likely he just wants to know about lads. . .

He pounds the ground with his fist.

"How many?" he demands.

"'Tis none of your concern mi'lord!" I pull my clothes on, angry blood throbbing in my cheeks.

"You act like there's something wrong with it."

"Tis a sin."

I march over and strike him on the shoulder.

"Tis not a sin! Only a fool thinks so! Swiving makes the crops grow!"

He puts his head in his hands, grimacing. Pity for him turns me gentle. I stroke his shoulder softly.

"There's no grief in it Sean. Tis a sacred thing."

"Witches and harlots say so!" he replies.

I push him and send him sprawling. Before I know my own thought, I have seized Coal's reins and mounted him, kicking him hard with my heels. I ride off, leaving Sean to walk many miles back to the village.

As I tie Coal to the rail outside the Inn remorse is pricking me and I almost ride back. The word harlot keeps me from it though.

Chapter 29

Three days later Sean knocks at my door. I answer with my baby sister on one shoulder and a kitten clinging and mewing on the other. I am flushed and sweaty from cooking and nearly close the door right in his face, but he looks so pitiful I have not the heart. Anxious to keep Mother from seeing him, I agree to meet him on the morrow.

When I go to meet him at the well, my thoughts are as fiery as my hair. But when he kneels abjectly by the well and takes my hands, kissing them and pressing his brow upon them, my anger disperses like a reflection from a wind-ruffled pool.

"If you'll not forgive me, say it now," he implores, "that I may end my life right here in this well. For I cannot endure glimpsing the claret—and the sun—and the honey—I could know with you—and never have it again. Forgive me."

"Someone may come here," I say, moved by the tears in his eyes. I lead him to one of the hidden places where Annie and I frequently make love, the holy place near the scrying pool. Often the coven meets there to divine meaning from the patterns of the stars in the midnight water. But even if he saw the pool I knew he would think nothing of it. A secret is safe from one blind to it.

As we walk, he places a bundle in my arms which proves to be a whole loaf of the sticky buns which I coveted so.

"I have asked Elspet—you know Elspet who is one of our maids?—to make you a blouse broidered with the thistles that you liked so much on the feast-cloth; in hopes that then when you were angry with me you could wear the thistles on your sleeve and not in your heart"

"I'm not the bard here," I laugh, thinking of how he had called me a poet without a pen.

"Nay, and if you're not a poet then you're a poem, a walking poem. You could make any man with talent the greatest bard in all the world I think. Providing he could get over his tongue being struck dumb by how beautiful you are."

I breathe deeply, cool breeze flowing into my lungs. How good the pines smell here. We sit down on a grassy place, the grass almost as thick as a mattress. He is wearing blue, velvet and silk, that makes his eyes seem more brilliant than the sky. When I weep I get all red and swollen. His tears if anything have made his eyes more clear, his skin more pale and feminine. He's still beardless, still a boy. I run the back of my hand gently along his chin, over his face, and loosen, as I had wished to the other day, the clasp that holds his hair. His hair is soft, clean, silky. How clean he smells. Fresh as the smell of the grass and evergreens, perfumed with flowers.

"How do you come to smell like flowers?" I ask, bringing my nose close to his ear.

"Flower water," he replies, "tis style for men to wear it as well as the women in the courts, though I hear that lately King James is thinking that bright colors and scents like this are frivolous and possibly even—temptations of Satan. Not that they're—any so much as temptations go." He looks straight at me, his eyes deep and true.

"Fiona, I'm sorry—the other day—I was just thinking of— the other men in the village laughing behind my back."

"No one else knows," I assure him. "It wasn't a man of the village."

"Just once, just one time?"

"Aye. Just that one time."

"He took advantage of you! He took advantage of your inno-cence!"

I start to giggle, push him with my foot.

"And here you are, taking advantage of it again!" He finally begins to laugh.

"Aye, I guess I'm as much a rogue as any of them. Tis just that—I love you, Fiona. I don't want anyone else to touch you. I want you all to myself. If you'll be true to me, I'll be true to you in return."

"Tis not as if we could marry."

"No, I know. But for now—I want to have you to myself, at least for now."

"Sean," I say, looking him in the eyes, "there's no other man in the village I want right now. But I will not make any promis-es. I'll not go behind your back. If another man catches my fancy, you shall hear of it from me." Guilt twinges inside me, for I have no intention of telling him the nature of my relationship with Annie.

"The Priest exorcised me when I told him."

"What! You told the Priest?"

"Well, I had to confess."

"I don't want you telling the Priest about us!" I snap. "If you are willing to be true to me, be true to me in this and tell the Priest no more!" Sean cocks his head, staring at me.

"Well, perhaps what he says is true. Perhaps you are of Witchly blood. Perhaps you are an enchantress and perhaps you have ensorcelled me. Perhaps I no longer rule my own sense or know my own free will. But Fiona, after he had said his prayers and danced the candles around me and drenched me with holy water, I felt the same about you as I did before we started. It seems to me that the way I feel about you is closer to being with God than anything I've felt in his kirk, or anywhere else."

I sit close to him. He kisses my throat.

"If this be the work of the devil, then the devil's man I am." He rolls over on top of me, enters my body. Inside my head I am calling the Lady of Wildness and the Lord of the Dance to be with us, and for the sacredness of this act to run so strong and clear between us that he will think of the devil no more.

Chapter 30

Side by side, almost close enough to touch, Annie and I lie with the fire from Gran's hearth warming our feet, the vision tea warm in our bellies. Animal skins soft under our backs, lying between us and the hard packed earth of Gran's floor. Pelts piled on top of us, we lie naked, swathed in fur.

We have tranced together so often, it is all we can do not to have our minds blend and merge now. I feel her hands relaxing and know how the slow relaxing breath ripples along her ribs, raises her breasts and lets them fall. The nest of pelts so warm against my body, I sense the truth of what Gran has told me, that the center of the earth is fire. Fire at the earth's core, reaching up to me in singing tendrils of orange and gold.

Earth's voice, deep and vibrant, purrs through my Grandmother's throat:

"Feel the full moon shining in your belly." Easily my attention slides down into my womb. Once I thought of the moon as cold. But the bright light pulsing in my womb now is as hot and dazzling as any sun. For the last three moons, Annie and I have been instructed to trance at every fortnight, going within our wombs at the time of our bleeding and the time of our fertility. We have discovered that the bleeding time corresponds to the dark of the moon, to the ebbing of tides, to waning, to flowing outwards. My fertile time I feel both full as the moon and empty as a chalice waiting to be filled and to spill over with light.

"Now let the full moon flow and throb throughout your body, relaxing your lights—let the serpent of your spine breathe. Let the serpent move like light between each vertebrae; feel the serpent winding supple through your bones. Light flows throughout your buttocks, into your thighs, into your lungs now. Fill your lungs with light, let your breasts fill with it, now your hands, your knees, your elbows, your arms. Your calves, your neck, your throat, your feet and now your head form a being of light." I float in a bright pool of moon.

"Still feel your body on the earth," Gran cautions.

"And now, stand at the gate of your womanness. Stand before the portal of flowers."

Flesh flower, faery temple; I stand small and awed at the sacred opening.

"Enter now, bringing the light of the moon as a torch to guide you."

Dark at first, as I will it to lighten, I find myself in a rosepink chamber, sleek, warm ripples of flesh. At the north end of the cavern, a shining net spills from the mouth of my womb like a waterfall. Woven skeins of light glittering within it form a lattice. Like a salmon irresistably drawn upstream, I swim up the glittering net, finding myself in a second chamber. It is soft, peaceful, like the nest of a bird with rose petal feathers. Sound of my heart, at first almost unbearably loud, then so soothing that I feel myself curling, infant-small, longing to burrow into the soft pink folds of this nest and stay here.

As I watch, a glowing silver orb appears and drifts, shimmering like a wishing coin cast into a well. It settles in one of the folds of my womb and lodges there, glittering, beckoning as a lamp.

"A comfortable place indeed," Gran comments. "How welcoming it must seem to a spirit wishing to incarnate in human form."

"And now," she continues, "feel the moon between your eyes. Leave the womb and go to that place."

Reluctantly my consciousness moves and twists. I sigh, and find myself between my eyes, in the starless place. But where it is indigo dark three weeks out of four, now the moon glows so piercingly silver, it almost burns.

"Conceiving a child is more than the mating of bodies," Gran informs us. "It is the moon between your eyes, not the one in your womb, that signals to the spirit world. While the tea we have taught you to make shall help, and the two white stones we have taught you to hold beneath your tongue will help you not to conceive, even should you lay with a man at the time of your body's greatest ripeness—if you learn not to control this moon between your eyes, then all of our herbs and magic shall be of no avail.

"Now imagine that this moon is a scrying crystal. Look within, and see if there is a spirit who wishes to come through you."

Instantly, a beautiful baby boy swims into the center of my moon, smiles, lifts his arms. A deep sigh fills my lungs. How lovely he is, eyes as indigo as the eye between the eyes of sight. My breasts fill, longing palpable as milk, and I can feel him, soft and warm in my arms, gazing up at me with those trusting indigo eyes. The moon in my belly trembles.

"What is your will?" Gran asks sharply. I struggle to recall my will, remembering that there is no man who would be father to my child. That my life would be hard.

"Bring forth the clouds!" Gran commands. "Bring forth the darkness from the starless place. Shield your moon!" I bring clouds up from the deeps of the starless place and shroud the face of the moon with them. As I do this, all regret and attraction for the baby vanish. I breathe deeply, feeling the presence of the spirit child moving off from me.

"Talk to the being. Be clear with your intentions," orders Gran.

"*Perhaps another time,*" I think to the child, "*it is not well for us to come together in this way now. If ever I am wed and settled, I shall call you then.*"

I spend a few more minutes feeling the difference between leaving my moon wide open and shining, feeling how when I do that the world of spirit turns and focuses on me with answering brightness, and how when I bring up the clouds, the spirit world folds itself away from me.

"The most important aspect of choosing when to bear a child," Gran says, "is this part. The moon between your eyes. Keep control of this, be clear with any spirits that you will not welcome them, and you shall not be troubled, even if you should lay with a man at the peak of your moon and with none of the precautions that we have shown you so far. But if you are not clear in this wise, then your moon may go off course and you may find yourself unexpectedly with child.

"Feel your will now. Here."

Touch of Gran's thumb to my diaphragm. My belly responds with a pulse, a surge of heat. Here at this point I feel a bright yellow sun. While the light of the moon made me feel dizzy and giddy, the light of the sun in my belly makes me feel strong, grounded.

"Breathe into your power."

I hear Annie's deep breathing matching mine, then feel Gran's unspoken instruction to be in my body and not in Annie's. I focus fully on the strength of the sun between my navel and my lungs.

"Do not think," Gran's voice continues quietly, "that the sun is the ally of man and the moon is the ally of woman. One must have both balanced within, if one is to be a power in the world. It is easy enough to become ensorcelled by the moon, drunk on the moon's magic. And if you are careless, you will bring spirits into your body, willy-nilly. And while we have the art of casting forth, should such misfortune occur, tis hard on your body and your spirit both. So remember the sun in your belly, when the moon grows there also. A Witch who knows not her will is worse than no Witch at all. Now. . ."

She lifts her thumb, moves it back up to hover above the space between my eyes, drawing my consciousness with it.

"Now, there may be occasion when it is not possible for you to veil the moon between your brows. If you find your true mate, the soul who is like unto your own but in a male form, then you will not be able to shield yourself when you are with him; nor will you wish to. A beautiful bridge of light will join you, brow to brow, blending you into one being. And nothing calls so strongly to the spirit world as the mating of twin hearts. So if you are ever in this wise, laying with a man who you love with all your spirit and all your heart, and the light and the flames leap out from your brow to his, then take a care to control that light. Move the serpent of light throughout his body, through his cock into your body, back up through your heart and out through your brow again—create a loop, a spinning loop of golden light. Hold in your mind that all the power you are raising between you is going only to nurture this circle of light, that there is no space within that circle for any being to enter, that the passion that you conjure through your flesh be directed to increase and expand and deepen your love, and that the fluids of your coupling shall be like rain upon your spirits, and shall not fertilise your body. And if he is a Witch and a true Stag as well as your mate, then share your intention with him, have him hold the image with you. It will be easier if both of your minds are fixed to the same purpose, but even if he is one who is not versed in the arts, and you cannot share this with him, your will alone may suffice.

"Imagine this now. Feel your man. Imagine him looking deep into your eyes. Feel him inside your body. Feel yourself completely yielding to him, yielding to your passion; the power of being a woman with a man of her choosing, a man who is her equal in grace and power. Then move that loop through both of your bodies."

The passion evoked in my body by the power of Gran's word-conjuring alone almost capsizes my will. It is all I can do not to moan and writhe and lose myself in the dizzying swirl of the moon, to surrender to the passion of the earth and seas to bring forth. I breathe the light and color of sun through my body and into the imagined body of my lover. The great golden serpent of energy moves through my body, into the body of air above me and back through mine. My breath steadies. My body shakes with the power of choice and desire, magic of the silver moon, power of the golden sun, not warring with each other, but mingling, merging, one. I feel my power as a woman, priestess who owns herself, who chooses consciously, as I have never felt it before. And I feel in myself the power of the oak and the willow and the apple tree in blossom that may one day bear fruit. It is my choice.

Gran exhales a long breath. And with that breath, as if the

wind herself had caressed me, I feel my body beginning to cool.

"Are there any questions?" she asks.

"No," whispers Annie. "Thank you—with all my heart."

I nod, feeling that she has spoken for both of us.

"Thank you."

"Very well then." She passes her hands over us, brushing the heaviness of trance from our limbs.

"Now wiggle your fingers," she says, "and feel yourself in your hands. Into your feet now. . ." I stretch my feet. The bones make crackling noises as the muscles stretch.

"Feel your hair. . . bring your attention out through your hair, into your scalp. . . and into your face. . . and into your breathing, and into your heartbeat. . . and all the surfaces of your skin, coming up now, into your skin." I stretch and purr as if I were coming out of a deep sleep.

"Opening your eyes now. . ."

Surprising to find it daylight still. The fire in Gran's beehive shaped hearth buzzing as merrily as if the flames within had honey as their industry instead of ash.

Annie and I sit up. Gran brings out some herbs.

"Show me again that you know how to prepare the tea. For while spirit is the key, our green allies can help us hold our purpose."

Readily we select the appropriate herbs; the evergreen branches with their pungent acid; the black and the blue cohosh; pennyroyal leaves; the bayberries and bay leaves; the leaves of willow, tansy and rue.

"If you find the mixture makes you too wakeful," advises Gran, "do not hesitate to add chamomile; it will in no way detract from the power of your brew. Or if you find it hard on your belly you may add mint along with the chamomile. But you are both so young and healthy I do not expect you to have any trouble."

"Did you ever have a mate—a true mate?" asks Annie as we wait for our tea to steep. Gran's brief smile and averted eyes betray the truth.

"Well and if I did, he's not alive now. What I have taught you is truth, and should you find your mate, it will work for you as it has worked for women who have chosen their will from time

as far back as my memory will carry me, and perhaps farther."
She looks at us as we drink the steaming beverage.

"Remember girls, you are not breeders. One or two bairns if
you wish. Not so many as to turn you from your true purpose.
The world is full of women who can bring forth children, and
there are very few of us indeed, women of the sun and moon, wom-
en who heal the earth and midwive her bringing forth. We must
survive. Without our magic, all the cycles which seem so much
larger than us, the tides and the earth's turning, the bow, disk
and horns of the moon, the times of planting and of harvest,
without us, and our power, all will go awry. You have a responsibility beyond yourself and beyond the raising of bairns that is a
common woman's natural contribution to the times that are to
come."

I nod, feeling the power strong within me.

"Do not lose yourself for any man," she warns. "If he is a man
worth having, he will want a woman who knows who she is."

Chapter 31

I had intended to keep to myself during my fertile times. But who could resist Sean's offer of leftover leg of lamb with claret and mint jellies? As my hips and breasts grow, my appetite, both for food and for Sean, increases. After the meal, tipsy on white wine, Sean and I giggle as he sings me some chants in Latin the Priest does in the kirk, mimicking the Priest so wickedly that I collapse again and again in merriment. He swears he has kept his faith to me and not said another word to the Priest.

"I assure him that I submit myself to God's Will in everything," he laughs.

"Which God, of course," he winks at me, "I do not say. My father favored the old Gods over the new, and perhaps still would were it not so politically expedient to do otherwise. He got in his cups the other night and told me that he'd worn the horns more than once, more than one year he was the Stag. I thought it a great pity we practice that custom no more. I could fancy wearing them myself."

Sean refers to an ancient custom whereby once a year a maid-

en's virginity would be sacrificed to the Stag. All the maidens of
the village would gather into the fields and a man with the headdress of a stag, otherwise naked, would be loosed among them. The
girl he caught was obliged to allow him to cover her, and if a
child resulted from the union, it was always destined to grow to
be a being of great magic and power. Mina once indiscreetly let
slip that my mother had lost her maidenhood to the Stag before
she had even started her blood, and that while no child had resulted from the union, that Gran had considered me to be in
some way magically connected to that rite.

I find myself wondering if it was the old Laird who had laid
with my mother on her first time.

"Why do you suppose we practice that rite no more?" Sean
asks.

"I suppose your friend, the Priest, is at the root of it. Can you
imagine what he would preach should he hear of such a thing?"

"Aye," Sean agrees, "he's unhappy enough even with the
planting and harvest rites. But good God, you cannot ask the
people to let go of everything. I suppose the old Gods of the earth
need their due as well as the new Gods of the spirit. Suppose the
superstition were true and the crops failed? We've always had
good crops here, while not all of our neighbors have been so fortu-
nate. If the rites we practice do not help, at least they do not
hurt."

He laughs and grabs me, tickling me under the armpits.

"I feel a call to sacrifice to the old Gods again," he laughs,
"surely they must like maidens with red hair best of all."

"Might I have a few pence to buy some milk for my family?"

"Of course," he says, "as long as I am not wanting, your family shall not either."

I open the magic pouch I carry around my waist. There is no
reason for him to think that it is ought than a purse; it is cut no
different from that which any other lass might wear. I giggle,
hiding from him under my hair, drop the money in the pouch and
take the two white stones forth, placing them under my tongue.
Tis not easy to hold them there as I giggle, tickling him, refusing
to let him inside me until I can get all his clothes off.

I manage to hold him off until I have him naked, ducking my
head and dodging the kisses he seeks to plant on my mouth,

thinking that once he has mounted me he will forget about kisses soon enough. But it is I who forget, as the sweet shocks of pleasure jolt up through my belly. He catches my head in his hands, my mouth yields open to his.

"What—?" he breaks free from me. "Fiona, what have you got in your mouth?"

"Nothing," I mumble.

"Nothing and a hen's egg—are you eating *again?*" He reaches his fingers inside my mouth, capturing one of my stones.

"What in Christ's name—?"

I spit the other stone out.

"I'll not be having your bairns like my mother had your father's! Tis all well for sport and play and honoring the Old Gods, but I'll not be sacrificing my womb. Tis to keep me from getting pregnant," I say, indicating the stones, "and I'll not be laying with you without it! We can kiss after!"

He picks up the stones and hurls them.

"Who taught you such sorcery?"

I push him away, cursing, searching for my stones in the grass.

"Who taught you such?"

"Tis naught that any girl in the village might not know!" I snap, "Just as anyone knows that mint is good for a sick belly and feverfew is good for a sick head."

"I'll not allow it."

"You'll not—I'll not be saddled with a pack of your bairns like your father gave my mother! If you want me 'twill be on *my* terms, my lairdie! I'm not a stupid breeder. There are wenches of that kind in plenty. You have your choice."

He catches me by the wrist.

"I'm not your brother." His eyes have a dangerous glint in them. I stop, looking at him in amazement.

"Nay, indeed you're not. You're no kin of mine, nor of Eostre's. But your father sired many a bastard in my croft, and you'll not be siring any on me."

"As many as say I'm kin to Sean and Malcolm say that I'm your brother as well."

"That's a lie," I say flatly.

"Tis a lie your mother told my father."

"He said that? Oh, aye, he'll say anything to keep us apart."

"No one knows who fathered your mother's children," Sean says scornfully, "one for every passing tinker and braw lad in the village."

Swiftly my hand bloodies his mouth. I rise and sprint naked towards Coal. This time Sean catches me, pulls me off, pushes me to the ground. Coal rears, agitated. As we roll away from his flailing hoofs, Sean enters me again, pushing hard and fast. I cry out with rage; at him for daring to mount me, at myself for not being willing to scratch his eyes. I savage his back with my nails, bite his shoulder. He cries out, slamming into me as if he would drive us both into the earth. His cries and Coal's high-pitched neighs turn me ferral, feline. When he comes, he comes not alone.

"Ah," he rolls off me, grimacing, hands pressed to his bleeding back.

"Ah, I deserve that, I know. Forgive me, I went mad—I go into a madness when I see you naked Fiona—I'm not myself, I'm like a beast. Hit me again if you like if you'll forgive me after. Or finish me off with that wee blade you wear at your ankle and I'll be the Lord cut down for the harvest."

"Tis not the time for sacred kings. Lughnasad is the time for that, and we've two moons before that day."

I am disturbed at how bloody his back is. I did not know my nails could be that sharp.

"Bide here a bit." I run to the river and dive in, letting the cold rush of water cleanse my body and spirit. Comfrey, mallow and slippery dock in turn agree to give up their lives for me. I clean the roots and mash them between rocks, carry the poultice back to where Sean is lying, face down in the grass. Gently I apply the poultice to his back. Cool light coming from my palms makes the herbs potent. He opens his eyes as I lie beside him.

"You are a Witch," he says softly.

"I am a simple country lass," I say, looking deep into his eyes, "I know the things that any peasant might know. Poor people like ourselves can afford no physician; we must be our own. Any girl with as many brothers and sisters as I have, falling down and getting hurt all the time, would need to know something of how to heal, at least the minor wounds of everyday."

"And the other?"

"What other?"

He holds out his hand, cradling the two white stones.

"I found these while you were at the river. I'm sorry Fiona, I hope I get thee not with child—is it too late? Is there anything you can do—now?"

I close my eyes for a minute.

"I'm not with child. Neither you nor any man can force me to bear. Nor could you have laid me just now without some measure of my wanting you to. My nails in your eyes would have stopped you soon enough."

"You are a Witch then, if it is you who decides when your womb becomes full and not God."

"Perhaps I have an agreement with God."

"Perhaps thou hast an agreement," he says, the fear shining plain in his eyes.

"Sean! We're not animals! I'm not a heifer to bear a calf every year, nor a chicken to lay an egg every day. Anyone who spends time on the earth and with the plants of the earth might know—will quickly learn—" I pause, not sure of how to speak the partial truth, "—may quickly learn how to avail herself of the natural powers around her. There's nothing of Satan in this. Look at Coal," I say, pointing to the horse, now calmed, cropping the grass, "do you think he communes with Satan by eating the herbs and plants he finds about him?" Sean manages a weak laugh.

"Ah—I am—too much with the Priest."

"I'll agree to that. Can you not ask your father for another tutor than that one?"

"Ah, well, I think not," replies Sean, "No one from the court of James is going to come all the way up here to teach the son of a minor Lairdie like my father. Is this done?" he asks, indicating my poultice

"Let's go to the river, we'll wash you off and see."

The poultice has done its work; the thin slashes are closed now and will finish their healing quickly.

"There," I kiss his back, "now I have atoned. You were not the only beast today." He smiles, holds me to him, kisses me deep.

"Ah, Fiona, I love you so much, love you so much. If we were of a class I would marry you tomorrow, I swear it."

Sean walks Coal through the village, to avoid scattering dust over the people passing by on the narrow path. My arms around his waist, my cheek resting against his shoulder, I smile at everyone that we see.

Chapter 32

No eyes in my head, all my vision is in my fingers and grappling toes as we inch down the narrow path—no more than a well worn series of hand and foot holds—rippling down the rock face to the beach below. Only a few miles from the village, it is completely secluded; only egg reivers and Witches know the secrets of scaling such cliffs. Annie and I carry the large smooth invoking sticks, called 'clackers', strapped to our backs. Gran and Mina each carry a huge mysterious sack slung over their shoulders which they bear as easily as if they weighed nothing at all.

Once on the beach, Gran stands in the center holding one end of a long cloth while Sarah, holding the other, trudges the outline of the circle in the sand. The rest of us bound the circle with seawrack and shells. All preparations are performed in silence. Twilight, yet not a bird moves or calls out. With the circle drawn, we are no longer Annie and Fiona, but Nimué and Kyairthwen, gathering driftwood and dried tulse to lay the sacred fires. At Anu's bidding, Nimué constructs a small fire circle near the north-west periphery of the circle, while I build mine near the south-east boundary. We then pile the material for the bonfire in the center. Anu blows the conch, Sari strikes the bell, and Wind Mare clacks two of the sticks while Nimué and I light our fires. Usually fire-starting is hard for me; this night the spark leaps from the flint into the dried tangle of tulse so quickly it startles me.

Nimué and I light the large fire together, kindling the need-fire from 'the tree marriage'; rubbing a fire-awl into a cleft cradle of wood until the dry threads of moss and flakes of lichen laid in the cradle ignite. Against tradition, the older women have given us a fire-awl of birch and a cradle of rowan, both female trees. As carefully as we have tried to veil our thoughts from the coven, I cannot rid myself of the uneasy feeling that they know all that is between us.

By the time the bonfire flares, our breathing is short and hurried, our hands shaking. We part with relief, to stand on opposite sides of the blaze. Soft as smoke, full of power, Anu's voice comes through the flames.

"We call all the elements to be with us now, to support and balance our conjuring of fire."

Nimué and I invoke each direction wordlessly, clacking our sticks with the rhythm that enters them. All we have been told of the Passage of Fire is that we must keep solemn silence, speaking only when asked the visions our invoking calls in us. After we have finished going around the circle, we cross our sticks and lay them in the fire.

"What is the meaning of the crossed sticks?" Wind Mare asks.

Our voices as one, we reply, "The Lovers." Quickly we look away from each other. I hope the firelight obscures the color of my face.

"So. What did you see when you called the air?" asks Wind Mare.

"The air feeds the fire—as much as the wood does. So—the fire—needs the fuel of the—body and the mind both? To thrive? A bitter wind will kill it, though," Nimué says.

I try to think how to put my sensing into words, when it comes as pictures only.

"Well, I had pictures of butterflies, and rolling in pollen, and pictures of birds—a jeweled bird—one that dies in the fire and rises again. Tis a plain bird at first, the color of ash. Tis only jeweled when it rises." My mouth feels dry with the fear that my answers may not be good enough. They do not comment upon our answers, and I cannot sense approval or disapproval in them.

"And the south?" asks Wind Mare.

Nimué speaks first.

"I saw men preparing a pit full of fire. They covered the fire with huge leaves—sharp-fingered leaves, each one as big as a man—and the fire cooled but the coals were still hot, covered with only a fine layer of ash. And I danced across the coals, I danced and sang—or the Goddess sang through me. Something for all the people. I wasn't burnt."

"I had a vision of a great mountain that was wounded. It opened into a cauldron of fire. I stood on the top wearing a cape of green feathers. When the moment was right, I dived in." I stop there, not knowing how to describe that moment of meeting with the fire, the pain and the glory.

"It was like—the feathers turned into—green jewels."

"The water?" Wind Mare questions.

Nimué replies, "The tide is coming up. It will extinguish the fires. It is hard to see those two as friends."

I don't understand the connection between the water and the fire either. I know that it's there but cannot say it or see it. I shake my head.

"What of the earth, then?"

"The fire comes from the rock," Nimué says, fingering the flint, "out of the cold and the dark of it. Fire runs in the veins of the earth as it does in ours. All that grows on the earth may be fuel for the fire."

"Aye—green fire in the leaves and plants. Black fire under the earth, red fire in the veins of animals and people. That is how the water fits in!" I say excitedly. "The liquid fire that flows in us—there's a blue fire in the sea as well, a fire that sometimes burns white."

Sari smiles, "That is why we always do this ritual by the sea—to remind us that the water and the fire need not be enemies but can be the closest of friends—and lovers."

The bonfire has been reduced to a small heap of flame. We sit around it, almost close enough to touch.

Sari continues: "When you make love with a man it feels like striking together a flint and a stone to make fire, but the moment of ecstasy comes like the crest of a wave, and the delight of both man and woman spills forth as water. And if the tides and the moon are right, and if you choose and are chosen by a soul, your waters swim together into a spark of life, and that spark begins its journey into being in the watery chamber of your womb."

A shiver of realization goes through me.

"And that is the Cauldron of Cerridwen."

"That is one of her manifestations," says Wind Mare.

Anu nods. "For fire and water to work well together they must be kept a little separate. The cauldron is the vessel that makes the marriage a transformation rather than a death."

Wind Mare says, "We blow on fire to make it grow—if you blow too forcefully, you will lose it. The balance is everything. Any element out of balance is a danger, but with the fire element there is little room for error. So when you call fire, be sure to conjure all the other elements as well, whether it's lighting a hearth or laying with a man, call the balance."

"Aye," Anu agrees, "you must keep your passions contained in the fire circle you build for them, lest they consume you. Remember the Cauldron. It keeps the heart's feelings and the body's passion a little separate, for if they run together, one will always triumph over the other. Keep purpose as strong as the iron pot and the two can pull from one yoke."

Sari smiles. "Be aware that the fire is in everything that grows on the earth. In dung, in peat, in the cool green trees, the rock from the blackest caves; it is all in knowing how to strike it forth."

They have us return to the small fires we built alone. We are to take turns; I am to lie down first and trance with their guidance while Nimué gazes into her fire to scry. The three elders form a triangle around the blazing central fire. Clacking their sticks, they begin a chant which quickly builds in speed and intensity:

"Eko eko Cernunos, eko eko Manannan, eko eko Gwydion, eko eko Myrrythin, eko eko Cernunos. . ." They call the Gods of the four elements over and over until the names blur and whirl into one force—at the height of their calling, a great wave crashes on the sand, fingers of foam reaching almost to the western edge of the circle.

"Yo! Evoe!" they shout, hurling their sticks onto the flames. The fire leaps up. The long vacant air suddenly fills with birds, whirling and calling, finally settling into the cliffs as the sky turns from purple to black.

I lie down beside my fire. They open my cloak, exposing my nakedness. One of the mystery sacks is opened over me. Feathers spill from it, filling my cloak all the way down to my feet, warm and comforting. They slide their hands under the cloak and through the feathers, tracing designs on my skin. The shock of initially cold hands on my flesh is nothing compared to the surprise of being intimately touched. Caught between a giggle and a gasp, I swallow both and shiver. The light touches become firmer, rubbing more and more deeply, massaging muscles and stimulating all the little cords of liquid fire spidering out from my heart down to the smallest threads of light radiating through my fingers and toes.

Fingers press deep on my chest, over my breastbone, massaging the cauldron of fire at the center of my heart. Hands over hands over hands—it seems like so many—massaging thighs and hips and belly—right at the place where the thighs join the buttocks, fingers maintain a sustained, pulsing pressure. With every pulse I feel my legs widen and the cleft that goes up into my belly also opening. I quickly forget to be embarrassed. It feels as wonderful as when Annie and I are together, but these are not the hands of lovers. These hands are impersonal as fire, channels of God-energy only.

Hands squeezing my thighs apart, hands pulling up on the tips of my breasts—the hands are gone. A rumble to the south that could be hoof-beats or a practiced hand on a boran drum—female voices, familiar, yet void of personality, whisper:

"He is coming! He is coming! He is coming!"

One whispers, "He is fire!"

I feel a torch pass close to my body. The warmth of it makes me shudder.

"He is water!"

A hand on either thigh, pulling them open so wide I have no choice but to dissolve, my pelvis a cauldron coming to boil. Bubbles fluttering up through my flesh. A warm breeze, incredibly warm, breath of a giant scented with flowers, blows across me.

"He is air!"

A few feathers swirl in my face, intensifying the smell of flowers fused with the warm smell of my ripeness and dissolving, and another musk so powerful it roils across the borders between harshness and delight. A thrill both of terror and elation courses through me, followed by bold pride at the power of my yielding.

Then another voice, not from those around me, vibrating from the arch of my pubic bone, the portal cradling my openness as a wishbone holds a charm:

"He is the flint that cracks fire from the unhewn dolmen!"

In that moment I feel him on me and in me, my hands slip over hide of stallion, bull, twist in goat hair, ram's wool, fur of cat. Wings shudder over me, feathers shining like jewels. Smooth as a snake, smooth as a man, shimmering all forms, muscle and power, panting and wild sounds leaping from his throat to mine. Light as windbreath, heavy as earth, always the pulsing thrusts of fire thundering through me like the falls of M'hira. Clawing like a cat, moaning like a dove, spreading my haunches like a mare, cacaphony of all wild things and the violence of the elements surges through me in one great cry. . .

I am surrounded by white shimmering air. He is no longer a form, but pure white spirit, the heart of the fire that is all the passion of life.

Gradually I become aware of the hiss of the fire on my left and the low moan of the sea on my right. Then I hear dark, gutteral sounds, darker than the tones of the sea, the sounds Annie makes when the passion begins to take her.

Holding the cloak with its nest of feathers close around me, I kneel looking into the fire, knowing it is my turn to do so. Mandalas of things I cannot quite see, pinwheeling in and out through the darkness and fire. The God who is winged serpent and stag, ram and man. Nimué's moans coming in waves, each one flooding higher than the one before it, each one hitting my body with all the force of the black night ocean. The darkness of her breaking against my spine like water and the dazzling brilliance of the God in the fire push closer together until I am in the center of the fire and the center of the sea at once, red and gold waves crashing into cresting tides of black and silver flame. As she cries out in the peak of loving the God, thud and hiss of the ocean, crackle and hiss of the fire throb into a huge cauldron of silence. And in the heart of the fire I see the animals, the beasts and the birds, the hoofed and horned, the feathered and scaled, the Goddess and the God in human form all dancing together, whirling into a single pillar of light.

In the heart of the fire, they are the same.

Chapter 33

"Annie—" I swallow, trying to move the lump in my throat aside so the words can flow past it. She looks at me questioningly, hearing the tightness in my voice, the pressure of my fingers against hers telling her my fear before I can speak it.

"Are you not—afraid?"

"Of what?" We turn from the Waters of M'hira, panting only slightly as we ascend the hill to our secret meadow. We enter the clearing broken by outcroppings of granite and heather. Between the two tallest trees at the meadow's border I catch a glimpse of M'hira streaming silver towards the sea. The deft fingers unlacing my outer garments stop, her arms go around me.

"Afraid of what?"

"The—burnings. The whole—a whole coven in Berkshire caught and condemned and more being captured every day. The Witch-hunters. They're going everywhere with a free rein to. . ." My voice trails off, barely audible.

"They might come here."

She shrugs, pulling off her outer garments, stretching out on a soft slope of heather in her shift. Looks at me, amused smile, shrugs again.

"It matters not."

I turn away, not looking at her as I pull off my clothes, ashamed of my fear and angry that she makes so light of it. Instead of lying beside her I go and stand at the clearing's edge, watching the sun burnish the river to the color of a sharp blade. My vision swims silver, then black as I close my lids and swallow to stop the tears. Soft fingers lift the shoulder of my smock away, replacing it with a kiss. The sensation running along my neck and shoulder so delicate I cannot be sure if it is her lips or merely the close warmth of her breath. Her forehead resting lightly against my shoulder.

"Do you want me to be afraid?" she asks. Turn and hug, soft breasts, musky hair, comforting thud of her heart.

"I wish I was as brave as you," I whisper.

She leads me over to where she has spread her cloak. We tuck my cloak under our heads for a pillow and lie in silence watching the clouds play at shape-shifting. She begins speaking as if lecturing the clouds.

"If your neighbor's calf falls ill, that proves you threw a hex. But tis just as damning if you find the simples to cure it. If your children thrive, and another's die, why how is't that your bairns are above the will of God? Yet if your babe should die, tis plain you sacrificed him to the Devil. If you've too ready a smile for the lads you're a foul slut and a sorceress; but deny a Priest and it's all over with you!"

"Annie!" I turn to her, shocked, "Not the Priest—!"

She laughs, a rich contralto laugh from her belly.

"Him! I doubt he knows there's aught to do with a pecker than pass water through it! Nay, I've been mindin' what Staghorn and Old William say on how it goes in other places." She turns to me, eyes black and intense as a hawk's, but gentler.

"Ah, Kyairthwen, if they want you they take you, there does not have to be a reason for it. Our fates were set in the stars the day we were born, and there's no changing it. The wheel will have what the wheel will have, my lady." She lies back down, turning her eyes once more to the sky.

"So," she says, "I do as I please, and fear no man, and have no master but what my heart tells me."

The feathered offspring of a dandelion float by, as jaunty as if they, and not the wind, could choose their course.

"Perhaps tis because I've always known I was different from everyone else. Who's a more likely choice for burning than a half-gypsy bastard no man can own?"

"I'll not let any hand touch you!" I cry. "If they take you they'll take me as well."

"Ah Kyairthwen—be careful what you conjure."

I bury my head on her shoulder.

"I could not live without you."

She cradles me for a moment, then rubs her knuckles across my head fiercely.

"Let's not write the lament just yet—not on such a fine bonny day," she teases. We wrestle; a bit of fake snarling and we're giggling like children half our age.

"Even that old gypsy who read our palms when we were seven said I had Witch's hair, remember?"

The picture flashes clear in my mind; two girls quivering with terror and delight, clutching each other tightly as we ventured into the forbidden territory of a gypsy wagon. Annie's eyes big as saucers as the old woman ran a hand through her hair.

"Waterfall hair, Witch's hair, little black heart. Beware of jealousy!" She smiled at us fondly. "Sisters of the willow," she crooned, closing her eyes to little slits, "little sisters of the moon."

"I remember the thing she said about your hair being like a waterfall." The black pour of her hair ripples through my fingers, curling at the bottom like water pluming up from the rocks. I rub it over my face, inhaling its fragrance of woodsmoke, heather and musk.

"But why does waterfall hair make you a Witch?"

"Witches have a special affinity with water. That's why they use fire to destroy us."

"But Gran says a Witch must stay in balance with all four elements—"

"Aye, but *they* say a Witch has a special affinity with water. That's why they float Witches and if they swim they're guilty for it shows the water loves them."

"But why water—more than air or earth or even fire?"

"Lake, stream, ocean—ice, mist, steam—water changes. So do

Witches. So do women." She gives me her most knowing, cat-like smile.

"Watch me turn you into steam." And dipping her head to the place between my thighs, she makes good her threat. Ice in my heart melts and everything in me flows fast and hot and free. Gradually the current slows from dizzying rapids to a lazy pool.

"Sweet water," I hear her murmur between my thighs. I nuzzle my nose and chin into the crisp hair protecting her woman cleft.

"Your woods-place smells like magic," I whisper, stroking my palm over the crescent of her hip.

"An' yours is a pink rose—yours is much nicer."

"Tis not," I bite her thigh.

"Ow! Tis so—" she retaliates.

I gnaw on her knee. She pinches my bottom. We nip and nibble our way down each other's legs, giggling and arguing and insulting each other the whole time. The sky colors, and we know we must leave off our love-making, for the coven is to meet at dusk. But we are reluctant to leave off chewing on each other's ankles, and things never start right on time anyway. . .

At last we dare delay no longer or 'twill be too dark to find our clothes. We lace up each other's white undergarments, then my green kirtle and her black. Black is only for mourning, or old women, or Witch's robes for night invisibility; Annie would never have touched it before. But her mother drowned her cat for having another litter of kittens, so Annie dyed everything she owned black to spite her. I think she regrets it now, but she's too headstrong and stubborn to ever admit it.

She brushes my hair back, fastening the elder brooch on my cloak. I lean to fasten hers, the twisted Celtic knot of dark wood catches the last of the setting sun. I remember us, solemn children cutting the branches from the elder, fierce protectress of children, chanting:

"Lady Ellerhorn, give me your bones, and I shall give you mine when they grow in the forest."

John Staghorn stood by making sure we offered her the proper respect, and made the brooches right while we watched, muttering spells to help the elder wood keep us from harm.

We hurry down the hill, but it is dark by the time we reach

Mina's house. Her cottage sits squat and glowing as a Samhain turnip, leaking yellow light into the darkness. Everyone calls Mina the Widow Mina, but she has never married. How did she come by such a fine house, the strong latch-bar all the way across the heavy door as if it were a castle keep and not a humble croft?

Before Annie can touch the latch the door swings open. Jessica greets us with mulled wine and a kiss. We are the last to arrive. John and Peter, Mina and my Gran are involved in a heated conversation, William Shepard nodding his shaggy head as if keeping time with music. Sarah and Jessica sit quiet but attentive, sipping wine out of the ox-horn chalices given to each member of the coven upon initiation. Rose is not visible, but the scent of rambling rose announces her presence. Too crippled to walk, Rose attends Esbats in the flesh only at her own croft, but it matters little. Seventy years of magic have enabled her to travel whither and wherever she will, leaving her body as unnecessary baggage. She is one of the Twelve; the legendary old women who fly through the air and hold coven meetings in the stars.

The conversation hushes. The oxhorns all tip heavenward as we finish the wine. In one fluid motion the horns are put away, our hands join, and we are standing, eyes closed, heads bowed. A loud hissing noise fills the room; we shiver and seethe like bubbles in the cauldron of Cerridwen. The big snake who lives behind Mina's hearth is singing to us, and we become his song, amplifying the sound through our bodies as a grass whistle held to the mouth shivers with the air that passes through it. The fire sings through its damp logs until the room evaporates in hissing and we are in the room no longer but passing through the curtains that separate the many worlds of flesh and time and spirit.

An ancient voice rings out, "Serpent, Wise One, you who shed life after life yet remain the same within, Speak with your tongue that knows of turning and crossroads, Come to us. . ."

I open my eyes. We are again sitting in a circle, but now the circle is more than a physical boundary of benches, and we are more than ourselves. In the East, John Gardner has become Staghorn, the weight of invisible antlers altering the way he holds his head. Between us and not between us is Violet Rose. I feel the coolness of her palm; the image of her gnarled swollen joints, more tree-like than human, wavers transparently over my hand.

Her eyes not rheumy and veiled as in daily life but piercingly blue burn for a moment then fade. She has made her appearance and need not maintain the physical illusion. And I am Fiona no longer but Kyairthwen, apprentice to the Great Cauldron; bridging the East and South, wings of rainbow and fire sweeping around me.

On my left side Jessica holds the South corner. Like Gran, she alters only slightly in circle, her inner and outer life being a tightly woven cord of one color. Not quite nineteen, yet she seems so much older than Annie and me. Her seriousness is reflected in her craft name, Jesses, the thongs which bind hawk to wrist, the discipline which does not allow the mind to soar from the body without the conscious direction of will.

Beside her, Annie has become Nimué: Magpie Maiden, trickster thief, black-hearted Enchantress, Queen of the Night. Her insolent smile and indolent slouch are strange contrast to Jesses' clear gray gaze and ramrod spine. Sarah is Sari Snowflower, her presence so subtle that she is almost less visible than Rose. Peter holds the West, a brawny, warm hearted man, his name Bear-Hearth seems so fitting that his Christian name seems small and odd beside it. Mina becomes Wind Mare, her gray hair haning in a loose mane over her shoulders.

I can hardly look at my Gran. Always intimidating, her presence as Anu is terrifying and absolute. Old William, standing between her and Staghorn, is a relief. Even in his aspect as Winter, his hoary eyebrows seeming to drip icicles down to his beard, he is a gentle soul, as simple as the sheep he tends.

Usually Jesses opens and closes the circle with the Coven sword. It is illegal for common folk to possess a sword, but Wind Mare knows the arts of concealment and keeps it safely hidden. Tonight the circle has formed itself without that formality. Rather than invoking the four corners with words, Anu, Staghorn, Jesses and BearHearth embody them. Embodying the corners requires continuous concentration, but it holds the circle tightly. For the work we need to do tonight, we need all the safety and protection we can muster.

Wind Mare pours wine around the hearth to honor her serpent while I place a bowl of milk by the crevice where he dwells. Our wraiths remain in place as our bodies perform these services, so that when I look over my shoulder I see myself sitting in place, motionless, waiting for my body to return. When my selves merge again I feel briefly sickened. I am not yet adept at separating spirit and body and would never do it but for Anu's insistence that it is a discipline a Priestess must master.

Wind Mare takes the staff and pounds it on the floor.

"What do we know, what have we heard so far?"

William Winter takes the staff. He was out herding his sheep, looking after a young ewe ready to drop her first lambs—twins can be hard on a ewe if it's her first labor—the old shepherd's story rambles on interminably. My foot jiggles with impatience. Gran looks at it. It retreats under my skirt. My toes wiggle in secret. Staghorn is speaking.

"By special order of King James—six Witch-hunters have been sent out to scour the land. They are to seek out the enemies of God—practitioners of the foul arts of sorcery. The law that once condemned only murder or grievous injury by Witchcraft has been struck down. Under the new law, all magical arts, especially any involving familiar spirits, are punishable by death. These Witch-finders have been given free rein to clear out every county, every town of this 'loathsome practice', even down to the farthest cottages in the North. 'Even the smallest stones must be turned over to find the creatures wriggling there,' they say."

Nimué laughs to think of us as wriggling creatures lurking under rocks. I wish I could laugh, but I am too frozen with fear even to smile.

"Staghorn—are these Witch-hunters—paid by the head, or by a monthly wage?" asks Anu.

"That I do not know. Tis certain that James believes in truth through torture. He himself attended the trials of Dr. Fian and others of the supposed coven of Berkshire and was said to be mightily gratified at the proceedings."

Anu swears a dreadful oath. I startle, shocked at her profanity.

"Then we must practice the arts of silence," she says grimly, only her lips do not move so I know I have heard her thought.

I pass the staff to Jesses, feeling a pang of grief that she is soon to be wedding the Miller's son in Ail Fionn and will be leaving us for the coven there. She says that Colin MacPherson, her betrothed, has said that 'queries' are being held in Ullapool and Strathspey but two days' ride to the south. And on the eastern coast the Berkshire madness has caught fire as far north as Lairg and Dornoch.

"Aye," interrupts Winter, "so said this shepherd who had come from there, there was a case there where a mother denounced her three daughters, the daughters denounced the mother and all burned together—"

"It could not happen!" Jesses pounds the staff vehemently.

"My mother would betray me soon enough," Nimué says evenly. Heavy silence descends. Only the fire speaks with its sizzling voice. Nimué takes the wand, shrugging off the fear her comment has engendered.

"Tis said the Berkshire Witches baptized a black cat 'King James' and tossed it out to sea in a silver milking pail in order to call the storm which nearly sank the King's ship. But what sort of Witches would destroy a cat in their work? Besides, a cat might look *at* a king, but would it look *like* one? Likely the Priests invented the whole tale and there's not a true Witch in the lot."

Winter takes the staff back. This same wandering shepherd he shared his lunch with volunteered the information that a Laird hoping to please the king tortured a serving girl named Geillie Duncan until she betrayed the whole wretched plot. Pain makes for strange tales. Why a person in a fever will say anything. When Fiona was but a child that fever in her foot gave her all manner of peculiar fancies. . .

In Anu's hands, the staff seems to bristle with leaves. Dark wings move around her, then blur, as if she were seated in the midst of a thundercloud.

"The Christians do not hold that each being is a balance of light and darkness. They imagine all darkness to be evil, and under control of their Lord Satan. While one of our Priests would have asked James to look within, to see what storms in his heart threatened to capsize his sense, their Priests could only imagine powerful enemies making an attempt on the King's life through magic. So a reward was offered for the culprits. The man who tortured the serving girl wanted the money, simple as simple. Greed has made men do worse."

Wind Mare takes the staff. The way she tosses her hair back

makes her look, for a moment, like a young girl.

"During my travels I spent time in Berkshire, and I know well enough that at least eight of the twelve accused *are* Witches, for tis been in their families for years. Word has it that poor Geillie could not look in a glass of water without seeing the future in it—she carried the sight from both sides of her family. The seers, healers and madwomen are ever the first suspected—and even if the tales they tell are false, the names they are forced to give are real enough."

My fingers dig into the bench like a bird's talons gripping the limb of a tree. Torture. I try to imagine pain bad enough to make me betray the people in this room. My mind goes blank. I think of my mother in labor. Surely no pain could be worse than that. It is hard for me to remember the time I hurt my foot and was so ill from it. If someone had asked for names then, would I have given them?

"Kyairthwen—keep your roots in the ground," Wind Mare says gently.

"Let's hold hands and breathe," says Jesses. The deep breath helps my stomach unclench. I feel the secure strength of my roots in the earth, a faint golden hum holding our circle together in an unbroken ring. When we open our eyes the air seems sharper, clearer.

"Nimué is right about the cats—that's a strange way to go about it," Snowflower says.

"Nothing strange in it," Anu says crisply. "No surer way to do magic than with blood, and no blood more potent than the blood of the sacrifice. The blood mysteries are the most ancient mysteries, Sari. Surely I need not instruct the midwife thus. A willing cat could have bound the spell; but to use a cat unwilling would be a sin against the Goddess, and if they did such then tis small wonder all went awry for them."

"It puts me in mind of a bullock who willingly gave his life in sacrifice years ago. I raised that bullock from a calf. . ." Winter begins laboriously.

"A cat is not a calf!" snaps Nimué. Anu takes the wand and silences us with her upraised hand.

"There is nothing we can do to help the Berkshire Witches. Innocent or no, their lives are forfeit. The issue is this; how to protect our own place and keep out of the way of the Witch-Hunters. Some of us must survive, to pass on what we know to another time."

"Glen Lochlan seems safe enough. How does it happen? How does a village come to change, turning against its wise ones?" Snowflower asks.

BearHearth responds, "They come to the inns and talk to the drunkards about Witches, saying that if evil ones have grown so high as to threaten even the King himself, what chance have the simple folk? Whole towns have been swallowed up in darkness—what misfortune has come here? People remember their sorrows and begin to suppose and suspect—they go to the Priest—accusations are formed out of suspicion and Priests telling confession secrets. From one old beggar woman who is suspected of cursing a child whose father gave her no alms, the suspicion spreads..."

I feel faint. I cut an opening in the circle and seal it behind me with my athamé. Outside it is cooler, my breath comes more deeply. I squat down, thinking, "*All I have comes from Thee and I return it to Thee,*" as I offer the gift of my urine to the Earth. I look at the stars showering their light all over Scotland, all over the world, though half the world is too blinded by the light of the sun to see them now.

"*Half in darkness, half in light, always in motion, every living being is a world,*" Gran had once said. "*But the Christians so fear the terrible beauty of the night that they would stop their world and dwell always in light.*"

Tears sting my eyes at the thought of anyone wishing to banish the lovely stars. I focus on a particularly brilliant star.

"Let me never betray anyone I love," I whisper. For an instant the star burns brighter; then the quick flash of a speaking star dropping through space seems to answer my plea. Reassured, I return to the circle.

We hold hands and breathe to make the circle firm once more. I take the wand.

"I can journey to Faerie and ask the Little People for their help."

Anu nods but says, "The days when the Fay might aid mortals is past. Their power has dwindled to the hollow hills and the hidden pools. They are no longer of this world." The wand pulses in her hand. Again I have the illusion that she wields a living tree.

"As you know, Wind Mare and I were born far to the south of here. Once, years ago, the people had love and respect for their Wise Ones and supported them for the luck of the village. The Priests changed that. We foresaw that the madness destroying the continent would spread over the sea, and so we wandered and traveled, making friends but never settling, until we came to Glen Lochlan. Here the old Laird, who is dead now, was yet Pagan, and the people had need of healers. Though the place seemed safe, yet we undertook a great rite of protection to ensure its safety in years to come. Invoking the great powers of Ragni, we wove a web around the village to hold it safe against the madness of the Priests. With Violet's help, we bound every rock, every bush, every tree from Loch Inbhir to Loch Earn and the Waters of M'hira three miles distant. It took three years. Every new moon we walk the periphery in our sleep, checking the strands, repairing it when need be. . ."

As she describes the web I see it, realizing that I have spent my life under the spokes of this unseen net.

"How did the Priest get through the web?" asks Nimué. Anu shakes her head impatiently.

"A small enough fly passes through. But a creature large enough may break it. As the danger grows, our vigilance must increase. So we must all take care of the web now, walking the boundaries in our bodies as well as in our dreams."

We move the benches back and construct a map of the village on the dirt floor, using horns and handy objects. We section out the circle into nine parts, each of us taking responsibility for our portion. Should any serious weakness occur we will notify the others and repair it.

"Keeping the web strong involves awareness in every part of our ordinary lives," Anu says. "Discretion! Do not advertise your talents. In the excitement of learning a new thing, be not so bold as to brag on it. It is coming to be known that Nimué can stop bleeding—mothers are bringing hurt children for your touch, are they not?"

It was true. Nimué's power over blood was already legend. She would lay her hands over a wound and chant, "Old woman bleed no more. The bleeding is stopping. The bleeding has stopped." When she took her hands away, the blood would have congealed and the healing begun. It gave her a new status in the village, but the reverence was mixed with fear; often I caught people crossing themselves hastily as she passed.

"What use is a Priestess who keeps her arts to herself?" asks Nimué.

"More use than a Priestess of ash," returns Anu. "Better a fire with a few embers left than a fire cold altogether."

Snowflower holds up her slender, long-fingered hands.

"These hands were made to help birth babies. If they burn me for saving their children, then so be it."

Winter shakes his head.

"Whoever could have thought healing would be a sin?"

"Or bringing children into the world," murmurs Snowflower.

Wind Mare sighs. "The world is evil to the Christians, and our arts are of this world."

We stare at the toy village we have made, sadness settling deep in our bones. Anu stands up.

"Despair is a luxury of the wealthy. We who have learned to do with little must take our little and make do with it."

"Let us weave and make our web strong," says Wind Mare.

We place our fingers in the center, just touching, and begin to chant.

"Webster, weaver, spinner, slayer, webster, weaver, spinner, slayer. . ."

Over the warp of the chant we toss cords of our will to survive; naming safety, courage, protection, power, hope, love, magic. The words become a rhyming babble as we move and speak more quickly. Wind Mare calls out, "Feel the spider's belly growing at our center." And we feel a palpable ball of hot sticky light bulging where our fingers meet. Silky strands stronger than rope trail each finger as we pull our hands down and out from the pulsing ball, honey and hemp, sticky and unbelievably strong.

Wind Mare ducks in and out between the strands; a weaving dance like the May Pole rite follows. People blur as the web spins itself out of our fingers; the web moves as of its own will into a pattern of criss-crossing spokes. We crouch down, anchoring the billowing web to the floor. It peaks like a mountain at the center.

Anu cries, "Now weave the web underground, roots and branches, the village enclosed in a sphere of light." The great ball quivers as we join hands and spin around it. So dizzy I fear I will faint or throw up, but we are moving too fast for me to do either. The old ones are used to shifting center and shape. We call on Ragni, the Great Spider, to help us, then cry out and collapse. As our bodies fall around our map village the web and our spirits release as one.

We hang in starlit space, watching the web stretch out in a protective arc over our village. We hover in silence, each of us willing the web to anchor firmly to the part of the circle under our care. Beautiful, peaceful, the village sleeps under the shining spokes of our web, like a child unconscious of its mother's watchful gaze. Anu's hands float in a gesture of blessing:

"The work is done; no ill may enter."

Wind Mare adds, "Nor blade may sever."

Snowflower murmurs:

"That which is done here,"

"Lasts forever," finishes BearHearth.

The circle drifts down through the roof of Wind Mare's house. We bring our palms to the center of our map village and breathe. Jesses opens the circle:

"Wordless, soundless
Cordless, boundless
Open we now.
The world within
And the world without
Are one."

We leave without speaking further to walk the section of the web under our care. I slowly trace my part of the periphery, feeling rather than seeing the cords we have cast firmly rooted in tree, stone and earth. All through my childhood I had felt so safe, unconscious of the bubble of lattice-light so carefully wrought and preserved by the three old women, that hovered over me like a bird shielding her nestlings. Now as I trudge the shores of that inlet of sea named Loch Inbhir my mind flicks to fishes being circled by a net—do they feel safe from the bigger fishes, until the net tightens—?

I shake off the thought of our net as a trap rather than protection. Thoughts make the world, Gran always says. Rapidly now the sky over the eastern trees shifts rose and gold and salmon. Through mottled clouds, slashes of crimson reach like a thin hand from the south. The light could as easily be from flames turning Witches to ash as dawn turning night into day. The light is not reassuring. I want to crawl into the lap of the receding darkness and hide there where nothing can find me.

But the world will not cease spinning anymore for those who wish to rest in the dark than for those who would flee from it. And I am no longer a child to be shielded by a comforting lap. I traded my innocence for knowledge at the moment of Initiation, and there is no going back.

Chapter 34

"Who are these traitors, these waerlogs—John speaks of?" I ask.

"They are men who gain entry to a coven only to betray its members," Gran replies.

"Men? Only men?" asks Annie.

"So it seems. Women break under torture as readily as the men—and most betrayal is of that sort. But these men, these Witch-finders, and Warlocks, often do have enough of a sixth sense about them to know Craft when they see it. And, sad to say, they are often coven-trained as well."

"Young Lochlan has the making of a warlock," Mina says. "He was raised by the Priest."

Gran looks at me so kindly that the defiance in my shoulders droops.

"It is the work of their Priests to sunder soul and body, mind and heart, into ever-warring parts. If he loves you with his body he must abjure you for his soul; if he loves you with his heart he must curse you with his mind."

"The more his heart loves the more his mind fears," Mina

adds. I shake my head vehemently, but their pitying look silences me before I can frame a retort.

"Nay, and you have no such splittings in you. You are all of one piece and you are blind to that which is not," Gran looks through me searchingly.

"Do not forget that you are vowed to silence, Kyairthwen."

"And if there is torture? How may we be certain to keep our silence then?" Annie asks. I turn to Annie, worshipping her self-possession. Is she never afraid, that she can ask such things so cooly?

Mina and Gran exchange grim looks. Mina mutters a charm against evil fate. Gran leans forward, fixing us with her gaze.

"None of our family shall ever be taken and tortured alone. We shall practice blending with each other through the starless place. If one of us is deprived of water, we shall send thoughts of water to cool her thirst. If she is cold, we shall send warmth. When the pain is great, we shall take some of that pain and channel it back to the earth."

Gran regards us each steadily.

"Pain too great to be borne by one can be easily borne by many. None of us need ever bear this burden alone."

I am trembling. Annie lays a calming hand on my back and the trembling stops. Gran continues.

"If you must confess, confess only to the fancies the Christians have of us. Aye, say you signed a pact with the devil, that you converse with rats, and sleep with incubi—" she waves a hand dismissing my look of horror. "What of it? It is no sin to lie in the name of truth. It is our real rites we must protect; their lies matter not."

"Tell the most outrageous story you can concoct. Make sure it has lots of swiving—these inquisitors are so racked with sin they can think of nothing else," says Mina.

Gran silences her with a gesture.

"When they ask who practiced these arts with you—say there came a mist, that all assumed a demon shape, that all were hooded and masked. If you are desperate—the art of remembering can as easily be turned to the art of forgetting. Imagine yourself blinded by snow, surrounded by veils of white or black—allow your mind to go blank. Say the name of the Goddess over and over un-

til nothing else exists. Or go into the form of your power beast
and forget all human speech. There are many ways to forget.
Practice when you are alone until it is as easy as remembering."

Gran leans forward looking deep into our eyes.

"For those who betray the Craft, there is no hope for them in
this life, nor in that which is to come. But if you hold steadfast,
believe me, you will suffer little. Herbs will reach you and you
shall not feel the flames, but only sleep. And wake to the ecstasy
of the Goddess. And the peace between the worlds."

For all her bravado, Annie is more pale than I have ever seen
her. Shaken, I put my arm around her waist and lean my head on
her shoulder.

"Would you be released from your vows and choose a less haz-
ardous path?" asks Gran.

We shake our heads.

"Ah!" Mina snaps her fingers. "We're forgetting the most
important part! Flying ointment! If they ask about flying ointment, be sure to give a recipe strong enough to fell an ox. Curiosity kills Priests and Judges as easily as cats. No, girls, but really,
several Priests in France have met their demise by such means. I
know not how they came to be obsessed by such a dangerous substance when there are easier means to that end, but they are
nearly as besotted with flying as they are with copulating. Oh,
and speaking of copulating, remember, the Devil's cock is never
less than a foot long," she purses her mouth wickedly at our giggles, "and cold as ice of course, and never goes down but remains
hard as steel no matter how many maidens he may deflower in
the course of an evening..."

At that even Gran snorts, struggles futily to regain her
composure, then breaks down and guffaws. Annie and I laugh so
hard we fall off our stools. We laugh until all four of us have
tears running down our cheeks.

Annie reaches out and takes Mina's hand.

"If ever I am taken—send me a drollery through the starless
place—that I may die laughing!"

Gran shakes her head at Mina, her eyes still glittering with
tears.

"Ah, old woman—if the Priests ever catch up with you, I
doubt not that you shall be more torment to them than they to

you!" A look of such love passes between them then that I am both embarrassed and glad to have seen it.

Mina shows us to the door, making shooing motions with her apron as if we were still pesky children bothering her with our eternal questions.

"Forget this dreary talk. Tis a lovely day. Go out and pick me some heather. Pink, if you please, I'm sick of purple and white." Her eyes twinkle as if she knew well what other activities we might pursue.

"Aye," she whispers, leaning up against the doorjam.

"Aye."

Chapter 35

The talons shift back and forth on my forearm, clutching the leather gyves nervously. I send a wave of blue light through my arm; the talons relax. The hawk grows heavy, dozing in her hood. I gently transfer her to the hawk-bar attached to the pommel of my saddle and we set off. Sean looks fine galloping beside me on Coal, the plumes in his green velvet hat dancing in the wind.

We mount to the top of a tor overlooking Loch Lochlan. The sun weaves a lattice-work of gold along the ripples. The air feels intoxicatingly thin, washed clean by last night's rain.

We take the birds onto our wrists and remove their bonnets. Drowsy as they are when hooded, they are instantly clear and alert when freed of them. Sean has brought his favorite hawk, a male kestral that he helped the falconer gentle when it was fresh from the nest. I would be hard put to pick a favorite from among the dozen birds in the Laird's eyrie, but I am well pleased with Sky-dance, the female peregrine Sean chose for me today. She is small for a female, but so fierce she frequently brings down birds twice her size. She scans the sky with her golden eyes and her quick pulse throbs from her feet into my arm. We remove the jesses binding their ankles and they quiver, tense as taut-strung bows, waiting our gesture to fly.

Before I see even the flicker of movement, Sean makes a flinging motion with his arm and the kestral swoops, skimming low over the loch after the fleeing bird. Sky-dance's talons clutch convulsively as she stalks back and forth in excitement, but her wings remain tucked; it is the kestral's bird. A flurry of brown and slate-blue wings; the kestral returns, dropping its prey on the ground between us, snatching the bloody gobbet of meat Sean holds out to it in reward. The skylark is dead, blood oozing from the wounds in its chest, but its wings beat a few times more, until the spirit separates and the body begins to stiffen. I am sad to see it. Too small for food, good only for the cheer of its song, it seems a sorry choice for a target. To our left, down in the marshland by the Loch, we hear the beaters urging the dogs to flush more birds for us. A pair of doves fly by. I let them pass. Sean looks at me curiously. Can he not see what an ill omen it would be to separate a love-bird from its mate? But no, Sean never thinks of such things. He will loose his hawk on a songbird just to see the chase, to enjoy his hawk's prowess.

A duck rises from the water and again the kestral swoops. At the same time, I recognize a distinctive whirr of wings; Sky-dance is upon it before the bird can rise from the sedge-grass. The male pheasant she drops at my horse's side glitters like a jewel in the sun. The dogs flush more birds; grouse and ptarmigan, blackbirds and woodcocks. The beautiful carnage continues, Sean's kestral slicing silent and deadly through the air like a knife, my peregrine somersaulting like a swift, laughing her excited 'kee-kee-kee' whenever she makes a kill. The beauty of their acrobatics stills the pity I feel for the birds gasping and fluttering their lives out on the ground. I brush off the last of my remorse with thoughts of how good their flesh will taste, of the finery Annie can make with their feathers. Already I envision her in a head-dress made from the pheasant, invoking the powers of air.

Satisfied, Sean blows the horn he carries on his belt, signifying to the beaters that they may gather up the hounds and return home. We set to the task of dividing up the birds, putting them in sacks or fastening them to the carrying bar that allows the lucky hawksman to display his catch. Sean takes the brace of grouse, the ptarmigan, a partridge and three ducks his bird brought down, indicating that I may take the other duck and partridge, the blackbirds and the woodcocks. He stoops to pick up the pheasant.

"That's mine," I say, putting a hand on his arm.

"You cannot eat a pheasant in a cottage," he says.

"And why not?"

"A princely bird deserves a princely table," he replies, attaching the bird to his own saddle.

I grasp the pheasant by the neck.

"Twas my bird caught it. I took it, and I'll eat it under the hill if I like!"

"You shall not. Anyway, twas not your bird took it, twas *my* bird, I lent to you for the afternoon."

"A sorry lending it is that lends to the work and not the reward!"

He laughs.

"Tis not work, tis sport."

I cannot wrest the bird away by force, he is stronger than me. A bitter retort rises to my lips, but I swallow it and smile instead. I grasp his shirt, pulling him close, gazing at his eyes, then his mouth.

"I know another sort of sport."

He smiles his wide, lopsided grin, takes my head in his hands, kisses me, reaches down inside my bodice, caressing my breasts. Without speaking, we tether the horses and I lead him down the hill to find a more sheltered spot. A level swath of greensward behind a fallen tree invites us. Our mouths never leave each other as he unlaces my stomacher, I unbutton his shirt. Our lips sliding together are the birds in the air, the sun web glittering in the water. He pulls off his breeches, I throw my skirts aside. He is pressing me down on my back, coolness of the earth and the grass. . . I put my hand between his bird and the nest that it seeks.

"Is it worth a pheasant to you?" I ask sweetly.

"Thou art a wench and a bitch," he replies.

"But not a wanton," I say, crossing my legs tightly. He pulls away, lips pressed tight with rage.

"Ah! But I have a secret," I say, touching a finger first to my lips, then to his. "Pheasant flesh makes me wanton."

"And you would have the grouse, too?"

"I would not send you back empty-handed," I say, running a hand through his hair.

"Very well then," he says, pressing my mouth to his. He mounts me, pushing my thighs apart. My heart is surging with the fast blood of a hawk but I hold him back another moment.

"The pheasant in mine, then?"

He groans.

"All the birds in the sky if it please thee!"

Then I open, crying out with the passion of the pierced bird, spiralling into the rush of wings, the sun spangled water. . .

*   *   *   *

Proud as a warrior queen, huntress, lady of the wild things, I ride back, the horse so be-feathered and my spirits so light, with a bit more wind, I dare say we could have flown. I have birds for everyone, everyone shall feast tonight because of me. Peter and Sarah are not home; I gleefully tie a brace of wood-cocks over their door. I leave the sack of blackbirds on Rose's doorstep. She has a recipe for blackbird pie cooked with a claret sauce that is her passion. She is too old to cook it herself, but one of her daughters or grand-daughters will make it for her. Sean said I might take both hawk and horse home, he would send a groom to fetch them later on. A few of the villagers gawk as I pass by. I bask in their stares, conscious of how fine I must look with the fitted leather gyves on my wrists, the blouse made of the same linen Sean wears, the green velvet skirt. I have asked Sean to get me a page's clothing so I might ride more easily. He let me choose a peacock-blue cloth from his own stores and set a seamstress to work on it right away, saying how fine 'twould look with the glory of my hair tumbling over the back.

Lost in the fantasy of myself in my blue tunic, free as a minstrel or a lord, with a harp and a hawk and a sword and a smile, I canter up to Gran's croft. She is outside, kneeling in an herb bed. She looks up and frowns, shading her face from the sun. I swing from the saddle, grinning, and hand her one of the woodcocks.

"I brought you some supper."

She takes it without even a cursory glance at how fat and fine it is, looking me up and down with an odd expression around her eyes. Finally she speaks.

"I see you have taken up the game of High Toby*."

A spot of color rises to my cheeks as quickly as if they had been burned.

"I went hawking with Sean."

She comes over to the horse and stands, looking at the hooded hawk on the pommel. Sky-dance cannot see her, but she feels the penetrating gaze of eyes as bright and merciless as her own, and turns her head in agitation, making the bells beneath the hood jingle. Gran nods.

"Aye. The young Lord. The young Lord's sport." She turns her gaze to me. "And has he got a little hood for you, with bells on it, as his father had for your mother?"

As a child, I would have cowered. Now I toss my head, swing back astride the horse and kick my heels. Gran hurls the limp bird across my saddle.

"I have no taste for the Lord's sport."

Kicking the mare hard, I slam the woodcock against Mina's door without curbing my breakneck gallop. If she wants it, fine; if not, she can let it rot.

I tether the horse outside the croft, mutter a few words to calm the hawk. Tearing off the gyves, I then strip to my underclothes so I will not sully my finery with the work of plucking and cleaning the birds. Gran's voice is ringing in my ears, *"I see you have taken up the game of High Toby."* I'm not stealing from Sean! What does she think I'm stealing? I take the pheasant from the saddle. Echo of my own voice, calculating and cool, *"Is it worth a pheasant to you?"*

"The pheasant was mine! I did not steal it!" I shout into the horse's flank. The bay turns her head and eyes me curiously as I throw the birds in a heap on the ground. Taking a deep breath, I fold my clothes gently, stroking the velvet skirt. Soon I'll have a blue tunic for riding. He loves me, he gives me things because he loves me. . .

Elana hurries out of the croft.

"Oh, Fiona, they're so beautiful!" she cries, handling the

---

*High Toby—Highway Robbery, serious theft.

birds, stroking their feathers as if they were still alive. She gives another cry of delight seeing the horse, but dares not approach the hawk too closely.

"Och!" she whispers admiringly, "To have such a one to be your friend. . ." Her excitement smoothes balm over my hurt feelings, and I am grateful for her company and her chatter as she helps me pluck the birds. We fall silent, absorbed in the work. Plucking the brown-gold down of a woodcock, my mind flits to the meadow lark—pierced chest heaving—too small to eat—the body left on the tor—the young lord—the young lord's sport—a little hood—a little hood with bells—

Chapter 36

Jessica brings each of us a mug of the foaming brown ale. My mouth is watering with anticipation of the leg of mutton roasting over their hearth. It is Crosby's birthday; Spring Equinox is a fortnight past. Annie and I have been invited to enjoy their feast of lamb and turnips and the first spring greens.

Jesse and Annie take the food from the fire and bring it over to the table. Crosby smiles and smiles. Such a handsome man, I half-envy Annie, and fear also that his gray eyes and ready smile, his broad shoulders and large, beautiful hands will come to please her more than I do.

Jesse and Crosby live in a croft less than a third the size of ours, one room with the hearth and table, a little loft above it. Crosby sleeps in the loft; Jesse's bed is on the other side of the hearth from the table. Their parents both died six or seven years ago, so they have lived on their own since then. The croft is made beautiful by Jesse's corn dolly weavings and wreaths hung all about, and the smallness of it just makes it seem all the cozier. Crosby turns twenty-two today. Jesse is nineteen, but she often talks to Crosby as if she were an older sister rather than a younger one. Where he is brash and impetuous, wild ideas springing out of his mouth like startled stags, she is calm as the seas, her movements and speech deliberate and graceful as the circling of hawks.

We hold hands around the feast.

"Thank you Horned Lord," says Jesse, "for the sacrifice of your son for this meal." Silently we all reverence the young ram Crosby butchered for the occasion.

"And for the mild winter and the fine spring and the early greens, thank you Lady," adds Crosby.

We hold hands, eyes closed in silence for a few moments, feeling our gratitude. Then my stomach growls, breaking the solemnity, and we all laugh. Jesse raises her glass.

"To my dear brother Crosby," she says warmly, "may this year be the finest yet. May it bring him health, and wealth, and love, and—" she looks sideways at Annie, "—and everything he desires." We all toast to Crosby.

"Ah, thank you, thank you. And I have another toast," he winks. "And this year, may our garden grow more than the fine crop of stones it gave us last year."

We laugh and toast again to the garden. Jessica and Crosby's croft lies on a piece of ground that is one of the steepest and rockiest in the village. Without Jesse's knowledge of how to harvest wild potherbs, and Crosby's hard work in the common fields, it would be stone soup for them more often than not.

Annie has just turned sixteen. She and Crosby are both spring bairns, said to be children of the Ram and the fresh green growth.

Crosby bought her several yards of pretty blue material which she has already made into a new bodice and overskirt. She says she doesn't fancy blue, but I think it looks very good on her.

"You should embroider some blue-bells on your blouse," Jesse nods to Annie, indicating the white blouse that she wears under her bodice.

"Aye, I've thought on that," Annie replies. "Next time I have the coppers to buy the thread."

"I'll buy you the thread," Crosby offers. "If I can be the first to see it on—and take it off."

Annie smiles a satisfied, cat-like smile, accepting a slice of lamb from Jesse.

"I imagine that could be arranged," she responds.

I breathe deeply, trying to quell the spark of jealousy in my heart. I like Crosby. He is funny and smart and he loves Annie. But I feel panicked at the thought of their marrying; of her coming to sleep at my croft no more, soon perhaps having bairns tying her to home. I have never been as enamored as she of her dream of us raising babies together. Who should I have them with? Certainly I do not intend to have bastards by Sean and be left with a household full of children and no man as my mother has been. None of the other young men in the village interest me in the least. And now Gran has declared that it has grown too dangerous for covens in different districts to gather for the High Holidays, and so my hopes of seeing Pan again this Beltane have been dashed. Such gatherings were the best way for the young people who shared a love of the old ways to meet each other and marry. And I wonder how long this Witch-hunt will last, how long before I have a chance to meet anyone likely to be my match. Jesse is betrothed now to Colin Miller, the Miller's son at Ail Fionn. They met and wooed each other through such gatherings. They are to be married at the Harvest of Mabon and it is plain that they are much in love.

His mother and grandmother and a cluster of aunts form the core of the coven at Ail Fionn. Because the village is so close and the people are under Lord Lochlan rather than another Laird, we have kept our connections with them. Briefly I fancied Colin's next younger brother, Stephan, but he is already betrothed to another girl in his own village. And the brother after that is but twelve, and at fifteen I cannot imagine him ever being old enough for me. I push away my fears that my friends will both soon be wed and I the only one left alone. This night is for pleasure, not for worry.

Annie has brought Crosby a broach that she has made of stag horn and silver for his cloak.

"How did you come by this?" Crosby asks in wonder, tracing the crescent of metal that she had melted and beaten herself.

"I had a bit of luck," she smiles.

I swallow, knowing our secret; that her luck lay in her ability to wheedle me into stealing a silver spoon from the Laird's pantry on one of my visits to Sean, and how I had nearly been caught by the cook.

I have brought a crock of honey begged from Sean. Crosby opens it with delight, puts a finger in it.

"There!" he smacks with mock selfishness. "It's all mine. And I'm going to lick every drop of it off Annie's breasts tonight." He smirks at her across the table.

"And who's cooking you dinner tonight?" Jesse counters.

"Oh, all right then," he concedes. "But who'll be cooking my dinners after you've gone and married that Miller's son? Lord, I never thought I would see my sister turned into a bannock," he moans. "And me left alone in this croft—why could you not persuade Colin to move here?"

Jesse smiles. They have argued this many times.

"Because he's a miller's son and will inherit his father's mill and there's no mill in Glen Lochlan."

"Aye," Crosby grumbles, "no mercy, no mercy on me at all."

"I made it a year and a day engagement," Jesse reproves him, "in the hopes that would give you time—" she smiles significantly at Annie, "—to find someone else to cook your meals."

"Tis only April," Crosby concedes. "Perhaps it will be time enough." Annie smiles and lowers her head as if somewhat shy, but a subtle shift of energy inside her tells me that she has withdrawn.

Jesse has made Crosby a pair of homespun long trousers.

"You cannot wear a kilt in the fields," she says.

Crosby puffs his chest, still proud that a year ago he was one of the few chosen as the Laird's personal guard. He works not only in the fields now but takes turns keeping watch over the Laird's barn and house, and he is paid in coin for his labors. If there were a war between our Laird and a neighboring one Crosby would be in the thick of it, I think fearfully. But so would any man in the village. And there has been no war in this Laird's time nor in his father's before him, though there are rumors that the greedy McCleod covets our land and should he start trouble Lochlan would be certain to respond. I only hope the other rumors of the McCleod are true; that he is a coward who prefers scheming and slander to battle

After the feast is finished I help Jesse clear the table and clean the trenchers while Annie and Crosby cuddle in front of the fire.

"Fetch your lap-harp, sister," Crosby requests when we come back inside.

Jessica takes out her lap-harp, her most prized possession, carved and strung by her father, a sad-eyed man with a sweet lilting voice who often sang at the Inn while he still lived.

She begins to play merry tunes. We all sing. Crosby keeps time with his mug on the bench, and we have more ale, enough ale so that when I giggle my eyes fill with tears and the whole room quivers like a jelly of firelight and laughter.

"Guess who's throwing herself at me," laughs Crosby. "Little Jennet Turner. One of those who figures I'll need a woman after you're gone," he nudges Jesse. "And doesn't think I'm serious about this one." He tickles Annie until her haughty expression cracks and she giggles, struggling with him on the bench.

"As if I'd trade my black beauty for that little bucktooth rabbit-girl," he laughs. "She's passing herself off as a virgin when everyone knows she's been with her own brothers."

"Crosby!" admonishes Jesse.

"Her brothers have bragged on it! How they ever expect their sister to marry if they spread such tales I know not. Poor thing."

"Poor thing indeed," frowns Jesse.

"Ah, be not so solemn!" he takes a swipe at her ankle with his foot.

Jesse raises her glass again, thoughtfully.

"A toast to our mother and father."

"Ah, a toast," Crosby agrees, sober for a moment.

"Would they were here to see you grown," Jesse adds sadly. They are of Rose's family, so they have had plenty of assistance and advice from kind aunts and uncles, but I imagine nothing can replace the love of their parents. I feel grateful that my mother has survived all her labors and her recent illnesses, frightened to consider what should become of all of us if anything should happen to her.

Annie and Jesse have worked together to make a jacket for Crosby of the same homespun wool Jesse had made for his breeches. They surprise him with it now, and he struts and preens proud as any pheasant.

I try not to feel too much envy at the thought of Crosby's mouth sucking the honey from Annie's breasts as Annie dips a finger in the honey pot, then into Crosby's mouth for a long, sweet kiss. They've been seeing each other a year now. I console myself with the thought that it is better than when she was sleeping with a different man every fortnight. At least now when she's not with me I know where she is, and that she's being loved.

Crosby launches into one of his wild and improbable monologues and soon we are laughing so hard that my ribs ache with merriment instead of jealousy.

"And so, Annie and I shall creep up the great lattice of ivy to the high tower where the king doth sleep. Betimes, one of Fiona's potions shall have knocked all of James' guards into a snoring slumber. We shall force him to drink a gallon of red wine laced with toadstools, and then Annie shall fuck him until the stars ring and the tides shift and the earth opens and he sees the light of the Goddess at last." He nods at Jessica. "And we shall dust the flour off of Jessica and dress her in silks and velvets, and she shall marry him."

"What about his wife?" interrupts Jessica, her round, normally placid face merry.

"Och!" he waves his hand as if brushing away a particularly insignificant fly. "A foreigner, a mere foreigner! We'll pack her back to where she came from. And so, my sister shall marry the King, and when he dies without issue, *I* shall be King of *all Scotland!*"

"And suppose I should have twenty bairns?" Jessica counters, "I've no reason to think myself barren."

"Well then I'll be the—the glorious Uncle Royal, the—uh— Uncle Chancellor—the High Chancellor of Uncles—and I shall be sent as ambassador to the continent, where soon—with perhaps a bit more help from Fiona's potions—" he winks at me, "—I shall persuade all the crowned heads of the error of their ways and when they have quite properly repented we shall set them and all the Papist and Separationist Priests off to sea in a sieve, making all good prayers to Mannanon and Marianna* to escort them to their heaven as soon as possible."

---

*Mannanon and Marianna are the Celtic God and Goddess of the sea.

"And we'll all live happily ever after," laughs Jessica. "But I can't say that Colin will approve of your plan."

"Nor do I!" protests Annie. "I hear King James is a dried-up old prune, and you wish him on me?"

"He's not that old—besides, tis but for a night—it will not take you more than a night to persuade him of the beauty of the Goddess, do you think?"

"Some are prunes that have never been plums," quotes Annie darkly. "And it seems to me as if our beloved King is one of those. Assuming that they'll all take their potions so cooperatively, perhaps we should make them a poison and be done with it."

"Shhh—" Jesse hushes her, trying with futility not to show that she is still laughing. "Drunk as titmice on redberry wine and plotting treason," she cautions. "If so much as a mouse hears us, 'twill be Berkshire all over again."

I am too drunk to feel a chill at her words.

"Would we had another Elizabeth," Jesse sighs. "I hear she thinks God alone is to be the judge of men's souls. Why can the Kings be not so wise?"

"Aye, but if we had a queen you women would be totally insufferable," Crosby says, "You're insufferable enough as it is." He begins tickling Annie again and soon they are wrestling on the floor. "Ah, that's one place where I agree with what they say in the kirk," he says, pinning her down, "Women should be *under* the man—at all times!"

She growls and bites him on the cheek.

"I'll agree to *sometimes*," she concedes, "but get not too cocky about it or thou'lt have nought but little Mary five-fingers to order about."

"That's one wench I've had enough of," Crosby admits, laughing.

Jesse begins playing her lap-harp again and singing bawdy songs. I love seeing her like this. She is so serious in circle, only Crosby has the power to make her laugh like this, and I marvel at how different they are; her serene round face, tranquil as the moon; him with his sharp, pock-marked features and his wild schemes, expressive hands like scythes harvesting the air.

He stops teasing long enough to go fetch more wood for the fire. Then we all eat a little more and we go out to the yard, taking the wishing cake and wishing candle under the moon and stars. The moon is waning but it seems no less a well-omened night for that. We circle Crosby like the three gentle fates. He takes a deep breath and looks up at the stars, looks at Annie and then blows the candle out. We each eat a piece of the cake and leave the rest for the little folk, both furred and fay.

Back in the house, Crosby stretches.

"I'm ready for bed." He hooks the ladder up to the loft; he and Annie get ready to climb up. She hugs me goodnight. I hold her tight, feeling the softness of her breasts against mine. Crosby hugs me and ruffles my hair.

"Goodnight little sister," he says fondly.

Jesse unrolls her mattress by the hearth.

"Would you like to stay and cuddle with me?" she asks.

I shake my head, knowing I would not be able to bear hearing the sounds that Crosby and Annie will be making soon. I kiss her and walk out into the night. Annie's giggles and Crosby's deep happy laugh follow me down the path until it curves onto the main road that runs through the village.

Chapter 37

The night of his birthday was the first time Crosby asked Annie to marry him. But while I knew this was the wish he had made to the stars on his wishing candle, she had not been able to answer with an aye or nay, saying only that she felt still young, and must consider it. The longer she considered it, the more he pressed her; the more he pressed her the more resistant she became.

"Once we marry, I'm afraid he'll think he owns me!" she blurts to me as we gather spring mushrooms and herbs. "Who knows if I would ever see you—or if he would even allow me to go to coven meetings!"

"Of course he'd allow you to go to coven meetings," I reply, feeling the terror in my heart that she might be right about the other. "His sister is in the coven. And Rose—"

"Aye, but Jesse is moving to Ail Fionn. I asked him why he would not be in the coven. Certainly we need more stags."

"What did he say?" I ask, my hand hovering over a mushroom, its execution stayed by the intensity of my concern.

"He said it—frightened him a bit. He said—when he was a child he used to have uncanny dreams and that he knew when his parents were going to die and he—did not want such knowing." She sighs. "How can I be with a man who wants not such knowledge? After all the explorings *we've* done—I've no mind to stop."

I sigh.

"We'd have all day—when he was in the fields—but—if you were to marry him I suppose you'd have to tell him, would you not?"

"I'll not," she says, picking mushrooms so vehemently that she forgets to leave some. With mushrooms it matters not; their true life lies in their web under the ground. Still, Gran and Mina say it is not well to be greedy and that we must always leave a few 'mothers' of any plant that we pick.

"That's part of our magic," she snaps. "It's not as if you were a man. It's part of our magic and—if he learns not the magic, he has no right to know about it."

My heart sinks, thinking about my mother and the Laird, and how secrets have a way of coming forth when we least desire them to.

We turn from the decimated mushroom ring and move on to vibrant green clumps of sorrel grass and delicate meadow-treat and shepherd's share. Moving through the sunny meadow we harvest some cowslips and are lucky enough to chance on some wild garlic. As we are uncovering the wild garlic, Annie gasps and brings forth a mandrake root. It is a male mandrake, the bulge of his cock showing plainly between his root legs. One arm points towards the sky, one towards the earth in the magician pose denoting, 'as above, so below.'

We gasp. She brushes the mandrake off gently, sits with it in her lap looking like a child with a doll except for the intensity of her breathing.

"You think this is a sign I should marry him?" she asks in a high, frightened voice that does not sound like her.

"I don't know. It's the shaman," I say, tracing the outline of the mandrake without touching it.

"Ah, but Crosby's no shaman. Perhaps I should wait," she says. "Aye, it must be telling me to wait. I love him," she says.

"But there's something in me that's telling me it's not right."

"That is the voice you must listen to," I encourage her. "Gran says that's the Priestess voice."

"Aye," she sighs. "Would that the Priestess voice would say what I want to hear."

"What do you want to hear?"

"I want to hear that I could have you both—marry Crosby and have my babies and still somehow be a power in the world as well. Do you think my power has been less since I've been sleeping with him?" she asks worriedly.

"Less—no, why do you say so?"

"The other night I tried to call up the mists and they laid low," she confesses. "And little Roddy Strathan fell down and cut his knee badly and I tried to stop the bleeding and it wouldn't stop. Not until Sarah came and wrapped it tight with a poultice." She finishes with a shaky sigh. As we have spoken, clouds have gathered across the sun, darkening by the second. Soon it will rain, and indeed, the omens seem not well.

As Annie became more doubtful, Crosby became more and more persistent; shouting at her when he saw her standing with her arm around another man at the smithy, showering her with presents, more than his income could afford. And now he becomes angry if she chooses to spend any evening at my croft instead of his.

"As if a flame could chase a moth," Jesse shook her head after a bitter argument which resulted in both Annie and Crosby slamming out of the croft and rushing off in different directions.

"If he would but stay with his own light he would draw her to him," Jesse observed, but I could see she had little faith in her brother's ability to stay still and trust.

To show Crosby that he did not own her, Annie began sleeping with other men occasionally, out of rebellion rather than desire. This drove him more wild than ever. I pitied him deeply, feeling the jealousy that he expressed so wildly and freely to be the same as that which I had always denied and pushed away, knowing that Annie would not tolerate my voicing of it.

One lovely evening in early summer at their croft, our meal of pease porridge and oat cakes came to an abrupt halt.

"Whose bed did you grace last night?" Crosby asks Annie suddenly.

Last night she had been with me, but he assumes now that any night she is not with him she is with another man.

"I stayed at Fiona's croft last night," she responds truthfully.

"That's not what it smells like! You're lying!" he accuses.

"I am not!" she spits.

"I smell it on you," he insists, and I freeze, thinking that he has been able to detect the smell of our lovemaking on her.

"As if I would bother to lie to you!" she bridles.

"All that you do when you're not with me is a lie," he says, choking. "In spite of all, all the other men would say, for all that the whole village would mock me behind my back, I'd still forgive you and make you my wife. But you would rather be known as the village whore!"

"Crosby," Jesse says, almost sharply, but then her voice softens, "Annie is a Priestess. No man can own her. Her true husband is the Horned God, and what he bids her do, so must she do. If you would have a woman be your chattel, marry a Christian. A woman like Annie—or me—cannot be owned."

Crosby almost sobs, but laughs bitterly instead.

"If I must be cuckholded, could I not at least be cuckholded by a woman with some taste? This day Jim Strathan said he'd had you out in the newly sown barley fields last week. I smashed his face with my shovel. I'd of killed him if the others had not pulled us apart. Do you know what he thinks of you? Do you think he thinks of the Goddess when he is with you?" he asks Annie bitterly.

Too close to tears to talk any more, he shoves the bench aside and slams out the door. Jesse breathes deeply and looks steadily at Annie.

"My brother is a good man, a generous man. You need not torment him like this, and I ask you not to. If you show him gentleness, he'll show it back to you."

Annie bows her head before Jesse's gaze and for a moment I think she will cry. But she and Crosby are cut of the same stubborn cloth, and if she ever shed a tear, over that evening or any other, neither I nor Jesse was there to see it.

I had never understood Annie's willingness to sleep with the men who could not honor her for it. As their battle raged, I secretly sympathized more and more with Crosby's side. Though I was still terrified of losing Annie to him, I almost wished she would surrender to the marriage, thinking it would be easier for me to endure her being with one man than with many. More often than not now our evenings ended with shouting rather than merriment, and I often thought that if Jesse had not been there to come between them that they would have come to blows.

Beginning of the hot month of August; Jesse had gone to visit Colin in Ail Fionn and to help his mother with the initial wedding preparations. Crosby begged Annie to come and stay with him for a couple of days, to see if they could not mend their differences. I tried to pray for them, straining to convince myself that I could endure sleeping alone at night without the smoky tulse of her hair coiled around me, without the softness of her breasts breathing against my back. Secretly I still cradled my childhood fantasy of Annie and I sharing a croft, knowing the village would never accept two of its prettiest girls living unwed in a croft full of herbs instead of babies. Knowing that anything that unusual would be taken as a sure sign of Witchcraft. Knowing that in many villages that once tolerated old women dwelling together to ease their poverty and loneliness, widows and spinsters were now routinely burned.

The next day Annie appears at my door with a glaring bruise on her cheek.

"Come on," she says. I hurry with her to the woods.

"'Tis all over between me and Crosby," she declares, voice clipped and tight. "He hit me. Jesse was not there to come between us. If she had been he'd probably have hit her too. I told him I'd marry him. But I told him I'd only marry him if you could live with us and that—I would be his wife and you would be mine."

"Annie! You said that to him?"

"Aye." Touching her finger to her swollen cheek, "He fair knocked me across the room. And I broke his chair on his head!"

"You fought before—"

"He never laid a hand on me before," she says harshly, "and now he will never do so again."

"I don't care, I don't care," she insists as I try to comfort her. "I never wanted to be any man's wife anyway."

"What if he tells—the others—what you said?" I ask, feeling sick at my stomach.

"He'll not. He'd be the laughing stock if he did. My reputation can have no where to go but up from where it is. It's he who would be shamed if any knew I cuckholded him for another woman. No, he won't say anything—except that he did not—want to marry a whore. He probably will say that." She tosses her hair defiantly. "I don't want to talk about him any more, now or ever."

"Come back to the house," I coax. "I'll fetch a comfrey poultice for your cheek."

In the days that followed, often I wanted to go to Crosby and make peace with him. Other than Ewan, he was the only young man in the village that I felt was my friend, and it hurt bitterly to lose that friend. But every time he looked at me in passing, his look was a curse and I was afraid to venture past his angry scowl to touch the hurt that lay beneath it.

Even at Jesse's wedding near two moons later, when Jessica hugged us both tight as if we were her sisters of the blood as well as the art, leaving her tears wet on both of our faces, Crosby treated us as if we were of no more interest than the sparrows hopping about pecking at the grain that had been tossed about the new-wed couple. Jesse was dressed in a gown of dark blue and white, wearing a crown of poppies and grain and grapes. Colin, slender and shy but strong in himself, graced with horns along with his headdress of grain and grapes, was glowing with joy, a true stag strong for the Lady and a right match for Jesse. Happy as I was for them, my heart wept the whole time for Crosby and Annie and how they should be wed too; but for me.

Chapter 38

My flesh crinkles into bumps, then relaxes with an almost audible purr into the warm caress of the summer sun. A bird trills. Just enough breeze to wrap a few loose strands of hair across her throat. The combed wool of the sheepskin floats under my knees as if it were the pelt of a cloud mated with a mountain lion.

Ceremoniously we unfold the necklace and headdress each has made in secret for the other. I gasp when I see the intricate weaving she has made for my throat, the crescent moon of rainbow shell, polished wishbones of small birds set to hang over my breasts and heart. Ah, clever fingers, her fancy weavings are always so much finer than mine. But anything would look handsome around her neck. A loop of deer hide hung with scallop shells and disks of stag horn is simple enough not to vainly attempt to compete with the beauty of her unadorned nakedness. I run my lips down the arterial river to the pool at the base of her throat. What I would not do for serpents of silver to twine around the sienna of her neck and arms.

For her head, a leather band sewn with bright red berries, a puff of white feathers floating down over each ear. I crown her with it, lean back on my heels to observe the effect. . .

Ripples disturb the surface of my vision. I see her dark but scarred and older, seated on a horse with a lance in her hand and a bow slung over her back, sadness in her eyes, but that same familiar hot smile playing over her lips. . .

Her hands on my breasts, low laughter, call me back. She makes me lie down, taking white heather from her leather bag to decorate my auburn portal. A stalk of wheat grass flying a jaunty white breath feather conquers the curl above the cleft.

"My standard claims the forest," she asserts, but tis her kiss beneath the standard that does the claiming.

Playful and slow as clouds at shape-dancing, until a quick snarl of lust turns us feline. Crushed heather powdering our thighs, we fall into each other. Breast bone, pelvic arch and the red sunbursts behind them; our bodies heave and break like the waves.

Warm waves, dark, blue as grapes, blue as the portal between the eyes of sight. Memory of gray seas vanishes. The salt we smell here is warm and fused with the heavy scent of honey. She leans back on her elbows, so greedy for the grapes I press through her lips the juice trickles down her neck. Temple Maidens on a holiday, feeding each other fruits we must make new names for; the womb-fruit with its seeds of blood; the sweet-sticky-seedy one; dried ears of the sun. And the more familiar grapes, fat and heavy with sugar, as nectar-laden as bumblebees. Nothing but fruit and kisses, sweet and sticky, light and sustaining.

Making love is the gate. Falling out of myself into that grace state of molten fire. Touching each other until our bodies glow hot and dissolve into shadows of light and become mirrors where we see each other clothed in other flesh, recognizable only through the eyes or some nuance of movement. Beloved, there is no body you can put on that would hide you from me, so well I know the scent of your soul and the shine of your eyes.

In this dream she is also gypsy dark; younger, smaller breasted, hands that dance like birds when she talks. Eurynome, I call her, and my name on her lips, Evadne, is sweeter than harps or flute. Exhausted, breathing deeply under the hot sun polishing our bodies, her

*breathing slows her into honeyed sleep. I breathe into her hair a poem
by the island Priestess whose legend we worship: "You may forget; but
let me tell you this; someone, in some future time, will think of us."**

She nuzzles me back into our own time; each of us holds a
hand cupped over the other's belly.

"Remember, we planted the womb-fruit seeds there—we sacrificed an untouched fruit to Artemis, and a tree grew there
faster than anyone had ever seen such a tree to grow. . ." Aye,
and the sharp-sweet taste of it, as much Crone as Maiden, the
flower-blown meadow opening to the depthless fall of cold black
air. . .

Nimué, spell-weaver, easily could you bind me as your name-
sake bound Myyrthin for the thousands of years. See how far the
sun has moved since first we lay here?

Annie laughs at my unspoken thought.

"Aye, there'll be hell to pay at my croft, and Eostre will scold
you for your shirking. We'd best away, dear as I love the heat of
that far-off sun."

We dismiss the circle we had cast and hasten back, picking
herbs along the way so as not to come back empty-handed—as if
no one could guess how hastily we might come by such things.

Eostre is angry, as Annie predicted. Rightfully so, my serious sister is too often left doing her work and mine too when Annie lures me away. Mother is stuffing sausages, Eostre is taking
loaves of bread from the fire. Elana is keeping the younger children busy weaving corn dollies to decorate hearth and threshold.
Tonight all the village will celebrate the harvest of the first
fruits; every cottage door will be open and every hearthside flowing with whiskey and laughter. The villagers may forget the
Lady or think only on that crumb of her called Mary the Priests
allow them, but no one dares forget Jack O'the Green at the seasons of planting and harvest. Not to honor the grain is to court
starvation, and even the Priests want to eat.

The littlest bairns have been neglected. I clean them up and
take them out with me to play while I churn the cream into butter. I sing to them and pretend to dance with the churn and grab
them and tickle them with my feet. Every so often I give them
tastes of the thickening cream. The cats stalk out to join the expectant throng. Work can be a merriment, especially on a day of

---

*Sappho

harvest. John brings the goats in early. I milk them, feed the little children to keep them from getting too hungry before the feasting. Then Elana and I work together to make them as beribboned and bonny as any flock of elflings. At last we are ready. We walk down the path to the common fields singing:

"All among the barley
Who would not be blythe
With the ripe and bearded barley
A-smilin' on the scythe."

They are harvesting the last of the grain. Nearly half of the village is there, cutting and binding and distributing the sheaves. Those not busy at the actual labor of it sing and chant to encourage the workers. The barley, wheat, rye and oats are parceled out to each family. We have no man to work the fields so our portion is small. But even the old maids and widows get a bit. This village has seen hunger between Imbolc and Ostara*, but none have died from it.

Peter takes our portion in his cart. He will take it to Ail Fionn to be ground by the miller there. I may accompany him so as to see Jessica. If Annie comes along, we'll have a party of it.

The last bunch of heavy stalks in each field is bound but left uncut. All grow solemn. Even the babies hush. Twisted of joint, gnarled and unsteady of limb, short of wind, Rose walks towards the sheaf, sickle in hand. Slow as fate, tis like watching a tree walk, each step a pulling up and replanting of roots. The men do all the harvesting but this. For lifetimes, none but the oldest woman in the village has dared to cut the last sheaf. For the spirit of the grain takes refuge in that sheaf, and it is slaying the God to take it. None but the Crone have the right to sever the God and remain unscathed.

As the God-sheafs are cut, the men drift away from the fields as if they too had been cut from them. The women rush in with wild cries, tearing the sheaves apart and then mixing them together into a braided man decorated with flowers. Cornflowers for his eyes, an ear of corn for his phallus, our doomed beloved God is carried in a painted cart through the village. All who have remained in their homes until now come out to bid farewell

---

*Imbolc and Ostara—between February and the Spring Equinox in late March.

to the God, not in sorrow, but with singing and laughter. Bleat-
ing, barking, crying, singing, cheering, whooping, a happy swaying serpent of women, goats, men, dogs, chickens, children, follow
the cart, the noises blending into a cacaphonous paen to the Lord
of Summer. Only the Priest looks glum, but he's ever dour.

The men have built a bonfire of stubble and cut wood while
the women wove the God. The God is hoisted to the top. The
Priest has his moment where he says how the Grain God is really Jesus who died so that our sins might be forgiven and the
grain might grow. He seems to feel much better once it is clear
that 'twas Jesus who died for the grain. Everyone nods politely,
happy that all Gods are on our side for the harvest.

The old women start it, the low wordless hum that soars and
crests into a peak of sound. As it peaks, the sky darkens enough
so the first star blazes through.

"The first star!" a child cries.

"The God is Risen!" Mina and Gran say together. The fire is
lit; the Grain God turns to smoke and travels to the stars. All
are dancing and singing, mugs of beer and brandy and whiskey
pass from hand to hand, the women pass out fancy breads, shaped
like men, or suns, or braided, decorated with dried flowers, stuffed
with fruit and nuts, glazed with honey. They are eagerly dis-
membered and devoured, though there is far too much to fight
over.

The Goodwives return to their homes then and prepare to en-
tertain the young people who pass from house to house eating
and drinking.

I see Sean looking at me with wistful eyes. He's looking fine,
but tonight I have no taste for his velvets, his feathered hat, his
chivalrous manner breaking into impatient lust when he kisses
me. I nudge Annie and we dodge through the throng. Hands
reach out to try to stay us, or merely caress us as we pass by, but
we slip through, otter-sleek. On such a holy night, we prefer each
other's company.

Flitting from croft to croft, we drink and dance and fly away.
Traditionally, the visitors bring a token of money or food as payment for each house's hospitality. Annie had the outrageous notion that we should make magical talismans of bone, feather and
twisted herbs to leave as payment. We give them out; "For the

luck of your house, for the luck of your hearth, for the luck of your bairns, for the luck of your barn." The tightened line around their throats, the eyes glancing away; hands afraid to refuse the tokens yet holding them as if they were woven of fire. We laugh and dart out into the night.

A few lads are determined to track us from croft to croft. Drunk as we are, we stifle our giggles long enough to lose them in the woods. We retreat to the meadow, stumbling and weaving. We'll sleep off the drink and have time to sober before our coven gathers for its ritual by the sea.

But by the time I wake, the night is far along. Annie is worse off than I, shaking me off and burying her head in her cloak when I try to rouse her. At last I get her on her feet and we stumble towards the cove to meet the others. We celebrate the harvest rite at the seashore because it corresponds with the ebb and flow of the tides, being at once the time of the God's dying and the flood of earth's bounty swelling our larders, promising survival through the winter to come. As part of the ritual we make wooden rafts a palm or two wide. We charge them with our wish for what we would harvest in the next year and adorn it with a gift for Mannanon and Marianna. We light the reed tapers dipped in fat and secure them in the center to guide our boats into the dark halls of the sea. Tis my favorite part of Lughnasad to see our small stars drifting out into the vasty deeps.

We arrive at just this point of the ritual, as they hand the sea-craft hand to hand, the oldest covener holding the circle's center on the beach, the youngest standing in the water. Violet Rose, strong as the World-tree, holds the center, but Winter is ill at home and without us the line into the sea is too short, Sari's outstretched arm just short of the breaking waves. Annie and I should be the farthest out to sea, reaching across the breakers to where out boats would have a better chance. We rush to the edge of the circle and ask permission to enter. Everyone ignores us. We ask again. Silence like a stone wall. We watch dumbly as the waves snatch the light from each of the boats, pushing them under the foam.

Like a snail withdrawing its horns, the line retreats to the circle marked with grain on the sand. They talk of the approaching time of balance at Mabon*. Again we ask to cross the bound-

---

*Mabon—Celtic harvest Sabbat occurring on the Autumnal Equinox.

aries of the circle to join them; again we are more invisible than the will 'o wisps for all the answer we get. They pass the chalice and food. Annie and I exchange disconsolate looks, sitting like hungry puppies locked out of a warm house. They close the circle, dismissing all the spirits and leave, still not deigning to acknowledge our existence.

We're so down-hearted we curl up and fall asleep on the sand together without saying a word, waking up sore and miserable to a blustery wet morning. We go to Gran's house to apologize for being late. She is at her most harsh and distant.

"Tis apparent you have no understanding of the meaning of harvest," she says, "or you would be more careful to sow what you desire to reap."

She scolds us for our behaviour, not in a way that leaves us any room to reply. Our harmless teasing and carelessness begins to look very serious indeed. She says we are to be banned from the next harvest Sabbat too.

As we turn to leave, bearing our remorse and resentment, Gran asks, "Fiona, Roxanne; have you ever heard tell of a man who planted a nut tree and grew it as a cherry?"

Chapter 39

"Fiona!"

Mina is at my door sounding very sharp and cross. What have I done to annoy her so? Is she still wroth with Annie and me for our Lughnasad* pranks? I wipe my hands on my apron, leave the loaves of bread I've been kneading. She takes my arm in a talon-like grip, pulls me outside of the croft. She snaps at the younger children trailing after me:

"Back in the house! We have private business to speak of."

My heart sinks.

She walks me rapidly into the woods. At the well we stop. She is breathing hard.

"Bad news girl," she pants, "one of the Witch-finders is in town."

My mouth goes dry.

"He's going about asking questions. Make sure there's no herbs or simples anywhere in your house. I lost my whole supply, buried it in the compost—" she mourns bitterly. "—I dared not even take it to Ann's for fear it should be seen. Get rid of anything the least bit—uncanny. Tell your brothers and sisters to

---

*Lughnasad—Celtic Harvest festival celebrated at August 2, also known as feast of the first fruits.

269

watch their tongues if they value their lives."

"Has anyone been named?"

"No. Just came in. This morning. We have no reason to suspect—any betrayal."

I curse myself and Annie for the foolishness of the charms at Lughnasad. Has one of our neighbors spoken out of turn and condemned us?

"I won't betray you," I promise Mina, suddenly certain it is I who will be betrayed. She hugs me and I hear how hard her heart is pounding.

"We shall all hold fast together. The web is strong. He will leave."

We go back to the croft. Gran is already there, the children sitting in a half-circle around her. The table where we were kneading bread has been pushed aside. My mother sitting white-faced, nursing Mark, the newest baby. Myrrh sits huddled under her skirts, sucking her thumb. Malcolm so pale each freckle stands out like a pebble. Colin is there, standing, looking grim and stangely old for his eleven years. He must have seen the Witch-hunter entering town and came to tell Gran and Mina.

"You go back to the fields," Gran says to him. "I know that you know well the quality of silence that is needed. Your absence must not be noted."

He nods and leaves.

"As for the rest of you—we must have no word of herbs, teas, charms, poultices, healings, midwives—"

"What's wrong with midwives?" pipes Sarah.

"No word of it!"

"How would the babies get born?" demands Sarah.

Gran stands up, marches over to Sarah and shakes her. The child bursts into angry tears, too frightened to kick or bite as she might if another had treated her so, but clearly enraged.

"Would you like to burn?" Gran asks her coldly.

"No," sobs the little girl.

"Then do as I say and do not badger me with any questions! It is not important for you to know why, it is important for you to do as I say!"

She turns to the others.

"Keep to yourselves and stay in this house. If anyone comes

here asking questions, the cat has your tongue. You may not speak. You must say, 'Ask my mother.' Can you say that?"

She tests each of the children.

"Alright now, here I am, a stranger. 'Tell me my little lassie, do you know of any herb women in these parts?'"

Sarah starts to nod; freezes. "No. I mean—ask my mother."

"Again," coaches Gran. "'Ask my mother.' I'm not asking you to lie. I'm merely asking you not to speak. Tis not so hard."

Sarah scrooches her face to stop the tears.

"There now my pretty lassie," says Gran again, "do you know where I might find an herb-woman or a cunning-man? I have an injured horse that needs tending."

"No," breathes Sarah, "Ask my mother. I'm only a bairn."

"Good," says Gran. "Good." She tests the other children. Elana bursts into sobs, then chokes them back.

"You must not show terror either. Tis as damning as anything you might say. Breathe. Look at your sister Eostre, she never shows anything she feels if she doesn't want to. Let that be your model."

Eostre straightens with pride.

"Do a spell," my mother pleads, "Do a charm so that he comes not here."

"Easier said than done!" bristles Gran. "If you were so interested in charms—" she bites back the bitter retort.

"Forgive me," she says. "One cannot force another on a path that is not theirs. I assure you that I am doing the best that I can—we must all do our part. Be *polite* to the man," she looks pointedly at Malcolm. "If there is any incident as there was with that Priest and the snowball—" she glares at him with a fierceness that would quail me even now. Malcolm bites his lip and looks at the ground. It was only last winter that he hit the Priest in the back with a snowball, and when my mother shook him and demanded that he apologize, he would only say, "I'm sorry I hit you in the back with the snowball. I meant to hit you in the head."

Dear God, I think, please let him know there is a difference between the Priest and the Witch-finders. His bravado could destroy us all.

"You fancy yourself a young man," Gran says harshly. "Behave like one! Now if ever." He raises his chin and nods, meeting her gaze. And I breathe a sigh of relief, knowing that in this crisis his judgement can be trusted.

Gran kneels by Myrrh.

"You understand what is happening here my dear? My pet? My pretty?"

Myrrh shakes her head, thumb wedged firmly in her mouth, hand gripping my mother's skirts as if she feared that Gran would wrench her away at any moment.

"If anyone asks any questions, just shake your head prettily, like you just did for me. All right?"

Myrrh nods.

"Keep your thumb in your mouth and all will be well and— I'll see to it that you have a bit of a treat—all of you—when the Witch-hunter leaves we'll have a treat of—magnificent proportions," she promises.

I nod. "Aye, that we will. Something special. For now we must be as invisible as we can."

"All right," sighs Gran, "let us go about our business. And— if you're feeling any fear—children, just remember to put your roots down into the earth. Just think of the trees. If they fear, they never let it show. They let the earth take their fear and their fear passes from them. Calm as the trees, rooted as the trees. And we shall remain, like the trees."

She nods to us all. "Bring me a loaf of that bread when you're done." She smiles at me though she cannot disguise the tenseness behind the smile. I smile back, kiss her, hold her tight. Who in the village might not identify her as the woman of herbs? What will I do if—

She pushes me away. "No if," she admonishes. "No if. Come out with me a bit." Outside the door she says to me softly, "If any of us are to be sacrificed, let it be the old ones."

I shake my head, tears starting to come. She holds my face in her hands.

"I'm not offering myself. No matter what happens Fiona—do nothing foolish. The future of Glen Lochlan is with you, with you. Without our powers this village itself would not survive. Even the seasons would go awry. Protect yourself, at all costs."

She looks me deep in the eyes. "I love you."

While I have felt her love always, I do not know that she has ever said it to me. The warmth of her love pours through my body, washing the fear away, grounding me.

She kisses me on the lips. She and Mina walk off together, holding hands. As I knead the bread, Elana and the twins helping me, I breathe deeply, remembering to run my breath in through my nose and out all through my body as if I were breathing down through the soles of my feet into the ground. I imagine the light of the Goddess pouring into my body, the dark solidity of the earth anchoring my feet. I breathe my calmness out into the house and feel my siblings relax and begin breathing in rhythm with my breath. Elana especially is gifted with breath. Soon she is completely relaxed, absorbed in the bread-making as if there was nothing else in her mind except making the most perfect loaves possible.

Outside the croft, the pool of calm ends. Quietly I step outside. Malcolm is chopping wood so furiously he does not hear or sense me. I walk in front of him so he will see me and not be startled. Chopped wood lies scattered all around like fallen foes. It is plain he is imagining hacking up the Witch-finder and all his kind.

"Malcolm," I say, as I kneel, looking right into his eyes, "these thoughts you are having will draw him."

He looks down and his lip quivers.

"I understand," I say, touching his shoulders, "I understand. But this is what they live on, and he will be here quickly if you do not control your mind."

He looks at me, hazel eyes clouded. "Help me."

"All right. Let's pile up this wood." As we stack the logs and kindling the tension in his body eases.

He grins. "It sure did make the chopping easier."

"It is not a wrongful thing to do with your anger, but dangerous now. We know not how powerful our enemy is. We must be careful not to give him any of our power." I sigh, feeling the soreness in my hands and shoulder from all the kneading, wishing that the day was warmer, though one cannot expect much more from September. Suddenly Malcolm is in my arms, his face pressed up against my shoulder, body shaking with sobs.

"I'm so afraid," he confesses.

I hold him tight. "They're not burning anyone your age," I say, trying to comfort him.

He pulls back, looks at me astonished. "It's not me I'm afraid for, it's you. That thing you did with the charms—I thought it was so funny, but—" his mouth trembles, "—don't let anyone hurt you."

"I won't," I assure him, wishing I had more certainty. "Not if I can help it. Believe me, I'll do nothing foolish—while he's about. I don't think we'll be betrayed," I say hopefully. "A third of the village is kin to Rose. They'll have too much to lose. The Laird—surely he'll not tolerate a Witch-finder here for long."

"You trust *him*?" Malcolm asks incredulously. "The *Laird*?"

"It's hardly in his interests for that man to be here. He's not the most Christian Laird in James' Kingdom. And his son consorts with a Witch." I smile. "No, he'll do all he can to get free of him. Go and do some fishing today," I suggest, "Sit by the stream, let it calm you and cool you."

"I think I'd best stay here. You might be needing a man—"

I shake my head. Is he truly six going on seven?

"All right," he concedes, reading my smile. "I'll go fish. Just think to me if you need—something."

"You'll know," I say, pleased with his confidence.

"Take the twins with you?" I ask as he fetches his fishing pole and gear.

"I'll never catch anything with them around," he grouses. "Oh, all right, if it will help," he relents.

They bound out, having wearied of kneading and pounding, ready for adventure by the stream. Elana offers to complete the baking.

Hoeing in the garden, my thoughts circle around to Annie. Glad that she is at Ail Fionn with Peter and Sarah to get some of the early grain ground. But they left yesterday, they should be back by this evening. Tightenings of panic around my throat. Annie has never blended in; her blood is clear, and the gypsies are the most persecuted of all under James' new edicts. Gran and Mina will be sending them word of the intruder through the starless place. I pray they receive the warning. I pray they stay safe in Ail Fionn.

Later that night, a sharp knock on the door.

Mother stands up, white-faced; the newest baby, accidentally jerked from her breast, begins to cry. I recognize the knock as Peter's, however. I run to the door and open it, fall with relief into his big bear hug. Their three children pour in. Sarah follows, looking weary, supporting the curve of her pregnant belly with one hand. Annie enters last, tight-lipped, and shrugs me off angrily when I try to hug her. She pulls up a bench and sits by the fire, lips pressed together, looking through narrowed eyes into the flames. Sarah takes off her scarves and shakes out her brown hair. She sits beside Annie and takes her hand with such gentle assertiveness that Annie does not push away from her as she did from me, but instead, puts her forehead on Sarah's shoulder and begins to sob hard, tight sobs.

"Time for bed, bairns," Peter says. "Aye, ye can all fall asleep here, come along, all in a pile, all in a pile. Nah, nah—" he brushes off any protests, picking the children up two and three at a time, carrying them into the other room. "Aye, of course I'll sing ye some songs, quiet down here. Naw, ye do not need yer mommy—I'll not sing if I'm not to be heard," he growls in his most bearlike fashion.

Mother sits on the bench opposite Sarah and Annie, holding baby Mark. Elana is standing with her knuckles pressed in her mouth, trembling like grass in the wind, watching Annie cry. I must look as shocked as she does. For Annie to shed a tear, it must be serious indeed. Has someone been taken? Have we all been accused? Could Peter sound so cheerful with the children in the other room if we were all to die? Don't let it be Gran, I pray. I realize with anguish that I cannot bear for it to be any of us.

"What happened?" My mother's lips move around the question we can barely hear. Annie has stopped crying. She is shuddering.

"Bastard," she whispers.

"When did the Witch-finder come here?" Sarah asks softly.

"This morning," Mother replies. "Colin heard a couple of the men talking about him and came to tell us."

"He stopped us as we came in," reveals Sarah.

Peter has finished his songs for the little ones. He comes out, sits on the bench, pulls me and Elana down on either side of him. Eostre and Colin have taken on the job of managing the smaller children and keeping them quiet. I hear Eostre hushing them and Colin telling stories.

"Aye, the Witch-finder stopped us on our way in," sighs Peter. "He's too canny, that one."

"Perhaps he stopped us—only because of how she looked. James has practically condemned all gypsies outright," suggests Sarah.

"I hope you're right," says Peter. "He asked us what we were doing with a gypsy. I told him she lived right here in these parts with her mother. A lass was entitled to make a mistake," he says, referring to Mairead's obvious indiscretion with a gypsy lad. "Sorry if I offended you," he apologizes to Annie, "I was nervous—thought I could joke him off—and he asked her—what sort of fortunes she told. We were in front of the ale house—Ian McTavish was there, and Orrin Argyle, the Turners. So was Crosby, thank God, we'd one ally in the crowd. You answered him well lass."

"What did she say?" asked Mother. Annie is quiet, head still on Sarah's shoulder.

"She said her face was her fortune," Sarah smiles, patting Annie's cheek.

"Good answer. Better than I could have thought of," nods Peter. "And he said that—from the talk he'd heard in the tavern, perhaps she'd been using her *charms*, her glamourie, to ensorcell the men of the village. Orrin smiled at that—I could have smashed him." Peter's hands clench, his eyes smolder. I have never seen the gentle bear look dangerous. A string of dark profanities rolls from him.

"Thank—Goddess you did not," whispers Sarah.

Peter continues, "Crosby stepped up then, and laughed the Witch-hunter to scorn. He said, 'Since when does a girl need more than a pretty face to lead a man astray? If you see Witchery in that, you must see it everwhere!' Then Tim Brede, bless his heart, said, 'That's right—don't be taking our pretty lasses from us—burn the old women if you want, we've better uses for the young ones.'"

"Was he satisfied then?" asks Mother.

"Black-hearted—" another string of extravagant profanity issues from Peter.

"Aye, he went on then, saying there was not a gypsy alive who had not Witchery and thievery in their blood, and that James had no intention of leaving any of the blacks alive. Black folk practice black arts, he said."

Annie lifts her head off Sarah's shoulder.

" 'I hear it takes a sorcerer to know one.' That's what I said. It was foolish. I should have held my tongue." She reaches down and takes the little knife from around her ankle.

"Perhaps I should kill myself now," she says, holding it with the point towards her chest. I am on my feet, but Sarah has gently reached her hand around the blade, cupping the point against her own palm.

"To what purpose?" she asks kindly. Annie presses her lips together in anguish.

"That I not betray you."

"Are you accused?" I ask.

"No one's accused," says Peter, "No, nor will they be. You said nothing to incriminate yourself," he assures Annie. "You did well, I told you, you did well. He has nothing to go on."

"Which of the men in the village may not betray me to the Witch-hunter?" she says hopelessly. "I am lost. My life is forfeit."

I look imploringly at Peter. He struggles for something to say.

"We create as we believe," reminds Sarah softly. "You must not think such. You must not think such. You are strong, and you are a Priestess. None of us need choose this death. I have life within me, not death." She puts Annie's hand on her belly. "Choose life," she urges, "choose life."

"What choice does one have if one is accused?" she asks. "Staghorn says that none escape—"

"No one has been accused—you have not been accused," reminds Sarah, "merely questioned."

"And Crosby defended you. You have a friend there you did not know that you had," adds Peter.

"Aye," Annie says softly.

"Aye, he's a champion," continues Peter. "Of course, he's Jesse's brother, he's got the blood. Rose can be proud of him. He came right out and laughed at the Witch-hunter before the crowd. He said, 'An old stick like you, you've forgot what a pretty girl is for. There's always a man wants to smash what he can't have.' Then he accused him of simply being in it for the money, asking, wasn't it true, didn't he make a set piece of money off of every person killed, and wasn't that why he was causing so much trouble, just to make his fortune that way? And then more of the men came out of the Inn and Sarah asked that they respect the needs of a woman with child and her weary bairns who needed their supper and bed."

"Ah, Sarah," he says, "I was so proud of you. If you were afraid I never saw it."

"I was not afraid," Sarah replies. "I've been at worse births. No one is going to die," she assures me.

"How long will he stay?" asks Mother.

"After the ribbing he took from the men at the Inn this night, not long, I hope. He's lost face, certainly. Laughter's the best weapon against his kind," Peter concludes.

"Except love," Sarah corrects gently.

He smiles fondly at her, beams his warmth on Annie.

"Are ye all right lass?"

Sarah has taken the knife out of Annie's hand and strapped it back on her ankle. Annie nods.

"Can she stay here with you tonight?" Peter asks Mother.

"Of course," Mother says loyally.

I take Annie up to bed in the loft. As I rub her shoulders, she says only, "I don't want to talk about it," before falling into exhausted sleep.

*   *   *   *

"Fiona."

Sean's hiss awakens me. What in the world is he doing here, in the loft, kneeling between my sister and me?

He holds his finger to his lips. Leads me down the ladder, outside to the cold night air.

"Sean, what are you doing here?"

"Do you know about the Witch-finder?" he whispers.

"Aye. Thanks for coming to tell me. I know. Brrr—let me go back to sleep!"

"What were you doing with your arm around her—your hand was on her breast!" he accuses.

"What?"

"Don't you know that—repudiate her!"

"What?" I demand sharply.

"The Witch-finder was—talking to my father about that—about Annie—tonight. He wants permission to try her."

"What did he say!"

"Father said there were no Witches in his district and he'd know if there were. He said he has no problems with crops or cattle, murrain or blight. He said the girl can't help her blood."

I sway with relief.

"Still," he cautions, "still, it's a danger. For how close it was—I come here and find you curled up with her—as if—" he stops, unable to voice the accusation. "It's not natural. People talk."

"What do they say?" I ask coldly.

"They say—" he shrugs, trying to mask his fear and disgust, "—they say it's not natural."

"Last I heard, friendship was a natural thing," I respond, icier than the bitter autumn air. I turn on my heel. "I'm freezing out here. I'm going back to bed."

He grabs my arm. "Fiona, be careful. I love you."

I relent. "I love you too. And I'm cold. Good night."

The next morning I go over to Mairead's with Annie. Knowing she is in danger I am determined not to leave her side. She has told me she would rather go alone, but I know that for the lie that it is.

The minute Mairead lays eyes on her, she begins screaming about the danger Annie has put her in, how she wishes that Annie had never been born. What an unnatural child she has been, more like an animal than a child.

"I won't burn because of you!" Mairead shrieks at her.

At that moment I feel a dark presence outside the house. Without thinking, my hand flashes up, claps over Mairead's mouth.

Annie turns and walks towards the door. She waits for the knock to open it. "Ah, good day."

The man who bows is so dark-complected I wonder if he has

not some of the same blood he feels so free to malign. He is small, twisted, though whether from joint fever or some birth injury I am not sure. His arms and legs are spindly, and one shoulder is a bit higher than the other. Small and slight, the sort of weak un- wholesome being folks generally regard as a changeling, though no one who knows the Fay could mistake him for one of theirs.

"Ah, good day mistress—" he raises his eyebrows, waiting for Annie to supply the name.

"Douglas," she says softly.

"Douglas?" His expression is an exaggeration of puzzlement. "Not a gypsy name that I know of."

"It's my name," Mairead says. "And I'm not a gypsy."

"Ah, but your daughter—"

"My daughter was a mistake. One I have already paid dearly for."

"Ah, I see," the Witch-hunter is wide-eyed. "Perhaps there were—strange circumstances surrounding her birth or concep- tion?"

"No," says Mairead. "Nothing strange. Only a mistake. I would ask you in," she lies, "but the truth is I am ill—" and here she coughs, "—I've a violent catarrh. Many have died of it."

"Oh," he nods sympathetically. "And so is this girl here," he nods at me, "a healer who has come to help you?"

"Her?" says Mairead, snorting contemptuously, "She never helped anyone in her life." She begins coughing again and goes into such a spasm that I begin to think fear has made the attack real, though I know that she was not ill, but only drunk a few minutes before.

"I'm a friend," I say.

"A friend?"

"Aye. Annie and I grew up together. We are friends. Have you never had a friend?"

"Ah, well," he says, smiling a secret smile, "there are some in Glen Lochlan who think your friendship is—unusual."

"There are some who think anything when they drink enough," retorts Annie. "If you spend your time talking to drunks at the Inn, I wonder not that they tell you some strange and curious things."

The Witch-hunter smiles at Annie. The silver cross on his

chest sparkles against the black of his clothes.

"Friends—ah yes, it's good to have—friends." His look chills me, as if some malevolent alien being stood there mocking us, a nightmare in human frame. Christians believe in devils and demons, I remember Gran saying, *"more than they believe in God."* Terror in the pit of my stomach. Perhaps there are devils and demons, and perhaps this is one of them. Surely no human ever bore such empty eyes.

"Well," he says, "I have much ground to cover. I think I will not tarry here long. The hospitality here has not been—all that I could wish it to be. But I'll be back."

He looks at us again, nodding. "Friends—" he muses.

He clucks to his jennet mule, takes its bridle and walks down towards the center path of the village toward the main road.

Is it a trap? Have we escaped?

After he has gone from our sight, Annie turns back to the bed. Mairead is gasping, retching and coughing, the beginning of a death rattle in her throat.

"He's gone now," Annie says. "You can stop dying."

Mairead sits up right away. "Get me another drink!" she croaks. For once Annie doesn't argue, pours some into the cup at her own waist and hands the rest to her mother.

"It's mine!" her mother shouts.

"Today you are sharing with me."

"Long life," Annie toasts, "and any death but fire."

She offers the cup to me—I sip from politeness, unable to stomach liquor so early in the day. She drains the rest. She pats her mother on the shoulder with more affection than I have seen her show Mairead for a very long time.

"Thank you Mairead," she says. She turns to me, "I think I'll go find Crosby. I owe him something."

The sky is blue. I feel light-headed, giddy enough to fly. As we walk, Annie weaves a crown of ferns and ivy and wheat grass for Crosby.

"I may marry him after all," she says to me. "If he'll still have me. After all our bitter words he still defended me, risked himself for me."

I follow her through the town to make sure the Witch-hunter is truly gone, and wait outside Crosby's fence until I see him embrace her and draw her in, and the door close. When I know she is safe with him, I walk home.

Chapter 40

"There they are."

We stand on the crest of the hill looking down at the bright yellow and blue and red wagons shining in the sun. We can just hear the snap of the banners in the wind. A scuffle of dark haired brats and dogs tumble yelping through the center of the encampment. They had appeared overnight like a circle of faery mushrooms, nestled between the two hills known as Anu's breasts. The bright colors of the wagons and the column of smoke from the cooking fires combine to give the little camp an air of cozy defiance against the coming cold. Tis not yet October, but anyone who can read the signs knows that this winter will be a bitter one.

Word has spread with the smell of burning grain stalks in the fields:

"The gypsies have come. They mean to spend the winter."

And there was grumbling and talk among some of the men of driving the cursed Egyptians off with torch and blade, but those who threatened such were least capable of acting on their threats, and it was said that the Laird cared not so long as they kept from town and did no thieving, so we knew that they would stay.

It has been so many years since a gypsy tribe passed near that I can scarcely remember it. Annie and I are set on getting our palms read. Of course we could have gone to Snow Flower for a reading of the leaves, or to Old Woman Wedlaw who rolled balls of bread across the table and divined from them in her strange English accent. For that matter we could have visited the scrying pool ourselves or eaten the mushrooms that opened the gates to faery. But no one can read futures like the gypsies, and our mothers forbidding us to have dealings with such dirty and dangerous scofflaws has made us all the more wild to waste no time making our way to the heart of the gypsy camp.

As we stand there, silver and courage clutched tight in our hands, some bright-eyed child spots us and a swarm of youngsters pours up the hill. Grubby hands fingering our clothes.

"Mistress, mistress, a ha'penny mistress?"

"Puppies, d'ye want to buy puppies, we have six, bonny and spotted and good hunter dogs to be sure—"

"Are ye wantin' to sell that cloak, mistress? My father'll gie ye the best for it."

Just as the urchin tide threatens to drown us entirely, the young lads arrive. Six of them, as much alike as six sleek ravens or six black cats, their names as alike as their faces to one unfamiliar with the tongue. They call the bairns off us, their gestures lordly and courteous as if they had been raised in a castle rather than in a tribe of landless wanderers.

"Here now, here now, a whole sky full of air and ye give these bonny lasses no room to breathe it."

"Aye, ye must mind yer manners about these fine ladies."

"By the five, this lass is one of our own!" says one of the lads, gesturing to Annie. He takes my arm, laughing, "We're supposed to steal *your* bairns, yer not supposed to steal ours!"

"My father left me willingly enough in my mother's womb!" Annie says tartly. Whereupon the lads all whoop and offer to leave me one just like her.

"And ye need not cross my palm with silver," purrs one, running a hand through my hair, "for that gold and copper that ye bear is currency finer than will ever pass the hand of James."

"Curse his eyes," amends one.

"And his black heart," agrees another.

Well, they've as little reason to love the king as we do, for the laws against the 'Gyptian folk have been harsh for the last fifteen years. Tis one thing to wander; tis another to be driven.

"Tis a matter of palms—and silver—which brings us here," says Annie, cool and unruffled as any queen.

One of the boys takes her hand. "Ah, yes, I see it here, plain as plain. . ."

She snatches it back. "We serve the Lady. Think not you can trifle with us or make us take guesses and dreams for the true sight. We came for the words of your oldest and wisest and have no mind to settle for less."

The eldest and most serious seeming of the group raises his palm. The gesture is slight, but power ripples from him like water over the back of the king salmon, leaving a hush in its wake. Even the smallest children grow still. He pauses, and I see that he is not so accustomed to the power as to be beyond enjoying its effect.

"Ah then," he says softly, "tis Rawnie ye want. She is my grandmother." He looks into Annie's eyes. "I too am of the Durriken clan. But I will not presume to tell your future—though I might well wish to be part of it." Had they each held the end of a spit they could have roasted a bird in the heat that passed between them. My heart kicks like a rabbit caught in a snare.

The spell passes quickly. The children race to be the first to announce our arrival, while the lads escort us at a more ceremonious pace, flirting and joking as they lead us to the old grandmother's wagon. Once there, Annie avers that she would like to see the ponies that Yarb and Beval and Verado were bragging on. Perhaps I would like to see Rawnie first? I nod, doubting it is so much her passion for horses as has caught her interest. A sigh catches me as I watch them move off, seeing strand after strand of interest weaving an invisible cord between her and the eldest lad, the one they call Verado. Ah well, so she'll sleep with him. She'll tire of him soon enough, I tell myself.

A kind-looking woman of middling age beckons me inside the wagon. Gold-broidered cloth covers the walls. Strong smelling herbs hang from the ceiling, so low that they catch in my hair. She sits me down on a leather hassock and gives me some tea. She crushes some herbs in a mortar and pestle and puts them to burn in a white scallop shell, then lights some candles. Perhaps there is something dizzying in the tea she gave me, or maybe it is but the closeness of the air, but I realize suddenly that an old woman is seated at a small table in the corner surveying me through the incense with beady eyes. She inclines her head slightly; I rise and move towards her, wondering what kind of tea it was that would leave my mouth so dry.

"I thought ye wore a neckpiece of white and yellow feathers when ye came in. But you are not one to keep a bird in a snare, are ye lass?" she says this more as a certainty than as a question. White and yellow. She must mean something about Annie. "Have ye come for a charm then, to hold a wandering lover?"

"No, Rawnie," I reply, knowing that Rawnie is simply the Gypsy word for Great Lady, and means she is a wise-one.

"Why then," she says, fumbling with a sack of herbs, "tis a medicine for melancholy you'll be needing."

"No my Lady. I'm here to have my fortune told." I hold my palm out to her with the three overlapping pieces of silver on it like the three phases of the moon. "I'm told you're very good," I wheedle.

She holds out her palm then, stubby gray fingers with joints so gnarled no ring could ever pass over them. I pass the coins over her hand three times and place them in her palm. They vanish as if dropped into a cloudy pool. She takes my palm, squinting at it through eyelids so swollen I wonder if she can truly make out the patterns of lines. Sharp intake of breath; she closes my fingers over my palm, pressing my hand between her two hands as if she could make it disappear.

She puts my hand in my lap and turns her head away.

"I cannot read ye." She looks at the floor. "I'm getting old," she says. She tries to give me back my money. Tis terrible bad luck for a gypsy to refuse your silver, I'll not take it back.

"Well then, I have some herbs for ye, cinquefoil and rosebuds and mugwort, a sovereign remedy for nightmare—"

"Grandmother, what did you see?"

She shakes her head. "I am getting—old. My eyes are not

what they were, Chavi."

She turns to the other woman. "Narrila, have ye not some bright buckles for this girl's shoes?" I know she's lying but I can do nothing about it.

"Good day, Grandmother!" I leave the wagon quickly, feeling cross and frightened.

Her wispy voice floats behind me. "Ja develesa, Chavi."

Outside the sun is high, the breeze pulls the stale smell of the wagon out of my hair. A boy of seven or eight tries to sell me an amethyst which he asserts belonged to a powerful ababina, a word I take to mean sorceress. I hold it up to the light, knowing little of stones but suspecting that it is glass. It is pretty though, and I think of buying it for Annie, but I cannot haggle him down in price to the few coppers I have remaining. Some smaller dark-eyed girls approach me with a black and white kitten. They all remind me of Annie, especially the one with the sassy tilt to her chin who likes to show off. The old woman's words are still in my mind. I ask the child what Ja develesa means. She purses her lips together and studies a fast moving cloud, trying to look as if she need not struggle to make the translation. She turns to me with a self-satisfied smile.

"It means, 'Go with God,' mistress."

We tease the kitten with yarn. I remember Annie and I playing with her cat's kittens, but the pleasant memory is followed by a harsher one; Annie, weeping over the bodies of the kittens and their mother Tawney, all drowned by Mairead.

Annie returns flanked with her retinue of lads. As they approach I am struck by how she walks the same as they do, head high, that free easy swing of the shoulders. It's not just her coloring that makes her stand out in the village, it's the way she moves. . .

I wish I could be as cool as Annie. The boys' attention turns me shy. But I have not long to suffer. Annie emerges from the wagon after a very brief time with only a curt farewell for the boys she had found so charming only minutes before.

We climb the hill in silence until we reach the crest.

"What did she say to you?" I ask.

Annie laughs and shrugs. "Oh, the usual. I'll meet a tall dark man and travel and such. Of course—" she casts a sidelong glance back at the encampment, "—there might be a bit of truth about the dark and comely lad. What did she say to you?"

I shrug, "Oh, the ususal."

She laughs sardonically. "The lads probably pay her to tell the lasses of their charms."

We walk in silence until we are well into the woods.

"Shall we gather berries on the way back?"

"Aye, why not. Mushrooms as well if they'll show themselves," I agree.

As we move through the forest gathering fruit and fungi in our aprons I steal glances at her, realizing with a rising sense of panic that I don't know what she is thinking. Why did we lie to each other? Has the old woman cast some enchantment on us? I blurt my question before I think it: "D'ye think your father is there?"

Her lips tighten into a white angry line.

"The bitch won't tell me. I slapped her and broke her chair but she won't even tell me his name!"

"Annie! Your mother gave you life, you mustn't—"

She turns on me violently. "My mother gave me no life worth living! I'll priestess my own conscience, Kyairthwen, be sure of that! I owe her nothing!" She turns from me, blinking hard, breath shaking.

"But for you I'd be outcast in this village. Only because your family takes me in do I have a place, and if they treat me as one of their own tis for your sake and not mine." She hushes my protests with a vehement gesture.

"Oh, Elana loves me well enough, but—" she breaks off, face working to keep back the glittering tears, "—even Mina and Gran, even the coven—d'ye think I know not that my place there is only by your sufferance?"

She turns and runs through the bushes then, while I stand mute and motionless, too stunned that she should run from me to follow.

Chapter 41

I stand on the cliff, looking out over the sea and the promontory of land that cradles it. Jagged crescents of silver sweep in lightning patterns over the bent grass and draggled blossoms, moving in great scouring arcs over the darker gray of the sea. Clothed in gray, I blend with the storm. Water streams from my saturated hood down my face. The deer-fur lining of my brogans have matted into mossy beds for the small ponds squishing between my toes.

My clothes are heavy, but inside I feel as wild and free as the whipping rain. The rain keeps the villagers close to their hearths, curious eyes bent to whittling and sewing. No birds fly in this weather, but I soar, running down hills and tors, flapping my cloak, screaming the shrill imprecations of hawks.

Such lightness makes me think I shall soon be ready to learn floating, that drifting on a cushion of air my Gran does so effortlessly. I remember her comforting me after my first vain attempts: "You were born in the hour of the fish, not the hour of the bird. The hour in which you are born is the gift you begin

with. As a Priestess progresses around the Wheel from Maiden
to Mother to Crone, so she must learn to shape-shift into the
forms that are harder for her. If you stay too long doing only
what is easy for you, you will remain out of balance."

"That is why we are born then—to learn balance?" I asked.

"Aye. When you are off center, look for the learning in it.
And do not expect the balance to come all at once, nor to stay
when it has come. It is the nature of balance to be fleeting. If you
spend an entire lifetime, or several lifetimes, deeply learning but
one point on the wheel—it is well enough."

The sea cliff stretching into Loch Inbhir blurs, then changes
into a different promontory many leagues and centuries distant
from here. A huge black back cleaves the water beyond the head-
land; smaller flukes tip beside it; a mother whale playing with
her child. Water crafts smaller than the whales knife through
the water, their sails billowing black, or gull white, or stained
with the color of dusk.

I come here often to see visions of another place, one that
opened to me when I was a child. The fear I felt with that first
unbidden vision has changed to pleasure in my ability to make
my seeing 'go soft' at will. Rain or mist provides the blur, the odd
focus of the scrying glass that opens me out of one world and into
another.

"You have a great art for this journeying," Gran said, studying me with narrowed eyes after I described the details of an old
temple to her. "Only, be-a-ware—" her eyes flicked shut as the
trance voice rumbled in her throat. "—be aware—that your
greatest weakness and your greatest power—grow from one
stalk—and the seeds—of—your—destruc—" the timbre of her
voice grew lower, then snapped off abruptly. She shook her head,
eyeing me with frank irritation. "The seeds—what *did* you do
with the milkweed seeds I asked you to gather for me?"

There will be no gathering today. I toss my head, exulting in
the pelting rain. Today is a day for scattering. I move through
the darkening evening towards the manor.

It is dark by the time I enter the kitchen. One of the scullery
maids nods toward the stairs.

"He's waiting for you."

Normally I pad up the curving stair to Sean's bedroom as

soundless as a cat. Tonight I squish and slop up the stairs as if the very spirit of the frog folk had broached the castle with me.

The door opens immediately to my knock.

Sean gapes at me. "Holy Mother of God, you're half-drowned!"

I strip off the cloak and scarves, setting them on the grill before the hearth to dry. Unlace the draggled shoes, drape my over-dress on a chair beside the fire. The fire gleams from the knobs of the brass screen, reflecting from the ornate bed warmer and fire tongs beside the hearth. All the while I have been arranging my clothes to dry I have been feeling his eyes slide over me, feeling his wanting to touch the places where my dampened petticoats cling to my hips and breasts. I sit back in a chair, cross my ankles and stretch lazily before finally meeting his gaze. He's leaning up against one of the posts of the bed, clad only in his tights and a white linen shirt. The tightness in his breathing tells me he's aroused. He begins unbuttoning his shirt, the candle-light flickering in his eyes.

"How do you feel about a kelpie* in your bed tonight?" I'm shaking the rain from my hair, drops flying off and popping in the fire.

He comes closer, leans back against the mattress.

"You look more like a mermaid to me." He goes to the book-shelf and takes out a book of poems. Kneels beside me and begins to read. The book is illustrated with detailed engravings; I am so taken with the pictures of the merry-maid that I scarcely hear the first few stanzas.

"That Tiamat, who with her tail doth turn—"

"What? Say that name again."

"Tiamat."

"Tis an old Goddess name, is it not?"

"Nay, tis the name of the mermaid."

He shakes his head impatiently and continues reading. I hush, but my thoughts race, listening to the poem with one part of my mind, thinking of Tiamat, the cruel and beautiful sea Goddess transformed to the capricious merry-maid. . .

The ship is sunk, the sailor who loved Tiamat is drowned. Languid and heartless, she sits on jagged rocks, alone with her mirror, combing her seaweed hair. I close my eyes, keeping for a

---

*Kelpie—Celtic term for a sea or loch monster such as the one reputed to lie in Loch Ness

moment the smell of the surf, the images made vivid by my lover's voice, I hear him lay the book down on the table behind us. Still kneeling, he kisses my breasts through the thin chemise, pulls my face down to his.

"Sweet mermaid," he murmurs, hand tightening around my waist. He picks me up, carries me to the bed. He rips my blouse taking it off. I cry out in protest, thinking of the tedious hours of sewing to repair it.

"I'll get you another, I'll get you another!" he whispers.

Unable to wait until we are naked, he wrenches my skirts about my waist, pulls his breeks to his knees. As always, his wildness rouses mine. Once inside me he comes quickly, but his silent spasms cause me to crest and break as well.

He lies beside me, hand between my breasts. Our hearts pound so hard the bed seems to shudder with that rhythm. Before our hearts can slow he is hard again, pressing his stiffness against my thigh.

"Aye, again," he murmurs, rolling back on top of me. He gasps, then sets his teeth, thrusting in silence. When the feeling begins bursting in me I care not if the whole household wakes. He pushes his hand against my mouth to stifle my cries. The fleshy part of his palm between my teeth is irresistable; I bite down, taking a sharp pleasure in his muffled cry of pain. Then I am lost to everything but the swirl of rainbow spinning me upside down, heartside out.

He rolls off me gasping, examines his wounded palm.

"Christ, Fiona, thou art a very wildcat! I thought thou wast a mermaid!"

I sigh and stretch complacently.

"I told you I was a kelpie."

"Aye, a monster in a beauteous form." He rolls over, kisses me and sighs. "I'll take the beast with the beauty."

"You have no choice," I say smugly, pulling the sheets up to my chin.

"Tis true. I'm not in my right mind since I started laying with you." He flops on his back, arms akimbo. "Ah, I pray to God I may never be in my right mind again."

I snort, "Small chance o' that."

"Get me that book and I'll read you another poem."

I fetch it, sliding back beside him, reveling in the texture of the sheets against my skin. Such fine material, and the washer-women keep it so clean. I rub the top sheet between my fingers as he reads to me, watching his profile against the hearth. Large bent nose, chin narrow, slightly receding with a small cleft in it. Long bony fingers—there's such a delicacy in him, so different from the Laird. They say his mother looked uncannily like mine, blonde and slender, so slender she did not recover from his birth-ing but died within a few months of it. I can see why the village whispers that we are brother and sister; he could easily be one of my mother's brood. . .

He is finishing an English love poem about a nosegay of flow-ers:

"The rose is all a-crimson
And the violet so small,
But the lily of the valley is the fairest of them all."

I have learned quite a bit of English from hearing him use it, and some French. The Latin still escapes me, so he always trans-lates for me when he reads that. It seems a pity that there are no books in our own tongue, but Sean says that the King himself speaks only English and French and says that Gaelic is a fay language that must die out with the faeries that taught it to us. I think the Scots' language and the Scots' heather are fairer than all the English words and English lilies in the world, but I do not say so. Instead I ask Sean to read me the poem about the heart of the rose in the book of erotic poetry he has that is in Lat-in. I like that poem. It says just how I feel when we make love, the luxuriousness of all my petals spreading open, blushing crimson. All the honey and powdered gold at my center open for the tak-ing.

Sean reads a couple more poems and then blows out the candles by the bed. The ones on the wall over the hearth are gut-tering blue. We let them die of their own accord. We cuddle down in the sheets, listening to the pop of the fire and the battering sheets of rain against glass and stone.

Most of the spring and summer we bed each other out of doors, but when the rains of fall settle in Sean smuggles me into the castle. The Laird has not actually forbid it, but Sean fears angering him and thus the charade of my sneaking in and out through the kitchen continues.

Sean puts his hand over my heart.

"I hate to send you back out in that."

"T'would be most ungrateful," I agree. The mattress has nestled into all my hollows like a warm, comforting cloud. I'm sinking into sleep. Sean is going to try to persuade me to leave, but I'm not going anywhere tonight. I turn my back on him.

"Fiona—I'll never get to sleep with you here."

"Mmmm. . ." I pull my sleepiness around me like a blanket, ignoring his urgent whispers.

"Fiona! Fiona!"

I smile, settling deeper, thinking, "Go to sleep Sean, tis a use-less endeavor."

Just before I drift off altogether I hear him whisper with res-ignation, "Mother of God."

*   *   *   *

Sean makes sure I've crept from his bed well before dawn. I do not argue, for the rain has stopped, and the clouds are playing a game of touched-ye-first with the sun.

As I pass the smithy, Ewan is washing his hands and arms outside in the horse trough. I wonder why he bothers. The soot of the forge is so ingrained in him he will never lose it. Tis a pity—save for his blackness and his bad teeth, he would be a handsome man with those blue eyes. He wipes his arm across his forehead. A trickle of soot glides down his cheek. He gives me a shy smile, able to meet my eyes only briefly.

"Yer up early."

I nod. He shifts uncomfortably in the short silence.

"Ah. Nice, but cold?" he says awkwardly.

"Aye."

He nods his head towards the forge.

"Come and warm a bit?"

Once he is busy at the forge, we both relax. His workmanship has all the assurance his conversation lacks. The smells of iron and leather and smoke are comforting. I look around. The walls of the smithy are smoke-stained, all dark but for the forge glowing like the spark of life at the dark center of a womb. At the Inn I sometimes feel uneasy when the men have drunk too much and the conversation turns lewd. But I always feel safe at the forge, even when there are knots of men gathered here drinking their home-brewed ale. For even when the talk gets rowdy there is something in the quietness of the Smith that keeps it in bounds. Something peaceful in the strength that bends the iron to use.

The firelight catches the wet sheen of his bulging arms as he strains to shape his wish into form. He's working on a piece unfamiliar to me, a decoration of some sort with three leaves coming off it.

"What's that bit?"

"For the Laird's carriage."

"For the Laird's carriage?"

"Aye. He's havin' a carriage—all made right in these parts, mostly in his own shire. Aye, he says his own workmen are as fine as any in Inverness, nay, as good as any in Edinburgh. He's a good man. He takes care of his own."

As long as they take care not to offend him, I think grimly.

"Well, I'm sure tis true, Ewan. I'm sure you're as good as the best of them. Everyone says so." I step back from the fire. "Thank you. I'll be heading back."

"They say the manor will be having a new mistress."

There's an odd tone to his voice, but I can see nothing in his expression but concentration on his work.

"Who says?"

"Well, why the carriage then? The way the Laird likes being astride a horse? Who is he getting a carriage for?"

I shrug. "Perhaps tis just another thing to own."

Despite my care to appear uninterested, I am troubled by his words. Suppose the Laird marries again? How fares my mother then? How fare we all?

*   *   *   *

I thought surely if the Laird planned to wed, Sean would let me know.

A fortnight passed and he said nothing. But when I mentioned that Elspet Turner and Sean McInnes were to wed, an uneasiness passed over him. I waited until we were through pleasuring ourselves that night to ask.

"Is your father thinkin' to marry again?"

Sean looks startled. "Why d'ye ask?"

"Ewan Smith said he was making a carriage for the Laird. Something so fancy-like he said 'twas sure the Shire would be having a new mistress—"

"The man talks too—are you lovers with him?" he asks sharply.

"D'ye see the hand-prints?" I tease.

"Ah—" Sean laughs with relief. "Of course not. Well—I meant to tell you anyway. Tis not father who'll be wed."

It takes a moment for what he means to sink in. Even then I do not believe it and stare at him blankly. He turns his eyes away.

"Father's made me a match with a girl from the Lothians. She's lots of money, and her father's in favor with the King. Tis a big family so they don't mind packing a daughter off to the wild hinterlands. Not much dowery since they have four more girls to be free of, but the connections—"

"To a lass you've not even met?"

"Tis the way it's usually done."

"Suppose you don't like her?"

He shrugs and turns back to me. "Suppose I don't. You're the one I love, Fiona. It doesn't matter about the wife. It's just another duty." He sighs and crushes me fiercely to him. "As long as I have you as my pleasure, I can do my duty."

Chapter 42

Coming over the crest of the hill, it is the dogs I hear first. Then the bells, tied on horse's bridles, tinkling from the eves of the little crofts on wheels. Coming closer, I see the dogs are fighting over scraps; Jack Green found his largest hog dead this morning. The gypsies bought it from him cheaply, seeing as how the beast must have been ill, and the flesh perhaps not good to eat, saying they would feed it to their dogs. But if my nose is not mistaken, the larger part of that pig is now simmering in the stewpots of several cooking fires about the camp.

At the cooking fire outside of Verado's wagon, the smell is not of pork, but of lamb, and I find myself wondering about the sheep that Winter complained of being absent from his flock a few days past. A woman with several teeth missing smiles at me and offers me a cup of the dried bean and mutton stew. I take it gratefully. My feet, wrapped in brogans and layers of wool, feel half frozen and the wind is blowing bits of sleet right through my tartan and down to my skin.

A number of people in the camp have noticed my presence.

The women ignore me, the men occasionally turn to watch. While I have no real sense of being welcome, my presence is no longer a novelty.

"Is Annie here?" I ask the woman by the fire. One of Verado's aunts, I think, though the family connections in this tribe are seldom clear to me.

"Annie? Ah—Chanda. Chanda-Mala." She makes a rude sign with two of her fingers. "Better bring a broom." She smiles, wrinkles fanning from her eyes over most of her face. Their custom of jumping the broom to signify a hand-fasting, or year-marriage, as it is sometimes called, must be the same as ours.

Verado is the eldest son of Rawnie's eldest son, and therefore a person of some importance. He already has his own wagon, which he shares with his younger brothers, Beval and Monda. Beval leaves off currying a black horse when he sees me, and the way he moves towards me is somehow much like a young stallion would move, the power and the grace.

"Greetings, Copper," he says in his own language, running his hands through my hair as if I were his sister and he had every right to touch me so intimately. His hand is as warm as if he had been tending a fire, and in truth, his familiarity has not offended me.

"I came to get Annie," I say, as if it were a question.

"Ah," he nods towards the wagon. "You might be waiting a while. I'm glad Derlina has given ye to sup. Thank you Derlina." He bows respectfully towards her.

He puts both arms around me. At fourteen, he is a head shorter and two years younger than I, but lacks no confidence for that.

"If ye like, I'll take ye somewhere and warm you, as Verado is warming Chanda."

I shake my head, ignoring the hollow ache between my thighs that responds to his offer.

"Not until we jump the broom first? Derlina, might we borrow your broom? Sweet Copper is shy."

"You'd never treat a gypsy girl like that," I say to him.

"If I treated one of ours like that her father'd cut my throat," Beval admits candidly. "Chanda says ye have no father. Yer white as something found under a rock," he continues, "but I hold it not against ye. In yer own way yer quite comely."

I pull away and knock at the wagon door.

"Annie!"

She opens the door, tying strings of her bodice, cheeks ruddy, eyes bright. She looks at me, or through me.

"My name is Chanda," she says haughtily. "Why are you here?"

I look at the ground. "Your mother's causing a disturbance at the Inn. You have not been home for four days," I take a deep breath, "and she's saying you've been kidnapped and trying to rouse the men to come and fetch you and drive the gypsies off. I thought you might want to know."

I turn and walk quickly away, hoping that I can be over the hill before the tears spill out of my eyes.

But I'm not so much as a quarter up the hill before her hand is around my waist. I pull from her and run. Just over the crest, in view of the stones, she catches my arm. I hope she will think the tears running down my face are from the sharp sting of the wind, but a treacherous sob betrays me.

"I'm sorry I was rude to you," she says, "I'm glad you came to tell me. There, don't be hurt," she pulls me towards her. I stand stiffly as her hands massage my back, the muscles knotted tight over my heart. "There now, are you going to sulk?" she asks. "All the time you've spent chasing after Sean and you begrudge me Verado?" Her face close to mine, coaxing. "Will you help me get my drunken mother home to bed?"

I nod, breathing shallowly so the tears will not come again. She links her arm through mine.

"Perhaps I'd best stay home a night or two. After Mairead falls asleep maybe we can be together in the barn. Tis coming on to my moon time anyway."

As the winter wore on, Annie came to our croft less and less, sleeping with me only at her fertile time and during her blood when Verado would have nothing to do with her.

I spent more time with Sean. He taught me to play chess that winter, and again and again I cheerfully surrendered my queen. I learned to quote a few of Sean's favorite poems in English, and even learned to have a bit of halting conversation in the

Sasanach tongue, but trying to make sense out of the letters on a page made my eyes and head sore. Lessons or games, the end was the same, and I would be able to forget about Annie for a few hours.

Whiskey, wine or ale; rich food, poetry and kisses; any and all could deaden the ache and make it fade. Whiskey worked the best. With Sean's money, I became a regular patron of the Bluebell. The mixture of heart's ease and mistletoe and all of Mina's herbs for complaints of the heart did nothing to ease my spirit's sense of having been torn in two. How long can a light live unmated, unsheltered by its companion of shadow? I knew the whiskey was no healer, but it seemed a friend. My only thought was to dim my light enough to survive until spring, when the gypsies would leave and Annie would return to me at last.

Chapter 43

Annie and I sit in the loft of the barn that had been her grandfather's, that the Laird now claims. Below us, the sheep stir and shift; their huddled warmth rises up to the loft, making it a cozy place to bed, even in winter-deep, as it is now.

We sit embroidering. She is working on a fancy amulet for Verado. I am making some new charm packets for my brothers and sisters, stuffed with garlic and vervain and other herbs that will help keep them healthy throughout the winter. It is well to make them every two moons so their potency will not wear thin.

Tallow candles placed on the cross beams of the barn cast their flickering light over us. The light from the flames dances and sparkles from the bracelet around my wrist; the red from my hair that catches the light, the black of hers that holds the shadow. We wove and exchanged them at the time of our initiation; one strand of her hair, one strand of mine; one strand of the two, mingled. Talismans of our love, our oneness, our commitment to the Lady. After weaving them we went out, standing under the maiden moon, seeing the horns of the Priestess etched on each

other's brows in sigils of blue light. Spontaneously, the song coming from us:

"Lady, lay me down
Rock me in your crescent arms,
Lady, lay me down
Rock me in your crescent arms. . ."

The bracelet on my wrist gleams not only with the light from
the candles, but from its own light, the light of all the times we
have lain cradled in each other's arms. All the fire that has been
between us, and all of the deeps and the darkness, the journeying
to the core of the earth, the mingling of the starless place.

I have not dared to ask Annie what she had done with her
bracelet. It has been missing from her arm since she began going
to the gypsy camp.

The light moving from the braided charm on my wrist catches her eye also.

"Burn that," she says.

I cup a protective hand around it. "No."

"Tis too Witchly a thing. I burned mine."

"If this burns I'll burn with it."

"Obstinate as a mule," she snaps, "and as foolish. And you'd
have me feel guilty for not being as stubborn and foolish as you."
She puts her sewing down. "I'm too tired to sew anymore. I'm going to sleep."

She makes a pillow out of the sack of cloth we have brought
up, takes off her overclothes, leaving her chemise on. Always
ready to leave off sewing, I pack my work away. I take off all my
clothes; I will not be cold lying next to Annie.

I crawl under the woolen blankets. Put my hands on her
shoulders, rubbing until the stiffness in her back eases. She
purrs and murmurs. When her back is soft, I reach a hand
around to her breast, nuzzle my lips against her ear, gently biting the sensitive place between her shoulder and her neck.

She takes a shaky breath, then pushes my hand away firmly.
"We're too old for that now."

Too old? I never thought we would be too old to touch, to kiss.
I had envisioned us, old as Gran and Mina, withered as Rose,

sharing a cottage, sitting on one bench beside the same hearth.

She hmmphs and shrugs and yawns, snuggles up to her pillow and breathes evenly, feigning sleep. Hesitantly I rest my
hand on her waist. She takes it, squeezes it, snuggles up spoon-
wise with me. Long after she has truly gone to sleep, I lie awake,
feeling the warmth of her body through her clothes, aching to
move and cry out with her, not daring to ask again. Thinking it
must be a fancy of hers, moody during her blood and all. Verado
will not sleep with her during her blood. Against gypsy law. At
first she sulked about the gypsy taboos against women's blood,
laughed at their fear of owls, scorned their jealousies and ready
quarrels. But now she says they have reasons for all, reasons no
one outside the tribe would understand. It has been a long time
since she has mocked or complained of their customs.

I convince myself at last that this is a fancy that will pass,
that soon she will want to make love with me again.

*   *   *   *

But she does not change her mind. Most of the time when
she is with me, she is not truly here. I begin to feel that while
her body returns from the gypsy camp, her heart no longer returns with it. She no longer wishes to journey through the starless place with me. And she, who has never been sick enough to
miss a coven meeting in three years, is now absent more than she
is present.

One time only, in late January, she is braiding my hair for
me, and as she brushes, I feel her mouth, hot along my shoulder,
my neck. Her breasts pressing against my back.

"Kiss me," she says, and it is the wildness again, the dark
wild fire, pleasure so fierce and desperate it hurts. Howling wind
driving the dark fire before it; thought and sense swirling away.
Shrieking wind battering the barn. The sheep, frightened, wailing like infants below us. I fear she'll change her mind at the
last; but the storm drives her also. She buries her face between
my legs, the Cailleach* who destroys through ecstatic fire.

Dark wind pummeling through the caves of my body; passion
stinging, biting my skin; sparks of ice, a hailstorm of fire.

She spreads herself over my mouth. Holding her hips, dark

---

*Cailleach—a Dark aspect of the Goddess; The Scottish Kali.

intoxicant taste of her blood flushing my mind crimson. Blood-winged butterfly, lost in the heart of her rose. Willing my tongue to butterfly narrowness, could I but penetrate the heart of her flower, spiral my tongue into her womb, into her heart, to the heart of her heart, the heart that pumps the blood of fire and shadow through her body. Could I but touch her that deeply, she would never want to stop making love with me again.

Thunder shakes the barn. Her cries, the battering power of the storm. Lightning and snow. The crest hurdles me to a trough of darkness so deep, I welcome it as death.

Gasping, she collapses on her back beside me. We clasp hands; silence, punctuated by our breathing, plaintive murmurs of the sheep below us.

"Verado never does that with me."

Hot star of jealousy piercing my belly brings its bitter tidings: I am alive.

"Has any man ever done that with you?"

"No. But I want Verado to do it." Her face darkens. "He says it's not manly. Or natural."

The pang deepens. I cannot even imagine asking Sean to touch me like that. But she kisses me and the pang eases, her smoky hair falling over me, her mouth smelling of my womanliness and I of hers we kiss and kiss. Annie, never stop touching me again, without your touch I cannot live.

*   *   *   *

But in the two months that followed, she did not make love with me again, saying that that had been fine when we were girls, and now we were women and she had her man and she wished me luck and Godspeed in finding mine. The star of jealousy twisted hot under my ribs, grew into a bruise that ached all through my bones, and I so frequently burst into tears over my work that Mother asked me if I was with child.

Chapter 44

Beginning of March; the snow is melting, the run-off sluices down the hills, thawing the fields to marsh, standing in puddles on the muddy road. Annie and I slog along, holding our sopping hems up to our kness, bare feet squishing in the cold glop sucking at our ankles. We are nearly out of the village when Tim Brede and Jim Strathan accost us.

"Gin ye hold yer skirts a bit higher we'll take ye to my barn and warm yer bones," Tim says.

We go to move around them. Jim reaches out and closes his hand around Annie's arm. His lips are drawn back over his teeth as if he were smiling, but there is nothing in his eyes that looks like a smile.

"Are the gypsy lads so much better looking then we are then?" he asks.

She regards him calmly, radiating scorn.

"I heard a droll rhyme about yer friends—" he chants with malice:

"The Romany chi
and the Romany chal
love luripen
and lutchipen
and dukkeripen
and hukipen
and every 'pen'
but latchipen
and tatchipen."*

Annie's face could be carved from stone, but I watch the air around her grow dark. She smiles at him as if she only now recognized him.

"Did we not lie together in the fresh furrowed fields before planting last year?" she asks.

A lewd grin splits his features. "Aye lass, we did—"

She pulls her wrist free from his grasp and touches her other palm to his crotch.

"It's too small," she says coldly.

Then she's walking away, with me stumbling through the mud to keep up with her, the two men hurling insults and curses; and I know that if they dared, their words would be coupled with stones.

We walk along the crest of the hill slowly, allowing breath and pulse to slow. I expect her to be angry, but she is relaxed, swinging her arms loosely. She smiles at me so warmly I know her calm is no facade. I hand back the package I had taken from her when Jim grabbed her arm. She had just picked it up from the Smith. I long to know its contents, but Annie has taken to snapping at me when I ask too many questions, so I remain silent. My curiosity is plain enough, however.

She strokes the burlap wrapping as if it were satin.

"It's a present for Verado. Tack for his horses." She looks so happy and flushed, my black rose. At this moment I do not begrudge her Verado, or anything else that could make her look so content. She breathes the air appreciatively; the salt from the sea, the new budding smell of the trees.

"It's going to be a beautiful spring," she murmurs. The yellow broidered flowers on her bodice dance with the rise and fall of

---

*"The Gypsy woman, and the Gypsy man, love stealing, and fucking, and fortune-telling, and lying, and every 'doing', but shame, and truth".

her breath. The sun is clearing a larger and larger hole in the sky, bursting from its swaddling of clouds like a child newly walking that thinks he's a man. It gives me the courage to reach out and take her hand. She smiles and I feel both dizzy as wind and clear as flame. For awhile it seems like old times, walking the ridge with our hands interlaced, the wind blowing our hair together like the marriage of midnight and morning.

We have not yet come to the roll-right stones when Annie stops and turns to face me. She has long since made it clear that the gypsy camp is her preserve and that I am not welcome to accompany her there. But when she takes her hand from mine I feel as cold as if my skin had gone with it.

"Could I not come with you today? Perhaps I'll find a lad there to—ease my sorrow," I finish ruefully.

She shakes her head. "You do not belong there—any more than I belong in Glen Lochlan."

I bow my head, pressing my lips together. Her touch on my arm.

"Kyairthwen. . ."

I look at her, face so close to mine, the invisible chasm between us so deep that if I cast my heart into it I would never hear it hit bottom.

"Try to understand," she says into my eyes, "I've found my people. After so long a time—I've found my people."

Am I not your people Nimué, are you not one of the Nine? More sister than any I have. We've eaten together, slept together, quarrelled together, loved together, done magic together, and everything together. Am I not your people?

Distant and veiled though her thoughts have grown to me, she reads me as easily as ever.

"You shared your family with me. But they were never my people." Such gentleness in her touch, her voice. She smiles into my eyes, kisses me on the forehead and walks quickly away.

I watch the thin arms of the bushes bend for her and spring quivering back. Even after I can no longer see her I continue to watch until the last shivering twig is still.

She never looked back.

Chapter 45

A week past Ostara* Mairead comes to our croft complaining that Annie's horse has been stolen. I haven't seen Annie at all in the few days since we had picked up the tack for Verado's horses. Several of the little ones have the spring fevers and I have been mopping up baby crap and vomit day and night, making teas for them and singing them to sleep and hushing them when they wake up whimpering in the night. Mairead makes a face at the stench and noise and won't come in. Can't say as I blame her. The company of that cantankerous old woman is the last thing I should wish for anyway. I go back to stirring the chicken broth and rocking two brothers and a sister at once.

I wake up before dawn the next morning. Not because a baby cried. They are all asleep, the sound of their featherlight breathing floating up to me from the room below the loft I share with Eostre and Elana. My belly is tight, heart pounding. I must be sickening up myself. I stare up at the twisting braided pattern of dried leaves and ferns pasted with mud on the wall over my sleeping place. Annie had helped me, remembering with me the

---

*Ostara—Spring Equinox

ancient temple with patterns of tulse and fern pressed into pillars and Eostre and Elana had eagerly imitated us, transforming
the loft into a bower of intertwining shell and bone and dried veg-
etation that was like a dance of spring into winter. Two moons
ago Eostre had pried off the part that undulated over her sleeping space and thrown the shells and weeds in the dung heap,
scorning it as 'baby stuff.' The unmarked layer of mud she had
replaced it with is scarcely dry. The smooth, trackless space separating my part of the pattern from Elana's fills me with terror
like the sensation of falling that sometimes comes between waking and sleep. I touch my fingers to my forehead and cheeks, surprised to find no trace of fever.

I get up to go piss outside. It's gray and cold and drizzly out.
Squatting down in the garden I have a vision of Annie asleep in
Verado's arms in a swaying wagon. I stand up; my sense of panic
is still there. Instead of going back to my bed I start over to Mairead's croft. Leaning up on my elbows on the cold stone dyke
around the pasture and fruit trees she has, I keep thinking I see
Bonny in the fog's shifting shapes; but the pony is gone. I'm wide
awake, yet the fog coating everything like snow fur makes me feel
like a sleepwalker treading through a phantom world. Too early
for anyone to be up and about; I pad unseen on soundless ghost
feet through the freshly furrowed fields. I surprise a bunch of
sheep; they hustle off, gray balls fading quickly into the fog. My
mind floats. My feet are taking me to the gypsy camp.

I start to skirt the circle of roll-right stones, change my
mind and enter. Inside there is no fog; the finely carved pillars
stand solid in their proper places, tracking the motion of sun,
moon and stars, casting spokes of shadow and light to intersect
at the altar which is the circle's hub.

I walk to the center, run my fingers lightly along the cool
polished slab. The altar stone shimmers with a faint bluish
pulse, magic that has passed through so many hands and minds
moves in it like the silent blue cords of blood flowing beneath the
translucent flesh of my wrist. How many times Annie and I
stood over this altar, miming the sacred marriage through chalice and blade. How often we wove the web of invisibility around
these stones and lay here at their heart, opening our bodies to
each other and our minds to the long stone stair that led us to

other bodies, other circles. I pause before stepping over the broken stones at the northern entrance, imagining myself passing under the lintel that is no longer there. As I step through, other temple thresholds and doorways flicker through my mind fast as a shuttle darts through a loom.

It is almost audible, that sound of a door closing behind me forever. I turn to go back; a curtain of mist solid and white as stone blocks my way.

My dew-heavy skirt clings to my legs as I struggle to the crest of the hill. The fog is so thick I cannot see the wagons. I hesitate, then stumble down the hill. Fog rising off the land like smoke, the wagons still invisible. I walk on a bit further, then stop. This is no trick of the fog. The wagons are gone. No dogs, no horses, no children, they've packed up and gone, Annie and Bonny with them. I stand, halfway down the hill, staring at the trampled muddy earth, the wheeltrack and hoof prints, the mist rising, the sky growing lighter and lighter gray. A curtain black as her hair closes over my heart.

I close my eyes, putting all my concentration into a picture of the camp still being there; smoke curling up from the campfires, men laughing around one, women cooking over the other. The horses whickering in the corral, children and barking dogs dodging around the wagons, chickens scratching the earth, the slanty-eyed goats wandering freely. I can see it all so plain, just as I had seen it last, a thin powder of snow dusting the ground.

I open my eyes. Nothing but silence and mist, the sky growing lighter but the sun hidden, as her thoughts had been hidden from me for so long.

Chapter 46

I tie another salmon bone hook on the tightly rolled strand of wool. Place my hands over it, blow on it three times: "Maiden, Mother, cunning Crone, fetch this salmon for mine own."

I bait it with a bit of pork fat, then tie a silvery leaf next to it to flutter like a small fish. I place my hands over the bait, breathe on it, imagining with every breath the sweet silver flesh of the fish the salmon likes to eat. I cast it over to the dark emerald water where the salmon I want is lurking and pull it slowly back to me. Cast again, slow flirtatious return. Again, letting the bait flutter awhile and release its scent in the current flowing fast from the falls. My arms are a little shaky from casting all afternoon, from pulling in the six trout now churning weakly in the thatch jug by the oak tree.

"Come—oh come—to the heartbeat's drum," I whisper.

With the next cast I see clearly the small silver fish leaping at the end of my line, diving into the dark pool. Sharp bite of the hook jerking under the jaw bone, line straining taut from the wooden dowel blistering my hands; I have him.

The fight is not long. He knows his death and goes to it gracefully, like the King in the fullness of his time. The last gasping heave shudders silent and the shimmer dulls on his skin. I put my hands on his body.

"Thank you for giving yourself to me. May my love guide you to the pools of the afterworld." I see him happy in a pool of peace.

"Forgive me for fooling you. My family is hungry." I know it is wrong to cast an enchantment on another, particularly on a being whose will is less strong. But my stomach cares little for the fairness of it. I share what I catch with Gran and Mina and they never say aught about it.

I hang the salmon from one end of the carrying pole, the jug of trout from the other. The burden is heavy. The pole chafes the back of my neck, my shoulders ache with the weight. I keep my eyes on my feet, breathing in rhythm with my steps.

As I near the bridge, the sound of dogs barking makes me lift my head. A large, heavy-set man kneeling to fix the wheel on his wagon stands, shading his eyes against the sun to see me. McTavish. Of all the men in the village, McTavish is the one who frightens me most. He is one of those who attends Kirk every Sunday and believes what the Priest says about women. He trembles when I come near and flatters himself that I will it to be so. I surround myself with a veil of chill air, remembering how Annie described her easy scorn; *"Just pretend you are the Queen of Ice and Darkness and none may touch you."*

Though no longer squinting into the sun, McTavish keeps his eyes shaded, gaze fixed on my chest. If he ever looked into my face, perhaps he would see what little care I have to rouse him.

"I see ye've been poaching the Laird's salmon," he says.

"This fish here? Nay, he jumped out of the water and begged me to take him home and warm him by my hearth." I see he has mutilated a nearby ash tree cutting a new lynch-pin for his axle. I start across the bridge, wishing he would get in his wagon and move on. Instead, he takes a step toward me.

"Planning to run off with the gypsies like yer friend?"

I turn sideways to slip past him. He bars my way.

"Let me pass!"

His hands circle my waist, thumbs pressing against the pulse over my navel.

"Ian McTavish." The voice of command Gran taught me is soft but strong, like the invisible undercurrent that pulls the unwary out to sea. Unwillingly, his eyes meet mine.

"Let me pass," I repeat. He releases me. When I am safely to the bend in the road, I loose the spell.

"You ought to get wed, McNair," he growls after me.

The little ones rush to greet me as I approach the croft, wild with anticipation of fish for supper. I scowl and snap at them: "Be off wi' you!" I take the fish to the midden heap to gut them. As I slice open their bellies and tear out their entrails I imagine gutting McTavish, spilling his lights into the waters of M'hira to wash clean to the sea. Angry as I am, I stay clear of working a spell with my thoughts. "You may *think* harm so long as you do not *cast* it." Gran and Mina had explained the difference to us over and over when Nimué and I were learning magic together.

I salt the salmon and hang it in the smokehouse. Elana takes one of the trout to Mina, Malcolm takes one to Gran. The others will feed the rest of us. After supper, the small ones in bed, I pull on my cloak. Mother sighs, busying herself with a hearth that needs no further tending.

I hardly need the cloak, the air so balmy it might be mid-May rather than April. Gran says we're due for another cold snap, but how she can guess that from the fine weather we've been having I know not. The pale eyelash of a new moon vanishes in the deepening sky. I knock at Mina's door.

She hugs me. "The wee trout was *wonderful*, dear. What a blessing that M'hira favors you so."

I take a mug of hot vegetable water and sit sipping it with John and Gran while Mina flutters about clearing her house for the ritual. She and Gran occasionally exchange a sentence in a language I do not know, bursting into laughter. John does not understand their talk either, but he smiles, puffing from his pipe like a contented dragon. William enters, hugs for all, puts clippings from the wool of the new lambs on the bench that serves as our altar. John lights him a pipe and then there are two dragons and two crones weaving a silent conversation of eyes over and through the talk of lambs and spring and the maiden moon. I burn my mouth on the second cup of hot broth. Equally scalding liquid scorches my eyes. I pretend it is the roughened tongue that draws my tears and not the way my heart contracts when I look at the door Nimué will not be coming through. It is a relief when at last Peter helps Rose through the door, Sarah trailing after. Sarah has just sat through two night's labor with Bessie McAwe. Her eyes are puffy but she smiles, "A fine new lad we have in Glen Lochlan, braw as his father an' bonny as his mother."

"A big broth of a boy," Peter says, "Bran's beside himself."

We cast the circle. Wind Mare asks if I would like to Priestess the purification of water or fire. I shake my head. It is hard enough simply to be here, feeling the hole where Nimué should be. We send a cone of power to bless the newborn lambs. Bear-Hearth plays the pipes, invoking the Horned God to protect them as they grow. Staghorn is excited.

"We've lost but two lambs in the lot, and all the others are as healthy as we could wish. Four sets of twins!"

"Glad I am to leave the sheep to you lad," Winter says to Staghorn, "And glad I am for such a fine spring as this to be my last."

"Nay then good Winter, say not so," admonishes Bear-Hearth.

Winter shakes his head. "Next January I shall be four score and one. That day shall be my last. He shakes his finger at Bear-Hearth, silencing him. "I have asked the stars for it." He coughs, winces. "When a man cannot breathe with ease, tis time to stop." He smiles at Violet Rose. "Are ye thinkin' of stepping off with me Rosy?"

She snorts. "I havna made up my mind."

"I've courted ye fer years auld woman—this is yer last chance to jump the broom wi' me."

"Impertinent pup!" Violet snaps, but she is unable to hide a smile of satisfaction. "Tis too late to make an honest woman of me, Will."

"Tis not too late for our Kyairthwen," Staghorn says.

"How is your heart healing since our cord-cutting with Nimué?" asks Sari.

I press my lips together and look down, suddenly so angry I would leave the house if the circle had not been cast.

We had held a circle soon after Nimué left where each of us

talked out our bad feelings about her leaving, released those feelings to the earth, and sent our blessings for her journey. Jesses had come from Ail Fionn for the rite. She and Sari held me while I sobbed, but I could not cut what frayed strands of cord still bound us, and I could not truthfully wish her well in leaving me. I finally said, "I wish ye well Nimué," but in my heart I wished her no peace until she returned to me.

All hold silent, waiting for me to speak.

"I've little enough time to think on it," I say sullenly. "With planting the garden and fishing and care of the wee ones."

"And what of the young Laird—are ye too busy to think of him as well?" creaks Violet in her rusty voice.

Sean has gone to his Wedding Feast in the Lothians, marrying a girl he has never met. "Tis a good match," he said in that cracking voice that showed him still to be a halfling lad. "Her family is far more wealthy and powerful than ours. I shall still have my own room, Fiona. An' father says—after I get a son on her I may seek her out but seldom—"

"Tis to be expected. He must do his duty," I say.

"There's a time for that," says Wind Mare.

"A year next spring would be a braw time for a wedding," BearHearth smiles playfully. "Staghorn and I shall have a mighty quarrel for father's honors."

"A wedding! And with whom? Tim Brede who has less brains than his ox? The McConnells who think a woman must be beat like a nut tree if she is to bear?"

"Ewan Smith is a good man and lonely. He thinks the sun rises and sets on ye," BearHearth says.

"As soon a lump of coal as Ewan Smith! God's death, what is this talk of marriage! Would you bind a hawk in a henhouse?" I stare accusingly at Anu.

For the first time, it is she who hoods her eyes and looks away. I glare around the circle. Only Violet can face my gaze unflinching through the cataracts webbing her eyes.

How dare they think to order my life so! We never speak so personally in circle, unless someone is ill and we are seeking to understand the cause of it.

"Fiona—ye've come to an age where a woman needs protection," Sari says gently.

I note bitterly her use of my given name rather than magical name. How often Wind Mare and Sari and Anu all said that a woman's magic is only as strong as her heart, that a Priestess must dance to her heart's own drum and no other. Would they strip me of all power?

"Tis time," Wind Mare says.

"You never wed!"

She sighs, avoiding my look. "Things were different then. I traveled when I was young. Besides, I was not so well favored as you. Tis hard for men to leave a pretty lass alone."

"When a bonny lass lives unwedded then men feel free to look—and if they look they may see more than tis well for them to see," explains Staghorn.

"Tis too plain that ye *are* the hawk in the henyard," Winter adds.

"Men tolerate the barn cat for the sake of the grain, where they'll not abide a lynx. Tis your safety we seek," says Wind Mare.

"And ours," whispers Sari.

The candles swim before me in a liquid blaze of light.

"So you would have me tamed and broken."

Wind Mare grasps my forearm. "We would have ye take more care to blend with your surroundings."

The only conversation for a time is the pop and hiss of the candles.

"Have ye made your partings with Sean?" Wind Mare asks.

"I see no reason for it."

"A jealous wife is reason and more," Anu says.

"Tis custom for a Laird to have a mistress."

"Tis custom for the wife to be jealous of it," warns Staghorn.

"Mother was as good as wife to the old Laird for years."

"Aye and it was the ruin of her," Anu says bitterly.

"And you the first to call her foolish, Kyairthwen," reminds Wind Mare.

"Sean's not like his father." I try to ignore the elders' exhange of glances. Wind Mare shakes her head.

"Kyairthwen is right. There is no fit mate for her i' the Smithy or the High Hall or in any croft in Glen Lochlan."

"Maybe the McInnes boy," suggests BearHearth.

"The McInnes lad is but twelve," says Sari.

"Ye could come with me to Ail Fionn," says BearHearth. "Jesses made a good match there."

Quick arc like a hawk, my athamé dips its point into my left palm. I stab the blade into the dirt floor, and slap my bleeding hand down beside it. "Diana defend me! I shall die a maid!"

I jerk my head up at Anu's cry of fury. Wind Mare catches her wrist to keep her ready slap from connecting with my face.

"I am not a child to be cuffed!"

Her eyes hurl black fire, but I am too far gone in my rebellion to back down now.

Sari begins breathing deeply. Instinctively we all begin breathing with her, responding to the commanding flow and ebb of the midwife's breath. I recognize the pattern of the centering breath Sari uses for that time just before a woman's womb opens completely, the time when she is most likely to let the pain make her forget what she is doing. We breathe. Ocean fills us, and recedes. In. Out. Open. Close. Sari's thoughts ride like dolphins through the crest of our breath: "*We are near the time of opening. Pain and confusion are greatest here. Soon we will open. Soon we will be ready to push something new into the world. In. Out. In. Out. Keep breathing.*"

At last our breath comes without effort, and when we open our eyes the room glows with a gold both softer and brighter than the candles can cast.

"Kyairthwen—with your permission—might we send out a call to draw a love that would be true, a love that would heal your heart?" asks Sari.

A part of me wants to remain sulky and inconsolable. But another part of me asks—why not? So I assent.

Wind Mare takes the fine velvet coverlet from her bed and lays it beneath me.

"And now—imagine that you are on a cloud, riding free above the waves—" I drift in the cloud, setting my mind free to ride with her voice. "—and the cloud calls to the spirits of the sea—and they rise to her—" Violet spumes of water spiral up from the sea and whirl about me in the air. Slowly the diaphanous plumes of water take on the graceful shapes of the water Fay. Then they are touching me, gliding a film of salt water over my lips, nose, eyelids, throat, breasts, all along the length of my body. I recognize the hand over my womb as Sari's, but the touch is so much like Nimué's, how she could put her hand there and take me back through the blood black cave into other lives, other bodies, but always my heart turning towards her as a plant turns its leaves to the sun. . .

I weep uncontrollably. The hands stroke my tears into the other salt water, and I weep harder, the hands of the water spirits, of my coven, stroking my tears all the way down to my feet, down to my fingers, out to the ends of my hair.

After the purification of salt, the water spirits dissipate and the spirits of the air swirl in their place, blowing streams of soothing breath over my body. Gradually the water dries and my body stops shaking. I am light, floating, no more than a feather cradled by the wind. Anu's voice rolls like thunder:

"Ashtara[1], who daily renews herself in fire—" Fire swirls around me, red and blue and gold, edged with violet. I whirl in it laughing, the Mistress of Disorder, Queen of Desire, dancing the dance of passion as it was danced by the Quadishu[2] in the oldest temples. As I dissolve in the dance of fire, an image comes. I see myself as a web of nerve strung from a harp of carved bone. Alone, silent, I hang in the starless place. Then a pair of strong square hands, calloused and sure, reaching for the center of my song. . .

Dissolved in a chord of music I quiver above the meadow I would be touching if I were yet flesh. Dimly I feel a brush fanning my hair about me like a flame. Dimly I hear them call Blouwedd, the Goddess made from flowers. Then I feel the flowers lightly laid on my body, becoming my body. They name them, part recipe, part incantation. . .

"Scarlet swordflower for the hair. . . fern for the green green eyes, rose petals, pink and white mixed, for the body. . . poppies for the heart and heather for courage. . . applewood for the bones, blossom and fruit, teeth and breath. . ."

I float in a bliss composed of feathers, flowers and light. Then they are sending a call to my true mate, conjuring my image to appear before him in dream, setting the flame to draw his fluttering spirit.

"Come hither: These are the hands, heart, brow, that you seek. Come hither: here are the feet, knees, thighs that you seek.

---

1. Ashtara/Ishtar/Astarte—a Goddess of passion, love, and fire. Anciently known as a creator Goddess. 2. Quadishu—ancient Priestesses who practiced sexual magic similar to Tantra.

Come hither. . ."

As they name and touch the parts of my body the flowers shine like a light set behind colored glass. And I am the bounty of the earth, and the beauty of the stars. The sea is my womb, and the moon is my mirror.

I come back to myself, flowers and music, cloud and carved bone. As I look around the circle, there is no need for thanks. My transformation is mirrored on each face. Even the yellow haws over Violet's eyes have a weird, perfect beauty.

As we pass the mulled wine, each of them utters a prediction, the sort of blessing magic done at the seining of a new child.

Wind Mare raises the chalice.

"He'll be a man with a song in his heart."

"Iron in his spine," growls Anu.

"As gentle as a ewe with a new lamb," says Winter.

"But with the rowdy passion of a Tomcat as well," winks Staghorn.

Sari takes the cup, laughing. "He'll have a merry face."

"A ready laugh," adds BearHearth.

"Older than you—and wiser," Violet quaffs and passes the chalice to me.

I raise the glass in a gesture of gratitude. "So mote it be."

"So mote it be," they echo.

The spell complete, we settle to a feast of scones, cheese, and dried fruit bread. Staghorn and BearHearth talk a little of what news has reached them—a Witch burned at Inverlochan, three more at Dornoch, a family imprisoned in Lairg—they talk hopefully of towns like ours where it has not happened.

"The web still holds," Anu affirms.

Walking home, I kneel by a thicket where the web seems particularly impenetrable. I breathe the power of the strands into myself and cast it, not as a net but as a moon-bright cord of rope. I release my end of it and bless it in its going.

"No tricks. No traps. Nimué, I love you. I wish you well. Take this cord that bound us. Remember to keep a web about yourself as you travel. Be safe. Be well."

I ground the energy and quickly stand, before I can lose my purpose and beg her to return.

Chapter 47

We should have known not to eat meat that had thawed and frozen and thawed again. But after a long winter with so little, the offer of a hind quarter of a stag from one of our neighbors proved irresistable.

Eostre and I have not eaten it, nor has Mother. We tend to the other children, who are sick with gripe in their bowels from having eaten the spoiled meat. The boys are the worst off. Malcolm is especially wretched that he will miss the minstrel who has come into town this day.

"God, what a piece of luck it was, too," Malcolm mourns, "He only came into Glen Lochlan because his horse had lost a shoe. He'll probably only be here the night. I'll have missed it."

Bluebelly, the Innkeeper, has sent his boys to our croft, and no doubt to every croft in the village, to spread the word that a famous minstrel is staying overnight at the Bluebell. I feel sorry for Malcolm and Colin and the others for missing it, but I have no intention to stay at home. Travelers of any sort are uncommon enough; a real minstrel is a rare treasure indeed.

Unseasonably cold for the end of April. I drape my green and white plaidie over my green dress, wrapping my hands and feet against the frost.

Caring for my brothers and sisters has made me late. The Inn is packed. Bluebelly must have sent one of his boys all the way to Ail Fionn; Jesse and her husband are here, and I recognize others from that village as well. A big fire stacked with peat and pine blazes in the hearth. Smell of smoke and sweat; wet earth, packed bodies, spilled alcohol.

I look longingly to the front of the room where my friends are; Peter and Sarah and Galen and his Bhari are sharing a table so covered with children they have not even room for their cups. John and William, Crosby, Jesse and her husband are squeezed together on one of the narrow benches. There are so many people standing between here and there I doubt I could even wedge my way up to them, much less sit once there.

Ewan Smith looks guiltily at me and then away. He is newly betrothed, and his intended, Jennet, seems to fancy I have intentions to steal her man from her. No chance at sitting there. Then, to my luck, Bluebelly shoves his way over to a center table where Jim Strathan and Tim Brede are drunk and raucous, grabs each of them by the arm and muscles them to the door. Gratefully I slip into one of the chairs at their table.

One of Bluebelly's boys appears at my elbow. I order whiskey, giving him one of the coins that Sean has left for me. He left me a pouch full of silver, "in case I should want for aught" while he is gone to his wedding in the Lothians. I look down, tracing a formless design on the polished wood table, wondering how things will be when he comes back with his bride. For though he has told me that nothing will change, I have taken the words of the coven to heart, for now if I continue with him it will be at the cost of betraying another woman.

The applause and laughter following the minstrel's last song is just dying away. The minstrel is tuning his lute, smiling and winking at some of the lasses calling to him to play a song of love.

Hard to say what age he is. He has a boyishness to his smile that seems quite young, scruffy dark curls alight with glints of both copper and silver; yet his confidence, both in the way he handles his lute and the way he chats with the crowd would seem to belong to a much older man. He is clean-shaven, as is the style for bards, face sunburned, laugh lines fanning out from his eyes.

"Well now, when I play, I do not like anyone to be sad," he says, "with the finest spring coming in that anyone's ever seen, and the nights soon warm enough for—" he pauses, sly smile. A ripple of laughter goes through the room. "—planting rituals," he finishes. "Surely no one has cause to grieve."

He begins playing a funny bawdy song. When I look up he is looking right at me. When he smiles irresistably and gives me a wink, I start to laugh. It *is* a funny song. Everyone in the room is laughing and singing. I see how he sings to everyone in the room; and yet he comes again and again back to me, as if it were my grief he wished to cheer. And suddenly I am not feeling lonely any more, but feeling like I have a friend, a friend whose name I do not know, but a friend nonetheless.

He sings a song about the Witchburnings in the towns to the east. The room hushes as everyone listens very intently.

"And when the old women die," he sings,
"The crops begin to fail.
And if we honor not the earth,
What rites will us avail?

And where the young women die,
The stock do cease to bear.
And if the seasons unmarked pass,
What harvest shall we share?"

He sings about how we need rain for the crops, and yet the fishermen are sometimes lost at sea during the storms. And is it the results of curses that a ship be lost or is it the nature of the weather to change, regardless of the cost?

"I am a messenger only," he sings,
"My duty to bring you the news.
And if it does not please you
Don't take it as my views.
For know that all my heart's desire

Is for thy pleasure—and the truth."

The last notes of his song fade to nothing in the room. A moth's flight would be audible in the hush that follows.

"Enough of solemn talk," he cries. "Stay seated if you can—"

He plays a fast dance song. There is no space to dance, but the people sway and rock back and forth and call out delightedly the refrain we all know. Soon we are all clapping our hands. Then he puts his lute aside, takes a little drum and a recorder forth from his pack. Using one hand to hold the recorder and tapping with the other on his drum he plays a pretty tune.

"And what about love, Minstrel?" cries one of the women, her arms about her husband. "Sing to us of love."

"I'll sing you a song of my own composition—if I may be so bold. The song came to me in a dream only a brief week past, a dream so real—this girl came to me—so fair I thought she was one of the faery kindred. She doffed off her clothes and slid into bed beside me—" he looks around the room roguishly, "—and I kissed her passionately—" he smiles, enjoying the expectant tension in the room his tale has created, "—and then I woke up— and I was kissing the nose of my own horse."

Everyone bursts into laughter, but the room soon hushes as he plays the opening notes to his song, and his voice shifts from the deep laughing songs he has sung to one strong, high and resonant, sweet at the crest of it like the gray sea alight with silver before it breaks.

"The Lady of love and the twilight kindred
Who wove the crimson sunset through her hair—
Wove she that crimson deep into my heart—"

From the first his eyes join with mine. And do not leave. As he sings I have the uncanny sense of entering his dream, being the dream, as born to hear the song as he to sing it. His hands moving on his harp, I suddenly know how they would move on my body, and I feel him reaching inside me with those hands, plucking melodies, my body turning into flowers, soft and open, his hands golden with the pollen. And his eyes. Such serious eyes in that roguish face.

"It is the Lady of the West that I love the best
None in the land of Faery do so fair.
For the look in her eyes of the sea I would die
And her bonny sunset hair."

The song ends and he is still looking at me, lips parted
around the last word, air between us charged like the air before a
storm.

Chairs scraping, heads turning to stare, looks of envy, admiration, lust. I blush hot to my ears and the roots of my hair and
look down, damning the minstrel for having focussed the attention on me so, cursing myself for not having put up my hair like
any respectable woman would have. Annie is always so cool in
these circumstances, snowflakes would not melt in her mouth.
But she's not here. If she had been sitting beside me I could have
looked right back at those people and pretended I did not care
what they thought. But now, without her cool confidence to
shield me, the angry, jealous glances scald.

Quickly the minstrel is chatting with the crowd, laughing,
asking the people to clap along, playing another bawdy song about
the Blacksmith and his reluctant leman and the shape-shifts
they go through until at last:

"She changed to a sheet
A-laying on the bed
And he changed to the coverlet
And gained her maidenhead."

Gradually the whiskey eases the deep pang of missing Annie.
Better to look up and blush than to look down at my glass and
cry. By the end of the song about the Smith I am also clapping
my hands and laughing, relieved that all the attention is back on
the minstrel and no one is paying me any heed.

He tunes his lute, looks around the room innocently.

"I hope I'll not offend anyone by singing a bit of an old song—
God knows I'm a God-fearing man—and I fear his Priests even
more than I fear Him—but I learned a bonny tune they sing
around planting time in Stropshire—everywhere I go a few people
seem to know it."

He plays the opening bars to The Lord of the Dance.

John rises to his feet, red-faced, drunk, waving his tankard excitedly, "Aye, laddie, we know it!" he cries and joins in singing lustily with the lyrics and soon everyone is singing along, the kirk-followers singing loudest of all. I stare with amazement. Here, where people have grown so cautious—to see all the caution of the last two years tossed aside as if it had never been, to see all the people singing the old songs together as if we were still all of one mind, as if half of Scotland was not on fire with the vengeance of James' campaign against the Witches. . .

What magic does he have to come into this town where no one knows him, to make himself loved and sing what he likes and have the others sing with him?

"Break the ground
not once alone:
Once for Maiden
Once for Crone
Once for Mother.
Even stone
Will yield
When the thrice-broke field
Is sown."

As he utters the old incantation for planting a great prayerful silence washes through the room. He sings a song about the Green Man, followed by one about John Barleycorn. After the song about John Barleycorn he raises his tankard of ale and makes a toast to the grain and the God who grows it. And most toast with him.

He sings another love song, a pretty thing about a young man begging his mistress to take mercy on him, for:

"Between your thighs
Salvation lies;
I aspire to no higher heaven—
Therefore take pity on this sinner
Who can be redeemed only through your love.

"A man within a woman makes a kirk
A heart within a heart
Sweet heaven's kingdom heals."

He sings it so winsomely I wonder how many women could say no to him after being wooed so. He lets his eyes brush by me, not lingering too long, aware of my earlier discomfiture, not wanting to embarrass me again but wanting me to know it is me he is singing to.

He sings a song about a wife playing her husband false, ending with many a ribald warning for the husbands in the crowd to keep their wives close to them. He tunes his lute again, talking all the while. He says that sometimes he sleeps on the faery mounds, and he keeps hoping some immortal lady will come and enchant him.

"But I'm too coarse for such," he laments. "Though often I hear wonderful tunes in my sleep and I wake up remembering how to play them—so perhaps there's something to the tales after all. I can't claim to have written this one—someone dreamed it long ago."

He begins to play the song, one I have heard only at Sabbats or in the crystal hall itself, called "King of the Faeries." One family towards the back leaves, but no one else stirs. I am staring at his hands, the way they caress the strings of his lute, fine square hands, calloused fingers touching the lute so gently—my body throbbing, wanting to be touched with that sureness, that delicacy. Whiskey sliding like little flames down my throat. The minstrel's eyes slide by me again, his gaze as warm as hands on my breasts. He puts the lute down without disturbing the spell and plays another fay song on his harp that he claims to have learned sleeping on the faery mounds.

I sit transfixed. I recognize that tune. I have heard it often under the hill, and no where else. He knows the fay. He knows them. For all his dissembling and saying he is too coarse for them, he knows their music. My breasts are hot, my belly is hot. Then he sings another love song, glancing at me secret-like under his lashes. Aye, he sings to some of the other lasses as well, but even when he is turned to them I can feel that it is me he is playing for, me he is wooing. I stare openly at him, no longer caring who sees. The way he holds his lips around the words as he sings, the way his mouth and eyes glisten in the firelight. His broad shoulders, ruffled yoke of his shirt open, dark hair on his forearms and chest gleams with an occasional glint of copper. The way the sweat glistens in the hollow of his throat, on his brow, the firelight dancing off the pewter, copper and glass in back of the bar, whiskey flames dancing inside me, flame of desire licking the candle of my flesh to liquid and longing. Wanting him to touch me with the competence and grace with which he touches his harp, wanting to make music for him as sweet as any he can conjure from his lute.

Bluebelly's boy brings me another whiskey. Four or five is my limit, and this is my fifth. Is the whiskey making me foolish? If he is a sorcerer, so be it. If he is here for one night only, so be it. I keep looking at his hands, thinking how much I want to feel them on my body. He has already entered me with his eyes, his voice. I will not deny the rest of him.

He takes his recorder and plays, like a bird calling out in a dark wood. And without song, my heart returns the call. He sings more songs that still dare talk of magic, of the old ways, balancing them with more ribald tunes, casting me glances from under his lashes as if he were not sure of me. He has no need to arouse me further; all the while that he sings, him playing to the crowd, sharing himself with everyone, me wrapped in my solitude, sharing myself with no one, the heat dances out of our bodies, twining between us like coupled snakes. Now he is laughing and joking, flirting with the married women, lifting a glass to toast to the men. Yet I know well that part of his mind is thinking of nothing but me and whether or not I will lay with him this night.

Soon I can wait no longer. My blood is on fire. It looks to me as though he could go on all night. Certainly the crowd would have him stay and play all night for them if they could. I stand, slowly adjust my bodice, letting him catch a glimpse of my breasts, wrap my plaidie around, covering them. As he sees me preparing to leave he sings quickly, all the words sliding together and piling up on top of each other like bairns at gutty ball. I wrap my hands, make my way towards the door. He is telling the crowd he is tired, bone-weary, he has journeyed long to get here. Cries of

"No! No! Play on Minstrel!" Coins thrown at his feet. He thanks the crowd, picking up the coins. This is such a wonderful crowd, wonderful village, best crowd he's played to in months—he'll not leave right away, inclined to think he'll stay a fortnight or so. So there will be many times to hear him, but for now we must forgive him, he feels so weary. . .

I stop by a table in the back where Mina and Rose are sitting. Mina must have come late with Rose who walks so very slowly. I stand there chatting idly with Mina while the minstrel sings a last, rollicking song that has the people on their feet, roaring with pleasure.

"And how is it with you?" I ask.

"Ah, well. And with you?"

"Mm, very well. A fine voice he has, does he not?"

"A fine voice! It that all you've noticed?"

I have less than half an ear on our conversation, listening to the minstrel, judging how close he is to done.

"You're not talking to me," Mina accuses in mock indignation. "You're just waiting for that Minstrel."

"It's you as wants to take my mind off the young lord, is it not?" I smile at her. She smiles back, unable to hide her delight.

I wait until the crowd has sat back down, making sure that he sees me, and then walk out the door, hearing the anxiousness in his voice that he tries to cover as he bids good-night to the crowd.

Ah, the night is so cold, so piercingly clear. The slender moon has gone down, the stars glitter. I walk slowly to make sure that he will be able to catch up with me.

Catch up he does, puffing, running across the fields from the back of the Inn, his harp and lute bound in a rucksack on his back. He walks the last few paces to catch up with me, trying to make it appear as if he had not run.

"May I walk with you a bit?" he pants, congealed breath making clouds.

"Aye, I hoped you would. I liked your playing."

"Did you for true? I hoped you did. I'm glad of it." He stops, seemingly embarrassed. He must be younger than I thought at first, boyishly pleased at my praise.

"I thank God for it," he continues. "I could ask no more than for ears like yours to hear me."

"You ask for too little."

He laughs, looks at me with conspiratorial surmise. How is it the way he looks at me makes me forget what it is to be shy with a man?

"So Alain, what brings such a skilled minstrel through such a far place as this?" I query.

"My name's not Alain—" he protests.

"Sure it is, Alain-a-dale, you're Robin the Good's Minstrel, I kenned that from the first."

He laughs. "Aye, Alain it is then, if you like. And you must be Maid Marion, then."

I nod. "I am the Maid of these woods."

As we enter the first copse of trees he catches me gently by the waist, looks in my eyes. Slowly he brings his mouth to mine, frost of our breath mingling, then the tip of his tongue along my lips, his eyes looking at me to see how I am liking it.

"What are you truly called, Lady of the twilight kindred?" he asks.

"Fiona."

"Fiona, Lady of the twilight kindred, Fiona, Lady of the sunset hair—" he sings, weaving my name into a few strands of the song he won me with.

"I swear that song was written for you," he declares.

"You said you wrote it a week ago," I remind him.

"Aye, but I said I wrote it out of a dream—if I dreamed not of you then it must have been a fair one under the hill who bears thy likeness."

A week ago. My coven doing the spell to call my mate, my flesh turning to flowers, my bones to a beckoning song. . .

Suddenly awed and shy, I look at the ground.

He touches my shoulder lightly.

"I hope I'm not being indelicate to ask for a place to sleep tonight?"

"There'll be nothing at my croft," I say, "crowded with sick brothers and sisters as it is. I can offer you nothing better than a hard stone bed out of doors."

"Ah, starlight and good company on stones suit me far better than a narrow feather bed in a castle."

"Starlight and good company you shall have," I promise.

I stop off at my croft to get some thick blankets. At the gate he catches me in his arms again.

"Thou wilt not tease me and leave me waiting here—" he asks, breathing hard.

I shake my head. "No chance of that."

When I come out I see him leaning up against the fence, softly fingering out a little tune. I keep one of the blankets wrapped around myself, he carries the others.

"We're proof against the cold stones now," he exults.

"Perhaps I know a mossy place more comfortable," I admit.

I lead him a long ways. I want to take him to the spring that forms the scrying pool. Tis one of the most sacred places I know and far from the village as well. He does not complain of the walk. We hold hands.

"Ah, the air is so clear," he breathes. "I knew a Witch once— she told me the stars are made of fire. I did not believe her at the time but tonight I can fair feel it."

"You had a—friend who was a Witch?"

"Friend—and a leman. Some of the songs I sang tonight I learned from her."

I nod. I thought as much.

The way his fingers stroke my wrist, up the inside of my arm to my elbow and back down to my hand makes me dizzy. The more I think about how much I want to lay under him, the harder it is to talk.

He talks ample for both of us, telling how he ran off to sea at a young age and had silver in his hair by the time he set back to land. And a minstrel's life is a hard life, living on the road without a tender lady's touch, why 'twill age you sure as sorrow. He is not at his most convincing with this tale of woe, and his calling me cruel when I laugh has no sincerity in it.

At last we come to the scrying pool. He immediately sees the mossy place I have intended for us and begins setting up our bed. He must have bedded many lasses out of doors; he is deft with making a soft place to lie.

I kneel by the pool, watching the reflection of the stars on its still surface. Dip my hand into the water, press it to the crown of my head, my brow, my lips, throat, heart, belly, sex, feet, consciously bringing the fire of the stars and the blood of the earth into each of the gates of my body. Silently I bless each part, affirming as I bless my womb that I will conceive only when I will to.

"I consecrate this act to the Mother, that all life thrive, that the wheel of life yet turn. Bless me Mother, for I am thy child. Let me serve you in this way."

I place one hand on my heel, one on my head. "All between my two hands belongs to the Goddess."

The silent rite takes only a few moments. As I finish I see the Minstrel watching me.

"Is it all right if I wash my hands and face?" he asks, nodding towards the spring.

"Aye, take a drink of her as well."

I slip under the covers. He begins tuning his lute, thinking to court me under the stars. But I have my clothes off in a matter of moments.

"Tis too cold for that. Come lay with me instead," I urge.

He needs no second bidding, comes to me with that candle behind his eyes, rubbing his hands together and blowing on them.

"My hands are cold," he says ruefully. He slips between layers of wool, we blow hotly on each other's hands a bit. Then I pull his hands to my breasts; they will warm up faster on my body. He gasps, smiles, pulls me to him, a long kiss. His mouth soon warms the chill his hands had left on my breasts. He pulls off his shirt, his leggings, another deep kiss. His chest is curling with dark hair; I rub my breasts up against him, he groans into my mouth, presses me closer, I moan in reply.

"Ah, Fiona, thank you," he gasps. He pulls my hand to his crotch, rubs it against his hardness. I'm startled, and delighted—Sean never lets me touch him there.

I am so used to Sean's quickness, his kissing me and then mounting me with so little touching. Alain rolls me on my back, kissing my neck, sucking my breasts, his whole attention in his mouth and hands, every inch of his body alive and conscious of mine. He lifts up his head, kisses me.

"Oh God, you are beautiful," he breathes, rubs his head along my belly, breasts, nuzzling, licking. So used to Sean's impatience I had almost forgotten Pan's teaching me the playfulness of a man. It is I who am impatient and cannot wait now.

"Take me now," I whisper, roll him on top of me, tipping my pelvis to meet him, wrapping one leg then the other around his back, rubbing my calves along the curve of his buttocks. Even here he is slow, entering me a little at a time, watching my face. Oh, I am not used to being seen so intimately by a man but I surrender to it. I wrap my arms and legs around him, opening easily.

His hands are everywhere, buried in my hair, opening my thighs, squeezing my breasts. He moves in me, slowly at first, rocking, then thrusting, faster and faster. He moans, whispers my name and moans again as we move together. His sounds excite me. Sean always grits his teeth as if his life hung in the balance of his silence, every groan I elicit from him a victory over a miser. The minstrel lets his excitement out as much as I do. Oh I like the way he moves; I knew he would be good; so good I dig my nails into his shoulder and cry out loudly as the feeling bursts over me and through me. He is murmuring something and kissing me; maybe he is just moaning. I twist under him, running my hands along his strong body, wonderfully taut back, muscular ass, yet he rolls me gently, so gently, thrusting faster now more urgent aye aye lad I'm with you I'm with you oh oh him calling my name over and over almost sobbing, we are galloping together, stallion and mare, elf locks tangled in the wild night wind, our bodies moving as one body, the God enters us and we shape-shift, first into horses, then into fire. . .

Afterwards we lie panting together, hearts still galloping. He raises up on his elbows, looks at me—tenderly, seriously, with a touch of wonder. This is nothing like being with Sean, more like being with— I skirt around her name as if it were thin ice on a loch. There is no grief in me now.

Who is this man that I can open to him so easily, looking at me as if he had loved me and cherished me for a lifetime? What magic does he have? And yet without knowing any of the answers, contentment flows like a peaceful river through my blood. Thoughts cease. Again I am drawn in and lost in the beautiful green of his eyes. His lips running so tender along my jaw, my cheeks, the lids of my eyes and sleep comes to me almost as softly as his kisses.

Chapter 48

Blankets bunched warm around my face. Snuggle down deeper. Warm arm pulling me close. What was I dreaming? Dreamed I was sleeping near a road—waking on wet leaves between towns, smiling into the warm eyes of a harper. I was a harper too, a woman dressed as a man, concealing my true identity from my traveling companion.

His hand circles my breast; my breast nuzzles back. I open my eyes. Sleepy eyes swimming with forests and mists. Hair touseled, bits of moss sticking to it. Dream or memory? Surely this is the harper of my dream. But if there was ever a life where he was deceived as to the nature of my sex, it is not this one.

Last bit of pink fading from the east. The gold follows it, leaving the sky blue. His cock presses hard against my hip. He slides an inquiring hand from my belly to my cleft. I smile and push his hand away, yawn and stretch. It smells as if one of us is fermenting, and since I bathed not a week past, I think it must be my new friend.

"Would you like a bath this morning?"

He sniffs under his arms. "A bit gamey for you?"

"I'll warrant you've not bathed all winter."

"Not so!" he says in an injured voice. "I bathed for Yule."

"Tis almost Beltane—" I chide.

"—and I'd like a bath," he smiles. "D'you think your mother—"

"Not there," I shake my head. This morning I know that Mina and Gran will be over at Rose's planning our Beltane ritual. Mina will not return until well after lunch which will give us plenty of time to bathe at her house, with her none the wiser. We fold our bedding away and dress.

"Thinking of going back to the Inn?" he asks.

I shake my head. "Wait and see." I kiss my hand and make the sign of the horns to the place, startled when the Minstrel copies my action.

As I had thought, Mina's house is empty save for the weft of concealing magic blurring the unwary vision like a fog. Her cat comes up and brushes against my legs.

"Good morning Cailitie." I press both hands to the cat, letting her purr vibrate the air clear for me. Gradually the hidden things in her house come into focus; the staff leaning against the hearth, chalice on the lintel. The minstrel imitates my actions with the cat. He reaches up, brushes a finger across some of the herbs hanging from the ceiling.

"Your friend is a—Wise Woman?" he asks.

I freeze. How can he have seen through the protective mist? Gran's warnings of false cowans and waerlogs come to my mind—the way he enchanted the people last night with his songs—

"Ah, forgive me," he says. "I meant no trespass. It matters not. Where's the bath?" His obvious anxiety over my fear eases me. No false man could bear those eyes.

"We'll have to heat the water."

We fill the largest cauldron from the rainwater barrel outside Mina's back stoop. He builds up the fire and sets the cauldron over it. We drag in the old cow trough for our tub and I prepare a pot of oats to put on the fire after our bath is hot.

We sit opposite each other on benches before the fire. I am still unsettled by his calling Mina a Wise Woman—a politer term but no less damning than Witch in these days. Foolish to have become so intimate with a stranger based on nought but loneliness and whiskey. Gran is always saying I must learn to think beyond my feeling. I strive to calm myself. He is as he seems; a wandering minstrel, better than most. He'll stay another day or two, then be gone. He's no waerlog. I'd lay my life to it. A bit of fear cramps my belly still, for I have laid my life to it.

He tunes his lute, tightening and loosening strings until the discordant noises he plucks from them turn sweet, and he begins to play. Each note rolls into me, a wave of warm air, a wave of feather and fire. I am opened and ensorcelled again, unable to do aught save stare at the feral grace of his fingers, the sound guiding my breath in and out, my breasts rising and falling under my bodice, aware of my skin as acutely as I would be if he were touching it with his hands instead of his voice.

"The breasts of the maiden are fair as the sun
And the candle of her mouth soft as flame
I would go into that country and with journeying be done
And would never fare forth again."

No cowan, but a sorcerer surely. He has cast the net of his words over my body, a net of fire so sweet I capitulate as thoughtlessly as the fish I sorcell out of M'hira.

With his next song he answers my unspoken question, saying that the only magic he possesses is that of lute, harp and voice:

"And what is that against the magic of a lady's glance?
And what is that against the magic of a circle dance?
And what is that against the magic of the Stones?
And what is that against the magic of the runes?

Barrows and dolmen, circles of night
Standing stones weaving the shadow and light.

I have not seen the faeries dance under the hill
But when the wind whispers my heart will not still.

"They say what I seek is uncanny and fay;
All curious cats meet the same fate one day.
They say I'll go mad sleeping under the moon
Dance with the Fay till I've worn out my shoon.

I have nothing to show for my quest but my dreams
Yet some say that's enough to condemn me to flames.

I have not seen the faeries dance under the hill
But when the wind whispers, my heart will not still."

"I am not of the old blood," he says, looking at me. "Neither am I Christian. I know where my sympathies lie." Our eyes lock. Silence. Gradually the whoosh of the wind comes up outside, rushing at the walls of the croft, billowing like the ocean. Movement in my body like the rocking of a ship.

"A better shipmate I could not ask for," he whispers.

The lad has read my mind. If he is not of the blood—perhaps he knows not his own blood. Perhaps the faeries have touched him, more than he thinks, not knowing how subtle their ways may be.

As if he again knew my mind, he begins to play "The King of the Faeries." I close my eyes, hearing again how that song is played in the hall of crystal, seeing myself dancing with the Fay. Is he telling the truth? Has he truly never been there, only slept above? Surely they've come to him in his sleep then. Sensing the presence of the Fay as close as they ever come to a croft. Does he know that he calls them?

"I am ignorant of the ways of crystal. But I had a—leman once—who was a Witch. She taught me—a few things. She healed my hand." He stretches out his hand to me. I see there is no use dissembling before him; he has seen me for what I am.

"I see nothing wrong with your hand."

"No. Not now. It was broken here, across the thumb. Twas in Edinburgh—the Separationists there are worse than the Papists. They fire up the young men with spiritual zeal so they break into a decent alehouse and overturn the tables, beat the patrons, particularly if there are any—ladies of light virtue about—they seek these out and beat them mercilessly. I was playing at the

Black Cloud—and a black day it was—the clods came in and smashed up my lute—smashed me up as well. I tried to give as good as I got. Not a physician could cure me, only bled me until my purse was empty and I could hardly stand. My hand smashed—I thought I'd never play again. Someone told me about an old Witch woman—I went as a last resort, being afraid as any superstitious fool—by that time my money was gone and I'd no way of earning more. She told me once I was better I could trade by cutting her wood for the winter. And it seemed—" he pauses, blushing like a boy caught in some misdeed, "—it seemed she had another use for me as well."

"Did you love her very much?"

"I—liked her fine. I was more in awe of her than love. She was old enough to be my mother—but at night—all cats—are gray—except for you—you blush so hot I can see it in the dark."

I push him. "Go check the water."

"Ah, tis blessedly hot."

I steady the trough—he pours the water in. I hand him Mina's best soap and a scrubbing brush. Mina is not as impassioned of baths as Gran is but she does it right when she does them. He takes off his clothes and sinks in, ducks his head, comes up sputtering, lathers his hair full of soap, ducks under again.

"Out little lousies. Ride's over."

He groans contentedly as I scrub his back, but then catches my arm as if he would pull me in.

"False lass," he accuses, "you said you'd bathe *with* me."

"There's no way two can fit in that tub," I laugh.

"I'll make room," he insists. He sticks a leg out. "There. Lots of room."

Blushing, I strip off my clothes, precariously seek my balance astride him. He soaps my breasts as I clutch the sides of the trough, giggling. Straddling him awkwardly, I keep bumping up against his cock, and giggle more. He swishes the soap down to my nether hairs. I squeak and grab his wrist. The tub rocks and sloshes, he keeps trying to pull me down deeper in the water my knees slippery on his chest we giggle madly as the tub begins tipping, a wild scramble to regain balance—crash!— water flooding the dirt floor. For a moment he looks like a ludicrous turtle, trough perched on his back. He pushes it off, grabs me, my breasts soapy and slippery against his wet fur, rolling in the muddy puddle of Mina's floor, we cannot stop laughing, we laugh and laugh he starts kissing me breathlessly between gasps of giggling and then we're not giggling; he is moving inside me and the noises are sweet but not laughter. He holds me so tight oh he feels so good between my legs oh all the way up in my belly fill me oh yes I move under him like waves, breasts gasping tight against his chest his hard thighs spreading me open so far so open for you lad take me as deep as you can; my pores start breathing rainbows my bones turn to light, moon and sun crash like waves together, like bells, like lute, like prayers of thunder.

Our cries go on and on until my bones ache with the echoes. Singing of all creation in my blood. Wolf and fox fade out of his face and he becomes human once more.

Our bellies plastered together with his come, our chests plastered with soap, our hair draggled in the mud of Mina's once-immaculate floor. It looks as if a mother sow and all her piglets had rooted for their breakfast there.

The door opens—Alain bites his lip in dismay. I twist my head to see Mina staring at the carnage in the midst of her house, her mouth open. She shakes her head.

"I do not see it, I do not see it," she mutters devoutly as she backs out of the croft, slamming the door behind her.

"Oh Christ." Alain peels himself off me and staggers to the hearth. I realize the unfamiliar smell I have been ignoring is that of burned oats. He snatches the kettle off the fire—groans at the unrecognizable charred mass within.

"Christ, what a mess!" We drag in the rain barrel, fill the trough with cold water. In our haste to rinse off the mud and sticky residue of our love-making we manage to tip the trough over again, flooding Mina's floor anew.

We burst into a paroxysm of helpless giggles, pull our clothes on over our dripping bodies and flee out the back door, laughing like loons, sprinting over Mina's wall and back to the woods. At last, panic and wind exhausted, we collapse, deep in the forest.

"Oh, that was wrong, that was very wrong, Fiona," he moans, clapping his hands to his head. "Christ I hope thy friend will not—over-look us—"

"Nay, nay," I assure him. "She's not overlooked me yet and she's had cause before."

He opens a pouch by his side and draws forth a couple pieces of silver.

"One of these will buy her a new pot—perhaps the other one will atone—" he starts laughing again, "—for how incredibly rude—" he plops down on the grass laughing too hard to speak, and I flop down next to him.

"Ah, tis great to be clean," he exults, "great to be clean and better to be laid." He rolls over on top of me, pats the wet hair out of my eyes. "Thou art a very wildcat," he says admiringly.

"A wildcat *and* a kelpie," I warn him.

"Ah, is that your secret then?" he says, "Ah, you look a bit like a kelpie with your hair all draggled like that. Either that or—the most desireable water rat in the history of the world." He kisses me.

"Watch who you call a water rat," I say when I come up for air, tugging at his own soggy curls.

"Wouldn't mind being a water rat or even a sly stoat had I you to be stoatly with," he asserts. "But are you sure your friend will not curse us, or me at least?"

"Mina never curses without need. Curses or blessings are strongest at their roots." He looks at me as if he did not quite follow.

"Whatever you conjure passes through you first," I explain, "It's one of the first things you learn. Did your Witch friend not tell you that?"

"I never asked her to teach me spells. I knew I was not worthy for that. And it frightened me. I was afraid the power might go to my head and—I might do evil." He wrinkles his brow so seriously I stop laughing, and shake my head.

"You have not the aptitude for evil. Foolish perhaps—" I giggle, "—but not evil."

"Don't you think that foolishness is the source of most evil in the world?" he asks.

"I know not—I think good and give no power to the other. That's what—" I stop, thinking perhaps I should not identify Rose as the author of this teaching. "That's what a friend of mine says."

"Art thou truly no more than sixteen?" he asks.

I nod.

"Thou art wise for thy years."

"And thou gray for thine." I run my hands through his curls. "And wise, too," thinking again of his music, and how he charmed our whole village and held them in the palm of his hand last night. .

"I would I had your way of getting people to love me."

He shakes his head in disbelief.

"Surely thou canst not have any trouble with *that*. Is there a man in Glen Lochlan who would not give all he possesses for thy love?"

I turn from him.

"Did I offend thee? Forgive me," he says, "perhaps thou wishest to be loved for thyself alone and not thy beauty."

How can one separate one's self from one's body? Is that why I do not like the way the men in the village look at me? Yes, perhaps that they lust for my body without really seeing me. . .

"Art thou widowed?" he asks.

I shake my head. "Nay, I've not wed—why did you think that?"

"You looked—you had a bit of a widow's air when you came in last night. You were not wearing the weeds but—there was a darkness about you."

"I was lonely," I admit. A smile. "I'm not lonely now." I get up and stretch.

"My mother will be wondering where I am. I'd best go back and make myself useful."

"Perhaps I could help? I'm very good at chopping wood."

"Wood chopping we can always use," I say, glad that he'll not be leaving right away. What did he say last night to the crowd—a fortnight he would tarry?

"Is your father—alive?" he asks cautiously as we walk down.

"No. Dead many years. And no older brother either." I smile at him. "You've no one to account to for my virtue—or lack thereof."

How natural it feels, having him around the house, chopping all the wood, hoeing in the garden. How quickly things go with a man's strength to do them. Playing on his harp when we cook, equally at ease with stirring the pot, kneading the bread, bouncing baby Mark on his knee. Malcolm adored him from the first, fascinated and awed at the minstrel's instruments. Alain sat with him, whenever there was a lull in the chores, teaching him the beginning of harping and lending advice on his whistles and Pan pipes. Together they carved a recorder for him that sounded sweet as a lark. He brought his magic with him, and not a heart in my family did not warm to him immediately, except for Eostre, who did her best to maintain her coolness. But when he poured the entire contents of a small sack of coins he had earned playing at the Bluebell into my mother's hands, a light came into Eostre's eyes and from that time on she served him first out of the pot, addressed him respectfully and even giggled at his jokes. We never slept at home of course, but took our leave of the family after dinner and went off into the hills or the forest.

In apology to Mina he gave the silver and chopped and stacked a fair winter's worth of wood for her. We took a trip one day to Ail Fionn to buy her a new pot and a new sack of oats to cook in it. Strange to say, Mina seemed jubilant rather than put out by our escapade. Soon she and the minstrel were insulting and teasing each other as easily as if they had several lifetimes of jokes between them already.

He played a few nights at the Inn and then tied his horse up at our croft. He agreed to play at the Inn five more times before he left and arranged the times with Bluebelly. Knowing he was there, many of our neighbors came when he was visiting us, sat around the fire and he played for them for free. When they offered him coin or provender he would refuse, suggesting that they might instead give my mother the chicken or cheese or sack of grain they had brought, and she would blush and look as proudly on him as if her were her son.

Chapter 49

A bonny dinner indeed; between the minstrel's money and some that Sean left me, we have laid a fine table. Three roasted chickens, scones with currants, tulse and tangle, old turnips kept throughout the winter.

"Would that we always had a minstrel to visit us," Malcolm beams, gnawing happily on the drumstick which has been allotted to him.

"Perhaps you shall," the minstrel smiles back. "There's much about here that needs a man's touch."

"And some that doesn't," sniffs Eostre.

"And some that *does*," the Minstrel insists pointedly. "Some that does and doesn't know it yet."

Eostre flushes furiously and quickly rises to put a pot of water on the hearth. Ever eager for a chance to tease their most superior and reserved sister, Colin and Malcolm begin arguing on how much the minstrel should owe them for our favors.

"If you take two sisters off our hands, tis a special rate," they finally decide. "Two chickens a day for the loan of one, three chickens for two, agreed?"

The dinner is merry and laughing as I cannot remember a meal at our croft being since the Laird left us.

After the meal is over and the others have gone to bed, Alain and I sit by the fire, wanting to stay warm awhile yet before venturing out into the cold night air. He seems to have lost the gaiety of our supper; the songs that he sings me are sad songs about lost love.

"Is all well with you?" I ask.

He smiles wanly. "Ah, no one's fault but my own if it is not." But then he sings another mournful tune.

"It sounds as if you are missing someone," I say, sad to think that he would think of someone else while he is with me.

"No," he says. "It's just—I thought—when I first laid with you—'twould be for our mutual pleasure and sport. It seems I have grown more fond of you than is fit."

I snuggle up beside him. "I'm glad you are fond of me. And why should you not be?"

"A man in the tavern today—told me that your love was plighted to the Lord's son, the young Lochlan—and if I knew what was good for me I would be well clear of this district by sun's height when it is time for them to return."

"Nay, I am free to love who I like," I say. "Sean is gone to marry a girl of his own class. I do not know how things will be when he comes back. But what of it, wanderer? You will be gone by then and I but a song and a memory. When I am in your arms it is of you I think and no other. What more can you desire?"

*   *   *   *

Entering the woods this night is like diving into the deep pool at M'hira, the gibbous moon thrilling the forest to tones of emerald with shadings of silver like the depths of the salmon pool. Smoke curls and snake twistings of ground fog lead us through a labyrinth of pines to a small clearing unfamiliar to me. Owls call to each other, and soft as owl feathers the woods breathe with the potent magic of Beltane. The veil between the worlds is thin, a gauze only, and I long for the realm of Faery. But the barrows have closed to me since Samhain; the visions the mushrooms gave me that night so disturbing I have not dared to take them again since. At times the Faerie Queen's sorrowing face comes to me in dreams, but she does not speak.

Equally silent, the minstrel takes me in his arms. Our love-making is slow, reverent. By the time we have finished, the stars and moon have vanished, and we float in the soft gray belly of a cloud.

"Is your coven all women?" he asks, "Or are there men?"

I hesitate. We have known each other a week. I have not spoken directly of being a Witch, though I know he knows it.

"Don't you trust me?" he reproaches. "You trust me enough to let me take you like this. You can trust me enough."

"Mostly women," I admit. "But not of our own choosing."

"Tomorrow is Beltane eve," he says. "If you vouch for me, will they let me come to your Sabbat?"

"Oh—" I reply, "—we never have strangers."

"Am I still strange to you?"

"No, but—" I stop, thinking how much the members of our coven enjoyed his music and how pleased they seemed to be, even Gran seemed pleased rather than put out with the suddenness with which I brought the traveler into my bed.

"I will ask," I promise.

"I thank you," he says. "I want to learn more of the old ways. I always have but—it seems that a coven, like a farm, is a settled thing. And now, there is so little trust in the land. Me not staying in one place for long, I've had little chance. I swear you can trust me."

I run my hand through his curls.

"I do trust you. Did you go to Lizbet's coven when you lived with her?" I ask, curious to know more about the Witch paramour who had healed his hand.

"No," he says. "She—worked alone. She was as solitary as a cat. I was only twenty when I left—I thought it would be easy to find others to teach me as she had taught me, but I found no teachers. Except for you. And the Fay, in my dreams—"

"When you were twenty—you told me you were twenty now."

Caught, he looks at me shamefaced.

"Ah, forgive me—I did say I was twenty when you asked my age that first night—"

"You would lie to me about something so small and ask me to trust you with the large?" I ask, shocked and on guard.

"Ah, Fiona, it was—it was vanity. I—you're so young and—I thought a younger man would be more to your liking. I'm nearer to thirty."

I remember Mina's reaction when, describing my new love, I told her he was twenty. "Twenty!" she snorted. "Aye, if he be twenty, I be twenty-nine!"

"I'm twenty-eight, close to twenty-nine," he admits, seeming more ashamed of his age than of the lie that concealed it. "Does it matter to you?" he asks, voice full of worry.

"A friend—in my coven—wished me someone older—and wiser." I tell him about the spell my coven did to call my mate to me, laughing at how all their wishes for me are embodied in this man.

He hugs me in his arms after the telling.

"Ah, it's what I've been feeling—well surely if they conjured me here they should have me, should they not?" He laughs. "I knew I felt differently about you than any other lass. You've been in my arms less than a week, yet—I cannot imagine you not being there." He strokes my cheek. "Is it really true? Have we been charmed to marry?"

"The spell was to bring my mate hither," I say, "what happens after that—is our choice."

"I'll choose it," he says readily. "I'll make you a dulcimer and teach you to play—you have a sweet voice, Fiona. And you—teach me, Fiona—about the Goddess and the God—for I am weary of singing about what I barely understand. I would be—a man of power."

"You are that already," I say to him. Wind rustles the fresh green leaves about us. The weather is changing; already our love-making has been conjuring the summer in.

"What did Lizbet teach you?" I ask.

"Well, she taught me a lot of the songs—and some chants. She had some fine weather-working chants—that woman could bring up a storm!" he remembers admiringly. "Aye, or lay one down, or move it to the north or to the south. I saw her do things with clouds and rain that had to be seen to be believed. And she taught me about the tea I told you about—what herbs to gather, the charm to say as they were picked, the rhymes to say when they had dried—so that the woman could drink the tea and not conceive even if the man did not pull out but stayed within her the whole time. Every girl I've bedded since then, I've blessed Lizbet for that gift. I've never gotten a bairn on any woman who did not want one. I have one daughter—in the east—a woman who was new widowed who had miscarried and desperately wanted a child. So I know my seed is good but—I would cause no woman shame. And Lizbet helped me in that. I know something of the druaderia*—the other ways to make love to a woman and not get her with child. But with druaderia one must convert the baser passion into spirit and—" he laughs, "—there are times I would prefer to keep it base."

I laugh with him, feeling my desire for him again and smile, knowing that a feather touch from me would make him ready again.

"And she taught me to cast a circle. She did not tell me much about it though but only had me play various sorts of music at the four directions when she invoked. When she was doing rituals she often used another language that I spoke not, and so I missed much of what I could have learned. Once I was marvelling at how she had healed my hand—she took a coal from the fire and laid it on my palm—it burned me not."

I nod remembering how I have danced through the coals in the hall of faery. It must have been a faery spell that Lizbet knew.

"Why did you not go back and learn more from her?" I ask.

"I did go back," he says, "a year after I left. Aye, I did go back. And I looked all about—she lived out in the country by herself— and I kept looking and not finding the place. Finally I found a bit of blackened timber all grown over with fresh vines and flowers and grasses. I went to the nearest town and asked as casually as I could and found that she had been burned." He shakes his head. "She said it would be so—"

"She knew it would come to pass?" I ask, a chill not of the wind raising the hair on the back of my neck.

"Aye," he says, "she predicted it to me before I left. But I— took it not—I thought perhaps she said as much to try to get me to stay. She always said that everyone chooses their own destiny.

---

*Druaderia—Gypsy Tantra which teaches various sexual mysteries, including ways to avoid or promote conception.

But if we could choose, would we not all choose for the best?"

I shake my head, remembering Mari. "I know not. There is much I have not learned. And I fear if you are looking for a wise woman you will be disappointed for I am young in my years and in my learning. Gran says I am still very foolish."

He shakes his head. "You need not years. You have a wisdom in your body—when I walk in the woods with you—I see things I never see when I walk alone. You move like a deer, and the trees—all seem to know you."

"Well, of course they know me. This is my place. They are my friends. It is probably just that you never stay in one place long enough to make such friends. You pass through and—"

"Aye," he sighs, "perhaps it is time for me to settle. I never thought I would—I would love to travel. But certainly there are things I have not been seeing and—" he presses my hand to his heart, "—things I have not been feeling—" he pauses, "—and the way you caught that fish!" he says, referring to the afternoon we had spent fishing the day before. "That was extraordinary. I don't care how many salmon are in that pool—I've fished for salmon, they're canny beasts—I've taken two or three days sometimes and not caught one, for all that the pools are full of them, or caught a young one not yet wise. But you—you took a fish practically as big as you, girl!"

"Aye, I was glad for your arms to help me draw him forth."

"And that cat!" he says, referring to Oberon. "He's a lynx, is he not?"

"Part lynx."

Alain shakes his head. "He's like a wee man in a fur suit. I swear to God—you said you had no father or older brother but that first night I came to your croft I swear he crawled up my chest and asked my intentions about you."

I laugh. "Aye, Obie loves to talk. He's the best ally anyone could ask for. He helps my fishing."

"And was rewarded well," the minstrel interjects, thinking how Obie demanded his share of the salmon as soon as it had been taken. "Well, when we leave we'll take him with us. Or one of his kittens if he wants to bide here."

"Leave!" I exclaim. "Leave to where?"

The minstrel shrugs. "Where I know not, but this is a small

village. I doubt if I could make a living settled here. For to bide together we must find a place, I must find a patron, a lord that I can work for who'll give me a croft and an income."

I shake my head. "Don't tease me, Minstrel."

"Are you still in love with him then?" he asks. "The young lord? They said you belonged to him—"

"I don't belong to anyone," I bristle. "I belong to myself."

"You are not pledged to him?"

"What pledges can there be between us? We are not of a class," I say, feeling my old anger that Sean should be placed above me; that my brothers and sisters, who are as much the Laird's children as he, should want, while he has everything.

"Are you much in love with him?" the minstrel persists.

I shrug. "Aye."

Uncomfortable silence, both of us staring up at the thick shifting fog. Night animals rustle in the brush. Call of the hunting owl.

"Have you enjoyed many lads?" he asks.

I shake my head. "No. Just one other. Just one time. My first time. Just that once."

"Was he a scoundrel then—did he betray you?"

"No, not at all." I tell him about my Beltane with Pan.

"So the other men keep their distance for fear of offending the young Lord?"

"I'm always shy with men. Except for you."

"Me?" he says happily.

I nod.

"Ah, well—I know tis early—but do you think you could leave your young lord then?"

"Leave? This is my home."

He turns from me and begins playing on his lute—a song so sad my eyes fill with tears.

"You've no right to be so sad," I say, "tis you who'll be leaving me."

"No," he says. He puts his lute aside, pulls me down under the covers. "No, I'll not be leaving you," he promises. "Not in a week's time. Not—I'm not leaving until you'll be leaving with me. And if it takes a month or two months. . ."

It starts to rain, a light sprinkle. Then the drops come harder. Alain stretches his forest-green cloak over the rest of our blankets and we huddle under them in a dark tent, listening to the rain.

"I may be mad," he whispers, "or I may be ensorcelled, but I want to marry you."

"You said you never played the scoundrel with anyone," I hiss back.

"As I do not!" he protests.

"Minstrels will settle when barley will travel, everyone knows that."

"I used to say that myself," he admits. "I said it to all the girls who wanted me to stay before but—Fiona, it's different with you, I swear it."

"Let's find a more honest use for that tongue, Minstrel," I say, kissing him deeply as we huddle under the covers, oddly content that he will tarry longer than he had originally planned. All the warnings of my mind, everything I have heard about the fickleness of minstrels, how they are all married to their harps and faithful only to the road, fades beneath my unreasoning happiness.

The rain comes down. Heaven and earth merge through the magic of water, their green marriage giving birth to summer. Heaven and earth, surrendering to warmer waters, we merge; and the branches bare in me since Annie left, bloom and again grow green.

Chapter 50

I thought it would take all morning, but it has taken the better part of the day. It was Nimué's design, the butterfly with vulval wings, the outline formed of bent willow-withes, strands of lover's-knot across the body, pink and red flowers threaded through. Our private tradition which we created together each Beltane for the past three years. This year I weave it alone and hang it on the special tree where we always hung our wreaths and garlands and pretty offerings when our rituals were over. I kiss the butterfly before I tie it deep in the inner boughs where it will not be seen, imagine it flying, high over hills and valleys and lochs to wherever Nimué travels now, lighting on her shoulder, rubbing its pussy-willow antennae along her jaw, whispering its wings against her cheek gently as we used to flutter our eyelashes against each other, calling the feathery caresses butterfly kisses. . .

Across the miles, she shivers. Perhaps a real butterfly has landed on her shoulder, perhaps a fluff of milkweed. Perhaps only the wraith-form of my charm. Brief flicker of her longing for me, then the gate up, the door slammed, the starless gap between us wide and empty as the night-black sea.

As I withdraw my head from the sweet scented pine, sun sweeps the blackness away, startles my thoughts back to the minstrel, and my heart and belly flutter a butterfly dance of excitement. I gather the rest of the flowers I have picked in my apron and fly to the meadow where we promised to meet.

The coven elders decided it was not yet time for him to come to our ritual, but they have given me permission to take him to the standing stones at midnight to perform the Great Rite there, and to teach him whatever I think it is well for him to know for the power of the rite to be whole.

Cuckoos and finches carol with noisy exuberance as I make my way to the clearing. I step through the bushes and see him kneeling there with such a choir of birds singing around him, he might well be the Lord of the Woods. His curly hair, his beautiful square hands. And then his green eyes meeting mine. I have told him that we are to meet in silence, to weave each other a garland of flowers and to part without touching further, not to set eyes on each other again until our rite at the standing stones.

We kneel, facing each other, almost touching, and weave each other the garlands. Is it always my fate to have lovers whose hands are more artful than mine? How can his hands, so much larger, move with so much more delicacy and grace? But I have more experience than he, so while my garland for him is simpler, white and green with three blushing roses, I am finished more quickly. His garland includes woodsmoke to hang down over my ears and long strands of ivy wove with Bridget's lace to hang down my back and tangle with my hair.

We crown each other, and I see in his parted lips and the mist that comes over his eyes that I have become the Goddess in his sight. As for me, I half believe that if I touch him now, he shall turn into a stag and bound away.

It takes every bit of discipline I have acquired so far in my training to rise regally and back away, turning only when the bushes have closed over between us. Hard to regard the Coven's meeting with ought but impatience, for the real magic tonight will be between me and Alain and the standing stones.

We have celebrated with none but ourselves and Jesse's coven in Ail Fionn the last two years. We miss meeting with the other covens, but it has grown too dangerous to do so. I make a flower offering to Pan, who took my maidenhead so gently and well two years ago, and give it to M'hira to carry to the sea.

"May your eyes never fail you, nor ears, nor taste nor any other sense, may your manhood ever rise strong. Swive and live long!"

*   *   *   *

I climb down the steep cliff to the beach, my haert pounding as one hand-hold after another crumbles under my grasp. No one comes to this cove, but Gran has deemed it too dangerous to light the bale fire. At winter solstice the village built a Yule fire on top of the highest tor, and the Laird himself lit it, despite the pressure from the Priest and the fear that was in everyone since the Witch-hunter's visit last autumn. But outside of the Laird's sanction, without the cover of the entire village's presence, we cannot dare it. We shall rely on vision flame tonight, that warms and conjures without traitorous smoke.

I am the last to arrive. Jesse runs and hugs me. She and her man and her man's family have come from Ail Fionn to join us. Our Maypole, a long piece of driftwood worn white by the waves, has been decorated before I get there with long strands of ivy woven with flowers. We dance the weaving dance, chanting and laughing, singing the Beltane songs. When we are finished all the strands are wove into one cord which pulses with light like the umbilicus of a new baby. Each of us in turn presses the end of that umbilicus to our heart, to our navel, letting the love and potent virility of the God, the love and fecundity of the Mother pour into us. The wind has come up; the pole vibrates and sings in the sand, the phallus connecting earth and sky as they make love. As I press the cord to my heart the power of all flowers fills me; dizzy with a thousand scents, skin soft as petals, I am intoxicated with my own desireability. As I press the cord to my belly the strength of the ivy and the power of all the good green life on the earth, marriage between earth and sky, fills me. I am the Queen of Air and Darkness who makes love with the Horned and Green Man of the Earth. I am the Goddess whose breasts are mountains, whose womb is the sea, opening herself to the Lord of the Sky, winged serpent, piercing light. Each of us now in the circle around the Maypole vibrates with all the fire and light and flowering communion of earth and sky.

The elders have already built a driftwood mound. Each of us has brought a piece or two of one of the nine sacred woods to add to it. Gran and Mina lead the chant:

"Fire from the Earth
Fire from the Sky
Meet and mate
Consume and die."

Purple fire, dragon fire whirls up in a spiral from the center of the pyre. A shock of lightning cries out in the sky above us. We breathe into the fire, rubbing our hands together, pouring the energy of our vision into the flames.

"The fire takes hold!" cries Staghorn.

"The fire is strong," says Colin, the young miller.

"Purple and green and yellow and blue," murmurs Jesse.

"Fire of life, burn eternal," adds Colin's mother.

"I bring birch for birth," says Sarah, placing the sheaf of white twigs on our imagined fire. "May all the births in our two villages this year be safe ones." She looks significantly at Jesse who smiles and puts her hand on her belly, not yet round with the life she carries.

I offer ash, "For the songs and for the Fay, may they thrive— and for all singers of songs as well."

Mina, Gran and Rose each place a black branch of elder, the hag wood, in the fire.

"Death to those who will death to us and our ways. Let all those pass from the earth who do not love her." We all echo them.

Colin and Jesse put in a twined strand of ivy. "Ivy for love which grows, strand on strand, heart to hand." It is good to see them so happy. Soon they will have their first child and be happier still. A lump grows in my throat as I imagine looking across the fire at the minstrel, imagine bearing his child in my womb.

"Oak for our strength. We shall endure," declares Winter.

As each of the sacred trees is added to our fire, it burns higher and brighter. We plant the Maypole in the center of the pyre. The Bale-flames run up and down the Maypole but nothing blackens nor curls nor withers. Our vision pulses sharper and clearer and more bright than before. As we dance around our vision of the flames the Maypole becomes a great tree spreading out branches; bright green leaves, soft flowers, fruits of every kind swelling and ripening, the tree bearing both flower and fruit at once, as if beauty and fertility would last forever, as if there were no death.

We scry through our wreaths into the flames, for the Beltane fire seen through a circle of flowers may speak as truly as crystal. I ask for a vision of my life with the minstrel. I see us meeting as Goddess and God at the center of the standing stones—surging power of gold and silver, sun and moon—then the fire goes white, and I see nothing beyond it.

"We'll have a girl," Jesse proclaims softly, scrying through her wreath. A murmur of delight and approval goes around the circle. I forget to be disappointed with my vision.

"A Samhain girl with a green spring heart," her husband agrees, "And a brace of boys to follow her."

"Do you see two?" she laughs. "I see three. What a busy croft we'll have!"

Our enchanted fire is so powerfully woven we feel warm sitting beside it, despite the cool sea air. We pass the food and drink, watching the play of colored light within. First the Beltane cake, adorned with a dozen nipples, each knob a charm to protect crops, livestock, hearths and children. We each eat part of the cake and then throw the rest into the fire, conjuring the unseen hosts to care for and watch over what is dearest to our hearts.

The rest of the feast appears, passed from hand to hand. Special sweet rolls with crosses and spirals. Lamb and venison and smoky pork, tulse and tangle, oat cakes and cheeses, wild mushrooms cooked with onions, bowls of young turnips and young greens and loaves of delicious breads. I save a bit of each of the best delicacy in a jug I have brought to share with the minstrel later, so eager to be met with him that I can eat only sparrow bites of the feast, my body quivering as if I had fasted for days.

Staghorn beckons me over to him. He brings out a helm of

deer hide crowned with antlers from a two-point buck.

"Tis for your laddie. Tis his for the night. Go now." He addresses the group. "Let's make a blessing for Kyairthwen."

They toss me across the top of the bonfire.

"The advantage of a vision-fire," snorts Rose, "is that not even a sow gets singed by it." All laugh; I am gathered into the center of a warm, loving spiral.

"The blessings of heart and belly be upon you," whispers Jesse, placing her hands on me. "May you be mated as well as I."

"If it is the will of the Horned One to bless you with a man in his image and to bless our coven with him as well, then so be it," nods Winter.

"We need new men," says one of the three old women from the Ail Fionn coven.

"And may all men be turned from the way of war to the ways of the hunter who is seed-sower as well," says Sarah, "Men who love their young—and their mothers."

"All the power of the Goddess go with you, Kyairthwen. So be it. So be it. So mote it be."

The warmth of the circle and the vision fire glow bright in my heart. The cliff that seemed crumbly and frail on my way down now opens handholds out of her flesh, making it as easy for me to ascend as if my shoulders bore no pack, but wings.

Chapter 51

Strange that it should be clear at the beach, yet misty here, at the stones. Well, mist is the Witch's friend. Thoughts travel easier from one to another when the mist is thick, visions appear more readily, and the mist serves as a friendly cloak to shroud that which is no longer safe to pursue in the light of day. I can sense Alain long before I can see him, kneeling beside a rock cairn at the north of the circle. I am all dressed in gray, save for the wreath of flowers around my head, so when I step out of the fog to stand before him, I know it is as if I had materialized out of the wet, shape-shifting air. He rises. I take his wreath and put it on the cairn, place mine beside it. I incline my head, indicating he should follow me and begin to run deosil* around the stones; an easy canter at first, then to a gallop, hair and cloak streaming out behind me. Soon we are flying; I can no longer feel my feet hit the ground. The ninth time around the circle the air takes me and spins me, floating me down to the ground, standing again before the wreathes left on the granite shelf. I nod to the minstrel. He takes the circlet of flowers, places it on my head. His fingers

---

*Deosil—clockwise, sunwise.

are so warm, my skin throbs where he has touched me. Taking the horns Staghorn has given me, I fasten the strap underneath his chin. I must undo and reweave the wreath to go over the horns; it takes only a few moments, fingers moving effortlessly.

It is my turn to be awed; the God standing before me, Stag and Man. I have an eerie sense of foresight; remembering the vision I had of the God as a child. I had been here at the stones, gathering herbs and blossoms. Catching a glimpse of a stag, I had stopped and shaded my eyes. But when the stag turned to look at me he had this face, these eyes, green with the warm love light pouring through them, these broad shoulders, in place of hoofs, these hands. Long moment of locked eyes and silence. Then another child laughing up the hill—he turned and bounded away in a flash, moving on four legs, not two.

This time the God will not flee. I stretch my hands out to him; his hands are already out and waiting for mine. Our hands clasp, melting, merging; conversations buzzing in our blood, my body a hive dizzy with sweetness and churring wings.

"On the first day of May
The Queen has no sting
Then shall the bold one
Swift on the wing
Heart of the butterfly
He shall be King."

We turn and walk through the North stone. Within, the inner circle is completely clear, no mist, moon shining down into the circle of stones, the stones themselves standing whole, glowing with blue fire. His astonishment jolts through my hand, my wrist, my shoulder, sweeps my body, leaving me shocked as the first time that Annie and I accidentally created this magic ourselves.

At the circle's center we spread our cloaks on the ground by the altar. The chalice and athamé gleam silver in the light of the waxing moon. The wine for May Eve is always white, spiced with woodruff. Not knowing why, I have brought red. Gran has always said that instinct must be trusted beyond tradition.

I take him to the east point of the circle, where we both kneel. Distant and far-away, the faery music vibrating under the hills.

"Feel now the powers of the East," I whisper to him. "Lizbet was right to have you play for the directions. Playing your music you are a mage already, though you know it not. Take a deep breath. Now the air is breathing you. Life begins when the infant takes its first breath. We may live without food a moon or more; without water, half a moon. Without air, only a few moments. Air is one with thought, mind and music. It was the beginning." I pause, sensing him beside me, breathing in silence.

"Feel the East, which is birth, breath, wings, flight. Air. Let the East come to you. And when you are ready, let it play you."

Brief wait in silence, eyes closed. . . then the sound of his recorder. Sweet callings in the wood, the bird to its mate, its mate's answer; darkness opening into dawn. The two birds flying, spiralling, soaring high above the sea, the rising sun coloring their wings rose and gold.

We rise. I lead Alain to the South.

"Fire," I invoke, "corner of the South. Sun, the All-Father, as much the source of life as Earth. We ignite the fires on Beltane to celebrate the healing powers of the light, the strengthening and waxing of the light. All the sun and all the fire." I kneel, feeling I have not been strong here, feeling still my fear and uneasiness with this element.

His lute sounding; at first the tune is that of the "King of the Faeries," then it is as if the strings are alive with white strands of flame. Through the gate between the eyes prance stag, stallion, and a cat so large Oberon could sleep on one of its paws. Rutting call of the stag, neigh of the stallion, roaring snarl of the great cat whose love is a forest full of flame. I become one with doe and mare, mounted, mated, terror and lust jolting through my loins, light breaking me apart, leaving me empty and shuddering. I can barely rise and lead him to the West, where we kneel again.

Before I can say anything about the West, womb of the Mother, twilight, autumn, the minstrel has taken out his harp. I melt into water as he calls the waves, sounds that conjure the great surging silences of the sea. Alain has said that the first harp was the gift of Mannanon MacLir; a poet on a beach, he said, was drawn by strange music; coming upon the rotting body of a whale, he saw that the sound was made when the wind whistled through the ribs and decaying tendons of the beast, filling the twilight with unearthly music. He took one of the ribs, went into dream and carved, and the first harp was born. The tale must be true; within the resonances of the harp I hear the whales calling and calling. Though I have never heard aught except for the gasp they make when they breach, and rarely that, I know from my dreams that under the water, they sing. And then I am a child again, safe in my mother's womb, rocking, rocking, gentleness, gentleness. It takes me some time after the last chord to realize it is the last. I stand, whole and graceful in my self, free of the hollow feeling from the fire.

I lead Alain to the North. Here we do not kneel, but stand.

"Deeps and the Darks. The crystal caves; fruit breaking the branches of apple and quince; the vine heavy with grapes, fields thick with grain; and under all the great caves of crystal, vast caverns of air, underground streams, and under that—fire and the center." I kneel, but Alain remains standing. A great numinous, shuddering sound comes through him. I bless the presence of the mist which keeps the sound within the boundary of the stones. The sound is like rock thrown into the center of the circle; the echoes of it ripple out and out, splashing and breaking against the perimeter of stones at the edge and rippling back in and coming forth in another huge surge—like the deep resonance that comes from my Gran sometimes when the Goddess Anu speaks through her and her wand becomes a living tree.

The sound flows into words, Taliesin, Amergin, the God voice chanting through him:

"I am fair among flowers
I am the ruthless boar
I am the salmon in the deep green pool
I am the hawk that stoops and strikes
Who but I circles both in pond and sky?

I am the perilous roar of the sea
I am the head ringed with smoke
I am the flame beyond the eyes
I am the eyes beyond the flame
Letters are none can spell my name.

I am the Leviathan; the great deeps are no mystery to me
I am the owl, and the waning moon is my branch
I am the piece of night named Raven of Dagda
I am the songs of all the seasons
And of none.

I am the corn on the threshing room floor
I am the barley ground between stones
I am the need-fire and the bale-fire and the charm of smoke
Who but I bright bird and coal that does not die?

I am terror and laughter
Drunkenness and sobriety
Who but I travels the sun for a day and a year?
Who but I knows the secrets of unhewn dolmen?"

He fixes me with his eyes, twin bale-fires burning behind green glass, and as he moves towards me I move back until we are at the center of the circle. I am no longer his teacher; he is possessed by the God and past instruction now. I take off my kirtle, naked except for my crown. Slowly he rips his shirt down the middle, casts it aside, strips of the rest of his clothes, eyes never leaving mine. I hand him the little ball of faerie crystal, motioning for him to hold it up to the waxing moon. As he holds the orb up to the moon, fire from behind his eyes, silver fire of the moon meet in a burst of light in the crystal; when he turns it towards me it is a shimmering transparent disk, as if the moon herself inhabited his hands, sea-foam churning across the surface, silver script of an ancient grimoire*, songs, chants, invocations, every language and before language a chaotic babble in my blood, water's gentleness ripped away, perilous roar of the sea in my skull—

And he brings the moon down, down upon me. Drowning in crashing billows of silver; as I gasp for breath to scream he holds the moon directly opposite to my face. I breathe in the moon and become one with the light, waves crashing through my head, sea-foam and silver fire out through my fingers, waterfall hissing light down through my breasts, my spine, light pouring from my nipples, down through my belly, red foaming churn of blood in my

---

*Grimoire—sacred book of magic.

womb, belly and breasts swelling with moon, waterfall of light pouring down hips and legs, earth hissing as if it were scalded by the silver pour of moon and moon-led ocean. My hands extend in the position of invoking. I am dream, moon, Goddess; sound like a whole choir of faerie whistles pours through the top of my head and out my mouth. Nothing exists but the sound of that pure light.

Something cold and round between my breasts. My hands go to my heart. The crystal ball, the minstrel's fingers. I see him, gray-green eyes, flower-decked horns, his arm connecting us, his cock rising up to his navel, aching to connect us deeper.

I place the ball on the altar. Take the chalice. After a brief hesitation his hand closes around the haft of the athamé. The waxing moon now floats, a point of light, on the blood-dark wine. Chalice cradled between my hands. He slowly brings the knife down. As it touches the wine the moon breaks into rings of light, the red fluid parts, opens to the blade. Deep ache of my body longing to be opened also. Tortured breath escapes him as the blade sinks into the wine. Tip of the blade contacting the bottom of the cup. Shivers spreading from the mouth of my womb, capturing heart, belly, throat.

"The Goddess and the God are One," I whisper.

"The Goddess and the God are One," he responds.

For a moment he is human, eyes mutely entreating what he is to do.

"Put the blade on the altar."

Slowly he withdraws it, his hand trembling. I offer him the cup. He drinks, holds the cup to my lips. I hold some of the wine in my mouth. As we kiss the wine flows back and forth between us, swirling first cool, then warm as blood.

The cup tips, spilling over his erect phallus, splattering my thighs like moon-blood. He moves to embrace me, but I push him gently so that he is leaning back on his hands, kneel across him, slowly lower myself onto his lap. Our eyes meet, wide, acknowledging the enormity of the magic, the vastness. We touch, crown of him throbbing into my openness, warm mouth of my vulva swallowing him, cup receiving blade, unbearably long sheathing, long sliding. . .

We scream, shatter; our mortal bodies torn to pieces of hot

light and scattered through the stars.

Sobs. Silence. Blinding silver. Slowly the splintered mirror of moon settles and sighs to pools of water. He is on his back, gasping as if he were the King cut down, I straddling him. No world beyond the curtains of my hair, our two faces. I breathe out and he breathes in as if my breath would give him life. He breathes out and I breathe in as if he were the source of all light in the world.

His eyes are closed, his gasps diminishing in strength. Have I killed him? Am I dead myself?

His eyes open, the air breathes his chest out and then in. His hands soft on my breasts. I have never been more glad to be alive.

Chapter 52

Alain works deftly with the Lady, tuning her, restoring her delicate balances. It's a fine spring day, white clouds fat and lazy as sheep at the end of summer grazing in the blue sky. Alain sits with his back up against the wall of the croft, Malcolm squatting on his heels beside him in a rapture of concentration.

"The Lady is delicate," Alain informs him, "like a virgin. Each time you must be as sensitive with her as if it were the first time."

He finishes tuning the lute, strokes its curving belly and gently puts it aside, taking up his harp.

"Are harps so sensitive too?" Malcolm runs a reverent finger along the gleaming wood.

"A harp needs its share of attention too, but it falls not so easily out of tune. More like a comfortable wife or leman of long-standing, used to your touch and easy to respond—" he glances sidelong at me, sly smile. I finish wringing out and hanging the morning's washing, pouring the water leavings over the midden heap.

"What sort of lesson is this?" I query, hands on my hips, mock indignation, "Music or sport?"

"Aye," he gives me his most winsome smile, "music is the fairest sport, excluding one—and that sport makes the fairest music." He catches his lower lip in his teeth, eyes caressing me as intimately as if I were clothed in nought but air.

Quick to notice the current of flame between us, Malcolm stands, stretches and busies himself in the garden yanking weeds.

"Ayè, Captain McNair. Take no prisoners," growls Alain, his stern voice belied by the grin that follows it.

"Aye, sir," Malcolm pulls his forelock in mock deference. "None shall be spared, sir."

Alain pushes himself up from the wall, stretching and flexing like a cat. The power in his shoulders and thighs makes me tremble. He stores his instruments inside the croft.

"Time for my lesson?" he asks hopefully.

"What sort of art would you be learning?" I tease.

"The art of being a man," he says, using the phrase meaning a man who is a shaman, a God-link, possessed by the God and given over to his service. Softness settles around his face and mouth as he strokes my hair.

"Teach me whatever thou wilt. I am thy novice."

I kiss his fingers. "Bring your harp and recorder."

We walk, holding hands, breathing in the fineness of the day. I lead without any plan of where we shall go, nor yet what we are to do when we arrive, following the scents of flower and pine weaving like a laughing stream before us.

We thread our way through a labyrinth of little tarns and ponds that dot the flat land beyond the hills. We call this district 'the stars' for there are nearly as many small pools here as there are lights in the night sky. He stops and picks purple heart-flowers, fixes them in my bodice, kisses my breasts, catching my nipples in his lips.

"It's too open here," I warn.

"Is it open here?" he asks, nuzzling his curly head against my groin.

"Soon," I promise.

The tallest pine in the area welcomes; surrounded by water,

flanked by a semi-crescent of its smaller children, it almost forms its own island. Not much concealment, but we can magic the rest.

"Would you learn how to cast a veil?" I ask.

He hovers on the edge of an erotic response, then bites his lip and nods.

"All right. This is like what I taught you about casting a circle. When we cast this, the circle must be like a wall. Rather than seeing the round inscribed by blue fire, we feel it as a curtain, not quite of darkness—" I hesitate, not ever having had it described to me in words, merely showed me. Alain's inner sight is not as keen as mine; he must have a description before he will be able to see it. He takes the recorder out of his pack and holds it, looking at me expectantly.

"It's not quite of darkness, it's more of a gray—sort of mist— that's not quite right either. It's a veil. See if you can see or sense it—as I pull it."

He nods. I half close my eyes and move my palm back and forth in a slow circle until I feel my palm hook as if onto some unseen fabric. Then slowly, pull the fabric out of the air, a yard of palpable gauze. As my hand hooks the invisible weft, Alain's recorder sounds a deep note behind me, the air sounding through the wooden tube as if it were one long continuous breath. Alain's magic is with his ears, his hands; while I see the weft, he describes it in sound. Long slow turning of the circle, the weft flowing out of my hands, straight and clear. At last connecting the place at the east where the cloth began, I move my hand up and down over the seam until the seam vanishes and is smooth, the curtain snug around us as a cocoon. Then I turn again around the circle, moving my hand up and down around the walls, barely visible save for an occasional wrinkle of irridescence. Satisfied, I sigh and shake out my hands, put them flat on the ground and lie full length in the grass. Our island is secure now as if guarded by fort as well as moat. The minstrel lays down his recorder.

"I am in awe of you," he whispers.

I sit beside him, running my hand through his curls.

"Can it work the other way?" he asks, "Can you make it a window or a door to draw someone in as well as a wall to keep someone out?"

I raise my eyebrows. "I don't know. I've never seen that done but—what one desires one can always do. Desire makes its own path." I pause, trying to imagine how to create such an opening, unable at first to think of why I would want to.

"I would make an opening between us," he says, "one that would never be veiled or closed—" he picks up his harp. "—I can feel the power in my fingers. Perhaps the magic will come if I play—" As he plays, the harp sounds different than I have ever heard it; he plucks one note and lets it fade, and plucks another, each note so far apart from the next that it is barely connected to the echo of the one before it.

My breasts feel hot. Unlacing my stomacher, I free them.

"Open yourself to me. Open a door that will lead me to your heart, come out of the cocoon. . ." He calls me through the harp, a song of butterfly coaxing.

Slowly I take off my clothes, making small gestures with my hands as if bringing the sun and the sounds of the harp into my body, my flesh dissolving to a window of air, clear as a pathway of light.

I stand with my legs far apart, my arms outstretched, open, in the posture of invoking and receiving. The air resonates with the power of yielding. He puts down the harp, undresses, lies on the ground before me, caressing my feet. He runs his lips up one leg, over to the other, presses his brow worshipfully against my portal, hands cupping my buttocks. I expect the five-fold kiss I have taught him that Witches used to reverence the Goddess in each other's bodies. Instead he slides his tongue deep inside my cleft.

Shock brings my hands down, pushing his head away.

"Open a door for me," he breathes. Alain nudges his head back, nuzzles me, his tongue igniting a white-hot flame flickering through my body. Dark pain twisting my heart douses it; Annie's mouth against me; our secret, our magic.

I push him away and kneel beside him, pulling his head to my breasts. He catches me passionately to him, sucking and biting. We kiss, rubbing against each other wildly.

"Kyairthwen!" he whimpers. I gave him the gift of sharing my magic name; now he makes good use of it, calling my soul to pour through my body like colored light. My smell on his lips—

exquisite—Annie—Annie—dark pain of losing her cramping me, taking me out of the pleasure.

"Oh Kyairthwen," he begs, "Open your heart to me. I want to be your mate," he whispers against my body, "I want to be your man."

Lying on my back, ground trembling under me, I dig my heels into the earth, arching.

"Take me," I whisper. Instead of mounting me he is kissing my body, tongue hot on my thighs, between—

"No. No."

He looks up at me, desire like pain in his eyes.

"Och, don't deny me. You're so beautiful. Let me worship you."

"I can't," I plead.

He lies on top of me, supporting himself by his arms. Tip of his cock caressing the softness where his tongue had been.

"Yes, that way," I urge.

He penetrates me.

"Is that what you want?"

"Yes."

"Have you never done the other?"

What shall I say?

"I—did not know—men and women did such."

"Ah then let me teach you. Let me teach you," he coaxes.

I hold his shoulders to try to keep him inside me.

"Lots of girls are shy about it at first," he says. "It's as natural as the other. You smell wonderful."

He puts his fingers inside me and rubs them under my nose. I sob, the ache of missing Annie more than I can bear.

"I promise you'll like it." He runs his lips down my midriff. "Ah, you said you'd open to me—" he pushes my thighs open. I put my hands over my face and moan as he puts his mouth against me. I sob as my body shivers into orgasm, and then sob harder and harder, turn over on my side, head in my arms, sobbing and sobbing until the sobbing turns into a high keen of loss and terror at feeling so in love and vulnerable again. What a fool I am to let this minstrel touch me so deeply, knowing he will leave me as he has left every girl, leaving my heart torn open again. Then I wail again, missing Annie so physically, desperate to feel her breasts, her hair, to hear her voice, to feel the soft touch of her fingers and lips on my body. The minstrel is holding me, hugging me. I sob more, feeling ashamed to look at him.

"What did I do?" he whispers in my ear. "Oh, Fiona, please look at me."

I bury my head in the cloak.

"Please, I thought you would like it. Did I hurt you? Please don't hide from me like this." I press my face into the cloak, wishing he would leave me to my grief.

"Kyairthwen." He whispers my magical name. I told him that if he called my true name, wherever he was, I would hear, and in body or wraith I would come to him. I have no choice but to turn and face him, hating myself for how red and blotchy I must look from crying.

"You're beautiful," he says, unconsciously responding to my thought. "Why are you crying? Please forgive me if I offended or hurt you in any way."

What shall I say? He pulls some of our clothes over me, stroking me in a comforting way.

"What happened?" he persists. "Where did you go?"

I shake my head. "I can't tell you."

"*Can't?* Ah," he sighs sadly, "are you drawing a wall between us then?"

I nod. "Aye."

He rubs his hand lightly over my heart. "Is there someone you didn't tell me about?"

I look at him. He'd asked if I had enjoyed many lovers. I told him he was the third, told him of my initiation with Pan, my relationship with Sean.

"Ah, that's it." He looks ready to cry. "Why did you lie to me?"

"I didn't quite lie. But it was a lie, too."

"Is it a man you're—still seeing?" he asks, unable to disguise the pain in his face.

"No. It's not a man at all." I tell him about Annie, thinking to be brief, but one story spills into another until he has heard about our magic and our passion, our childhood thefts and mischief, her leaving with the gypsies. At the end of the telling I cannot tell if he is shocked or only surprised.

"I knew men did with each other—at sea of course—and traveling players are known for it." Shakes his head. "Stupid of me not to think—stupid to think a chalice—needs a blade—to make a stir." He laughs at himself. "Just never really thought of it. But—why not. You loved each other." His smile vanishes. "And you still love her. You love her more than you love the young lord."

"Beyond compare," I admit.

"That much." He bites his lip, looks at the ground. "Do you think you'd ever love a man—as you loved her?"

"I don't know."

He rubs his curls over my body, takes me in his arms. "Well, if you could—please love me."

I hold him to me, his suffering deepening mine. Gran's voice at Initiation: *"Remember every wounding is an opening—"*

As I surrender, going deeper into the pain, it runs to its depth and eases, and the wound fills with peace. I open my eyes at the same instant Alain opens his. Doors of love, pure as the trees leaning to each other, green to green, pure as the love of the tarns called stars holding and reflecting the sky. My heart opens, flowering, flowing into love, pure and sweet and clear.

Chapter 53

Mina nods. "Aye—aye—he's ready. The mushrooms are a powerful ally. They will serve you well."

Gran says nothing, staring into the fire. Through some trick of the firelight the lines in her face are erased, merging with the shadows. How beautiful she must have been thirty years ago.

"What do you think?" I whisper.

"Mina speaks for us," she says. She turns to me, pupils of her eyes enormous, hypnotic. "Take him to the top of Cuadhain Ben More."

"Is there a faery gate there?"

She shakes her head slightly. "This journey is not to Faery. Think not you know this quest. It is the future you are weaving here. You are rooted enough. You are a tree in blossom and must consider how you will fruit."

I feel excited. It is a long walk and a steep climb to Cuadhain Ben More. Rituals at that site are rare. Only those rites which require visioning into the future are held there; Sarah has made the ascent each time she has found herself to be with child, to scry the child's future and learn its true name. Once when I was seven the coven took me there. We built the watchtower cairns to the four corners and had a bonfire. They laid a quartz egg in each of my hands and put me into trance, invoking the wisdom of the Child Goddess, the Sooktart Machlana Shaumone. But what questions they asked her, or what she spoke through me I know not. I vaguely remember voices talking and the comforting warmth of BearHearth's arms around me as he carried me sleeping down the mountain, and for a year after that she appeared often in my dreams. And that whole year that the Sooktart Machlana blessed me with her presence, pregnant women in the village would ask me to put my hands on their bellies and bless the child within. And each time the Machlana's warmth and magic flowed through my hands, and each of the six bairns blessed in this way was born healthy and beautiful and wise with the purity of the Machlana.

"Build the four cairns together with him. Let him lay and build the fire. Take your chalice—whatever water is in the working you be responsible for that. Invoke your air ally. The osprey can see a long ways and can see deep as well, deep into the heart of things. Use that vision to see into your heart, to see the heart of this man and what your destiny with him is."

Her voice is so like mine, deeper with wisdom, thicker with age, but the resonances so like that if her lips had not moved I would have thought it the speaking of my own deep self.

Gran takes some of the dried amanita mushrooms out of her sack. She and Mina bless them with burning herbs and salt water, making all the magical sigils for protection and opening of gates over them. Staghorn comes in so softly it is as if he had always been there and had just become visible. He holds the mushrooms in his hands:

"By the God who is the Shape-Shifter
By the Magical Lord of the Dance.
You Who are always in Motion
On Earth
As in the Heavens,
Teacher—Healer—Changer;
Fill the gift of these mushrooms

With your blue fire.
May we always use it wisely and well.
Heart's ease—Sorrow's end.
Knowledge beyond pain.
Ecstasy beyond death.
We invoke You.
We are humbled before Your power.
Support our Kyairthwen
And the Man who carries Your magic
In his hands and voice
By whatever name You choose for him.
Let them be healed and receive true vision
Through your ecstatic fires."

He draws a series of sigils over the mushrooms with his ritual stag horn. Male mysteries perhaps, or deeper mysteries of the mushrooms I have not yet been initiated into.

I take the mushrooms and place them one by one in my magic pouch. The three of them surround me, arms linked.

"Holy spirits of earth and sky
Guide you.
Sacred heart of water and flame
Guard you."

That night the minstrel and I begin our fast. After hoeing and planting a new section of the garden the next morning we set out. Once in the woods, the love of the trees shimmers out to us so tangibly it is like walking through water. Our pace slows as I frequently stop to hug and kiss an especially dear tree, and kiss my hand to others as we pass.

"You move like a doe in these woods," Alain says admiringly. "Are the trees always alive like this or do they only become so when you pass?"

"Always," I smile and caress a branch of elder.

"I think you're more at ease with trees than you are with people."

How not? I wonder. Trees give so much and ask for so little. They do no harm. . .

That night we walk a long, long way in the moonlight, the moon casting eerie blue lights and shadows throughout the forest. Seeing in the flickering shift of light and shadow an occasional faery-face smiling by at me, spinning and disappearing. The woods are alive with their faces, their barely heard steps running beside us, darting off, bushes rustling, subdued giggles. The minstel takes my hand.

"The shadows are alive tonight," he murmurs.

"It's the Fay," I whisper to him. "Curious about you. Can you ses them?"

"Where?" he stops and looks around.

"Everywhere," I say. "Don't look too hard or you'll miss them."

"I feel—something," he stops again as an unmistakeable peal of faery laughter comes through the clearing.

"Is that—God's name—"

"Shhhh—you'll frighten them," I warn.

"Surely it was a bird—a nightingale perhaps—a nightingale—it was a nightingale."

I giggle, pulling him along the path.

"Are we going to the land of Faery tonight?" he asks, full of excitement. "I'll go. I can believe anything when I'm with you. I always have. I always have believed in them really. Sometimes they sing for me in my dreams."

"Tomorrow we hike up the mountain and tomorrow eve we'll take the mushrooms. What happens then is in the hands of the Goddess."

"As I am in yours," he responds.

We stop. Between a weft of branches an enormous spider has spun a perfect web, shimmering crystal against the moon. A light breeze stirs the web. Ecstatic, I ride with the spider on the pulse of the air.

"One time," I confide in Alain, "when I was in the realm of Faery, the Queen of the Fay showed me how to take a spider web apart and put it back together as cunning as ever Ragni could spin it. But when I came back to this world—and I tried to do as she had taught me—I made a mess of it—Gran slapped me and told me that Ragni would spin me a bitter fate for my meddling."

Alain takes his harp from his back and plays a weaving song for the spiders, for the great Weaver whose loom is the earth.

"Ah—look—over by the moon—" I point to my special star as she steps forth, shining in her white nakedness against the deepening blue. I kiss my hand to the star.

"Why is that star special to you? Is it particularly sacred—the evening star?"

I sigh, happy. "That star is my friend. I know not why that one shines so in my heart any more than I know—why you shine there so. Stars make constant friends, Mina says. It is well to have a friend who can be yours life after life. Eternal in beauty—the friendship of a star. The trees I love will pass—and you and I in these forms. Whenever I come to earth I can seek this star and know that our love is eternal."

"Suppose your star should fall?"

"She will not. My love will keep her there in the sky."

The minstrel's long fingers stroking the inside of my palm, tracing the patterns on my fingers. Our hands dance together, touching lightly, warming the air between them. The star. The web. Our hands. Braid of our breath.

"Mina says that—the fixed stars and the speaking stars are not the same. The speaking stars come as messengers, quick and fleeting as the powers of the mind and the air. The fixed stars are the heart—constant as the earth."

He catches my other hand. "Ah, if you be the earth, then—let me be that other star, our hearts fixed, star to star and flame to flame, from now to the end of time."

I catch my breath. The world hovers, delicate as a web or a breath, soft and strong as the light of my twilight star. My heart glows into a pearl of flame, arcing into a rainbow of moon and dew, crystal and foam, starfire and snow, meeting the flame in his heart, as like unto mine as a mirror. Nimué embodied all that I lacked, and wished I had. The minstrel embodies all that I am and am becoming. Our bodies close, hands entwined, we stand, feeling the echo resonate between our beings. He brings his mouth down to mine. Our lips almost touch; breathing each other's breath; kiss of spirits, the flame between us so palpable we need not touch to call it forth.

*   *   *   *

That is what I remember; not the walking after that, silent except for the occasional brush of the leaves, the sigh of wind. Not the finding of a soft cushion of moss in which we made our bed for the night. Not even the passion that we shared together, sweet as it was. But the weaving between us of that moment; the silence; the star; the bridge of crystal light between us; the kiss without touching.

Chapter 54

Next morning at the foot of the mountain we find a stream pouring into a tarn. We bathe there. Cold and refreshed, light from fasting, we ascend. We are silent much of the way. Alain occasionally breaks the silence, playing on his harp, his recorder, or singing. The path is too steep much of the time for him to play or sing or do anything except breathe deeply.

Near the summit I point out an osprey's nest on top of a huge, wind-flattened pine. As we watch, the male osprey returns, the female rises from the nest to greet him, and they do a dance of greeting, momentarily oblivious to the cries of their young. They sweep by us—wind from their wing tips brushes our faces. We watch as they return to the nest, feeding the young the fish that the father has brought.

"That is my air ally," I whisper to him. "That one came to me when I was but eleven. Gran says that the water is my power element, and that is why even my creature of air is a lover of the sea."

"Is that where you learned to catch fish?" he jokes.

"No. I learned that from the fish themselves. I told you the salmon is my water ally."

"And the lynx your earth ally. Thank you for sharing this with me. Is there an ally of fire?"

I turn and smile. "If I have an ally of fire, I think it must be you."

When we reach the top of Cuadhain Ben More, the sun is still high in the sky. The minstrel sets about finding wood, breaking it into pieces for our fire tonight.

"We can do that later," I suggest, taking off my clothes and lying down in the sun. "Let's rest."

"Aye, in a bit," he agrees. But by the time he comes to lay with me I have dozed, and in my dream I have a pair of wings. Tucking and hurtling through the air, I plunge into the cool dark sea. In the sea I turn fish, salmon migrating upstream to the sacred pool. Swiped from the pool I become the big-pawed cat, padding soundlessly through the woods, my eyes as green as the sun through the leaves. From there, loping up the mountain, returning to the top to prowl and purr beside my lover, who is feathered, who is sleek, who is furred. Mating we dissolve into shimmers of light, becoming a quivering hive of twilight stars.

I wake, expecting twilight from the coolness, but the sky is still blue, the days as long as they will ever be.

"How glad I am to have you when the days are long," I say as he opens his eyes and smiles at me.

"Ahh—I shall be glad to have you when the nights are long," he says, holding me to him. "And cold," he adds thoughtfully. "We'll need our own croft by then," he asserts happily. "Perhaps this winter—I'll get you with child."

"This winter! Too soon—too soon," I shake my head.

"Ah, but someday—someday—Fiona, what a bonny child we'd make between us, would we not?"

"Easier to make them than to feed them," I warn.

"Ah, I will feed them well enough," he promises. "Feed them on love." He stretches, beautiful, cat-like. Cells of my body laughing into desire.

"Can we do the rite or—must we wait for dark?" he asks.

"Aye, we can begin." I say.

"Shall we take the mushrooms first or build the cairns

first?"

A loud growl from his stomach makes us both giggle. I put my hand on his furry belly and warn, "This will not fill you up— it may make you sick. But 'twill be a healing in the end, I promise."

We build the first cairn, hunting for the flat rocks that are always scattered after they are used to make the watchtowers for the directions. Fitting them together, the rocks have been used so often some of them have been worn to a place where they interlock as if carved to do so by some master hand.

"Are these shaped by the Fay?" he whispers.

"Perhaps."

The first cairn complete comes about to our chest as we sit beside it. We take out the mushrooms. He gives me the ones he has been carrying next to his heart, I give him the ones I have carried next to mine. We chew them slowly. He makes a wry face but does not joke. We drink water to wash them down and go to the second quarter, finding the stones and fitting them in place.

Nothing but his hands, square, strong fingered; my hands, matching in shape but half the size. The stones that mesh together as we place them, just so.

Walking over to the third point in the circle, I become aware that I am feeling sick; but the heft of the stones in my hands grounds me, and soon I lose myself in the activity of stacking the stones, creating the western tower. The stones begin to shimmer; I find the minstrel sitting and staring at a stone he has in his hand. I guide his hand over to stack it on top of my stone; our hands begin to nuzzle each other like coupling snakes. We complete the cairn slowly. I feel him looking at me but I do not look at him, knowing we would get lost in the looking, and there is yet another cairn to complete.

We walk, picking up stones and sliding them together, moving so slowly, the world's most slow and exquisite dance as we shape the final cairn. Our hands brush. His lips are wet—he is smiling and our eyes and our eyes and our eyes. . .

The cairn is complete and we sit, we sit—though neither of us hears the bird, the feather floats down between us, landing on top of the north cairn.

The sea eagle.

He takes the feather between his fingers; my fingers bracelet his wrist. He brushes it over my face as if with that feather he willed my face into being for the first time. Then I guide the feather to his face, brushing him to being. *Eyes. . . eyes. . .eyes. . .* As if I were looking into a quiet stream or loch, seeing my own reflection. His face shimmers, dances; movement and light.

A wave of nausea. I close my eyes and open them again. Alain, my minstrel. And also myself. We are close together now. One flame. One heart. We are in the middle of the circle. The sky is purple. I stand, searching for my star, fixing my gaze where she will appear and raising my hands in a gesture of welcome. He stands behind me, his chin resting on top of my head, his arms like wings floating behind my arms. I feel the pulse of his throat against the back of my head. Our arms together, one pair of wings. Then the star breaking forth, impossibly bright like a jewel, scattering, scattering beads of light, light streaming out, streaming into patterns of the most complex and ornate web that the universe ever spun, white lights streaking across the sky. A cry shivers through us. Our voices one voice. We stare with amazement, the spider-weaving of our star glittering, hanging over us.

I turn and cry out, thinking we are in the fire. But the bonfire has not been lit; the wraith flames dancing around us part of the great star web. I press my mouth to his and we kiss. Blaze of flame white as the starfire fills our heads.

"I am a fire in the head." The voice of the Goddess, deep as a God's voice, fills me. We merge. We have always been merged. We have always been one.

"How do you know he is my mate?" I had asked Mina.

"How do you not?" she had asked me. "Child, clear as this is, can you not know it?"

I will never unknow it now.

Peace. Absolute darkness. Blackness. At the heart of the earth lies the fire. . . At the heart of the fire lies the darkness. . . At the heart of the darkness lies the light. . . At the heart of the light. . .

Shivers. Waves of colored irridescence shining through my body. I have a body. Body is cold. The minstrel's voice, sounding both far away and in the center of my skull. We rise. He fumbles with his flint for a moment only and then the fire catches. I feel a moment of panic, shake my head, "No—"

"It's all right. Here, come close." He wraps our cloaks together, making a pocket of warmth for us by the fire. Yes, I'm shaking. I realize it is not with cold but merely the shaking the mushrooms bring.

"Water," I breathe.

"Ayë, where is it?"

"Mmmm—I left my skin here—" Journey over to the west cairn to fetch the water. Stop and watch him tending the fire, beautiful light on his face, his hair. He stares at me with widely dilated eyes.

"Come," he coaxes. "Come."

And I feel like a deer, watching a human, suddenly shy. But more curious than shy, I step closer and closer, sideways steps as a deer would take. He tucks his chin, staring at me. His beautiful eyes, rippling blue, rippling black, rippling green. And I see the horns growing from his head. He is stag. Man. My mate. His hands caress a deer horn he has brought which he recently found. I remember his exulation at this sign of having been chosen, being acknowledged as a son of the Horned God, the God blessing him with his image, his token.

I kiss his brow, his forehead, his eyebrows, his closed eyes. He smiles at me, moving his jaws to ease the tightness. I yawn and stretch. And then the surface of the air between us ripples and he shifts again, to a beautiful woman, a Goddess, and then back to the God. And then woman and man and God and Goddess again. And I feel myself ripple and change—have we breasts, horns, a skin that slips off when you touch it? He puts his hand, my hand, on our cock. How long have we been naked?

I am not cold anymore. Warmth from the fire, warmth from our eyes, meeting and melding. Male and female is nothing; a game, a dance. We are one creature; we have breasts, we have phallus, we have fur and silk smoothness, womb and the womb's open flower.

And eyes and eyes and eyes. . .

We have been sliding—mouths, teeth, lips. We have breath. We are the white starfire. The pulsing web of nerve and vein. Blood of Moonsun brightness. Glittering web of star spinning out from inside us. We are one being, the bright constellations within him matching those within me. Each of us map of the stars and the still water that holds it. Woven together. Woven together. A web of crystal fire. Our differences fall away, shed like skins. And what is left. And what is left. Not serpent. Not spider. Not web. Only the vast whiteness. The vast white fire of stillness.

A single star.

Chapter 55

I serve the minstrel another bowl of hotch-potch. We have been wealthy since he came; anyone can have soup before bed that wants it. Malcolm and Colin are also drinking a cup of bed-time soup. The other children cluster close to me for their good-night story. I like telling stories to the children. Sometimes they ask to hear a particular tale they've heard many times over again, but what I like best is to just sit and look in the fire a bit and let the fire tell me a story which I then say out loud. It's as new to me as it is to them, and often I have no idea how it is to end before I get there.

This tale has a happy ending. All of my tales since the minstrel came have ended happily: "And so the two of them settled down in the croft, with the magic quern that made butter and cheese whenever they wished, and the magic millstone that ground flour from chaff, and the magic well that never ran dry; and they sat before the fire that could burn forever on one clump of peat, and they and the children they bore between them lived happily ever after."

Sprawled half-asleep on my lap, Myrrh gives a satisfied sigh, wraps her arms around my belly and nuzzles her head up against me.

"Ah, I wish I was your child and I could sleep with you," she asserts.

"You're just jealous of the new baby," says Sarah knowingly. "I felt the same way when you came along."

"No!" responds Myrrh angrily. "'Tis not that! If Fiona was my mother we should always have plenty to eat and live happily forever after. That's how the stories are and that's how it is."

I hush them. "No one is going to live happily ever after with such quarreling. Come along then." Myrrh wraps her arms and legs around me and I carry her off to bed, the other children trailing reluctantly after.

"I might as well go too," sighs Eostre. Mother is already in bed with the new baby. I feel warm thinking about him; Mark is such a pretty boy. I begrudged the extra mouth to feed when Mother was pregnant with him and could barely conceal my impatience with her for deciding to bear again. But the moment he was born and looked up at me with that unfocussed indigo stare new-borns have, I lost my heart to him. Now he's eight months old, as healthy, bright and bonny and cheerful a child as anyone could wish for.

The children tucked in, the minstrel joins me and together we sing a couple of songs for them. I was shy to sing with him at first, knowing my voice could not compare with his, but he urged and cajoled me, and now I like the melodies we make together.

We go back in and sit by the fire.

"That was a braw tale."

"Ah, that was no tale. Just something that came in my head just then."

"You made it up?"

"No, no, I don't make them up. Not like you and your songs. Just—sometimes the wind or the fire or someone in my head tells me a story and I say it out loud. That's all it is."

"Why so it is with any maker of tales or singer of songs, love," he says. "That's how I feel about my songs often; like the song is already formed and it's just up to me to listen carefully so I can bring it out of the dream place into words." He slides off his bench and kneels before me, his arms around my knees.

"You look so pretty with the little ones on your knee. I would love to hear the tales you would tell the children we made between us."

I blush. "I've raised enough of my mother's children without making any of my own. Raising children is too hard."

"I don't mean to get you with child and then be parted from you," he says. "I'm asking you to marry me."

The old saying comes again unbidden to my lips: "'Minstrels will settle when barley will travel.' Tying you to a farm would be like putting a bird in a cage. I am a Priestess—bound to the land. And a harper is a creature of air—bound only to his songs."

"But birds do both. Fly away with me; I'll build the finest nest you could ask for. We'll fly and nest both; we'll have our babies and sing our songs and travel our travels. I want you Fiona. Enough to settle. I never thought I would meet my match, but I have. And am I not the Green Man, laid out in the threshing room of your heart? Cast me not aside, to be lost to the ravens of the air—"

I stop his speech by covering his mouth with mine, trusting his kisses more than his fancy words.

"Let's go find a place to lie for the night."

We put on our cloaks and take our blankets out into the night. The moon is waning, there is little light to see.

We say little until we are under the blankets.

"Do you believe me—I do want to marry you."

"I'm not the marrying kind."

"Then I'll bed you out of doors forever. I'd jump the broom with you tomorrow, I vow it. I can get a position as a court minstrel. I've been offered more than once but I always wanted my freedom too much to accept."

"I don't think the Laird would do that," I say hesitantly.

"Will young Lochlan be expecting you to be his mistress still?"

"Aye. He'll expect that."

"And do you want to be?"

"I've hardly thought of him since you came. I don't want to think of him now either." I snuggle up to the minstrel, take his face in my hands for a long kiss. I hush him as I would hush the children as he tries to talk some more.

"I'm yours for the taking," I say. "You don't have to promise me anything."

"In the north country I just passed through there's a couple of Lairds there who would be happy for me to stay. It's a poor district—I cannot say we would live like kings, but—the people there still practice the old ways."

"Have you been in Ross-shire? Over by Linsay's district—just to the South? They're both pagan Lairds, unlike McCleod. McCleod burned some old women last year and a well known sorcerer and his family the year before. Some say that he did it only to please James and not out of any real fear of Witchcraft. Mina says that he's an unchancy man—and would that he were a great deal further off."

"Aye, I felt something of that, passing through his district," the minstrel says. "I'd heard of Ross, and that's where I was headed until Epona lost her shoe and split her foot and—I came here. Stopped here thinking it was just on the way—when it was really my destination." An odd look comes into his face.

"What is it?"

"I just remembered—a gypsy told me once I would find my love through a crescent of iron and lose her—through a circle of gold. Perhaps you are right—perhaps we shouldn't marry." He laughs uneasily.

"Either that or make sure the ring is of brass," I laugh.

"Or silver," he suggests. "Would you like a silver ring?"

I stroke him erect, cuddle close. "I'd like less talk."

*   *   *   *

Alain is as persistent as an autumn wind.

"You never answered me about the silver ring," he reminds me the following day.

I swallow and take the brush out from the pouch at my waist, brushing my hair over my face. Through its red-gold curtain I watch him take his lute out of his sack and start tuning it. A bee flies and tangles in my hair. Careful not to hurt her, I hold my finger up to her so she can walk out on it, then blow slightly on her wings to guide her off.

"Flower I be, but not for the likes of thee," I admonish.

I brush my hair back down my back; Alain takes the brush from me and examines it.

"It's beautiful. What's it made of?"

"Rosewood."

"Rosewood, shame to use that for anything but a lute. It's a pretty thing, though. Where did you come by it?"

"Sean gave it to me."

"You'll not come with me when I leave?"

Leave Gran, my family, the coven, the land? Suppose Annie comes back and I'm not here? How would I ever find her again?

I shake my head.

"Travelling can be hard," he acknowledges. "But—when I find a patron—suppose Ross or Linsay offers me—a place at his table. Or if not there, one of these Lords in the north? I'll come back for you—and would you come with me then, knowing you had a place? Knowing it was a safe place?"

"It's just—I've been here all my life."

He presses his lips together, eyes downcast. "Only a week before the Lochlans come back I'll play for them. If they'll hire me here—I'll stay on here. But—if young Lochlan is as jealous as he is likely to be I—see no future in it. I can see you not wanting to commit until I've found a place. You can come back and visit your family whenever you want. It's not taking you away forever I'm thinking of. And the coven too, I know. But—you said there were covens in Ross-shire, and another in Linsay's district—so surely they'd take us in, would they not?"

"I don't know," I say. "A coven's like a family. It usually *is* a family, not something you can just—walk into." And my family is *here,* I think to myself with vehemence. I don't want to leave.

But I look at the minstrel's beautiful sorrowing profile and feel I cannot bear to have him leave me either.

"I'll be faithful to you Fiona," he promises, "as faithful in my body as my heart if you like. I'll not be leaving you and going off with other girls. I know you think a minstrel is—a certain way."

"The Goddess that I serve has no love for such vows," I tell him, though my heart has leaped up in response to his promise.

"The young Laird?" he asks again busying himself with his lute and not looking at me.

"Ah, I know not," I say, miserable. "You're a clever man, Minstrel. You've fair ruined me for any but yourself. Watered ale to whiskey, Sean is to you."

I turn from him, heartsick and confused. Mina says he's my mate and I would be a fool not to go with him. But I saw the stricken expression on my Gran's face before she could conceal it. Where could I find another teacher like her? And how can I leave my mother when she needs my help so much? Leave everything I've known to go with Alain who I've known little more than a moon. . .

I feel his strong fingers easing my shoulders and relax totally. If only my mind could trust as completely as my body.

I catch one of his hands and hold it between my breasts, turn and look him in the eye.

"I almost curse you in my heart for how lonely I will be when you have gone," I say. I take a deep breath. "But I bless you instead."

A single greenfinch leaps from a branch of a tall pine and flies singing over the clearing. Another flies out of the tree after it.

"Bless me in my freedom as I bless you in yours, Minstrel."

He presses his lips together again; his face clenches with effort. After a long moment of struggle inside himself he opens his eyes.

"I bless your freedom—Priestess."

We hold each other; one of the rare times that we have simply lain together and held each other without making love.

As he lays his head on my shoulder his body slowly relaxes and his breathing becomes deep and regular. Easily I could leave Sean; I have left him already. I don't ever want to stop holding the man lying on my breast now.

What about Gran, and Mina, and the coven? Am I to leave aside my magic for a man as Gran has warned me so many times not to do? And over and over I see Annie coming back to look for me, discovering me gone, with no way of finding me.

Unconsciously I dig my nails into his shoulder and he wakes.

"I have to stay," I whisper.

Chapter 56

Loops and circlets of white and yellow and green twine everywhere. Flowers have been picked for miles around for the rite; the Laird's garden utterly bereft of roses. Evergreen boughs laced with the blooms are draped all about the castle; the wedding pavilion and feasting tables drip with greenery and ribbons.

All the tables from the feasting hall have been laid in rows outside; planks set on stumps covered with linen and flowers augment them. Oh, the smells! I am instantly glad to have set my pride and jealousy aside to come. And glad I am also that the minstrel persuaded me not to wear any of the fine things Sean has given me, but to remain with the best dress that I sewed with my own hands. I stand out enough; raised eyebrows, knowing or deliberately unknowing smiles acknowledge my presence.

As my family arrives a stream of guests pours out of the little kirk. The families in service to the Laird looking proud and puffed at the honor of having attended the kirk service. Ross and Linsay glittering in black and silver; Ross' beautiful black-haired wife in a dress of cream yellow silk edged with scarlet. I recognize the McCleod of Assynt from Sean's description. Short, hard-faced, dressed boldly in yellow and blue, he is less well-favored than Ross or Linsay, but more the peacock. I wonder at his presence, for the neighboring chieftain is no friend, greedy and scheming for the lands about him.

The kirk disgorges so many guests I imagine it will collapse on itself when empty. Last comes Sean and his bride, walking under the arch-way formed by swords and staffs, hay-rakes and outstretched arms, pelted by flowers. But the little talisman sacks of grain pinned on the clothes of the couples at most weddings are conspicuously absent, as is a broom for them to jump at the end of the arch. I feel a moment of bitterness at the Laird for having excluded the old ways from his son's wedding. But then I remember Sean telling me that McCleod was poisoning the ear of James against the Lochlans, saying they were too pagan, and that was why it was crucial that Sean marry this girl, whose family was closely allied to the crown.

As they come to the end of the arch, my jealous curiosity to see Sean's bride is replaced by dismay at how ill-favored she is, nothing like the small portrait Sean showed me. Her skin is beautiful, clear and very white, but her face is so fat it makes her eyes and mouth look very narrow. Her dun hair pulled in a few limp curls about her face does nothing to relieve the plainness. Her gown is gorgeous, though, white and blue brocade set with pearls. A fat woman is said to be a healthy woman, a woman who can bear children easily. I envy her for how much she must have eaten for her arms to be so plump, for her elbows to be so round. Still, Sean looks like a bit of a mouse beside her. As she and Sean exchange the wedding cakes I see how soft and white her hands are, hands that have never scrubbed clothes or been burned baking or crushed orms in the garden. I find myself hiding my roughened hands under my shawl.

They turn to the crowd; Sean bows, the Lady Anne curtsies. The crowd responds with whoops of excitement. As the couple eats the wedding cakes and exchanges the ritual tokens which have been baked into them, the minstrel plays behind them some courtly tunes of love:

"What shall I do to say how much I love her?

What worldly baubles can true love express?
Angels in grace I could not place above her,
Mine an idolatrous passion I confess."

Sean and Anne are seated in two ornately carved high backed
chairs set for them in a little bower on a platform overseeing the
festivities. The minstrel kneels on one knee beside the new mistress of Glen Lochlan and plays as the Laird blesses the feast and
blesses the couple.

The food is wonderful. Lamb and beef, cisterns of gravy,
bottles of whiskey and imported wines. Soon I am pleasantly
drunk and stuffed as a goose without even having visited the des-
sert table laden with dozens of sweet confections, the result of
days of baking not only in the Laird's kitchen but in every hearth
in the village.

As the minstrel's cup nears emptiness I bring a skin of gold-
en ale and pour it for him. He smiles and as I hover near the
platform he sings one of the love songs he has written for me.
Feasting forgotten, desire hollows out my bones leaving me light
as a bird. Our eyes dance together, and it is our wedding feast,
not the feast of the couple sitting above us grim-faced and
strained. I set aside some of the best delicacies I can find on a
trencher for him; smoked pheasant, crusty slices of lamb and
ham, wonderful cheese scones the kitchen cook is so justly famed
for, oat and curdled-cream cakes, honey-nut rolls. I steal glances
at Sean, jealousy far behind me, feeling only pity for the story I
read in his glum, tight face, in the Lady Anne's thin lips that
tell of all she has eaten that has not nourished her, the frightened misery ill-concealed in both of their eyes.

As I compare Sean's slender paleness and sulky mouth to the
minstrel's beautifully muscled arms, his robustness, the alive-
ness and joy in his face, I can no longer remember what I saw in
Sean as a lover. I cannot imagine lying with him again, only pity
his ill-starred match as I would the misfortune of any friend. I
pray things will go better for him as the marriage progresses.

At last the minstrel takes his ease. Linsay has brought some
musicians; a renowned blind fiddler who has played at every Sabbat in that district for years, and a drummer who I also recognize
from our old joint Sabbats. The fiddler's sister with her dulcimer

completes the trio, and they play blithe dancing music. It is painful to watch Sean and his Lady at the first dance, so awkward they are in touching each other. It is a relief when a particularly loud roll of the drum signals the other celebrants to join them, obscuring their misery with flashes of bright colored clothes and laughter. The minstrel dances with me over to the garden where he exclaims and moans with pleasure as I push tidbits of food into his mouth, crisp-skinned goose and cheese scones and all the other tasty morsels I have culled for him. I have left a handful of strawberries soaking in a goblet of wine. Sated from devouring two trenchers of delicacies, we take the berries in our mouths and share the fruit and the wine with deep sweet kisses.

Coldness like a blade piercing the crimson of my brain. I turn my head as the minstrel is kissing my neck and see Sean looking at us with a murderous expression. I see his lady following his gaze, and watch her turn and look deliberately away, seething with cold rage.

"Let's dance," I urge Alain, pulling him into the heart of the happy throng. Alternating with bouts of the wild melee where everyone dances and swirls, the best dancers from neighboring villages come forth and perform some traditional wedding dances. I look over to the McCleod to see how he takes the dances, but it is me he is staring at with cold appraising eyes. There is something in the coldness of his eyes that reminds me of the Witch-hunter; quelling my fear, I smile and curtsey. He looks away.

I love to dance, but I love it better still when Alain pulls me around to the back of the castle and kisses my shoulders and neck and mouth. He presses against me, his hardness throbbing through our clothes.

"Ah, if I did not have to play again I would take you off and marry you in a field right now," he gasps.

Sean's look, McCleod's glance, come back to me with a twinge of foreboding. It is impossible to resist the minstrel's passionate bites and groans for long, however, and soon I am laughing with reckless joy, all thoughts of jealousy and plots forgotten.

The minstrel sings again, as dusk comes on, sweet songs that echo the gentle coloring of the sky, the soft blossoming of stars. Lovers put their arms around each other. Peter and Sarah are kissing passionately, ignoring the children tugging at Sarah's skirts. I catch my mother looking with such pure longing on the old Laird, who is red-faced and drunk and joking with Linsay that I ache for her undead love. I long for the minstrel's arms around me, but it is sweet to wait, knowing that he sings for me, feeling the tense air between us vibrating with desire.

At last his set is done. The old Laird makes a great show of filling Alain's hat with silver mixed with a few pieces of gold. I have never seen so much money in my life and am awed at the obvious regard and respect the other Lords accord to Lochlan for having hired such a fine harper to his son's wedding. More platters of food keep coming to replace those devoured. Alain and I abscond with an entire roast pheasant and flee to the vineyard.

We sit together under the curling vines. The waxing moon silvers the baby grapes into clusters of little pearls. We pretend to be foxes growling at each other, mock-fighting over the bones as we pick them clean with our sharp teeth, licking the grease off each other's fingers, lips, chins.

White and gray moths brush by our hair. Around us, muffled cries of lovers who have found each other. I hope that the passion of all the couples who join in love-making tonight will magically create a new beginning for Sean and his Lady. Unable to contain our lust any longer we toss the bones of the bird aside and couple, growling and biting like foxes under the swelling grapes. The vine God enters the muscles and sinews and juices of my lover, crushes all the sweetness of summer to a rich wave of purple pouring through my body and brain. As we arch and shudder to a gasping finish, his body sags happily onto mine.

Hot white flash of faery-fire, a speaking star traverses a quarter of the sky. I call out; Alain lifts his head in time to catch the last of it as it disappears, and we look at each other, eyes and teeth bright in the moon-light, smile, the message of the speaking star plain to each of us, and I know clearly that this is my man and my mate, and I will never be lovers with Sean again.

Chapter 57

We are surrounded by the dense yellow broom flowers that come up to my shoulders, breathing in their scent. I had sworn to Alain that the broom never bloomed so early in the year, and he swore back to me that if we made love near this thicket of it for three consecutive nights and mornings that it could not help but bloom; we see whose will prevailed. Bees move happily through the blossoms, humming with gratitude at this early source for their honey, the nectars we spun for them from the joyful sweat of our bodies.

Using my little crescent-shaped harvesting sickle I gather an armload, more than we need for the handfasting broom, sufficient to wreathe our brows as well. Alain is whittling off the branches from a stave of ash as thick around as his wrist. As I watch, he carves a snake curling around the staff from the bottom to the top; at the top he carves a three-legged cauldron, a star leaping from the arms of the waning moon into its depths.

"That is me, giving myself to our union," he informs me.

I smile at how he has blended himself into my magical sigil.

Now I shall never make my mark as Kyairthwen without thinking of him as well.

He fashions his own sigil, antlers emerging from a set of lute
strings. At the center of the antlers, a star shines.

"You are both; the lute that sings to my touch and the star
that guides my vision."

I laugh. "I thought at first the antlers were thunder-clouds,
the lute-strings the rain."

"Ah, let that be their other meaning then," he agrees.
"Thunder and rain, like our passion."

Finished with his carving, he takes the cloth that I have
braided, red for me and blue for him and a third strand dyed with
indigo and madder-root mixed, and uses it to wrap a bunch of the
bright broom flowers around the ash stave he has carved.

"Oh come buy my besoms*
Besoms fine and new,
Jolly greenwood besoms
Better never grew "

As he wraps the broom Alain sings a popular bawdy song
about a besom maker, and I join in. I have never laughed so much
during rituals as since I met him. He has the art of sacred
laughter; from his lips, the most raucous drinking song telling of
barnyard pleasures becomes numinous and glows with the hidden
meaning, the mating of Goddess and God.

Song finished, we squat, one on each side of the broom. We
hold hands and teeter on our heels, giggling like children. Tee-
tering, laughing, I pull him unresisting over on top of me.

"Alas! you have pulled me over to your side. That means you
shall always have the upper hand in this marriage. As I
thought," he adds ruefully.

"*I* shall have the upper hand?" I say doubtfully. "Tis you who
is on top!"

"Ah," he smiles, rolling his pelvis up against me, laughing
happily when I moan. "Tis not the plow that rules the earth."

"Think not for harvest so soon," I caution.

"This is my harvest." He rolls to his side, propped on one elbow, looking down at me, smiling, yet serious. "All the love I

---

*Besoms—brooms.

could ever want. Harvest and plenty, I should say."

He kisses my two hands. "Marry me."

Candle-flame of his eyes melts me.

"For a year and a day."

"Now and forever," he replies.

I hesitate, almost swayed, balancing on the thin cord of my caution.

"A year and a day," I insist at last. A wave of longing moves through me, cool green light under water, wanting to say yes, wanting to plight my troth for ever and aye to this man and his love-mirroring eyes.

"A year and a day—if you are not returned for me then—I be free to seek elsewhere."

"Never will I stay that long away," he shakes his head. "By your birthday—I have promised—whether I have found—but I will have—easily, easily, I will have a position by then. That gives me—four moons—a little more—two to search out the place and two to settle in it. But even if I should not complete my quest in that time I will return to you." He looks sad, strokes the line of my jaw "How can we marry if you will not trust me? I talk of eternity and you will not trust me for such an inch of time."

"I trust you."

He searches my eyes and then kisses my brow and eyelids.

"What rite shall we do—what shall we do to make potent this rite?"

I take my clothes off, and he strips as well. As always, my heart leaps up to see the beauty of his nakedness, as his cock rises to see mine.

We plant the staff end of the broom in the earth, sweet smelling flowers of the female end level with our faces.

"Staff that signifies the union of female and male," I breathe.

The minstrel finishes my sentence, "Come we here today to bring ourselves into like union.

"One staff from two woods," he adds.

"Two lives, one heart," I respond.

We lay the broom on its side, forming the lintel of a mysterious doorway. We face it, holding hands; pause, look at each other.

He catches his lower lip between his teeth, eyes wide, anticipation of the uncharted place we are to go. We hover for a moment, holding our breath. Then he nods, and we leap together.

Our leaping takes forever, as if the invisible web of stars glued us to the air.

Then we are on the other side, feet on the earth, facing each other. He laughs, joy, hugs me to him.

"Ah, Fiona, Kyairthwen, my bride, we are together."

He uncorks the flask of red wine he has brought and pours it into the hammered silver chalice I have worn at my waist. The beaten silver glows smooth between my palms. He takes his knife and slowly brings it down into the liquid. I watch mesmerized as the gleam of the blade disappears in the crimson depths, point at last settling in the deepest hollow of the cup.

The wave of power pouring from his hands through the knife into the cup is so great I can scarcely hold it. I summons my will, visualizing the chalice as a pool of clear water, place where the earth opens her sweet body to the sky, and a wave of earth power meets and matches his skyness. Slowly he takes the knife from the chalice. Carefully he runs his fingers along the blade to clean it, sucks the wine from his thumb, puts his power finger between my lips, offering me the droplets of wine as I would offer Oberon a taste of cream.

We sip from the chalice, two deer sharing a small spring. Cool liquid spilling into fire as it pours down my throat, past my heart. We sip again, mingling the wine in our kiss.

He pours half of what remains in the chalice over my body, half over his. I exclaim at the costly waste, but when he begins licking me clean of the red juice it seems no waste at all.

I sip droplets of wine from his chest hair.

"Thou art sticky as a very bumblebee," I exclaim, lapping his fur.

"Ah, this bee seeks your flower." He puts my hand on his cock, wet with wine. Hesitantly I bring my mouth down and lick the wine from his phallus, marveling at how silky tender the flesh beneath his foreskin is. Inspired by his cries, I suck and caress his sex long after the wine is gone.

He pulls me to him, moaning and gasping, hands flutter convulsively over my face like wounded birds. We both cry out again as he buries the root of his phallus as deep in me as it will go.

"The Goddess and the God are One!" he cries out, and my body overflows with his warm wine.

It is only a matter of minutes before he stiffens inside me again.

"I'm so happy," he murmurs. "Fiona, Kyairthwen, sweet Priestess, I have never been so happy."

Lost in passion, I now freely give the promise I have withheld before, "I love you. I love you. I want to be yours now and forever. Now and forever, my minstrel, my Priest, my man and my mate—now and forever. Now and forever."

Chapter 58

Alain has arranged a wild and beautiful mask of pheasant; the green iridescence of the neck feathers form the eyeholes of the mask, the wild gold of their tails sweeps up into horns on the top of his head. He has dyed the skin of his arms and face and throat a bluish-green, giving him an other-worldly look.

I have so much moss tied into my hair that it is more green than red. He has made me a pheasant mask as well of some of the gold-brown feathers to go around my eyes. He has painted a pattern of red and blue stripes on my forehead and cheeks and chin and made a lovely pattern of vines and serpents in green and brown dyes curling around my body. It seems a shame to put anything on over the designs. When they are quite dry I put on a white jersey and a white skirt that I have just made, and decorate the waistband and bodice with flowers. He has made a necklace of feathers to go around my neck. His necklace that he always wears, the little fish with the chain-mail body that shimmers like a real fish, looks well with the savagery of his costume.

On St. John's night, the summer solstice, the young people often dress in revealing and fanciful costumes. One of the aspects of this Rite is celebration and identification with the wild animals. The Horned God is in his glory; the Goddess we invoke is the Lady of the Wild Things. I think with longing of the days when we would have met with the other covens in Ross-shire, how much excitement and power there was in our rare meetings. But tonight it will be our coven only, and Alain will be there as our honored guest. It will be his first coven meeting, and he is champing with excitement.

He says, "For all these years I've played magical songs and seen the old folk and herb women in the hall smile secretly, but whenever I sought out those who seemed friendliest to the songs they put me off as they would anyone, saying that they knew Witches must exist, but bless God they did not exist in this parrish, or suggesting that I go out by the faery-haunted hills where I would wait all night and no one else would appear."

There will be a bale-fire tonight. After our caution at Beltane, Gran seems to think it will be safe to light a bale-fire for summer solstice.

"To not honor the light in this way before it passes," Rose had shaken her head, "would bring darkness on us all."

"More darkness if it attracts the Witch-finders to us," Gran had grumbled.

But Rose had prevailed. Every year, as far back as anyone could remember, the summer and winter solstices had been observed by the whole village, and Mina thought, and Gran finally agreed, that it might look more strange not to have the bale-fire than to have it, provided that it were merely the bale-fire and some dancing and that we kept the actual ritual secret.

They put Alain and me into John's wee croft to start the need-fire to light the solstice flame. After nearly an hour of working with the awl and the groove of wood, our hands blistered and sore, at last the tinder catches and holds. He carries the iron brazier of coals, while I keep feeding it with twigs and grasses and dried moss. We carry it up the hill. The young people from the village are there, dressed finely, or strangely, some masked or dyed or daubed with mud. Many wear combinations of fur and feathers, hair braided with flowers, everyone wearing at least some token piece of animal hide or fur.

The sexual tension in the air is palpable as the boys and girls eye each other with surmise, for all is permissible at the fire festivals; sex is no longer seen as the sin described in kirk but as the magic which helps the crops to grow and the animals to flourish. The fire lit from our fresh-kindled flame dances from branch to branch, and cries of excitement rise from the assembly. Some of the married couples are there too, Peter and Sarah of course, Galen and his Bhari, and several other couples, some who have obviously come to celebrate the rite together, and others, equally obviously, looking for what variety the night might hold.

The music starts with Staghorn and Winter pounding drums; we dance, leaping and flickering like colored flames around the bonfire. At times Alain sends wild bird calls trilling through the crowd with his recorder. The savage keening of McClanishe's bagpipes intoxicates us, all sense of what is known and familiar swirls away as the costumed dancers weave in and amongst each other. The children who climb the hill to attempt to join us are driven back; this is not a rite for children. They must settle for watching the blaze from the bottom of the hill.

More men and boys are attending the rite than girls and women, and the energy of the rite becomes charged with a competitive, predatory air. As the passion of the dance should be building I notice some of the other women and girls looking apprehensive and moving hesitantly.

Eventually people begin to pair up; Alain dances the courting dance of the pheasant before me, holding his arms like wings, preening and bobbing, strutting before me exactly in the way that a cock pheasant would appeal to his lady love. Captured by the mime, my arms stretch into wings; at first appearing to be unmoved, then fluttering in excited anticipation, swishing my tail seductively at him. I give thanks that Sean has not come to the ritual.

Even through the glaze of mounting passion I feel uneasy. A cluster of men who have not succeeded in courting a mate for the evening stand discontented and resentful in the circle outside the dancing shadows.

Before each of the pairs of dancers leaves to go off and couple in the woods they share a glass of whiskey, each taking a sip and pouring the rest in the flames, signifying that their passion goes to increase the flame of life.

We toss the whiskey in the fire and Alain leads me off, still clucking and strutting. We almost trip over Galen and Bhari making love under the roots of a great oak tree on the banks of a stream. We thread around a little clearing where Peter and Sarah are swiving passionately, quiet, gentle Sarah keening with pleasure, vociferous as any cat.

We come up onto the crest of another hill not quite so high as the bale-fire hill. The light from the bale-fire casts its flickering red-orange glow so that the bare stones at the top of its sister tor gleam like coals. Alain dances for me on top of the hill, feet bare on the red-glowing granite. A wind comes up, biting through the thin clothes I have worn, but it is a wind with feathers on it, and I feel more bird-like than ever. The wind picks up my moss-woven hair and I hold out my plaidie as if it were my wings spread, dancing until I think the wind will lift me clear off my feet and into the star-dappled sky. It is Alain who swings me off my feet, holds me in his arms, spinning me around and around, laying me down, dizzy and gasping. Falling on me more like a hawk than a pheasant, his cock pierces me to the navel, and he rolls fiercely with me in the heather. It is a dark night with little moon, and the strange fantastic creature mounting me with such intensity bears no resemblance to anyone I know. He feels my fear instantly, stops and pulls off his mask, gently taking mine off as well. We look into each other's eyes for a long time, him quiet inside me, until at last my cunt, throbbing, tells him to move, and he moves slowly, his spindle rubbing gently in my groove until the need-fire catches. My body contracts, rather than expands, into orgasm, feeling too out in the open, too exposed, to cry out and lose control.

No sooner has Alain pulled out of me, still lying half on top of me, holding me close, than a voice comes from the shadows.

"Do you mind sharing her?"

Tim Brede rises to kneeling from the heather, smiles to Alain.

"Not enough lasses to go around. Mind if we take a turn?"

Alain's hand tightens on my arm. Why is he asking Alain instead of me? His tone is friendly enough, but something in his

talking to Alain as if he owned me instead of courting me directly sends a wave of cold sickness through my body. Through the
nausea I sense Jim Strathan, predatory and malicious, lurking in
the shadows behind Tim.

"Some birds mate for life," Alain replies. "You'll have to look
further."

Tim pouts like a child denied a treat.

"Leave the lovebirds then," hisses Strathan.

We hear them scuffling and cursing their way down the hill.

"Put your clothes on," says Alain, disturbed.

"Let's go purify in the pool," I suggest.

"Will we get back in time? I'd not miss the ritual."

"Staghorn—John—told me we are all going to go over there
anyway. Surely they won't mind if we're first."

We go to the bonfire to tell the others. Galen and the other
piper from the village have volunteered to hold the bale-fire until
it burns out at dawn. The rest of us are free to come and go as we
choose.

We walk to the pools, the scrying pool and the large round
ritual pool bounded by rocks right beside the river Inver. Just being in the presence of the pool, still and star-reflecting beside the
turbulence of the river, calms me. We step into the water.

"Good-bye finery," says Alain. He pushes himself under water; only a few bubbles mark where he has been. A twinge of regret
for my moss hair before I plunge under water also, holding my
breath almost as long as he does before popping up.

I see the falling star on the surface of the water first, and
catch his arm; Alain looks up in time to see the last movement of
its tail whipping into darkness.

"Most people think it's an ill-omen," he says to me.

"Not for me," I assure him. "It always appears to let me know
that what I am doing is the truth."

He smiles. We notice that we are both shivering. Out in the
cold night air, I regret having gotten my hair soaking. My
clothes cling clamily to my wet skin, providing little comfort.
Alain pulls me into his lap and wraps his tartan all around us
and my shivering subsides. Our sliding mouths and sweet words
warm us soon enough.

He turns serious, frowns.

"Has that happened before?"

"Oh, they like to tease about it," I say, trying to sound lighter than I feel.

"Was that teasing?" he asks doubtfully.

When the rest of the coven arrives Alain disrobes again and is purified formally in the pool. Staghorn has brought yards of rough cloth; Alain is toweled dry, annointed with oil scented with wood betony. Whiskey for his mouth, the horns for his head, his arms bound to his sides by a loop of woven flowers.

Gran tells him, "Our bond is a rope of flowers; as soft, as yielding, and as powerful; easy to break at any time you might wish it."

We continue with the ritual purification.

Gran speaks. "This is the beginning; you have been received and purified. When you come back, your training will begin in earnest. And if you are settled in an area where there is a coven we know, we will ask them to continue your training. And if you continue in this path you will receive Initiation."

Alain kneels and thanks each one of them. Each responds with a spontaneous blessing.

"I trust you with my life," he says, "and I pray to be worthy of your trust in me."

He is gently unbound, and we continue with the Sabbat ritual honoring Litha, the summer solstice.

"The power of the sun reigns now," says Gran. "After this day we return to the power of the moon. The King will die but the dying brings forth new life."

"But for now the sun is at its height," says Staghorn. "The dance of life burns bright as the bale-fire."

We pass the chalice of whiskey around the circle, each of us asking the Goddess and God for boons of passion and love.

In unison, Peter and Sarah say, "We wish for the fire of our love to grow high in this year, and for the flame of life to burn brightly in our children."

Winter repeats the prayer he utters at almost every Sabbat, "Hoofed and Horned One, Lady who gives him birth, may the sheep have good health and many births this year, if it please you; I, Winter, your old friend, ask for it."

Staghorn takes the chalice next, pats Winter on the back.

"Well asked, well asked. Health and lust of the Stag in my body, and health to the new young buck in our midst tonight!"

Alain takes the cup next. Again I fall in love with his beautiful hands, cradling the chalice.

"I ask to be made worthy of Kyairthwen's love. And—Lord of Life, imbue me with your power. Lady of Dreams, send me your songs—and as long as I live I will remind each heart that hears me to open to your beautiful presence and love."

The whiskey comes to me, brown-gold spirit of the grain gleaming in the cup. What shall I ask? To go or to stay? For Annie to return, for a new life with Alain? My heart pulses when I think of Alain, yet I hesitate. I have held the chalice longer than anyone, yet no words come. At last I sip, press it to my brow and pass it silently to Mina.

"I pass my passion on to you girl—use it wisely!" she laughs, "But not too wisely!"

Sarah takes the cup from Mina and offers me a flower.

"Rose sends a prickly rose. She passes her passion to you, and says to tell you the fragrance of the blossom is always worth the sting of the thorns."

Gran, Priestess Anu, takes the cup solemnly.

"Lord of Life, Lady of the Wild Things! May our Kyairthwen be mated wisely and well. Love be the door, lust lay the bed, abundance lay the table, all the days that she is wed. So mote it be."

I am touched by their wishes for the success of my relationship with Alain, and I almost ask for the chalice back again, feeling clearly as his eyes whisper love to mine that he is my destiny. But the energy of the circle shifts quickly into chanting and then into dancing, and the larger mating of the sun and earth fills my being. We release the cone of power to keep the sacred marriage of sun and earth, male and female, strong and potent. We pant, recovering in the bliss that follows a magical sending, and then Alain plays midsummer tunes on his harp, the old songs that speak of the course of the sun and the moon, the mating of animals and humans.

At last the others go, back to their crofts, back to tend the bale-fire, to feast with whoever comes up from the village to do so.

Alain and I stay in the clearing by the pools, the place I had taken him to make love that first time. Tradition would have had us stay up all night to watch the flames of the bonfire leaping up like stags of light to honor the sun, but exhaustion claims me before we have even time to kiss good-night.

The next awareness I have is the brilliant caress of the sun through the pines. The sun is so bright all day, it is impossible to believe it has already started on its downward course into darkness.

Chapter 59

Yellow. Yellow pulsing with black.

All I can see is flames. Ropes tight around my body, hard pole against my back; my skin blisters and bursts in the heat, I am dying. . .

I wake screaming. Alain is gone. Alone by the scrying pool, black moonless night, I am alone, abandoned, I am dying. . .

Swift as an arrow he flings himself from the trees and shadows. Alain catches me in his arms, muffling my screams against his neck, his shoulder. As the screams turn to sobs he rocks me, strokes me. So gentle, sweet God, like a mother he is. I clutch him, sick with fear. Save me, change it, do not let it be so.

"Tis only a dream, Fiona, tis only a dream," the minstrel murmurs, patting me on the back. "What is it that troubles your sleep so? Every night now these last four—come now, share it," he coaxes, "if you share it it will have less power over you."

Finally I confess that my dreams are of dying in fire.

"Ah," his grip on me tightens. "So many are—but—Fiona— for all that neither of us respects Lord Lochlan—when I have played for him it is the Pagan songs he asks for and he makes no secret of his enjoyment of them. And what I have seen—it is the cities and fishing villages where the burnings are worst—in the country—the country Lairds cannot afford to lose so many of the hands that feed them. Only those few fanatics or those so craven as to seek James' favor in this way will decimate their own village. Tis usually a token, a few scapegoats—tis the old women who are little use any more that they choose." He strokes my hair, calms my shuddering.

"Nay, my love, even were Lochlan pressed to find a victim it would not be you—you have been too close to his son and he to your mother—they could be implicated and their lands taken thus. He could not risk it. If any are safe, your family must be so. And as for our travels—I shall seek out the safest place in Scotland and bring you thence. There be Lairds secretly Pagan to the north—and Linsay and Ross close by to here. I have not played for them but there have been no burnings in their districts—nay Ross burned one, supposedly a wizard but another minstrel did tell me 'twas a mere vagabond whose only magic was the art of making folk's purses disappear."

Soon he has me giggling with the stories he tells—the Priest who warned of sin and hell on Sundays and donned the horns to lead his congregation in the Sabbat dances—rumors he had heard of James' displeasure with Ross.

Content at last with my transformation into peace, he asks me to lie on my back, eyes closed, promising to surprise me.

A soft petalled cascade pours over me. I open my eyes, laughing. He must have been at work all night to gather these, sneaking off while I was yet sleeping and returning just as I woke screaming from my dream. From the number of roses tumbled over my body I conclude that most of the blooms he has reaved from the garlands hung all about the castle for Sean's wedding.

"There, lie still, lie still," he admonishes, adorning me with the flowers, weaving them in my hair, arranging circles of them over my breasts and belly, decorating my pubic hair with some of the smallest blooms. Streams of blossoms cover my legs, roses nestle between my toes.

"Ah, there you are," he smiles, standing over me. "Blouwedd herself could not be more lovely. That is how you enchanted me," he accuses, lying beside me. "After you told me of that spell your coven did cast to lure me here, I remembered a dream I had of the Goddess, all in flowers, turned into a living maiden. I must have had that dream the very night you did your working." He slides on top of me. His cock pierces to the heart of my female flower. Kissing, scattering petals from my face, gasping and laughing with sweet joy at how easily our passion comes to us. Soon the green bower above us is spinning as we laugh and laugh, light green as the trees and soft as the flowers echoes through our bodies. Tremendous warmth in our chests and bellies pours like water through our muscles and bones. Heat pulsing in the soles of my feet, in my hands caressing his shoulders and back. Ah, sweet sighs, sweet sighs. I feel so safe with him, the terror of my dreams belongs to some distant, other world.

"Ah, Fiona, I am happy, I am so happy," he laughs, sliding to rest beside me, cradling me to him.

"Ah, my little flower Goddess. Thank God your coven threw that enchantment and ensnared my soul. I had given up on ever finding my mate. And I had accepted it—I thought perhaps the solitary life was what I was suited for." His eyes are singing. His recorder sits untouched in his pack, but all the sweet bird-like tunes he plays on it dance merrily through my blood.

"I did not ensnare you," I correct him. "They did a spell for me to call my mate, to heal my heart. If you had not been he, the casting would have had no effect on you whatever."

"Aye, and what spell shall you cast on me when I be gone to conjure me back?" he teases.

My smile vanishes.

"I would do no spell against thy will. If you choose not to return—it will be your choice."

The desolation I felt at waking from my nightmare and finding him gone before the morning light sweeps through me like a cold northern wind.

He cups my face in his hands.

"No," he shakes his head. "I'll be back. I swear it. You have my heart, sorceress. Set it free and it will still return to you, I swear it."

I tuck my chin to my chest and close my eyes. He'll be leaving in a few days. He may not return.

"Fiona—" he coaxes my chin up. "Do you believe me?"

"You may change your mind," I whisper.

He shakes his head. "I'll not."

I tuck my chin again. "You may find someone prettier."

His sigh hovers on the edge of exasperation. "Prettier—no—no, Fiona—I love you. I've been with many pretty girls—it's not—it's not—I love you, all of you. I've been with enough girls to know—how rare it is to feel this way. I've only been in love once before—with a girl a year older than me when I was sixteen. We made love in the fields and she said she'd marry me. But her father arranged a marriage with a lad from a family that was better off—and she married him instead. It had been so long I—thought I'd never love again. Thought I'd never have another chance really. I'd be a fool to throw it away."

I tuck some of the scattered flowers into his curls. Already my fingers ache with missing him.

"You said—you'd ask Lord Lochlan—"

"I can't stay here."

"He *liked* your music—he gave you all that money."

"Fiona—can you truly see us living in peace with young Lochlan here?"

"I told you I want no more to do with him."

"Aye, but does he want no more to do with you?"

"He has his mate and I have mine," I insist stubbornly. "And if I say no what recourse does he have but to accept it?"

"He'd not force you?" the minstrel says, eyes clouding with concern.

"Sean? Of course not!"

The image comes to me of Sean throwing me to the ground that time by the river, mounting me when I was angry at him. Aye, but that was a lover's quarrel. I brush it out of my mind. If I had really fought—

"You're in no danger with me leaving?"

"No. I'll tell him it's finished and there's an end to it. Alain," I plead, "why didn't you ask the Lord if you could stay and play for him?"

"Do you remember the way young Lochlan looked at me at the wedding?" the minstrel asks.

I nod.

"What makes you think he would not—do what was needed to be rid of me?"

"Could he pay you to leave me?"

"Fiona!" he looks angrily at me for the first time. "No one could pay me to leave you. Would you be wed for more than our year? Small good I'll do you, poisoned in the high hall or dead in a ditch. McTavish had told me—if Lochlan wants me removed—he can pay to have it done."

I feel stunned. Surely Sean could do no such thing.

"I'll play for the Lord tonight," he says. "I'll neither eat nor drink from that table—when I leave three days thence—" At the look on my face he says, "—ah, Fiona, if you love me so, if you'll miss me so—come with me."

"I'm afraid," I sob.

"You'd be with me," he urges. "Fiona, I'll take care of you. We'll come back to see your family—as often as you like."

A surge of longing goes through me. I want to go. I want to go with him. But leave my family? Leave Gran, leave my mother— and what of all the Witch-finders in all the other towns that we might go to? Towns and villages where there is no web of protection. And Annie, if Annie returns. . .

*   *   *   *

Try as I would to slow the time, the three days vanished like dew on a summer morning.

Alain bid his farewells to my family that last evening, making a present of a piece of cloth for each of them, enough to make a shirt or skirt. I thought how happy Widow Corey must be to have so many of his coins in exchange for her linens. She is the best flax weef and dyer in the whole village. Anyone who wants a truly brilliant blue or yellow or green goes to her.

For Malcolm though he gave not only a piece of cloth but a small harp that he had been working on, a little at a time in secret, for weeks. Malcolm's eyes were so full of tears that he could not speak for several moments, but finally he slowly fingered out a tune the minstrel liked to play.

Alain hugged him. "Ere six months, brother, we'll play together again."

We knew now that Malcolm also walked a minstrel's path, and Alain promised that when he found a patron and a place and the two of us had been settled there for a bit that Malcolm could come and spend part of his time there learning the minstrel's art in earnest. Mother had not seemed pleased at the prospect of losing two of her children instead of one, but she tried to cover her concerns as best as she could, saying that perhaps when Malcolm was nine or ten that she could spare him the winter quarter of the year.

*   *   *   *

Baiting my hook. River above a mill, bordered by meadows and woods. These waters are strange to me, but I sense the salmon, silver and pink beneath the rippling green. Casting my line, hooking not a salmon but a strange blackened log afloat in the shoals.

Not a log, perhaps it is cork, bobbing so strangely in the water, black waterworts streaming from it—drawing it towards me, turning it over—it is Annie, body charred, blackened, burnt and drowned both; her eyes wide staring pain and horror beyond soothing mouth open in a soundless scream tongue missing mouth a cavern, eternal scarred emptiness mocking kisses, speech, the pretense that life could hold meaning or joy.

Again I awake screaming; the minstrel's calm, his scent, his soft words comforting me.

"Of course you worry of your friend, not knowing where she be, or if she be safe."

"If anything happened to Annie, I would know," I sob.

"Aye, of course you would," he reassures me. "Also—also— I've seen enough of the gypsies to know that they're a clever lot. Tis true they're much persecuted and harassed now but they've a way of sensing an uncanny place and vanishing just ahead of the pitchforks and tar-barrels."

I had gone back to sleep in his arms, but woke again, the other nightmare I've had over and over in the week past; myself bound to a cart, rattling over the stones to the stake, hated by all, abandoned to the flames. I wake sobbing and sit, biting my knees to keep from crying out, not wanting to wake him again. We stayed up so late, making love and talking. He should be rested for his journey, but we've had so little sleep in nights past, making love and talking the night through—and then every night the hag dreams and him comforting me.

At length I finish my sobbing, lie on my elbow and watch his upturned face, as light as if the moon shone behind it. I stay awake a long, long time looking at his face, committing it to memory in case I should not see him again.

Chapter 60

It seems I have only rested my head on the minstrel's chest for a few moments, the beat of his heart drumming me softly back into the maze of sleep. Only a few moments that I was happily lost in that maze when he stirs. I wake, peace instantly fled, fear twisting my lights and narrowing my breath. I hold him and snuggle closer, trying to will him back to sleep.

"Ah, Fiona," he breathes, kissing the top of my head, then snuggling down beside me, kissing my forehead, my eyes.

"Daybreak," he whispers, "is heartache.
Sadder than sad and sad am I
To go beneath the open sky."

He raises my chin and kisses my mouth.

"But soon," he sings, "I will return, and we
Shall fly together joyfully.
I'll find and feather fine our nest

And never shall my heart once rest
Until it beats again with thine.
Therefore thou lovest me not in vain
For I swear to return again.
When birds fly south and autumn rain
Falls like our tears upon this earth
Then shall our love enjoy rebirth
For winter's beginning shall be our spring."

He presses his cock against my belly.

"How will I survive four moons without your touch?" he wonders.

I rise from our cozy nest to go urinate. As I step from the bushes back into our clearing I see him standing, his back to me. Gray morning light shining on his shoulders, curve of his ass, muscular legs.

"Never again. Never again," insists an anguished voice in my head. *"I will never see him again."*

Cuddling back together under the blankets and clothes. Our lips and tongues slide together.

"Ah, Fiona," he says, voice on the edge of tears, "let us magic our love to be eternal." He rolls on top of me, slides inside. I feel fear like a stone cold in my belly.

"Do not close to me," he implores, "do the magic with me, that I return quickly and we be together again. You know the magic will not come from a closed heart."

I start to sob. As my tears flow, my womanjuices flow also, and soon we are rocking and twisting together, our bodies wet, tears and sweat, the juice of our loving. I cry harder and harder, as if we were swimming through tears and I can't tell if he is also sobbing or simply crying out in his passion.

Light fills us. We twist up into the light, bodies losing density. Shedding form, a snakeskin, a husk. Reaching a point of pure light at the center, bursting, vanishing into that light.

Warm. So warm. I rub my nose in the fragrant fur on his chest. He is still spread over me, a canopy of love. I nuzzle my head down against his chest as if I would hide forever, wanting so much to stay in that darkness, that peace. Feeling reluctantly our bodies slowly differentiating from each other, knowing the difference at last between his thigh and mine. The sound vibrating and filling my skull sifting into the sighs in his throat pressed against my brow. Our bellies and heart-beats remain merged. Then he moves, slides from me, reclaiming his body for himself. My brother, my mate. Would we could stay in this realm of oneness forever and never feel the sadness of one being split into two bodies. Where did we come from? In the round between lives is it like this always, where we are one being? And is that being male or female or bodiless, or is there another kind of body of which I have no kenning?

His hand cups, forming a cowrie, joining his mouth to my ear.

"I love you eternally. Our love is eternal," he whispers.

I press my brow to his, joining us at the starless place between the eyes. Often we have started and ended our lovemaking joined in this way. As our thoughts vanish and we again merge as one on the starless plane, I hear my whisper as if it were the voice of the Goddess: "I will love you eternally. Our love is eternal."

Pain in my head as our brows separate. His eyes an inch away. Then two inches. Three. Long unbreaking cord of light between our eyes.

"Mercy, enchantress," he begs at last.

I close my eyes, letting the cord of light dwindle away.

When I open them again he has already put on his shirt. He pulls on his leggings. Curlew crying in the marsh. I lie still, my body radiating ripples of calmness from our merging. He puts on his belt, runs his hand through his curls. Stands up, stretching.

"Let me dress you," he offers.

Kissing my breasts and belly as he puts on my chemise. Then my two skirts, more kisses scattered on my legs and faery mound. Then my belt, arranging my little pouches. Then my stockings, following his mouth from my ankles to my thighs. He helps me into my bodice, laces it tight, kisses the top of my breasts.

"Are you going to shave?" I ask, rubbing my cheek along the barely-peeking stubble of his jaw.

"Nay, I shaved last night. I'll wait on it. Unless it's too coarse for you."

I shake my head and then regret my honesty, wanting anything that will delay his departure.

He opens the pouch where he keeps his talismans and takes out the little silver fish that he wears about his neck. Chain mail in the middle, small as a faery creature, it twists in his fingers as if it were alive. He puts it around my neck.

"For the greatest fisher-woman in all Scotland. Thou hast captured my heart, little fisher-Witch, and you may let me play out a long long way; still I will return to you on this chain of love."

The fish rests so cool against the hollow of my throat. Yet that is where it rests on Alain when he wears it—*What magic does it have to fit us both?*—I wonder.

"I shortened the chain," he says. "I know the size of your neck by heart now—as I know every part of you by heart."

He kisses me again, my throat, the tops of my breasts, my mouth.

"The day is so gray," I mourn, "I thought surely we had conjured the sun."

"I have a light in my heart bright enough to shine my way on," he asserts, "and to brighten my way home as well."

He puts his shoes on. I press up against him and sob. Hold me, take me, make love to me again before you leave.

Very gently he pushes our bodies separate.

"You're witching me to stay," he says. He looks at me, green eyes swimming with forests and mists. "Mercy, enchantress," he pleads.

I struggle to hold my sobs inside and fail. He rubs me fiercely across the head with his knuckles.

"Your eyes are as red as your hair, girl," he says gruffly. He is being the man for me, holding his own tears in. I must not make it hard for him.

My breathing still shaky, I manage a smile. Tears still flow from my eyes, no more under my control than a fast-moving stream.

"There," Alain dries my eyes on his sleeves. "There. I'll not wash this shirt, but carry you with me thus until I return."

"I wish I had something to give you to wear in exchange for your wee fish."

"Here, I'll take a lock of thy hair and find a locket to put it in."

He cuts a long strand of my hair, kisses it, ties it in a love knot and puts it in his talisman pouch. I take my favorite of his curls, the one that lies in the center of his forehead, and tie the ends of his curl with a thread from my shawl before putting it with my magic things. As I slip it into my pouch I feel it nestling comfortably into the bracelet of hair Annie and I wove together, and a weight of sadness settles on me so heavy I can scarcely stand.

How the birds call to each other, criss-crossing from tree to tree, every tree and bush shining, sparkling; a pool of green watchfulness cradling our storm, our human reds and oranges. The pale gray quality to the light, sky polished like the inside of a shell. Consciously I slow and stop the time; his hand floats in the air between us—the birds' song hovers on a single note. He is luminous, shining. My heart notes every detail, precise as if I were carving it from something solid, as if I could stitch a tapestry of the moment and keep it forever.

Alain takes his lute and tunes it until the tarnished notes shine like polished silver and plays me his farewell song:

"Though our bodies shall dwell apart
Still our hearts shall beat as one heart.
I shall love you as well from afar
I shall love you as well from afar."

"No matter how far I travel, my heart travels within you," the minstrel assures me. "Between our bodies the distance may be great, yet our spirits shall know no separation. Mated we are forever."

"I still wish I had something to give you," I whisper, sad that I have no token to exchange for his fish.

"Give me your thoughts every day," he asks, "and your prayers—that my quest be over quickly. Give me your love."

I hold him tightly again, feeling how our hearts still beat in synchrony. But as we embrace, one of our hearts skips, and then his heart begins to beat faster with readiness for his journey. Still I hold him, feeling it is my life that I let go of when I let go of him, yet wanting so much to believe that we will be together

again. And yet when I try to extend my mind to the future, to
share his vision of us living together in some other shire, I see
only blankness between us and the blankness feels like death.

Terror makes me clutch him tightly.

"Priestess—" he whispers, "Kyairthwen. Let me go. Knowing
that I will return, rest secure in my love—there will be no moment where I do not think of you."

I release my grasp and take a deep, deep breath. I smile for
him, knowing he will see how false it is, wanting to have love in
my eyes only, but feeling the presence of death like a deep well behind my eyes, leaching the sparkle and light from them.

We walk together to the base of the hill that marks the
boundary of as far as I have ever walked from the village in that
direction.

"Keep an eye on Epona," he says to me. "Don't let that smith
sell her."

"Ewan's honest," I say. "He would never. I wish she were well
enough to ride—'twould speed you."

"Aye," he agrees, "but she was limping when we came back
from Ail Fionn that day, and that was less than a fortnight ago.
When she does get well—when that split foot heals all the
way—you can ride her as much as you like. She's very gentle.
Actually I look forward to being on foot again for awhile—but for
the pace, as you say."

We kiss.

"Fare thee well," he says. "And God bless you."

"Goddess keep you," I reply.

He lopes through the bushes, his plaidie cradling all the instruments so they'll not bang up against each other as he runs
up the hill.

At the crest of the hill he turns and waves.

And then he is gone.

Chapter 61

The sun streams down, gleaming off my brother's wet baby skin, shining in his brown eyes. He laughs and coos as I soap him, wriggling in delight at the unaccustomed treat of so much warm water and sunshine. Ah, the soft silkiness of a baby's skin feels so fine; tis no wonder my mother bears as many as she can. I used to think I would die a maid, but since meeting the minstrel I have thought more and more on having a child of my own.

A picture of the minstrel sitting by a warm hearth bouncing a laughing boy like Mark merges with the reality of the baby squirming happily in my grasp.

Suddenly the sun goes cold, then dark. Like a fierce north wind her cry hurtles through me:

"Fiona! Kyairthwen!"

Nimué! After four months of no contact the mind-touch burns like frost-fire. The starless tunnel contracts about me. The harsh clutch of her desperation knocks the air from my lungs.

"Help me, Kyairthwen!"

The contact cut off—as if she were clinging to me in a black,

fast moving current and the force of the water wrenched her
away.

Piercing scream shocks me back to cold sunlight. My brother,
red-faced, alternately shrieking and gagging on the soapy water.
I must have dropped him; soap in his eyes, he thrashes and
twists in the wash basin bellowing his outrage at this betrayal.

Nimué, Nimué has need.

"Eostre!" I call, "Eostre!" My next youngest sister Elana appears, frightened eyes.

"What is it Fiona?"

"Take him!" I shove Mark in her arms and run blindly into
the forest.

In all my knowing of Nimué I never had felt her terror, her
fear. She laughed away my nightmares, her easy courage and acceptance of fate shaming me to smile and yawn and sink back
into forgetful sleep in the strength and safety of her arms. Brave
one, Nimué, always so much braver than me. I see nothing as I
run through the trees, bang into twisted trunks, sob and run on.

Faeries glen and Maidenstone at last; I fall on my knees by
the stone, face down on the rough quartz, arms outstretched,
heart thudding from the run. I force breath into my sobbing
lungs, press my forehead and palms into the grainy rock, breathing down, and deep down and deep, deep, deep falling again into
that tunnel, gray deepening to black past the stars to the void,
the starless place, center of the world beneath the world.

Starless. Windless. I stand and wait in the high hushed
plain where no tree grows, no storm brings rain or wonder. Nimué. Tremulous into this hush of midnight blue I call her name.
"*Nimué.*" At last a moan, weak touching in return.

"Kyairthwen."

"I am here Nimué. Nimué?"

Again feel her violently wrenched from me. Alone in a dark
plane I reach and reach for her, this sense like a hand feeling for
a familiar shape in the dark, sifting for a shell in the sand.
Speak. Where are you? A touch, feather light. Was that a touch?
Sudden shock as if my fingers had brushed over her lips, her hair.
Nimué. The connection is so fragile, quivering, I feel her barely
conscious not as in dream but as the darkness near death.

"Fiona?"

"Aye I'm here Annie, I'm with you, what's happened, where are you?"

Connection crumpling, blows, she's being hurt, Nimué! The connection still there but her thoughts are nothing but lightning flash and thundershock of pain.

"Who's hurting you, where are you, answer, try, Nimué."

Interminable darkness. Finally her stirring, clasping with me weakly.

"Tis alright, I have you, where are you Annie?"

"Prison. A dungeon."

I feel the floor cold under her bare skin, shudder.

"Dinna blend wi' me," she tries to push me out.

I ease out of her, cloak her like a shadow.

"Nimué where are you?"

Her mind sends me a blur of images. I see her lover falling, swords in his belly, his chest, screams of women and animals, men attacking the gypsy camp. Hands stripping her clothes off, hands on her neck. Then shadows and prison, she blots the images not wanting me to see, pushes me away, being hurt now, not wanting me to endure it with her.

"Annie, where are you?" I persist. "Name the place." My mind forms desperate pictures, I'll steal Sean's horse, or maybe he'll help me, find a way to rescue her or die trying.

"Where are you Annie?"

"Dinna torment me!" she cries. "They torture me enough! Hold me."

I hold her, feeling her convulse with pain though blocking me from seeing the source of it.

"Just hold me Fiona," her weeping, Annie, my Annie, what are they doing to you?

She calls to Ashtoreth, the Maiden of shadows and fire, merging me with the Goddess in her mind. I begin a chant for courage:

"Millstone and barley
Cup and the wine
Let the love of my lips
Be the grapes on thy vine
Ashtoreth!

"Sweet sting of honey
Intoxicant mead
Here! Come!
We call at need
Ashtoreth!

Hunter and hunted
Arrow and bow
Dying and borning
These secrets you know
Ashtoreth!"

I will the power of Ashtoreth to her and she becomes it, rising from pain, hands firm on the bow of her will. Her thank you
calm and clear, her strong heart throbbing in my chest.

Clarity. Strength. Our hearts beating together like wings of
fire. The vision we have at the crest of lovemaking and always
forget when the passion is over. Wonderful suspension of love in
golden light. Then she snaps like a bowstring; clearly I hear the
crack of the whip; the moment breaks, pain like coarse salt in my
throat, each aftershock of the whip pouring over me like waves,
sharp smell of blood.

They'll kill her! The power of my own feelings pushes me
away like surf. Struggling through the churning salt to touch
her again—I am alone on this barren plane, she in a storm of
pain washed from my arms.

"Nimué."

I try to connect; hot flood of pain bursts around my head, incredible pain, sickness, trying to fight through it to find Annie.
This *is* Annie, this pain is all there is of her now. Caught in her
pain like an insect in a web, struggling until exhaustion washes
me limp.

Trembling, neck stiff, the rock cold under me. I stagger up,
piss, drink from the brae, wash my face. I return to the rock,
evening chill in my bones now. Dusk was ever our favorite time,
always at dawn and dusk we were together and through the long
nights.

"Dear rock, lord of the stones, take me down and through. . ."
to my tapping plea the door swings wide and the vision tunnel

opens. All around me the moon colors of sunset and dawn and dusk and images of Annie wavering like the dark sky mirrored in a scrying pool. Her despair reaches me before I can calm myself to the starless center, her grief clasps me, draws me in. Feeling her grief for Verado, his death becomes my grief also. She is being tortured to confess to Witchcraft.

"I confessed," she says, bewildered, afraid. "They promised mercy if I confessed. Now they say they'll put me to the test again if I will not give names. 'What names can you want, you have us all,' I said." The picture she sends me of the Witch-hunter who came through the village last autumn makes me wince.

"The filthy little bastard remembers me, says I belonged to a coven in Glen Lochlan and it's those names he'll have from me or my suffering will pay the price."

"Tell me where you are," I beg, holding fast to my delusion that I might somehow rescue her.

"Do not make it harder for me." Her voice pleading; I have never heard her sound so small and vulnerable, even when we were children.

"Do not make it worse for me. Comfort me." Holding her, ah Gods, the image almost warm and solid enough to be her body.

"Hold me," she weeps, clutching tighter.

"Can you forgive me for leaving you?" she sobs. "I never stopped loving you. I thought of you every night." Our spirits a braid of darkness and dying light, we huddle together, bodies sleeping, minds never losing awareness of our blending and touching.

Waking buckled over with pain, clutching my abdomen. Sinking down through layers of darkness, helplessly feeling Annie being beaten, and pain worse than beating which my mind refuses to comprehend. Her rage twisting in me. If only I had the power to blast them dead, if I had but a tenth of the power they fancy Witches to have, how their suffering would pay for this. Invoking the bleak Lady for vengence, the one whose name is never spoken out loud. Annie is hungry, thirsty. I drag my half conscious body to the stream and drink, sending every gulp to her; cool, wet, soothing, the image of water in her mouth, her throat. I imagine pressing a soaked cloth to her brow, her face. Beloved, beloved, take comfort. Wordless gratitude rushing back to me like water.

They are questioning her. I cannot hear the questions but I feel her stiffen, refusing to speak, her arm slowly twisted behind her back until the wrist snaps. Blinded by bursts of pain, grasping for her now is like groping through fire for the hottest coal. Can seared flesh feel? Realizing I have blended with her, willing myself to absorb her pain like a sponge. Her pain is so much greater than I can hold, her fainting snaps me also into darkness.

Weeping. Twin waterfalls pouring into a pool. Two circles of ripples that touch and shatter. Sunlight gilding the mist and turning rainbow between the two falls. Sunlit motes transform to colored sparks, floating up, perishing and drifting down to float up once more in rainbow immortality like the tiniest of fairies or gods. Thousands of rainbow flecks drift, swirl, dance, in a glittering cloud above the brown gold water gleaming like ale. For a time longer than time the water swishes by the ferns; green beards of moss stream from the rocks. Two small frogs bob curiously out to the center of the pool; they tentatively touch, then duck away, kicking with webbed feet below the surface to where I cannot see.

Cold; cold so cold; Annie's hand limp and cold as ice. I have been off dreaming and left Annie alone in hell.

"Feel me," I plead, "forgive me, feel me with you." More direct than I can be, the jailors rouse her by putting hot coals under her arms. She screams into consciousness; my insides shatter like glass at her screaming; they torment her and I can do nothing. Annie. Annie. They're stretching her, pulling her apart, relentless slow let me take some of the pain, let me at least take some of the pain. Trying to channel her pain through my own body into the earth; broken bone in her wrist slicing jagged through the skin—past all thought of channeling now, agony pushes me through cold water—drowning—letting myself go absent. Crawling back to her through a long narrow tunnel into the pain shaking me as a dog shakes a rat her shoulders wrenched out of their sockets tearing in knees and hips. . .

I lose touch with her and with everything for awhile; come to sobbing in the dirt by the stream. My body needs tending; defecate, wash. I drink from the stream, dropping through layers of darkness and feathered clouds, imagining the water in my throat to be in hers:

"I bring water, I bring water, feel it lady, it is for thee."

For a long time I try to feel her throat in mine, her consciousness of the water coming to her through my thoughts. I wake with my face in the stream, half drowned. Choking, sputtering, my body wants to sleep so badly it takes me without my knowing. I look around, disoriented in this familiar place. Black trees; black water; black sky. The moon wanes. I have no idea how long I have been here.

I crawl back over to the stone, lay my head and arms down. Sobbing through my teeth, God I want to sleep, I just want to sleep. Shamed at my body's weakness I leave my body behind—rapid descent through rings of blue lights to the still place.

"Annie—please answer me." Feeling for her—to the left—she must be there. . .

Silence. Years of silence. Moving through cold thick as wool, touching her at last, her body heavy and cold as no living body should be. Holding her hand. It feels so good to touch her. I sense that she is alone now. Not asleep. Not awake. Not really conscious of me.

"Nimué, dearest, sweet Annie, I'm here. Please say something." I feel her become dully aware of my presence.

"Talk to me," I beg, "tell me where you are."

One clear message and one only:

"I'm dying Fiona."

I cannot accept it. No. I kiss her brow, take her in my arms, cradle her on my breast.

"I'm here Nimué. It will be all right. Tis a nightmare, we'll wake soon, we'll wake together, sleep now, tis only a bad dream. Dinna fear—" There is no fear in her. She sinks colder and colder, heavy on my chest. I hear gurgling in her throat, deep tearing wheeze in her lungs. I realize that her mouth is empty, her tongue is gone. The images come without words. While I was unconscious, absent from her, she called to me thinking that she called with her mind only. But she had spoken my name out loud, and her tormentors had seized upon it:

"Fiona, who is Fiona, the rest of the name, bitch, give us the rest."

Her despair that her pain had spoken without her knowledge; thinking that she had betrayed me she set her tongue between her teeth and dashed her head against the wall. The guards finished severing what was left of her tongue, cauterizing it at the root. They botched it badly. After they left she hemorrhaged. She is drowning in her own blood.

I breathe with her. Her breath ever more irregular; stopping at the crest of the in breath rattling on the out breath in out slower colder colder slower no thoughts no feelings just the matching breath until the long stop at the top of the last in breath almost inaudible outbreath then silence.

Years or hours later, I twist and slide off the stone, heavy as stone myself Bright light slashes my eyes, I go back into the darkness, willing myself to finish my dying.

It is well known that the old Priestesses choose their time of death, their wills being so much stronger than their bodies. At sixteen, my body is stronger than my will. I wake to a pale gray sky that could be dawn or dusk or any time of day shrouded in fog.

I sit up. The weight of my hair almost drags me down. My body feels heavy, hateful. I cannot believe that I live while Annie is dead. I feel as though my shadow has been ripped away from me, like I've been eviscerated and a cold stone left where my lights had been. It takes a long time to move my heavy aching body to the point where it can stand.

I cannot remember the walk home, but walk home I must have done. When I arrive the mist has turned to light rain. It is afternoon, and they are just finishing burying my brother Mark.

Chapter 62

"D'ye scorn me then?" Sean catches me by the arm. One of the pails of water I fetched from the well sloshes over both of our feet. I had not seen him hiding in the bushes by the well, nor heard his step, but I am too numb to be startled by his appearance.

"D'ye scorn me for it then? Or is it shame that keeps you from me?"

Scorn? Shame? The Latin he had been teaching me made more sense.

"You had no complaint when I first told you I was to marry. Are you afraid of her? We meet as we have been meeting—she'll know nothing of it. Who shall tell her? And in any case, the man is the head of the woman. Tis I who'll tell her how to think. She dare have no thoughts that cross the will of her lord."

His hair. His mouth. His eyes. I feel nothing for him.

"Or is it that minstrel you cuckholded me with?" He shakes me. Water sloshes from the pails clenched in my hands; both of our feet are soaked.

"Has he your tongue as well as your heart? Answer me!"

"What was the question?"

"Are you in love with him?"

Smell of Annie's hair, feeling of her arms around me.

"No," I say, voice distant as my ability to really remember. The minstrel, the man in front of me. They both seem so far away.

Sean relaxes visibly. "Ah—leave your chores then." He takes the buckets out of my hands. "I need to love you. Christ, Fiona! It's been weeks—bitter weeks—away from you. More than weeks, two months! Who would have thought I could survive without you so long!"

"I have work to do. You've spilled my water. Will you fetch me some more, please. My arms are tired."

"Aye, aye, I'll fetch it for you." He pulls the water up from the well and refills my buckets. "There now, tis done for you. I'll carry it home for you if you like. Now, come." He takes my hand.

"No "

"Why not?"

"I don't want to."

"Fiona—what ails thee?"

"Have you not heard my—my brother has died? Scarce a week past. You may see from the color I wear that I am in mourning."

"Oh—" He falls to a sitting position, as if I had struck him. "I'm sorry, I suppose I heard—I forgot I suppose—it's just that it's been so long—the whole village is talking about you and that minstrel—" he says resentfully. "I saw how you looked at him— at my own wedding. You might have had more feeling for me than to flaunt your infidelity like that."

"I never told you I'd be faithful to you," I say, picking up my pails of water. "Good day."

Less than a week later he is at my door. My mother and some of my siblings are leaving for kirk. Sean is waiting outside, elegant in his black hose, his black and white tunic.

"Sean—young Lochlan!" my mother recollects herself. "Are you not at kirk? I feared we would be late."

"To hell with kirk," he says, brushing past her. "I need to have a word with your daughter."

"I have no word for you. I told you I was mourning." I cannot share with him the truth about Annie, her death and how I have known of it. Is not Mark's death cause enough? I indicate the scraped out bowl of porridge, the dirty trenchers.

"I have work to do. Get you to kirk. Your wife will be expecting you there."

"As I have told you, my wife commands not me, I command her!" He strides towards me. Instantly Colin and Malcolm are on either side of him.

"My lord," says Colin respectfully, "our house is in deep mourning. You must forgive us if we are not hospitable. My mother is not well—"

Mother standing at the door, red-eyed and coughing attests to the truth of his words.

"She has asked us to escort her to the kirk. We would be honored by the grace of your presence, my lord. My sister is—too—distracted to come."

"Fiona has never gone to kirk," says Sean. "She goes not to kirk because she is a Witch. She's a Witch who has enchanted *me*. And if she does not right by me—"

The threat hangs in the air.

"I shall come for you tomorrow," he calls over his shoulder.

He gallops off, his horse kicking dirt in my family's faces, my mother weeping and coughing, Colin patting her back, Malcolm, teeth bared, seething at the broken bushes churning in Coal's wake.

When the others have gone, Eostre sits in the chair cradling Myrrh and one of the cats in her lap. I sit on the bench before the fire holding Oberon. He puts one paw up on each of my shoulders, head nudging my chin, purring loudly. In the fortnight since Annie and Mark have died he seems to have taken it upon himself to purr me back to life. He scarcely leaves my side, and will not leave at all at night, even to hunt mice, or love. When I thought the ice in my bones would freeze me altogether, he would be there, melding against my body, lending his life force to me as I had lent him my breath seven years before, when he was born.

The next day Sean is back again. Oberon lays his ears back flat against his head and growls, and Malcolm comes close to doing the same. My mother weeps herself into a spasm of coughing such that Eostre and Elana have to put her to bed.

"All I'm asking is to talk!" he swears. "That's all I'm asking! Damn it Fiona, you owe me that. Don't look so strangely on me—"

"Get out of our croft!" demands Malcolm.

"Yours by whose leave?" snaps Sean.

"Does your father know you are here?" Malcolm replies.

The expression on Sean's face tells that Malcolm has found his target. He turns on his heel and stamps out.

*   *   *   *

Day after day, his knock on the door; his anger, my silence, my mother's tears. Finally he catches me again at the well.

"I do not desire you. I am grieving."

"For your vagabond minstrel?"

"For my brother." A picture of Annie holding Mark in her arms, smiling at me, grows large in my heart until it shuts breath from my lungs.

He begins pleading with me. He would not reproach me for my 'unfaithfulness' as he called it. He had been away. I had been lonely. He reminds me the marriage was not of his own will. He is miserable. I should pity him. He has never loved aught but me. I see but one way to stop the flow of words and get back to my chores. I take off my clothes and lie beneath him.

He makes no effort to pleasure me, entering my body as blindly as if it were an opening with no person behind it. My spirit crawls out of my body and sits hugging a tree until he has rolled off me. Then I curl in a ball, pulling my shawl over me. Leaving the body makes it so cold to return.

As I shiver under the scratchy wool his voice comes bitterly: "Ah, then, am I to be cursed with a cold wife and a cold mistress both?"

I wonder who he is speaking to.

"Is it to punish me you seek?"

Punish him? I roll the idea in my mind like a round pebble but can make no sense of it. A little wind stirs the grasses, fluttering like a field of faery wheat. He whines on. The edges of his words poke sharp corners into my mind as he had thrust uncaring at my body. I curl into a tighter ball, arms blocking my ears and eyes. I think of a mouse Tawney had brought in with its paws clenched over its eyes, as if it did not wish to see its end. I try to become as small as that mouse, hidden by the grass. I will Sean to go away. When I open my eyes, he is gone.

*   *   *   *

But he comes back, and back. He will not leave me be, and my mother near hysteria whenever he enters our croft to drag me away from my chores. Finally I promise to meet him every Sunday after kirk if he will come no more to our croft. After that first bitter outburst he seems not to notice that I am absent from my body when he touches it. I am past all hope of pleasure for myself. If he takes comfort in my body, what's the harm? How had it been with the Minstrel? Had he touched me as I remembered? Had we truly danced the Goddess and the God to incarnate fire in our flesh? This body that I wear now is like armor, heavy, unfeeling, impenetrable. But when I think of the minstrel, feel his mind reaching for me, hear his voice singing from far away, something feathered turns and moves in me, the ice in my veins cracks, ache of undead fire smoulders in my bones. I pull my numbness like a thick fur tighter around me, muffling the sound of his songs, the feel of his hands. He is gone; from the face of the earth for all I know. He will not be back. I can not think of him without feeling, and I cannot bear to feel.

With mother ill, there is plenty to do at home. Colin spends most of each day at work in the fields, so the rest of us have to take on his chores. At eleven, he is taking his place as the man of our house, working hard so that our family will have a larger share of grain this winter.

The twins take over care of the henyard as Malcolm spends more time fishing and trapping small birds. I teach him cat-patience and the other magical arts I had learned for fishing, and he proves so quick a pupil I begin to think of him as a young mage and send him to study with BearHearth and Staghorn as often as we can spare him from home. More to eat means more to cook, more to salt and preserve against leaner times. I welcome the tedium of chores, the more mindless the better, and even turn my hand to mending when there is no more cleaning to be done. I make salves for Mother's chest, poppy syrups to soothe her to sleep, teas to bring up the phlegm.

She never fails to thank me for my healing, and I never fail to notice the reproach behind it; if it were not for my neglect, Mark would not have gulped water into his lungs, would not have taken chill and died so suddenly. And it is clear that if he had not died, Mother would not be lying here, thin as a pressed flower, pressing her face to the bedclothes so her wracking cough will not wake the children.

The sun shines, day after day, yet I am never warm. Only at night, with Obie curled up beside me, golden pollen of his purr filling the air with sleep, is there comfort, and rest.

Chapter 63

I can avoid seeing my Gran no longer; she has sent word that she is ill. A jug of hotch-potch soup in one hand, a basket with a brace of oat-bread loaves in the other, I trudge over to her croft, Oberon marching in my wake. Once arrived I see that it is a trap. Gran hems and haws a bit, pretending to cough, but there is nothing in her wraith-field that indicates any sickness. Mina is there also, and Sarah, suckling her latest baby.

"Ah—thank you, thank you," Gran says, clearing her throat. "Sorry I am to make you work for it—sit down."

"I have much to do." I sit anyway, feeling how rude it would be to turn my back on them.

"How is your mother?"

"Not well."

"We have some more herbs for her," says Gran, "the same as the ones we sent with Malcolm. I hope they have more effect. I have nothing stronger."

"Thank you. I've been picking them myself; but I'm sure she would be glad for something—out of your own hands. My power is—not as it was."

"Well, of course not." Mina grasps my hand sympathetically as Gran sets tea on the table for me.

I have not sat and talked with them since I came to tell them that Annie was dead. I think perhaps they already knew. They had not asked if I was sure, nor seemed surprised. I can hardly remember that meeting now. All of my memory has become like that. The moment something has occurred and passed, it drops away from me like a stone disappearing into a loch.

"You need a healing," says Mina. "You've lost not just a friend, but a part of yourself. You must get that part back."

"Get it back?" I said. "Are you saying we can bring Annie back?"

"No, not Annie, but the—part of you that you gave away to her."

"She can keep it."

"No!" says Gran, sitting across from me. "No, she cannot keep it! You must have it back!"

"Ann—" Sarah cautions, "—go gently—"

"It does not matter," I say to Sarah. "Nothing hurts anymore."

Gran grabs my wrist, digging her nails into it.

"It should hurt."

I feel the pressure, then the sensation of her nails, sinking through the skin. But what I have said is true; there is no real pain involved. She releases her grip.

"Ah, I'm sorry child. I did not mean to hurt you. Forgive me. Forgive me." She gives me a look of such piercing sadness, I almost wish that I could hurt for her.

Mina's spotted hands reach over, her soft, stubby fingers massaging an ungent into my wrist.

"There now, there now, no one wants to hurt you. We want to help you."

"Would it could be so," I say, wanting to give them something back for their love and concern, feeling I have nothing to offer.

"Fiona." Gran takes my hands, looking into my eyes. "Believe you not that Annie dwells now in a better world than this one?"

"Tis not hard to find a better world than this one," I reply.

"'Tis we who make this world what it is," she says.

"I never did so."

"Aye but you do. We make the world anew every day." She pauses, eyes searching deep. "Annie has chosen death. You need not do the same. You *must* not do the same."

"She did not choose it! She did not choose it."

"Ah—forgive me—you are not ready for this," Gran acknowledges.

Oberon jumps into my lap, purring loudly, not in his soothing drone, but in short staccato bursts as if he too had something to say.

"He knows," says Mina. "He wants you to live."

"I eat. I drink. I am alive."

"But barely," observes Mina.

"We would do a ritual to heal you, to call the life back for you," says Sarah.

Her baby asleep, she holds her over a shoulder, kneels beside me, nuzzles her head against me like Oberon.

"Let us heal you."

"I am not ready," I say. I do not say that I do not believe it is possible. Our coven does not contact the dead. What healing can there be?

"I hope you feel better soon," I tell Gran. "I love you very much. I'm sorry I'm not—" words come through my mind—better—stronger—I lift my shoulders and let them fall. "I'm sorry."

Mina pins a bunch of herbs to the shoulder of my dress as I leave.

"Well, at least take this," she says. "Put it under your pillow. Let the healing start with dreams."

I walk to M'hira and scatter the herbs in the water before heading home. All the way back, Oberon is scolding, clucking, meowing to himself all the many things that he would tell me if I were there to hear.

Chapter 64

Eostre stacks up the wooden trenchers.

"Try washing with water and leave the mud to the Sow," she admonishes the twins.

"Aye, any more sand in our craws and we'll all shift into chickens!" Malcolm warns.

Peter juts out his chin and scowls. "Yer not so smart."

Sarah puffs her cheeks out belligerently, ready to back Peter up. Malcolm raises his eyebrows.

"Ah, now, I meant nothing by it," he says, trying to soothe the formidable pair.

"Quarreling and treats are not of an evening." My calm pronouncement dispells all warlike intentions. The children gather round, clamoring to help, as I pour the skin of ewe's milk John has brought us into a cooking pot and stir in a piece of the honeycomb Sean gave me.

Eostre goes to the door, carefully arranging her plaidie.

"I'm going for a walk."

"Will you not stay for the honey cream?"

She shakes her head and lifts the latch.

Colin frowns. "Are ye—meeting someone?"

She glares at him. "Och, aye, the Father of Lies and the Queen of the Fay and King James himself if the weather proves fair."

I wince. Would she *were* meeting a lad. But Eostre's sharp manner keeps the village men well at bay. I remember her snapping at the minstrel when he complimented her, "Oh, aye, all my life, so they say, what fortune have I to be bonny. We're supposed to be so delighted to find a man to give us bread and bairns and blows. Barely, I can wait."

I put the pot over the fire and hurry to the door.

"Sister—" I call after her softly, "—take care."

She turns and smiles. "Says the pot to the pan." On a rare impulse she turns back and hugs me, then runs, vanishing into the forest. The full moon is rising, yellow and rich as the cream John brought us. It is that which calls her, that which she goes to meet. Eostre has never had anything but scorn for coven and kirk alike: "If Witches cannot save themselves from fire in this world and Christians must face it in the next, what's the use?"

When I tried to share the magic Gran had taught me for the bleeding time, she brushed it roughly aside: "Pretend is for bairns. I'll take my whiskey neat."

Still, the moon mutters in her blood. Early in spring I had glimpsed her dancing alone under its full light, barefoot in the glimmering frost. Men may forget the Lady, imagining themselves as hard as the stone in the kirks they raise. But how can a woman deny the echo between her womb and the moon when even the great seas cannot refuse to dance?

The woods where Eostre has disappeared are alive with shifting blue lights and feathery shadows. Physical longing aches in my bones.

Elana calls from the door, "Fiona, milk is bubbling."

Back in the croft, the soft light and ocean smell of cuddy-fish candles. The children border me like lace on a skirt, each brandishing a cup of leather, horn or wood.

"Still as the stones, careful and slow," I warn, ladling a bit into each vessel. There's not so much to share, only half a cup each even with Eostre gone and mine left empty. Myrrh gulps hers down with reckless speed, licking the ring of cream from around her mouth with the self-absorbed delight of a kitten. She wants more, asks a sister, then a brother, then another brother if they'll share. They clutch their cups and scowl or smirk or quickly drain the last few drops. Her face goes scarlet as she bursts into piteous sobs.

"Tis all gone! And it was so sweet!"

Like a clap of jagged light splitting the darkness, her cry shatters me. I sob until I am barely conscious, gasping for air. Malcolm hugging me from the back, hands pressed tight around my middle. Elana holding a wet cloth to my face.

"Fiona, please don't cry. You can have some of mine."

Sarah holding her mug to me. Peter beside her, nodding, holding out his cup that has barely a sip left. If we had but a mouthful left, Nimué, the cream and the sting and the sweetness.

Malcolm and Elana help me to bed. He holds my feet and she strokes my head, as if between the two of them they would hold the soul to my body. Oberon stretches himself over my middle, absorbing the diminishing shocks of my sobs, his loud purr vibrating in my chest. As the sobs grow weaker, the purring grows in intensity, penetrating heart and veins, shaking the rhythm of my body into a pattern of silence. Threads of darker and darker colors, the loom of his purring at last weaves me into sleep.

*   *   *   *

A woman dressed in white, wearing an indigo shawl. She walks ahead of me, a crown of red poppies on her head, black hair swaying above her hips. Hair like a waterfall.

I quicken my pace but cannot catch her. At last I call to her, "Nimué! Please come back. Please wait!"

She turns to me, deep sparkling eyes shining like black stars, Nimué one with Vanthi, the poppy Goddess of peaceful death. She stretches her hand towards me and I reach for it, sobbing with relief. But as our fingers almost touch, a wall of white flame suddenly divides us and I am driven back by the heat.

Chapter 65

Orrin Argylle smacks the tankard down on the table, slopping a froth of beer over the wooden surface to drip unnoticed onto his lap. His red lips glisten slackly, his eyes hang on my breasts as if he believed he could stare my bodice away. The tightness in my belly makes my womb cramp harder with its monthly shedding. He licks some brown foam from his beard and takes another greedy swill from his tankard.

"Aye, but I do have a message for ye lass," he says as I turn on my heel to walk out. I spin back, trying to look haughty, telling myself they cannot hear the hammering of my heart. What's to fear from Orrin? He's a drunken sot but harmless enough. But what is McTavish doing here drinking with the town drunk, who he despises, in the middle of the day when sober men like himself are out tending their fields?

"A friend of yers is waiting for ye on the road just outside of town—between here and Loch Inver," Orrin says with a smirk. An ugly expression of amusement passes over McTavish's face as well.

Alain! He knew that I needed him, he has returned to me. Ah, let them jest then—I hasten out of the Bluebell, gusts of laughter and sobs warring in my chest. I snatch flowers from the roadside, weaving a hasty wreath to greet him as the God is greeted after his long absence in the winter following the sacrifice at Harvest. Purples and greens and blues, oh dandelions, yellow and white for the sun and the moon brought back together. Blood squeaking painfully through the cold rust that has clamped my heart since Annie's death. I still live, and my love has returned to me.

"Lady, seabirds fly
Sea to sea and sky to sky
Lady why not you and I
Shall we go, shall we go?"

Aye minstrel, I shall go with you. I am ready now, Alain-a-dale, Lord of the Dance, my Green Man. The clouds are lowering, heavy with rain and ragged bolts of fire, but I run lightly as if my feet danced towards the clearest of dawns.

Over the crest of the hill overlooking Loch Lochlan I see the man bending over his horse's foot. A crow caws overhead and my womb cramps with a violence that nearly takes me to my knees. Things freeze and for a moment each of us holds motionless; the hawk the moment before he stoops; the mouse flattened against a stone under the shadow of those wings. I do not know which of us moves so that but an arm's length separates us.

His eyes are bloodshot, the dull brown centers crouching like spiders in the scarlet web of tiny veins. The Witch-hunter stares with an intensity akin to lust, a lust that covets not the body but the bones beneath.

"The good folk of Clashnessie put a band of gypsies to the sword. Some fled, but several of their sorceresses were taken and burned..."

He takes it out of his cloak, holding it as casually as a child might hold a lighted turnip at Samhain. Through the ringing in my ears I hear him say that a lass named Roxanne named a Fiona during questioning. Had I not a gypsy friend named Roxanne? He holds the skull out to me, the blackened sockets returning my gaze. Aye, it is hers, there was no fragment of her, burnt or broken, which my soul would not have known. They must have burned her body after she died. Drowned and burned both. Clashnessie is but a day's ride to the north. So close, and I helped her not. The skull pulses in his hand like a dark crystal.

"Perhaps you would like to bury your poor friend's remains?"

I watch my hand rise to take it.

Her voice loud in my skull: *"No Fiona! Tis a trap! Turn and fly, turn and fly away!"*

Then I am walking swiftly away from him, the hills, the trees the Loch all bluring together as if melting under incredible heat; the roaring so great in my ears that if he called after me, I heard him not.

Chapter 66

Above the falls, the waters of M'hira widen and slow. The edges of the river grow thick with floating waterworts and the ankle-deeps, herbs that need a marshy spot to thrive. A meadow like a great disc radiates out from the stream and is absorbed by the woods. Woodsworts, meadow herbs and the water plants all within a small span; the perfect setting to teach wortcunning.

We sit in a small circle near the stream, a mound of butter-wort, cress, sundews, floatwort and lady's slipper in the center. Elana, Malcolm and Myrrh each take a bunch of the butterwort and close their eyes. I guide their breathing with mine, watching the colors around them deepen as they merge with the plants in their hands. The sun shimmers from their heads as from three bands of a rainbow; Elana's hair a blend of sun and moon, Malcolm's gold curls tinged with auburn, Myrrh's mop of crimson bright and unruly as the morning sun in summer.

"You are within this plant, knowing what this plant knows—how does it feel?"

"My eyes are yellow," says Myrrh. Her attention flutters like

442

the wings of a butterfly only briefly perched on a stem. She does well for a small bairn though; Malcolm never could have sat still so long when he was three. Chants and birdcalls were all the magic he had patience for then.

"I look at the sky, but my feet are in the mud," he says.

"I like to float," says Elana. "I like things to be easy. . ."

"And what purpose may I serve?" I prompt.

"I like to be cooked in a big stew for wee lasses to eat!" laughs Myrrh. Unable to restrain herself, she nips off some of the yellow blossoms.

"I think—I think tis good for the eyesight. Not as a poultice but—like Myrrh says—in a stew, eaten, tis good. . ." Malcolm says.

"Aye, tis a mild herb and can be taken in quantity," Elana muses. "Good for the bowel too—it likes everything to be easy and so tis soothing to all it touches—"

"Good. Very good. You're all right. You *can* use butterwort as a poultice, Malcolm, but cucumber and eyebright are so much better we keep butterwort as a pot herb."

"Twould be good with the floatwort," says Elana.

"Aye, so tis. In a broth for gas or cramping in the gut, tis sovereign. Now, taste the watercress—and tell me why we call this wort the health keeper."

Myrrh shakes her head. "It has an awful taste."

"Try it anyway—see what happens in your body."

She takes a bite and spits it out. "It burns my tongue!" She opens her eyes and pouts defiantly. A finger to my lips and a sideways glance silence her.

"It—like—puts sparkles in my blood," says Malcolm. "Makes me wake up—like a rooster in my mouth!"

"Elana?"

"It has—so much green. So much greenness. It feels like it cleans the blood. Even my bones feel—polished."

"It *looks* cool, but it *tastes* hot," says Myrrh.

"It is—it would be good for cold in the joints. Like Rose has," continues Elana. "And it makes my hair feel sparkly."

"It's the sparkles I like," says Malcolm. "Tis good with venison, Myrrh, you'd like it thus. Seems like it makes a balance— like meat is the God and cress is the Goddess?"

"Aye. Good, very good." I'm pleased at their progress. New blood for the coven in a few years time. What luck that three of my siblings should have the gifts.

Myrrh is still shaking her head vehemently, her face turning red. I forestall one of her famous tantrums by opening my rucksack.

"Time. for a bit of supper." I spread bannocks, dried venison and cheese on a cloth.

"To go with your cress," I smile, handing Malcolm some of the meat.

"From Sean?" he asks. At my nod he seems on the brink of refusing it, but hunger overcomes his pride.

I finish eating first. Even long walks leave me with little hunger. They say old people live on air. Perhaps I am learning that art.

"This is the most important part of wortcunning. Once you ken how to go inside the plant, and be it, it'll teach you anything you need to know of it."

"Like if it has an awful taste," says Myrrh darkly.

"Or poison, more to the point," says Malcolm.

"Most plants, like people, have both bane and blessings in them. Like the bittersweet, that makes the sheep so ill if they graze on it yet makes a sovereign poultice for drawing forth infection. If you hold two plants together, they'll tell you if they'd be good combined, or dangerous. . ."

"Like the floatwort and butterwort," says Elana.

"Aye, they're a happy marriage. Like with people, again, there's good matches and bad. Gran says plants and beasts and humans are the same. Each of us has two lives. We have the life in which all our striving is to make ourselves happy, and then the life in which we want to be the best use to that larger part of the web. Everything is the Goddess, complete and whole in itself—the smallest little flower and pebble. At the same time, each thing is just a piece with a part to play in the greater Wheel."

After lunch we return downstream, stopping to pick any likely looking herbs along the way. It is only a few miles back to the croft, but at our leisurely pace, much of the afternoon has passed before we arrive back at the well to fill the jugs we had left there on the way. As we approach the point where the woods give way to the grassy knoll sloping down to the croft, Elana suddenly halts.

"Stop. Wait. Stop." She stands trembling, face white. "Something's wrong," she whispers.

Malcolm takes her arm. "Aye, I feel it."

"I'm scared," Myrrh whimpers, burying her face in my skirts. I feel nothing but tiredness, though why such a short walk should weary me. . .

My annoyance gives way to puzzlement. It cannot be much, but if all of them feel it—

"Wait here," I tell Elana. "If ought is amiss, be sure the herbs are scattered and hidden."

At the edge of the woods, where the trees halt, so do we. An unfamiliar cart outside our croft. Cages in it. The sort to carry pigeons or chickens to market. Children crying in the croft. Nothing odd in that, but is it Mother's sobs we hear as well?

As we watch, a scrawny, twisted, stick-figure of a man bursts from the croft and wrestles Oberon into one of the cages, the twins right at his heels.

"You can't take him, he's our sister's!"

Eostre slaps them back and forth, bloodying their mouths.

"The man of God will do as he sees fit, you'll say no word against him! Get inside!" Terror radiates from her, bright as a halo of torchlight.

"I thought it was a wild cat no one dared touch," the Witch-hunter says, gesturing to Oberon snarling and biting the bars.

He goes back in the croft, returning to slam Seraphin in another cage. The gray cat adds her cry to Oberon's.

The Witch-hunter puts a gloved hand to his scratched and bleeding face.

"Get me that other cat up in the loft," he orders. Eostre nods and turns to enter the croft.

"No!" Before I can stop him, Malcolm runs down the hill to the cart. Moonsock is his cat. Eostre grabs him by the shoulders, her eyes like flint, hard with hidden fire.

"The man says that cats be a sign of Witchcraft and any not willing to give them up may stand accused."

I walk slowly down the hill, Myrrh dragging at my skirts as

if I were pulling her through water, sobbing, "Dinna let him take our catties, dinna let him—" at the top of her lungs.

The Witch-hunter smiles when he sees me, extends his hand. "I believe we've met."

I keep my hands busy stroking my sister's hair. Mother comes to the door. Myrrh runs to her. She tries to pick the child up but instead sags and folds to a sitting position on the ground. Her eyes are swollen, tears running down her face, staining the yoke of her dress.

"Must you terrify the children? They are so fond of the little catties."

Eostre comes back out, snapping at Peter and Sarah to remain within.

"I cannot get the other one. I've done my best."

The Witch-hunter shoulders her aside. Malcolm stands in his path.

"Has the Laird given his permission for this?"

"My orders are from the King," he replies, pushing in to fetch Moonsock down from the rafters. Mother beside the doorsill, quietly weeping. The twins tumbling out to bury their bruised faces in her skirts. Myrrh stretching her arms out to me, to the cages, "Dinna let him, dinna let him. . ."

Eostre looking right at me, her thoughts clear as a blade, *"If you make a move, we can all die. You have put us in this danger."*

And Malcolm looking to me, the initiated one, the one who should know what to do. . .

"Go help Elana," I whisper. Tears fill his eyes as trust wars with despair. He swallows and runs back into the woods.

Oberon isn't fighting any more. He's lying still, looking at me. The cages are shut with a little lynch-pin. Just three steps away. I could take those three steps, slip the pins out and he and Seraphin would be off as if flung from a bow.

Eostre's eyes on me, and Mother's; we could all die. . . just three steps. Oberon not flicking his eyes away as cats will if you're rude enough to stare, but looking at me, in me—he knows I can let him go, and he knows that if I don't let him go he's going to die. And I with no more power to move than a standing stone or the stump of a dead tree. . .

The Witch-hunter emerges, the black cat with the white

chest and paw biting and twisting at the leathered gloves clamped like talons around her body. He slams her into a cage, throws the lock.

"You have no more of these little demons?"

"That's the lot," replies Eostre.

He fixes me with his opaque, soulless eyes. "King James has been informed that a Witch be nothing without her familiar, and so if the familiar is destroyed, then the Witch may be more easily taken and destroyed also. And so we shall have a mighty cat burning. I daresay a Witchburning shall soon follow. Perhaps these cats are innocent. But I'm sure you will agree that their sacrifice is worthwhile for such a noble end?"

The taunt in his voice invites me to gainsay him.

"I take it you have no objections then?"

Eostre's strong arm pushing me back as she places herself between us.

"Other than that we'll be eaten out of house and home by rats and mice, what objections could we possibly have? Come and help me get dinner ready Fiona."

She pulls me into the house. Whip crack over the horse, sobbing calls of the cats, rattle of the wooden wheels echoing from a long ways off.

It is so dark in the croft. My eyes cannot adjust, flashing from bright to dark like the heart's steady pattern of thud and silence.

*　　　　　*　　　　　*　　　　　*

Just light enough to make out the film of cobwebs hanging from the beams. Morning. Eostre lying beside me, propped on one arm.

"D'ye want something to drink?"

"Aye."

She dips a ladle of minted water and helps me sit to drink it. I move my feet around, knowing that Oberon won't be there before I remember why.

"You slept for two days." Her eyes the deep warm blue of a candle's heart. People say she's hard and cold as a winter loch. They don't know her.

"I'm sorry." Sorry I slept so long. Sorry she has to be the strong one with everyone calling her hard because of it.

"I'll get up and make breakfast."

"Are you sure you're all right?"

"Aye."

"We dared not send—"

I understand. With the Witch-hunter near, the coven must lay low. He'd be drawn to magic as a carrion bird is drawn to the scent of blood.

It's so odd, stirring the oatmeal, no one purring and rubbing up against my ankles. The croft seems empty, even with all the people beginning to wake and stir. I keep my eyes on the porridge and bid my mind be empty as well.

Chapter 67

"A bonny wee coo. A bonny wee faery coo," Myrrh croons, crouching to examine the large snail she has found amidst the kale. All of us save for Colin and Mother are out tending the vegetable garden this morning.

"Yon bonny wee coo shall gnaw our supper to lace and tatters," admonishes Eostre. "Gie it a good stomp."

"No!" shouts Myrrh, scooping the snail up in her hands.

Eostre throws down her hoe and makes as if to snatch it. Myrrh runs screaming towards me, bearing her friend in cupped hands.

"The Morrigan is after me coo! The Morrigan is after me coo!"

Eostre nearly catches up to her, but the three year old dodges behind my skirts.

"Save me coo! Save me coo!" she shrieks.

I fend Eostre off. "Sister. . . sister. . ."

"Dinna 'sister' me, Fiona!" she snaps, trying to lunge behind me to grab the child. "I'll not be sharin' *my* supper with every scummy little orm and beetle she takes a fancy to!"

"Leave her be." I push Eostre away and block her with the handle of my hoe.

"You're spoiling that brat rotten!" she shrieks.

I let the hoe drop, hoist Myrrh up on my hip.

"Here now, we'll take your coo to greener pastures then."

"Aye, any excuse to get out of the work!" snarls Eostre, returning to the labor of hoeing decayed midden into the ground.

I take Myrrh to a clearing in the woods, and bid her set her coo out to graze.

"I'll build her a wee byre," she says, constructing a shelter of pebbles and twigs. The snail sits cautiously for a bit, then extends her horns and slides gracefully along.

"There. Tis a proper happy coo now," I say.

Myrrh sighs with satisfaction. "Tis the bonniest coo in the world."

Finally content that her coo was comfortably ensconced in its new pasture, and after many good-byes and promises to visit, Myrrh is persuaded to take my hand and return down the hill. She asks if we might not stop by the well and make a wish.

"If we can but find a white wishing stone—" she says, scanning the ground.

"Here. Use this." I hand her a copper.

"Wi' a real ha-penny? 'Twill be a famous wish indeed!" she cries.

She leans over the water, face squinched tight with concentration, so enraptured with her wishing that her body quivers and becomes haloed with light. At last she drops the coin and bends to watch it disappear, leaning over so far that I grab the back of her dress to keep her from tumbling in. Long after the coin has wobbled from sight, she remains staring, her face taking on the glazed look of a sleepwalker.

"Someone is coming to see us," she says dreamily. Is she scrying then? Elana has the sight, and Malcolm as well. . .

She pops out of the trance as easily as a curlew steps dry from the water.

"Are you not going to make a wish?" she asks. I trace the round cobbles of the well. My mind is as blank as the dark circle of water.

"I have nothing to wish for."

"Oh, but you must, Fiona, you must! Have ye no more coppers? A yellow dandelion will do for a small wish. Sarah and I use them and they work famously for us."

I have a belt full of coppers. Sean gives me more and more now, so much I need not spend it all on whiskey to dull me and help me sleep. Every night since Myrrh's birthday I make honey milk and sweetmeats for the children, plenty of it so no one has to cry. It is so easy to make them happy with sweets and ribbons and bells for their shoes. . .

To please her, I cast a coin into the water, and follow it with the yellow blossom she offers me. Satisfied, she hops down from the edge, saying, "Well, let's go see who it is."

Pursuing her vision, she eagerly runs ahead of me, her auburn curls bobbing in and out of the greenery. I remember Gran brushing my hair when I was small, saying, "Hair the color of beginnings and endings. . . the hair of one who can lift the skin off of one world and peer into the next." Then I hear the old gypsy woman whispering to Annie, "Witch's hair, waterfall hair, little black heart." I stop, clasp my hand around a birch to steady myself.

A pulse of blackness clenches my heart; all my senses go dark. The black pain blurs me, thins me to shadow.

Children's voices call me back.

"Fiona, hurry, hurry, tis for you! Someone for you!"

I move, floating wraithlike through the trees, feeling no curiosity, nor even my feet on the earth. Orrin Argylle in the bar, leering, "A friend of yers. . . on the road. . ." Less than a fortnight ago, the Witch-hunter's cart at our door, taking our cats.

"Fiona! Come quickly! Someone has come for you!"

As I step from the glade, sunlight blinds me. Slowly the brightness sorts itself into colors, patterns. A tall lanky looking man with a feathered hat, leaning on our fence, talking with Myrrh, who is narrating some drama with excited laughter and gestures. Not the Witch-hunter. A young man I don't know. He's not very comely; nose and ears too large, teeth crooked and yellow. But his brown hair falls nicely over his brow, and his hazel eyes are open and clear. He gives me a shy smile, admiring but not lecherous.

"Aye, you must be Fiona, then."

My brothers and sisters swirl between us, jumping up and down, roughhousing with a dog that must be his companion, pestering him for more sausage and cheese, which he had made the mistake of sharing with them.

He casts a worried glance at Malcolm who has wrested a harp free from his rucksack.

"Be careful with her," he cautions.

"Oh, aye sir, I will!" Malcolm promises. "Alain taught me how to handle a harp. Tis a friend of Alain's, Fiona! Another minstrel!"

The young man performs a courtly bow, removing his hat.

"Ian McGillicuddy, at your service."

It is so strange to see this man here, so like Alain, and so unlike. I keep seeing Alain in his place, coming through the gateway, leaning on the fence. Pain catches in my throat; block the vision, push it away.

"If you be Fiona McNair, I have a letter to you from Alain the Woods-walker," the minstrel says. Malcolm sits caressing the harp, looking up at the young man as worshipfully as he had regarded Alain. Alain worked so patiently teaching him to play, carving him his own recorder. . .

Myrrh takes my skirt possessively.

"This *is* Fiona. I know her, she's my sister."

Ian laughs. "She was just telling me how you rescued her coo from the Morrigan."

I can think of nothing to say. Silence sits between us like a moat.

He takes a folded parchment from his shirt and breaks the seal. "I have it by heart, but I'll read it direct. The ink's not three days old, barely dry. . ."

"Barely dry!" cries young Peter, jumping up. "Let's see!"

The minstrel fends him off, holding the letter high out of his reach. Good fortune that he is so tall—

"It starts, 'My Dearest Fiona, Lady of the Twilight Kindred...' "

Ringing in my ears. Everyone looks small and strange.

"I have been hired to the table of the Lord of Ross at Tain in Ross-shire. He is a good and able Lord, and my place with him is secure. He has given me a croft by a stream with woods on one side and meadows bordering the other two. Every day I feather this nest in hopes that my mate will soon join me.

"The Lord is a man of revels and requires my presence throughout the harvest holidays. But I swear that I shall come to you as soon after Samhain as my feet can carry me. If you like, we might be wed for your birthday.

"As if this good fortune were not sign enough that the Gods love us, who should be passing through Tain on his way south to Edinburgh but my old friend Ian McGillicuddy, as fine a minstrel and a gentleman as any in the land. Having more kindness in his heart than haste, he agreed to bear this letter to you. I pray you to receive him as if he were my brother of blood as well as art.

"The old herb woman here died recently, and was held in such good repute that no one should but be grateful for another as cunning in such ways. Here the people celebrate the old rites with no shame. They say the Lord himself shall don the horns for harvest. All that is required for this dream to be a waking one is your consent.

"I pray that this letter finds you in good health, and though 'I love you as well from afar,' my heart will not be whole until your touch shall make it so."

Ian folds up the letter. "He has bid me sing you a song." The song is long, only the refrain stays in my mind:

"Be faithful as the moon alone,
Who changes ever, yet is one.
Content am I, but one star in your sky,
Though you for me burn as my only sun."

I am still as mute as a mermaid on dry land. Ian seems a bit chagrined.

"He had more songs than that. So many we had not enough hours to sing them all. But he said he dared not put too many songs of courting in another man's mouth." He shrugs self-deprecatingly. "He flattered me there, I have neither his looks nor his voice."

"I think your voice is very fine," says Malcolm.

Sarah, ever blunt, nods. "Not as good as Alain's though."

Eostre has come out of the house to see the stranger. She seems softened by the song, her face more like a flower than a fine-carved stone. She takes Ian's hand and curtsies.

"Won't you come in and honor our humble croft? We have but little, but you are free to what we have."

By evening word has spread of his arrival, and bit by bit our neighbors drop by to sit with us around the fire and hear his tales and songs. Ian apologizes for not having a lute, saying after a day's ride he could as easy build a new one as tune the old, and his hands grew weary of it. No one complains. The magic of his dulcimer and harp are fine enough.

Mina and Gran and John join us for dinner. Then Peter and Sarah and their bairns arrive; the Widow Corey, William and his son Gabriel drift in. Every time the latch clicks I look up, expecting to see Annie. Once I actually glimpsed her arm opening the door, a strand of black hair falling over her plaidie shawl. But it was the Widow Corey, the long black ribbons from her mourning cap swinging over the shawl Annie gave her just before she left. . .

Everyone in the room seems so happy. They all have a roundness to their shape, and movement, where I am flat, and motionless. Like looking at one of the paintings in the castle where it all looks so real, from the gleam off a pewter tankard to the color of a man's cheeks; I am only imagining myself to be there in the picture, and a part of it. Everyone is as ebullient and congratulatory as if Alain himself was here and it was our wedding feast. But I have no faith. Whatever it said in the letter, we will never bide together.

I'd had Ian read it to me again, in private, so I would remember it and have it by heart. But the words made no more sense to me than the scratching on paper a learned man takes for words. Like so many cups empty of water or wine, there was no nourishment for me there.

Every night after that I would take the letter and the bracelet I had made of Annie's hair and mine and hold them against my heart as if they were a poultice or a charm. I put my whole self into my breathing until my thoughts became as thin as the parchment and the hair and I could slip through the cracks of the cold stone door that stood between me and sleep.

Chapter 68

One evening Malcolm asks if he could not have a word with me after supper. I say aye, thinking he wished to discuss his magical training with me. Staghorn had shown him how to make magical whistles from different sorts of wood, and Malcolm was putting his new talents to shrewd use, calling birds into the traps he set. He loves the birds, though, and I know it troubles him to deceive them as it has troubled me to deceive the fish into taking the hook.

We walk to a clearing in the woods.

"D'ye wish to cast a circle?" I ask.

He hesitates, then nods. We send a silent call to the four directions. He plays on his Pan-pipes to invoke the God. I watch him, eyes closed, bent to the task of calling up the whistling and sighing winds, and half see small horns budding from his red-gold curls; the small leather-wrapped feet almost clefting into hooves. The music casts a mist over my eyes and I feel the minstrel there in the circle with us. After the music stops, I keep my eyes closed, cupping the echo as long as I can, feeling Alain so physically there, knowing the sensation as a weft of the magic only.

Small cold fingers curl over my hands. I open my eyes to Malcolm's clear hazel gaze.

"And the Goddess?" I ask.

"When I am with you I feel—that the Goddess is already here. In you. You are the Goddess—Kyairthwen." He does not actually say my magical name; his lips hold the shape of it and then he stands quite still, eyes wide with acknowledgement of his daring. For I have never told him my circle name. How much does he know? I have taken no care to guard my thoughts from him. The intimacy of our magic has gone deep.

The soundless utterance of my true name leaves me shaken. I have kept apart from the coven, unwilling to face the pain I would need to face to be healed of Nimué's death, not believing that healing could come to one who has lost her soul's twin. I am no longer willing to suffer to learn. Better to keep within the small orbit of croft and yard, better to say that I dare not leave my mother's side while the sickness yet lingers in her lungs.

"What would you have, Malcolm?"

He sits beside me on the body of an old oak made velvet with moss.

"Yer still seeing the Laird. Sean."

I make a slight nod.

"D'ye wish—is't of yer own will?"

I want to say yes but find I can only shrug and look away.

"Is it? Yer own wish, or—"

I shrug helplessly. "What matter."

"It matters to *me*." He juts his chin out defiantly. "I'll put a stop to it! Colin will back me up. And Staghorn and BearHearth too if we ask them. He has no right—"

"And you no bigger than an imrock!" I try to laugh him off with Mina's old insult, but he is not fazed, and I see he has not missed the desperate tone in my laughter.

"Yer to marry the minstrel, will ye not? Then you are promised, and Sean has no right! Let him keep to what's his!"

I can only shake my head, wondering if the coven has put him up to this. But they would never have betrayed my name to him. He came by that honestly enough. I remember how I had craved to be a woman at his age, see how the magic has made him impatient to be a man.

"Tis—grateful I am for your protection. But—"

"When Alain comes back—"

"Tis but August. Alain may well change his mind ere November." I shut my eyes, hear myself speaking in the closed voice of trance, "I do not expect to see him again." My mind shuts like a seed. The starless place is cold, black, empty. Malcolm shakes me out of the blankness, shivering.

"He *will* be back Fiona. I *know* he will! Mina says you're as ill in your heart as Mother is with her lungs. If you would but go to them for a healing—"

"No more! No more. Please. . . Malcolm, let me care for myself. All—all will be well. As the Goddess wills."

"Then remember that Her will *is* yours. And you are Her."

"Very well, young Priest! Very well!" I stand up; this time my laughter is more genuine.

"What have I done that one who does not even come up to my heart should think to order it! If I have been chastized quite enough, might we not return to our warm hearth?"

When I go to meet Sean the following Sunday, I find my young champion has preceded me.

"She will not be seeing you this Sabbath or any other," Malcolm asserts. "Alain-the-woods-walker has asked for her hand. The Earl of Ross has hired him to his table and bids them settle in Ross-shire. As soon as he can get a croft built—"

"Is she at home now?" Sean begins to stride out of the clearing without waiting for an answer.

Malcolm catches his arm. "Leave my sister be!"

"You young pup!" Upraised arm, dangerous flash in his eyes, my God, he does look like his father—

I step out of the bushes. Sean drops his arm and strides towards me, pushing Malcolm aside.

"Come!" he says curtly.

"Leave this to me," I say quietly to Malcolm. "And thank you," I mouth silently. His countenance falls, his body droops, but he turns for home at my bidding, leaving me to follow Sean. When we are alone, Sean turns on me, seething.

"Is't true then? That ragged tinker—you're planning to run

off with him? A whore and a vagabond, a bonny match that shall be!" Rage bares my teeth, curls my fingers to claws. Hiss of an angry cat breaks through my throat. The grip of his hands leaves black marks on my arms as he shakes me.

"Is't true then? Is't true?" He is white with rage; for the first time, I fear him. He lets go of one arm, clenched fist cocked for my head.

"Answer me wench, or—"

"Hit me once and you shall never touch me again." The calm finality in my voice stops him. The stony glaze over his eyes vanishes, replaced by tears.

"Ah, Fiona—I never intended to hurt thee—" he releases me and sinks to the ground. "You will abandon me then, and leave me alone—"

"What of your wife? Surely she will grow to love you if you but treat her—" tears blind me, "—as ye treated me when first we—"

He curses and says something so low I cannot hear. I bend closer. He grabs my arm again, the look of hatred in his eyes makes me quail away from him.

"I am no man with her!" he shouts. "So what have you done to me, Witch, that I think of naught but you and lust for naught but you!"

Fear stops my breath; my senses begin to spin away. The brokenness in his voice brings me back.

"You never loved me as I loved you. You loved that gypsy slut more than you loved me. You used me, Fiona, and now you throw me over for a handsome scoundrel who will take you away—desert you when he wearies of you—"

"Your marriage is not consumated?"

"With enough whiskey in me I'd go up on a she-goat! Drunk every night and sick the next day and her crying and calling me a brute and having to look well contented to face her family every day—it was hell—" he rambles hysterically about his ill-starred honeymoon in the Lothians.

"And then I come back to my own place and see you fawning over that cursed minstrel—and now I am powerless to do ought with her—" he looks up, his eyes again beginning to glaze.

"The Priest says that all Witchcraft comes because of the insatiable lusts of women, so I should be grateful for the coldness of my Lady Anne, and pray that she turn my sinful mind to God! And father says. . ."

A picture flashes before my eyes, swift, terrible. A courtroom, Sean denouncing me before a magistrate.

"Would you have me burn then for the holy fire between us?"

Against his protestations I can but sob, "Swear! Swear you will never denounce me!"

"On my soul, Fiona—"

"Your Christian soul? On your Christian soul? Swear by your body, mi'lord, as much bound by lust as mine!"

"On my body then—ah, Fiona, do not cry, I cannot bear it when you cry. . ."

His eyes are inches from mine, brilliant with blue flame.

"None but you can content me Fiona—I am ensorcelled—have mercy—"

I shrink from his kiss but he catches my head in his hand, enters my mouth with his tongue. He begins sobbing as he kisses me, tears mixing with saliva; I sob harder in reply. Our sobs crack open the ice-locked moat between us. As he wrenches my skirts up to my waist, I arch willingly to meet his thrust. I welcome his roughness; alive, at least I feel alive.

Sleep fells him like an axe. I keep my arms and legs wrapped around him, rocking his unconscious form.

"I will always love you," I whisper into his ear. He snores in reply and I fall also into sleep.

Chapter 69

"Change your mind and come with us, lass."

Peter holding my hand, leaning over from his place on the wagon. My cheek still tingles from the scrub of his beard where he kissed me. He and Sarah are going over to Ail Fionn to help Jesse birth her first child. Sarah always knows when a child is about to be born.

"Sarah says 'twill be tomorrow when the child comes—we'll stay a few days beyond that to help Jesse get settled with the new bairn—though Christ knows with the mother-in-law she's got she'll have plenty of help with that—but, you know, Sarah never has enough bairns to mother—"

Sarah rewards him with a sharp elbow in his ribs.

"Aye, and you're the biggest of the lot," she says smugly.

In the back of the wagon the children bounce up and down.

"Let's go! Let's go! We want to see our new wee cousin."

"No one is seeing any new cousins until tomorrow," Sarah asserts. "I'll not be having you rush Jesse, although I think," she nods, "the labor will be easy enough. She's very ready. Very ripe."

I waver, tempted. Peter leans closer.

"I would sooner you came with us," he says huskily, "with that unchancy man about."

I wince. The Witch-hunter is back with his cold eyes and his jet clothes and the silver cross that practically spans his scrawny chest. A darkness has settled over the whole village with his coming. Twice he had come in the summer; once to show me Annie's skull, a fortnight later he took Oberon. Neither time had he lingered for more than a day. This time he has come with a companion, a man who is as large and bluff and well-made as the Witch-hunter is small and shriveled. And instead of coming on his mule only, the two of them arrived with a large cart, small limbs of trees like bars about its edge, as if they expected to return with captives.

They are staying with McTavish. Every day finds them walking up and down the street, stopping people, talking to them, pretending great friendliness of course, yet almost everyone here is afraid of them. They have spent the majority of their time in the kirk or in the high hall or in the tavern; how long before someone says something foolish and lives are forfeit?

Soft concern in Peter's eyes, worried pucker in Sarah's brow. I want to go, want to get away from the gloom and terror that he has brought to our village. But suppose Gran needs me, suppose Malcolm does not guard his tongue? Suppose Alain returns early? I told Sean I would meet him tonight; if I disappear he may make trouble at my croft.

Midwives are especially vulnerable under the new laws, for almost anything they do to help the laboring woman may be seen as magic, even if it is no more than the old herb teas, or teaching the woman how to breathe, or pressing her back. My absence would be noted, and if there is any possibility that my being with Peter and Sarah might bring danger to them I cannot risk it.

"I'll stay," I say to Peter, but I don't let go of his hand, wishing he would think of something to say that could persuade me otherwise.

"Oh, very well then," he sighs at last. "I know Jesse would be happy to have you there. But we'll bring you news of the wee one. I'm sure 'twill be a bonny babe, and healthy." He grins. "I'm looking forward to staying up drinking all night with Colin."

He calls to the cattle pulling the cart and they move off, trudging slowly. In the back of the wagon with the children is a pile of unthreshed grain and some weavings so it may be seen that they are going to Ail Fionn to finish grinding their grain and sell the cloth that Sarah has made.

As I watch them go, unreasoning terror rises from my feet, roots in my throat. The village darkens, contracting in a pall more foreboding than the grayness of the day can account for. It is all I can do not to run after them and climb in the back of the cart with the children to huddle down beside the grain, small as a mouse.

I shake my head, willing the panic to ease. It's no more than the winter sadness, I tell myself. The breath of the Crone chilling the leaves and frosting the fields. No more than that.

The Witch-hunter will surely leave again empty-handed as he has left before. Without the Laird's consent he can do nothing. . . I go up the steps into the Bluebell. A glass of ale will settle me. Crosby is sitting by the fire, orange flickering light battling with the shadows to own his face. Staring woodenly at the wall beyond his cup of ale, he does not notice me until I speak.

"May I sit with you?"

He looks at me almost suspiciously, then nods. I remember the fun we had teasing and joking at his house when he was lovers with Annie and feel a great longing to be friends with him again. It would be so good to laugh.

"You must be excited about Jesse," I say. "Soon you'll be an uncle."

His face softens and he nods. "Aye. Aye, I'm looking forward to seeing her babe. Jess and I—don't always see eye to eye but— she's all the family I have."

"Well, you have Rose, you have all your aunts and uncles—"

"I don't mean that crazy old woman," he snaps. "There's more to family than blood. Just Jess. That's all I have. My real family. Just Jess."

The ale and the warmth from the hearth have relaxed me. There are plenty of chores awaiting me at home, but they can wait a bit longer.

"Well, soon you'll have a niece."

"A niece!" he replies sharply. "What makes you think it

won't be a nephew?"

"Well," I shrug, "Jess thinks it is a girl—it's a mother's sense."

"Oh, aye," he snorts sarcastically, "A *mother's* sense."

He gives me a sudden sharp look. "Have you heard from Annie?"

"How would I hear?" I ask and swallow, feeling guilty for not having told him of her death, seeing the stress of the unconscious knowing etched in deep lines around his brow and mouth.

"Oh, do you not have the art of talking through the air? Jess always knew my mind well enough." He pauses. "I know all about you and Annie." His jaw locks hard, all friendliness gone from him. "I curse the day I laid her."

Compassion for him wells up in my throat. "I know you miss her." I put my hand over his. He takes his hand away.

"I curse the day I met her," he says, eyes sullen with gray fire. He pushes his chair back and stands ready to go, leaving his beer unfinished.

"I wish we could be friends again," I say to him, feeling the longing so deeply in my bones for someone I could call my friend.

He stops and kneels beside me, vulnerability coming into his eyes.

"Magic my sister a safe birth," he whispers. "Make sure she comes through all right and maybe we can be friends."

I nod reassuringly, "Jess will be fine. She's healthy and strong."

He rises and goes out the door. I stay, staring into my ale, for a long time. If Annie had married Crosby she'd still be alive. Perhaps if it were not for my jealousy pulling at her she would have married him and she would have been happily settled before the gypsies came and not been tempted by that gypsy lad.

It's my fault, I think, finishing my ale. He's right to be angry at me. It's my fault they didn't marry. It's my fault she's dead. Painful memories of the time since her departure; the anger I felt towards her. All the times I wished her no peace in her heart until she returned to me.

Glass empty except for a few lines of foam like the beach when the waves pull back.

"Something else?" asks Bluebelly, wiping off a glass.

"No."

Walking home I see two figures in black strolling down from the kirk through the grove of apple trees, the Priest's hands clasped behind his back, the Witch-hunter holding his elbow as if the Priest required some guidance on the footpath. The Priest looks up, sees me and makes the sign of the cross. What is he telling him about me, what can he know? Has Sean kept his promise not to talk to the Priest of me? I breathe a circle of light around myself, sharp with blue fire at the perimeter.

I am tempted to duck into the Smithy. Ewan's quiet strength, and his seeming shyer of me than I of him has always made the Smithy a reassuring haven. But after Peter told Ewan I had rejected his suit, he had quickly courted and married Jennet Turner, and things have been strained between us ever since. Yesterday when I went there I found him alone.

He looked coldly at me. "I've scarce seen you since I wed. I suppose you've no time for your old married friends now. Except for one," he noted, referring to my relationship with Sean.

"My mother's been sick. We've had much grief in our croft," I stammered. "I've strayed not far from home."

"That man's been asking questions about you," he whispered.

"What sort of questions?" I asked, trying not to appear afraid.

Ewan did not answer for a long time, strong arm pounding, shaping.

"He seems to think that—you'd bewitched me." The piece he was working on tore. He cursed and started over. "Perhaps he's right."

The thought of Ewan being cold to me again daunts me, but anything is better than the stares of the Priest and the Witch-hunter.

The talk in the Smithy stops as soon as I enter. A woman raises her nose, pulls her skirts aside and sweeps out, her husband closely following. One other woman there turns to her husband, whispers something in his ear. She keeps her head turned away from me. After a hesitation I walk the gauntlet of stares closer to the forge, my heart pounding so hard my clothes must be shaking with it.

Ewan pretends not to see me, working the metal. Sweat drips from his face, evaporating with sharp hisses in the flames.

For a long moment I try to brazen it out. The silence, the looks. Ewan continues working as if he had not noticed me, though I saw him look up when I came in.

I turn and go. A light rain is starting to fall. But I walk rather than run, until I've entered the small path through the woods and I am sure that no one is watching me.

Chapter 70

I wake up shaking in the middle of my nightmares, terror so tight around my throat I can scarcely breathe. Feeling of evil strong as carrion-smell in the dark barn. Night comes so swiftly now. I remember Sean pulling me into the barn, curtly ordering the Laird's vassals out, the looks of resentment and derision from the men as they abandoned milking the cows and currying the horses, Sean pulling my clothes off, pushing me down in a pile of fresh hay. The numb shame I felt afterwards at letting myself be used, wondering how I could face the minstrel if he returned, sure he would no longer want me.

Sean lies curled in the hay, his gentle snoring ruffling the lace on his shirt. I get up, hurriedly pull on my skirt, shaking, got to get out of here, want to go home.

As my blouse goes over my head, a rough hand grabs my arm, another hand twists my breast.

"Not so fast, lass, the fun's not over yet."

"Sean!" I cry out.

Blouse ripped off my head, McTavish grabbing my breasts.

Orrin Argylle leering over a rectangular iron lantern. Sean wakes with a start, cries out with dismay. The horses in the barn echo him with frightened neighs.

The Witch-hunter and his assistant materialize. The light from their lantern sets the silver cross on the Witch-hunter's chest ablaze with unnatural fire.

"You'd better come with me lad." The Witch-hunter takes Sean's arm. "It appears you've been bewitched. Perhaps there is still time to help you."

"Leave her alone," Sean says, his voice scared and small.

"Get the talisman off her neck," orders the Witch-hunter.

McTavish rips the silver fish Alain gave me off my neck. I scream, feeling Alain's love and protection torn away from me. I scratch my hand toward McTavish's face, he catches my wrist. Try to bite and kick. Glimpse Sean struggling with the large man, the assistant Witch-hunter pushing him towards the door.

"Get help!" I scream. My teeth connect with McTavish's thumb, he lets go and I twist away, free for two running steps, then the rope goes around my neck, burning as it saws back and forth across my throat.

On my knees, struggling like a fish in the harsh air, fighting against the rope, hands not strong enough to loosen it. Unable to breathe—I am sorry, I am sorry I call to all the fish I have ever taken as the light passes.

Then I am on my back, gasping, darkness lifting off from me. Heavy slamming down on my body.

No!

McTavish crashing down on top of me. It hurts. Orrin pinning me down, holding my wrists. Strain all my muscles taut with the effort to twist and throw him off.

"Sean—Sean—help me!" Demonic shadows, eerie lights cast by the lantern, can't see anything but McTavish's red leering face above me, teeth bared.

"Give it to her McTavish," urges Orrin. "Show her what it's all about."

Thrash my head from side to side trying to bite one of Orrin's wrists but he stays out of my reach. I scream in rage.

"Let me go! I curse you McTavish! I curse you! You will suffer for this, I swear it!"

I scream for help again and again. Someone has got to hear. The Laird's vassals cannot be far off, the Laird will stop it, Sean must be getting help—where are the guards, why doesn't someone come? Not calling with my voice, but calling as loudly as I may with my mind I send a call to Gran, *"Anu—help me—help me—Wind Mare—help me—I need—Staghorn! Help me!"* My mind flickering like the lantern, alternating between fierce concentration of the spirit call and shrill screams for Sean.

"Don't fret, Fiona," sneers Orrin, "you'll get plenty of cock tonight, you won't need the young Lord." McTavish pulls out of me and slams in hard. I feel myself tear, cry out.

"Stop it! Stop! You're hurting me!"

"Now you've got the idea," gloats Orrin.

Choking back a sob I growl instead, struggling so hard my muscles almost tear, helpless against the two of them, my struggles only intensifying my pain. McTavish pulls out, shoots his come over my body.

I get my legs free as they trade places, kicking hard, roll to my side, almost free. Then McTavish's hands closing over my throat. When I come back into consciousness it is not Orrin on top of me but Jack Turner, one of the Laird's vassals Sean had ordered away. My threats and curses have no effect on him. He shudders, clenches his hips and rolls off me. His brother kneels down, taking his place.

Screaming for Sean again, calling for help. God it hurts, it hurts!

"You're hurting me!"

He says something to McTavish who is holding my arms. Ugly laughter. Orrin leans over, pours ale in my mouth, up my nose.

"Drink up lass, it's a party."

Choking, sputtering, my cries are obviously terror now.

"Sean—"

Crosby runs in. Bright flood of relief.

"Crosby, help!" Thank God, thank God someone has come, there must be more of the Laird's guard nearby—

John Turner pulls out of me with a satisfied belch. Crosby pulling up his kilt. His cock is hard.

"Crosby—no—no—no—"

He doesn't look at me, eyes clenched tight, teeth set in a grimace. He pushes into me. Waves of horror and nausea shudder through me with each thrust.

"You must punish this Witch. You must purge yourselves in her evil flesh." The Priest standing to one side of me, holding a crucifix. "What you are doing is the will of God," he intones. Crosby shoving himself in and out of me. He's mad, they're all mad. The Witch-hunter has cast some spell on them.

I call him by name, "Crosby, Crosby, God—" Crosby I never hurt you. I never hurt you Crosby. Jesse's brother, Rose's blood, you can't, you can't do this! I cannot say Jesse's name or Rose's, cannot call him to his senses by betraying them. The Witch-hunter is right there, the Priest is right there.

"Crosby, Crosby." Sharp stabbing pain in my womb. God I can't believe how much this hurts why do they want to do this it's hurting so much.

"You're hurting me Crosby," I plead. Still he pounds away, no feeling, no feeling for me at all, as if he were the plow and I the soil that had to be broken. I rage and weep.

"Is it hot enough for you?" Jack Turner at my head, sneering. "Is it hot enough for you Fiona? Is this as hot and heavy as you like it?"

Crosby finally pulls out of me, bloody from his navel to his knees. I pull my legs together but the Witch-hunter's assistant is there, pushing them apart, thrusting into me, bludgeon of flesh bigger than I would have believed a man could have. Beyond shame now, screaming with pain.

"It hurts—you're killing me, you're killing me, you're killing me, God, you're killing me!"

My core, my center shredding to a pool of blood. Hay under my hips slippery with it. Pleading for help, for mercy. Mother, Dark One, strike them dead, take me away, let me faint or die, make them stop—I'm dying.

Unconsciousness. Perhaps for a moment. Perhaps for a long time. Another body on top of mine. Pain like being torn in half. Jim Strathan, face taut like a malicious bird.

"It wasn't big enough for Annie," he hisses over me. "Is it big enough for you? Is it hard enough?"

"I hope it falls off," I sob, "God curse you all and give you a bitter death!"

Tim Brede is next, white face, frightened by the blood that is everywhere now, and the curse. He loses his erection before he is quite inside me, grimaces, grinds his pubic bone against me, faking it.

"Don't go along with it Tim," I plead. "Help me. Get someone to help me."

He looks angrily at me, slaps me across the mouth, letting them all know he is not swayed by anything I have said.

The Turner boys are arguing about who among the three of them is going first.

"Here's Ewan," someone calls. "Let Ewan go first."

Ewan the Blacksmith kneeling between my thighs. His eyes flinch up from the bloody wound of my genitals, meeting my eyes. I look at him. No words. One of the few men in the village I felt safe with. One of the few that I trusted. One I thought was my friend.

He shudders, his eyes close to my mute entreaty. He pushes into me as if I were no more real or feeling than a figure in a dream.

The Priest piously murmuring benedictions over my slaughter. Why has no one come? Gran, Mina, I send pleading, pleading thoughts out to my coven. Please hear me. Do something, anything, get me out of this torment.

Long feline cry of despair tears through me. Surely they must have heard. Half the men in the village are here. Everyone must know.

Ewan pulls out of me, looks at his bloody cock, then at me, with a look of pure horror. Ian Turner shoulders him aside, mounts me, eyes gleaming with excitement. God, God, kill me some other way. The Witch-hunter and the Priest muttering obscene benedictions and encouragement.

"The Witch must suffer. The more she suffers the more the village will be blessed. Purge your foul lusts in her body and be cleansed! It is she who has tempted you, she who has put these thoughts in you. It is no sin to purge yourselves in this way."

Ian's teeth close on my breasts, mark my shoulders. He shakes me like a dog, growling over its kill.

"Just what you always wanted," taunts Orrin. "All the cocks

in the village. All in one night." Sloshes more beer down my throat. Maybe he'll drown me. Help me Annie, help me to die quickly.

Another of the Turner boys on top of me. The Witch-hunter's black eyes glittering with sadistic satisfaction. The Priest shaking, mouth wet.

"Come on lad, renounce the devil. This will heal you. You've been bewitched, this will help break the spell." The Witch-hunter hisses, "The bitch has laid hold of your senses—resist it, resist the enchantment, this will break it."

They strip Sean naked, push him to his knees. He gives me a look of blind terror. Two of the men pull my legs apart.

"For your immortal soul," the Witch-hunter breathes in his ear, "Your immortal soul is at stake. Purge yourself. Purge, or burn with her."

Sharp, stabbing pain. My voice soft, whispering his name.

"Sean. Sean. Sean. Sean. Sean."

Men's voices, encouraging him, ribald laughter.

"You're a real man, young lord, you're a real man. Look, she likes it. That's it, show her who's boss, show her who's in charge."

My voice soft and small, sobbing like my littlest sister would after a nightmare.

"Sean it hurts it hurts, please Sean."

Broken, humbled before them, unable to gather my pride to stop begging him as he jerks and thrusts, tearing me deeper. He gasps, spasms. In my torn and bleeding body he found pleasure. Let me die. Let me die.

He staggers up from me. My heart rips open, violated and torn as my body. I have not the spirit to scream anymore. I sob brokenly, not seeing who is behind the next punishing cock. Or the next. Or the next. Knowing the Witch-hunter's assistant by his size as he breaks into me again. Something else tears inside me, my bladder empties, wave of unbearable burning. I cry help-lessly against the brutal pain of my internal organs being crushed. McTavish, after him, gloating, gloating over me, daring me to look at him, daring me to curse him.

"I've suffered your kind enough," he snarls, "you've no more power here. Now you know who the master is."

Had he thrust the knife he carries on his hip into me I could not feel more agony. Another assailant, and another. I must be dying. I must be dying now. Even death by fire would be welcome now, any death, any death but this one.

They jerk me to my feet; sickening lurch inside my belly as my womb sags loose inside me. Christ they have butchered me. Someone twisting my arm behind my back. McTavish's gloating face next to mine. One of my hands breaks free—hawk-swift, I dart for his eyes, hear him howl and reel away. Then the sharp, heavy thunk of a lantern biting into my skull, and nothing more.

Chapter 71

Cold. Hard. Smooth cold stone under my face. Hot throbbing in my head. Slowly contact other sensations beyond the drumming of fire in my skull. My body feels shaky, empty. Sharp pain between my shoulder blades as I try to move my arms. Wrists unable to part. Hands numb. I shift position slightly and groan.

"The little red-haired queen is waking up."

Guttural low voice, strange accent. A boot pushing against my midsection, turning me over. Patterns of yellow and gold spin wildly behind my eyes. Icy water drenches me, sending my body into a convulsion of shivers.

"Ah now, is it cold you are lass? John lad, the little red-haired queen is cold—let's give her a good drubbing to warm her."

Open my eyes. Crazy slide of light and dark. Figures I can't quite see; hands, arms, blur of beard. Dark here, pieces of blurred fire clinging to the walls. Someone sawing at a cord between my wrists. My arms separate. I gasp at the pain between my shoulder blades as my arms are pulled and pinned over my head.

Hands pushing my thighs apart, waking bitter memory. The

men. The barn. No. No. Oh God. Pain—deep wrenching pain in my gut, breaking me apart. The Witch-hunter's assistant—not in the barn—it's so cold, where—icy stone bruising my back as he crushes into me. My head throbs agony with the pulse of his thrusts. The way I am twisting my body is making it hurt more. I will myself to lie quietly, biting my lip until my mouth floods with salt. Trying to will myself back into unconsciousness. I'm not here, I'm not here. I'm asleep with Alain; it's just a nightmare. Home. Take me home.

Pain keeps me. Pain binds me. Fire in my head and belly blazing too brightly to let me slip through into the darkness again. I pray for it to be over. Soon. Please. Soon.

"I see you find our little Witch friend amusing."

This voice I recognize. My eyes focus enough to see the silver cross gleaming dully beneath the Witch-hunter's dark malicious face. Behind him a fat Priest with a cassock and cross, trembling and sweating at the sight of my ravaged body. Clench my teeth tightly, not wanting them to have the satisfaction of my pain.

"Sit her up." The Witch-hunter squats as the others pull me to my knees before him. This must be a prison. How did I get here? I try to remember anything between the men raping me in the barn and this place. Only the pain in my head answers.

As if he read my mind, the Witch-hunter says, "Fiona—do you know why you are here?"

I focus on controlling my breathing, trying to slow the gasps.

"You are accused of Witchcraft. . ." he draws out the word, "a sin of treason, treason against God and King—has been discovered. From this place you will not leave alive. You get to choose— how quickly—and how easily—you will die. If you confess, you may earn the mercy of strangling before you are burnt. Should you not confess and name those who helped you—" he smiles, as joyful a look as I have ever seen on him, "—then your suffering— will be long."

Warm blood sliding down my thighs. I wish I could stop trembling.

"The Priest is here to hear your confession," he says. "If you confess and renounce your wicked ways—you may yet be saved from the Pit. But should you be recalcitrant—"

I close my eyes.

"This bitch stole the manhood of every man in her village," the Witch-hunter informs my captors. He lists my other offenses, saying that I have caused crops to fail, though our crops have been fine every year since I was a child. Saying I caused cattle to sicken, when I know of no sickness in the Laird's cattle, finally ending with the assertion that I sacrificed my baby brother Mark to the Devil and that the Priest in my village had observed this.

"Do you wish to confess and repent of all these crimes?" the Priest asks me. How would Mother feel if she heard I confessed that I sacrificed Mark? Ride with the breath. Ride with the breath.

"When did you first sign a pact with the Devil?"

Breathe in. Breathe out. No world beyond. My breath eases the shaking in my belly.

"The Witch is obstinate," the Witch-hunter says smugly. "Very well, McNair, we'll beat the devil free from your bones. A good scouraging will loosen your tongue."

Pain in my belly so intense I almost faint as they yank me up and press me flat against a wall. They struggle to chain my wrists to a pair of iron manacles set in the stone. The manacles are far too big and they slip off repeatedly.

"The bitch has cast a spell on the chains. They'll not take her!" mutters the smaller man fearfully.

"Use rope!" the Witch-hunter exclaims, pacing impatiently as they curse and fumble, securing me to the chains.

The first blow drives me up against the wall, my knees buckle, shaky legs give way under the force of the second blow, the third, hanging by my arms sheer agony in the shoulders. I stumble back on my feet, tears hot in my eyes, biting my lower lip, blood trickling over my chin, the volitional pain a small distraction from the stripes of fire scoring my body. Shuddering after every blow, determined not to cry out, all my will gathers into making no sound. One of the whip slashes opens the skin, warm blood running down my back, half-fainting but the pain of my body's weight on my shoulders brings me to; rising, falling, my body thumping against the wall with each blow—I am on fire—I hear them talking, threatening voices; they are frightened by my silence, tiny pulse of triumph before the next blow shatters me back to raw animal agony. Face hot with tears and blood, hanging by my arms, unable to rise anymore, silently begging the Goddess for mercy; at last the dark door opens and I fall.

Chapter 72

Someone else has been taken. I hear moaning nearby. A woman. What did they do to her? She whimpers with every breath. Suddenly I realize that the sounds are pushing out of my own throat. I am face down on the floor trembling and moaning. With a groan I stop my breath, stifle the catch in my throat, imagine a stone blocking it.

Hands turn me over. The Witch-hunter's ugly face leans close to mine.

"Had a nice rest?"

I hate him. He sees it in my eyes and smiles.

"Are you ready to talk to us Witch?"

My belly is shaking violently. I stare at him as if staring could turn him to stone.

"Cat got your tongue, Fiona?" Teasing, familiar. I hate him I hate him I hate him.

"We want the names of the others. Give us that and all this can stop. Give us that and you can die an easy death."

"God is merciful to sinners," the Priest intones solemnly.

"More luck to you," I whisper.

"Ah, she can speak. Barack, get the lass some water, she's dry sure."

He holds a bowl of water to my lips. I sip coolness down my throat.

Three small sips and he takes it away.

"There's more of this in exchange for names, Fiona."

I press my lips together, close my eyes, blood like a drum beating in my ears. When the man holding my shoulders shifts position fresh currents of pain ripple over my back and legs.

"Fiona, your grandmother is dead. Your silence cannot protect her."

Stone in a pool, the impact of his words send ripples of shock to my core. But it is not true because it cannot be true.

I drop my head and go limp, feigning faint, dropping my spirit into light trance. With great will I drop to the tunnel where the body ceases to be one with the mind. Hard to stay there, men's voices, pain crackling through. With will I center and try to touch. And try to touch. Like a hand groping in the dark to find a bed-mate not there, the blankets still warm where she should be—Gran! Gran! Anu! Signalling as strongly as I can, fighting the rising panic making me feel like a child awakening alone in a dark house, not feeling her, not finding her. . .

Back suddenly, face ringing from a strong backhanded slap, and another, and another.

"Enough," says the calm voice.

Hatred clenches my belly. I'm sitting, guard holding me upright by the shoulders, my head swaying from the blows.

With feigned sympathy the Witch-hunter says, "After you were taken, men came to your grandmother's house to take her too. Her Witchery was known." He pauses for dramatic effect. "They found your Gran hanging. With John Gardner. Killed themselves to escape."

"But nothing escapes the Lord's divine vengeance," hisses the Priest in the background. "They're screaming in eternal torment now. . ."

A ball of pain plunges through my center and explodes in my head.

This time, the faint is real.

*   *   *   *

Sound of soft, disembodied sobs. Again as physical sensations come slowly into focus I feel the sobs gasping up from my own chest, recognize the wetness on my face as fresh tears.

The Witch-hunter is murmuring sympathetically. Christ his lying sympathy makes me ill. Gran never cried, she would not cry, I've got to stop. I swallow the sobs, quiet my body's shaking as best as I can.

"The names, Fiona."

The softness in his voice drips menace.

I open my eyes and look directly up at him.

"Water," I whisper. "Water, and I'll tell."

The Witch-hunter lifts me up in the crook of his arm, puts the water to my lips. Just enough to wet my mouth and whet my thirst.

"More after the first name," he promises. "Owen—"

The guard who held me before lifts me up while the Witch-hunter produces a quill and parchment from the folds of his cloak. So much the image of their God Satan that I almost smile. He looks at me questioningly.

"McTavish."

A hardness appears around his mouth.

"McTavish is a God-fearing man," he replies.

"Fear God he may, but he worships the devil." I am ice cold with my desire that McTavish join me in my suffering.

"That is a lie, McNair!" The Witch-hunter's eyes are very cold.

"'Tis true! For all his piety he has a black heart. He was GrandMaster at our meetings. The cursed warlock has betrayed me to save his own skin. He's the Devil's man, I swear it."

A silence. His eyes hooded like a hawk's. He writes the name out slowly.

"Give her another sip of water."

The water is so good. They give me so little.

"Who else?"

"Orrin Argyle, Jack Turner, John Turner, all the Turners!" I cannot contain my fury. "Jim Strathan, Tim Brede—"

"You name the men who ravaged you McNair."

He puts the parchment back in his cloak.

"D'ye think you can lie to me then? Give her stripes on her front to match her back," he orders.

How eagerly they obey. My nipples tense with fear as they bind my wrists over my head. The bear-like guard, the Witchhunter's assistant, pinches them, "For good luck," he says and roars with laughter. He picks up the whip. I close my eyes.

The blow knocks the breath out of me. Oh God this is worse, they can see my face. I press my lips together tightly. Silent through the fourth blow the fifth the sixth the seventh past the point of counting. Pain takes me over, my back arches, the whip wrenches a deep cry from a place my will cannot reach.

I smack my head backwards against the wall to knock myself out. Again. Again.

I remain conscious but the scouraging stops.

There is no sound but my own ragged sobs. I fight for control, shamed that they can make me cry, terrified that if I start screaming I will go mad and betray everyone in my madness. I strangle the sobs to gasps, clench my teeth to stifle the moans bubbling in my throat. Oh Gran give me courage, Lady stand by me. I see an image of my Gran invoking the Goddess, being the Goddess, I calm enough to open my eyes and face my persecutors.

"Your courage is impressive, child. But how long do you think it will last? This is just the start, you know." The Witchhunter stands closer, smiling his false, cold smile. "This is nothing compared to the suffering you will endure should your obstinacy continue."

"Spare me your concern," I whisper.

"Ah well, so be it," he yawns and smiles. "Torture is a wearying affair and the hour is late. I will to bed." He turns to the guards; three of them now, not two.

"Amuse yourselves with her as you wish. If you have her ready with answers by morning tis money in your pockets." He saunters off and the Priest strides after him. A heavy door closes.

The three men form a semi-circle around me. The big man the others call Barack grins and rubs the whip over my bleeding body. Puts it to my lips.

"Kiss it," he orders.

I turn my head as far as I can.

"Kiss the rod that beats you girl," he insists. "By God I'll beat you until you beg for a chance to kiss it."

"By Christ, Barack, she's in bad enough shape. I want to fuck her while I can still stand to look at her."

My moans, their crude jokes and harsh laughter, slow unending torture of being bludgeoned to death from the inside. The dying goes on and on, and the death I pray for does not come.

Having sated themselves, Owen and Dirk do not object when Barack again brings out the scourage.

"Just enough to make her squirm," he promises, "not enough to tire my arm."

The lash on my belly is unbearable. I turn over, cradling my head in my arms. It is no less painful on my lacerated back and buttocks but my face is hidden. I clasp my teeth in my right forearm and bite down hard as the blows convulse my body.

I summon my will, my concentration, and try to numb my body to the point where I can darken my mind to the starless void where distance vanishes, where a call can be sent and heard. *"Mina, Mina,"* my mind calls. After Annie and my Gran it was Mina I clasped with easiest. *"Help me!"* Desperation sends the call strongly, but nothing but utter eerie silence answers. They cannot all be dead. . . fighting a wave of panic I turn my will towards Rose, dear Rose, deaf in her ears but not to inner calls— Rose, Rose, clasp with me I have need. . . I feel an answering recognition, a shudder, as if she woke from a nightmare. She fades. *"Rose, dinna go—"* BearHearth. . . Snowflower. . . Winter. . . nothing. . . nothing. So much of my will is going to stave off the pain that my reaching is weakened, but they should be reaching out to me. . .

Cold certainty kicks me in the chest, the frost of it congealing my veins. It is not that they cannot hear, but that they will not hear. They have deliberately closed to me, shunning my calls as if I were already dead and they feared my ghost. Like a cur shivering in a snowstorm I whine at one closed door after another. Do they blame me for Gran's death? Or—my mind twists like a fish drowning in dry air, trying to imagine why my coven would have abandoned me. Do they feel that I deserted them in my long absence after Nimué's death? Or do they think that I have already betrayed them? *"Help me not to betray you,"* I plead, *"Help me to die."* Desperate, I cast wildly to anyone who loves me, Mama, Eostre, Elana, help me someone please. . .

A flood of warmth, smell of touseled hair and a damp wool cloak—Alain, oh Alain, thank you, thank you. I realize he is asleep, dreaming of me, unaware that he is answering a call but answering it just the same. He's holding me in his dream, caressing me. I enter his dream shivering, feeling still the punishing lash.

"Shield me," I implore. He smiles in his sleep, holds his cloak over me, his safe arms around me. The blows fade and become raindrops pattering on the cloak tent so lovingly cupped and protectively held around me. Against the sweet warmth of his body I melt into blessed sleep.

*   *   *   *

Pain jerks me back to my body. I am being anally raped, each stroke like a spear thrust tearing my entrails. I vomit up bile, scalding my throat, and keep vomiting long after there is nothing left to come up.

One of the men stuffs some rags in my mouth. They turn me on my side so that Barack can enter my shredded cunt while one of the other men penetrates me from behind. Images of a doe I'd seen dragged down and torn apart by hounds, the fawn ripped out of her belly and devoured while she was still alive. I live that doe's dying.

Through my agony I hold one hope; that I might swallow the rags, block my breathing and die. By swallowing hard repeatedly and pushing back with my tongue at last I manage to suck some of the rags back into my throat. At once my body begins to struggle for air; blackness presses down on my eyes, wild happiness and triumph, I am free.

*   *   *   *

But I do not wake up to a fairer place. I return to my body, gasping for air on the cold stone floor. One of the men is upbraiding the other for having put the rags in my mouth. A hand on my brow feels surprisingly gentle. I open my eyes to the furrowed brows and blue gaze of a blond youth who looks to be no older than myself.

"Thank Christ we didn't lose her," says Barack. "Ian lad, we're indebted to ye. Take a ride on her if ye like; she's not so comely as she was but her quim's tight and warm."

The lad pays him no heed.

"Get me some water for her," he says.

One of the other men gets the bowl of water and comes over with it. Ian raises me up slowly and with care. The guard urinates in the bowl before handing it to Ian with a crude joke. I feel Ian's arm tighten around me as he throws the tainted water on the floor. From the slight upward motion of his arm I guess that he had started to throw it in the other's face but thought better of it.

"Filthy bastard, get me some decent water!"

"Water's against our orders," Owen says. "She gets water when she's ready to confess. If ye like the lass so much then bang her. Ye dinna have to court her first!"

Laughter from the others as they try to shame the young man into raping me. Ian lays me back on the floor and stands up.

"I can find lasses willing. I need not force myself on one who cannot say aye or nay."

They call him a womanish coward but it sways him not. He strides out. My eyes fill with tears. If Sean had shown but half of that lad's courage. . .

Chapter 73

"Had a nice night Fiona?" The Witch-hunter with his amused, predatory stare. "Ready to confess, ask Christ's forgiveness and name those who led you in these evil ways?"

To my silence he continues, "It seems a shame to suffer for those who have already betrayed you. Lord Lochlan has signed your death warrant, his own son having fallen prey to your sorceries. Tis well known that no Witch works alone; one as young as yourself has had teachers, Fiona."

"You look so thirsty," he whispers. "I'd like to give you some water."

I sob, bow my head with shame. I would do anything for water, even tainted water. Despairing, I cast my need through the starless place, knowing there will be no answer. They all hate me; not just the men who attacked me in the barn; my coven, my family. If they all hate me I must be evil indeed, as evil as the Witch-hunter says.

Faint scent of dried roses, heather, lavender and rosemary, followed by the sensation of water soothing my scalded throat.

Violet Rose reaching out to me, tentatively at first, then with the assurance of a midwife tending a laboring woman. Two more shadowy presences attend her. One is a future incarnation of Rose, and one my own future self, a Priestess reaching to me from a time when Priestesses are burned no longer. Courage fills me like the wind filling a sail.

Barack wraps a leather band around my head and twists it somehow so that it gradually tightens. Roaring in my ears, bursts of color. I link in with Rose when I have the peace of fainting. I tell her about the leather band, such a simple thing to cause so much pain. Alternating states of blind agony and calm. At times nothing exists but this world of bright pain. But in the intervals of healing twilight I hear Rose saying, *"Your death has a purpose, Fiona. This will make you stronger."* And the ghost of my future self whispering, *"What is remembered lives. You live in me, you live in me forever."*

My body is not comforted. Retching and moaning, I spin back to waking consciousness. The guards are speaking but I cannot comprehend what they say. Slaps, water in my face, a cruel hand pulling my head back by the hair to stare into the Witchhunter's unsouled eyes. I wish I had moisture in my mouth to spit at him.

"Fiona, the Priest is ready to hear your confession."

Only the hatred in my eyes speaks.

They put me on the rack, a monstrous machine that creaks and groans as it pulls my body taut. Sweat breaks out over my body. I am hot, burning with fever now. The Witch-hunter talks on in his soft, hateful voice, running his fingers down my tightening belly. My head twists back and forth as I gasp for breath. The whip comes down now across my flanks, ribs, breasts. Mother Mother Lady help me—Rose. . .

"I am here." Rose is with me, so calm, so strong. Help me, please I cannot bear it. *"It will be over soon,"* she promises. Feeling muscles tear in my shoulders, my knees. Hearing myself cry out over and over.

*   *   *   *

I must have refused to speak again. They have a thing like a cauldron or brazier of hot coals with metal bars like spokes. Barack slides one out passing its dull red glow before my face. Two men pinning me on my knees between them, bolts of pain up my legs, twisting through my back from the tearing inflicted by the rack. The Witch-hunter asking me to spare myself. The hot iron touching the web of whip weals on my back, the men holding me tightly, I can't escape or twist away from it, one of the men actually caressing my breast while Barack burns me over and over, little touches as first, teasing, then holding it there as I sob and curse. They extinguish one iron after another on my body until I can bear it no longer. I promise to confess.

Feeling shame, knowing I would crawl at their feet now and beg for mercy if I thought there was any chance they would give it, if there were any softness in them at all.

The Witch-hunter reads me a list of my transgressions. I have been accused of everything from souring milk and sickening kine to enchanting a long list of men and stealing their manhood, to killing my brother Mark as a sacrifice to the Devil. I care not what they say, I confess to every charge. What does it matter, they'll kill me anyway. I worship devils, consort with demons, anything, anything for respite. But the questions change. Was Wilhemina MacEnry my confederate? No. Alma Turner? No. The names continue. I shake my head. Did I enchant the Laird's son? Aye. Did I take him to a Sabbat? No. Did I ever see the Laird himself at a Sabbat? No.

I'm shaking with pain and exhaustion. I try to bargain.

"Let me rest and I'll tell you more. My head hurts so, I cannot remember."

He promises to hurt me far more if I cannot remember. On about the Laird's household, who practiced magic there. Was the Laird not really my father, and had he not promised me to the devil when I was born? Was he GrandMaster at our meetings? I see the urn bristling with its spokes of torment. Park slides another out, holds the glowing iron a few inches from my eyes. He threatens to gouge out my eyes with it, to rape me with it.

"We'll break ye McNair, tis only a matter of time and how much ye wish to suffer."

"All these people have already offered testimony against ye, why suffer for them that have already betrayed ye?" asks the

Witch-hunter.

I'm afraid, afraid of more pain, afraid I will break and name whoever they wish me to. Prickling at my neck, faint touch of Rose's hand on my hair.

"*I am here. I am with you. Can you tell me what is happening now?*"

I pretend to faint, use the opportunity to make linking. "*I think it's the Laird they're after more than anyone else. Maybe I should say aye—*"

"*You need not give them anything,*" Rose says. "I need not give them anything," I repeat. Relief.

"*I know ye will not betray the Craft,*" Rose says. Her serene confidence steadies me.

I do not have to give them anything. It will be over soon. I wake biting my lip fiercely as they shake me back and forth. Again the hot irons. They tell me how much more agonizing it will be for me when I am being eaten by flames at the stake. They will make it a hot fire for me, with no smoke to choke me senseless. They promise me a quick death by strangling if I give names. I hurt so much. I hurt so much. Please let me die, let it stop. I plead that everyone assumed a demon shape at Sabbats, I could not recognize anyone. I babble nonsense. We flew through the air, danced with devils in animal form. I tell them about flying ointment, making sure the combination of ingredients I give them is lethal. It wins me only a brief respite. I fear losing control, so I stop speaking, force the heavy stone to cover my throat like a dead well, a tomb.

They have me back on the rack. Animal sounds of pain bubble up around the boulder in my throat, but no words. My connection with Rose is a thin thread of sanity. Through the buzzing in my brain, past their leering threats and my helpless sounds I hear her saying, "*It will be over soon. It will be over. Your death has a purpose. We will meet again, be close again, closer, in another life. Everything hurt is healed again, Fiona.*"

Chapter 74

Barack keeps repeating my name, "McNair. Fiona McNair," like an obscenity.

I open my eyes, try to focus on him. My vision is fogged, like looking through a wavery gray glass. Two men are holding my legs apart, a third is holding my hands above my head. Barack stands, holding a glowing brand in one hand, his prick in the other.

"Which will it be, Fiona? The hot iron of your choice."

Moans fluttering in my throat, unbelieving, they cannot do this, I would die, they can threaten it, they cannot do it. . .

"Choose or I choose for you."

The terror, the certainty that he is inhuman enough to do it. Then pain searing me into convulsions screaming spasms of agony burning alive.

I am in the starless place, feeling the jolting of my body thrashing on the stone floor. Storms of ragged lightening sweep through my flesh. I feel sorry for my body, but I can no longer remain there. I abandon my writhing form, breathing at that calm place in the center. Rose is there, patient, unsleeping, like a mother rocking a new babe that cannot sleep. I tell her I have found a place beyond pain.

"Yes," she says, "*the center of the whirlwind. The stillness at the center. Soon you will be past all pain, safe in the Mother. The Goddess will free you. She is always with you and within you. She is always with you. It will soon be over.*"

Like a leaf flickering gold and silver in the light as it falls, drifting through dream and nothingness. I can hear them shouting at me, hate the sound of my name when they say it. I alternate between waves of fever, imagining myself already burning at the stake, and spasms of chills. Taste of blood in my mouth. The men unreal, like shadows. My own body like a piece of shadow, the blows seeming to pass through me. A woman screaming; the shadowy men transformed into black-cloaked women, coven sisters of my future self, holding her, holding me, screaming beside a fire on an isolated beach. From the damp salt air and comforting arms to the shadow dungeon and bitter blood streaming down my throat. Back and forth and through the starless place where nothing exists, to the rough feel of a coarse wool tartan and Rose's old arms around me and again through a long gentle space of nothingness. It is wonderful to feel numb to their torments, not caring anymore, no longer my body.

Feeling different women passing through me, of me and not me, all the bodies and minds I have been which are dust, which are ash, and I, this body of me, traveling towards dust and ash, and then on to another body, a Priestess in an age when Priestesses are burned no longer. And her pregnant in turn with people I cannot see except as shadows, like tree rings, spiralling outward. Realizing that all the bodies I have been are like flowers swelling to fruit, ripening and falling; the Motherself like a tree that remains after the fruit has fallen, bearing again and again, new orchards locked in the scattered seeds, ready to spring out of the shadow into the light when the old tree falls.

Dreaming, I huddle deep inside my body, a butterfly crumpled inside the chrysalis that must break apart before it can fly free. Like an unborn child moving backwards through time, I curl into a ball, growing smaller and smaller, growing towards a hard-shelled seed that could be buried and sprout again.

Pictures float by. A spider crouched on a torn web, fluttering in the icy midnight air. The pattern torn, the world falling to darkness. The old ways vanish. My people are dying with me. Seeds of new life scattered invisible on the scorched ground. The blue Goddess beckoning at the heart of the flame. My bones boiled and burnished smooth in a molten lake. A bird with wings of fire rising from it. Words of my consecration vibrating like music:

"I am thy Priestess. I give myself utterly to the Dance. May my life and death serve."

I regret nothing.

Chapter 75

Intense smell of crushed herbs. My nose wrinkles with the effort of sorting the pungent odor into recognizable parts. Rosemary. . . pennyroyal. . .thyme. . . savoury. . .wormwood perhaps. . . I squat on my heels, watching Gran grind the dried plants in her mortar and pestle, humming a wordless chant. She adds the powder to a small cauldron of sheep fat, beeswax and pine resins cooking over the fire, stirring the mixture to a thick paste. A drowsy syrup of belladonna, poppies and chamomile simmering nearby.

"One to soothe the spirit to sleep, one to revive it. It is well to make opposites together, because. . ."

"It keeps the balance," I say, proud to understand the importance of such things. She passes the ladle coated with the reviving salve under my nose—a sting like the shock of cold water flashes along the hidden web of nerves, my hands and feet vibrate with green light.

The smell grows fainter. I feel my head descend and touch the floor. The hand gently stroking my hair is not my Gran's. A young man. Someone I don't know. A wet cloth moving lightly over my face. Sound of splashing water. Again the cool cloth moving over the pulse in my throat, across my collarbones. Eyes closed, I tentatively reach out with cat sense to explore the room. I am in prison still. The hands touching me—that young guard—Ian, they called him. None of the others are here. I feel their absence almost like a light. Demons fled at sunrise. I flinch and moan as the cloth touches my breasts. He pours a stream of water over me and continues mopping my flanks, my belly. I start shivering uncontrollably as cold water sluices over my female parts. His deft hands tremble.

He rises quickly, steps across the room. I hear him vomiting in the far corner. My nose is not totally blocked with blood. Smells of urine, vomit, semen, mingled with the harsh odor of scorched hair and flesh. I must look as horrible as I smell. The young man returns to my side. His breathing is shaky. I force my eyes to open a slit. Soft blur of movement. Dimly I make out his face, set and hard, lips pressed in a tight line as he washes my legs Too much effort, I surrender and let my eyes close. But he must have seen my eyelids flutter Fingers just barely brushing my brow, the cloth cool against my lids, cheeks, my torn mouth.

"Fiona?" he whispers softly. "Little queen—I have clean water. Can ye drink a bit?"

He lifts my head, puts the bowl to my mouth. Nothing has ever tasted sweeter. So grateful for the water, for the gentle touch, had I tears left, I would weep. The cold water cramps my stomach. I buckle, vomit up blood. Ian wipes my mouth and gives the water more slowly.

"I gave ye too much. Let that settle now. Ye can have more in a bit."

As he finishes wiping me off I begin shivering violently again, sudden drop from raging fever to bone-cracking cold. He pulls a heavy wool blanket over me, holding it close against my body until my teeth stop chattering. Then I flush hot again and cannot bear the prickly blanket against my raw skin. He starts to apply some of the herbal salve to my body. My skin shudders awake to the sensations of the hot irons, the scourage. He stops when he sees my suffering. A miracle: He takes no pleasure in my pain. He dresses me in a rough white shift. I almost vomit again. He is getting me ready to be burned. A little kindness for the animal about to be slaughtered.

He tells me they will come soon to take me to judgement. I am to go before a judge, confess my crimes and be sentenced. I struggle to find language.

"Burn. . . right. . . after?"

"Tis already past noon. They will probably wait—tomorrow— is All Hallows Eve. It will be then."

I am to die on Samhain then. A sacred time. I try to feel like the Dying One, the King who is sacrificed each year with love and born again in the Spring. I do not imagine the King God dying in torment. I wish I felt brave. I feel like a frightened child.

Two of the other guards come to take me. As they enter the room, a calmness settles in my bones. It no longer matters what happens. I am at hard rock bottom. It is some solace to discover that there is a bottom point to suffering, that I will descend no further. The fire will be terrible. And I will pass through it. I have no choice. I will endure what must be endured.

They want me to walk somewhere? Bitter jest. This body is too mangled to move. They pull me up by the shoulders. I faint. They try to drag me again. I go limp, not struggling. Roaring in my ears, chasms of light, bright colors, and down again into velvet darkness.

Huge, gray-green eyes. Soft lap, sheltering arms. My mother singin me a lullaby. "Nonny, nonny, nonny nonny dee, sittin' on yer Mama's knee—" Her beauty passing suddenly, like a tree stripped bare by the White Lady of Winter. Gray settling like dust over the gold of her hair, a few wisps of white framing her face. Pinched in cheeks and jaw, angular body spent from birthing, shoulders slumped, but still that great light in her eyes. . .

Fast, now slow, light-hearted, now melancholy, the tune called *King of the Faeries* playing in my mind. When Jack Green was still alive he played it a light tripping way that held no menace, though it was the song played all night at Samhain, the song that opened the gates to the otherworld of faery and the blessed isles of death. The young people screaming with laughter and mock fear as we snapped the serpent through the ruined fields, stumbling over the broken stalks of wheat and corn, falling, the coarse cord of black, red and white wool yanked from my grasp. Dancing alone then, dropping my clothes piece by piece, dancing ever closer to the Gate of Passing at the far end of the field. The hooded crones holding the black veil nod, and I tumble through, naked, onto the other side. Another hooded figure dresses me in a black cloak, gives me a turnip with a lighted candle in it. Bodies invisible, ghastly faces illuminated by the bowl of weak light cupped in our hands, we newly dead wander past each other and off on our solitary paths to the seashore, the well, the slopes overlooking the sibilant waters of Mira. Crouching alone, attended by the murmur of water, scrying in my candle until it flickers its last weak pulse of blue and dies.

*　　　　　*　　　　　*　　　　　*

I no longer have the sensation of walking on fire. Enclosed in their frozen coffins of deer hide, my feet have gone almost totally numb. Tripping over hidden tree roots, arms too stiff to catch my fall, face full of powdery snow. Christ tis bitter, Christ tis cold. Trees bare except for the pines. The forest seems thinner. No scent of them by the frozen spring, the most impenetrable maze of thickets yields only a frozen bird. I call and call, voice and mind, for the Queen of Air and Darkness to appear. Silence. Only a still, white regret, a dusting of snow obscuring the rippled glass of a pond. Ache in my foot like the bite of cold steel. I will have frost-bite, I must turn back.

"I have to turn back! Ye must come part way to me!" I scream into the wind. Like the snow and the occasional dry blowing leaf they flee before my voice. And I, defeated, turn back.

*　　　　　*　　　　　*　　　　　*

Christ tis cold. Shaking. Stone floor against the side of my face cold as ice. Eyes unfocussed, fish looking up through a wrinkle of ice at the winter fishermen. I don't understand what's being shouted at me. I do understand the boot in my stomach.

*　　　　　*　　　　　*　　　　　*

"Blow the candles out."
Sean hesitates, so I roll over the linen sheets, blow them out

myself. The dark, that's better, no sight but dim, no touch but sharp and fine. I bite his shoulder, rake my nails down his arms. He moans, pins me and enters me, breathing harsh and hurried. His smell, thin muscular body, large awkward hands. His wide, sensual mouth, boundaries between us lost in wetness, both my mouths wide open to his tongue, his cock, devouring him. I am the cat, devouring, taking him in, turning him to water; I am the Witch of the rain, of the rain, of the hot summer rain. Pour into me I call; pull him in, milk him like a cloud, and am struck by lightning, flashing every nerve into feathers of light.

*   *   *   *

My eyes open. Nothing but hair. My face must be covered by my hair.

"D'ye want to kill her outright?" Angry voices. Like an argument among cloud spirits, so far up it hardly concerns me. Hands lifting me up, Ian awkwardly adjusts me in his arms as if he could make my agony comfortable.

I have been gritting my teeth for so long the jaw muscles feel frozen, the muscles that tore when they forced my mouth jumping and spasming where the jaw locks. *I hate him too, this gentle one, I think as pain blots me out.*

The ache in my jaws is the first thing I feel. Green pungent smell in my nostrils, like the midden heap outside the house, rich with the sharp odors of decay. I keep breathing it. Tis like Gran, like home, my brothers and sisters playing a game of tag in front of the croft, knocking each other down, screaming with laughter, then the wail as someone gets too rough. Twilight, blue and hazy, a strong south wind with a storm coming in.

"More bad news from England," the old people say.

Something stinging in this odor, making my eyes water. I open them and look up, my eyes going in and out of focus. Ian has me propped up against a wall, cupping a small jar under my nostrils. The lad knows wortcunning, and he's doing it right under their noses. With their permission? A warlock, traitor who sells his cunning skills to the men in power? An executioner's son who has not the knack for suffering but for healing instead? I feel a little sick thinking they may catch him at this earth sorcery and burn him along with me. He puts a pastille under my tongue, minty and bitter, bracing as the breath of winter. I am amazed at how much more conscious I feel. Both drugged and awake, a strange combination. I still have trouble focussing my eyes—everything blurs and runs together. He is talking to me in a low urgent voice. My ears are as unfocussed as my eyes, and the words run together and blur.

"Forgive me. I am watched now. I can do no more."

Forgiveness. Why forgiveness when he has not harmed me? I wish I could sort out more of the words. They make so little sense.

"Ye must try to keep standing. It will be over soon, I promise. Forgive us we cannot do more."

At length he stands me up and walks with his arm around me for support. The chamber we enter seems dark. A judge in black with a curly gray wig seated high above me. I am put in a dock, small square wooden box with spikes around the outside. I steady myself on two of the spikes at the front of the box. My head aches. Everything aches. I lock my knees. A stiff curtain of hair falls in my face, matted with blood. The sway of faces, voices, motion beyond the curtain makes me dizzy.

I close my eyes. I imagine the faces from my village who must be here, the looks of pity, gloating, disgust. I'll not meet any of those gazes. Open my eyes to keep from falling into unconsciousness. Purple swollen hands, pus-filled blisters, hands that can barely curl around the spikes for support. Not my hands. Not mine.

The judge asks if I know what crimes I have been accused of. I don't know what answer they want. Into my hesitation he rolls the long series of accusations. Do I, freely and of my own will, confess to these crimes? Freely and of my own will? I look up to see if he is smiling. He must be mocking me. He is not smiling, face tense and fearful, pinched mouth, frightened eyes. My vision blurs, then clears. I no longer see the frowning judge, but a lean woman of middle age, vertical grooves down her cheeks, the eyebrows pinched together, fierce hawk nose and gray blowing hair. She is clad in coarse brown cloth, but the winged headdress fluttering on her brow, the purpose in her eyes fierce as the falcon clutching her wrist, speak her as a Priestess. The stony beach we stand on rings an island, a temple where we both serve lies beyond these vermillion cliffs. Daybreak; wind from a passing storm ruffling the wings in her hair to mimicry of flight.

Deep menacing voice shatters the image as if it were wove on water. The harsh, proud Priestess dissolves into the judge's frightened face. Does he fear me, torn open and dying as I am? No, it is the dying that he fears, not me. And I, dying before his eyes, at his word. Another image comes, more faintly. An aunt, or some older relative who cared for him as a child, teaching him about the dance of the animals and the plants, about the sacred passages of the year wheel's round. His fear of dying has caused him to betray the deepest knowing of his spirit. And bitter and well he knows it.

I become aware that he has asked me a question and I have not answered. His fear is making him angry. My mind is wandering, I don't know what they want from me. I don't want to be hurt anymore. I'll say what they like, if it betrays no one.

"What would ye like me to say?" Even that whisper is such effort, each word gouging my throat, stumbling over my split lips and swollen tongue. In my mind I am pleading with him not to have me tortured any more; I am dying, you could let me die in peace. Wondering if he can read the asking in my eyes. His eyes crinkle. Yes, he feels my suffering in his body. Christian he may be but he is not dead on the inside like the Witch-hunter or my tormentors.

He repeats his question. Do I freely and willingly confess to the crimes which I have previously confessed to in prison? Bitter as the jest of my free will is, I cannot but smile.

"Aye."

My bones ache. Through the throb in my head I hear the Witch-hunter's voice. Saying something about a victim of my crimes being here to offer testimony against me. And then the soft, halting voice speaking is Sean's. I can barely hear him as he describes how I seduced him, led his soul astray, caused him to be faithless to his dear wife. I focus on him through the shifting curtain of gray fogging my vision. He is looking down at his hands as he speaks, the Witch-hunter standing by with a malicious smile. I sink slowly to my knees, lean my forehead up against the inside of the dock. It is so cold here.

Hands like steel clamps gripping me, pulling me upright.

Let this charade cease. We all know how it is to end. The judge asks me if I confess to the crimes Sean accuses me of. Was he my victim or my accomplice?

"It is as he said. I bewitched him. I worked alone in my art. None helped me."

"Was he not your accomplice? Did he make covenant with Satan at your bidding?"

"He is innocent."

Sean shudders at my words, not daring to look at me. False cowan, I give you your life. Never draw breath but know it as my gift. I try to will him to meet my eyes. Please look at me. Let me think you still love me. Let me think you betrayed me only out of fear. Let me know you do not believe those things you said of me. He will not look. Weak, they all told me you were weak, unworthy. How I persisted in thinking you a gentle soul, misunderstood. Coward. Even as I think these harsh thoughts I know they are but a bridge to keep me from falling into a bottomless well of grief. I still love you poor lad, I wish you well. I wish you joy. Fare thee well, Sean.

The judge asks me to repent. The Priest will hear my confession. The old lie about their merciful God.

"I repent nothing."

In the name of the holy church, in the name of the King, in the name of God, he sentences me to be burned quick—alive—on the 31st day of October, year of their Lord 1595.

Alive. I expected it. The mercy of strangling is for traitors. It will be the last pain I must endure.

As they start to pull me away, Sean finally looks up at me. For a long moment our eyes lock; we are as naked as we have ever been together. He covers his face with his hands and groans.

Someone shoves me roughly. I am gone before I hit the floor.

Chapter 76

I jolt briefly back to consciousness as I am thrown back in a dark cell. The door slams shut, the bolt is thrown. I am alone. Brief gratitude for this mercy as the tide rolls through me and bears me away on smothering currents of shadow.

*   *   *   *

Lolling about at the bottom of M'hira, hair tangling together, black and red mingling with the water-wort we clutch to keep us submerged. Eyes bulge salmon-wise as our breath runs out. We push up to the surface, gasping in great gulps of cool morning air. We are at the twin falls, where the ale brown stream pours silver cold over the rocks. My new-budding breasts are swollen, Annie's breasts already rearing small mounds above the ridges of her ribcage.

"They're getting big," I say admiringly, sliding my hands over her chest. Circle her hard wet nipples with my fingers. We stop our giggling, weave deep into each other's eyes. Eyes that go so far back. I see her shape-shift into other women, other girls, her body changing under my hands, under my gaze. How long I have loved her, in how many forms.

"Ky-air-thwen," she says, smiling into my eyes.

"Nimué." I slip into her embrace, brush my tongue through the soft slide of her mouth, across the ivory temples of her teeth. Yes this is fine, so fine. Moving out of the water, slow motion of dream, sinking to the tousle of tartan clothing tangled at the water's edge. My breasts hurt fiercely under her tongue, her merciless bite. Slender hand, muscled thigh, slide between my legs, flesh shivering and bumpy from the cold stream then the incredible warmth spreading out from the inside. Pebbles crunching underneath us as we twist and gasp on our tartan cloaks, the wool like fire crackling under us.

"Touch me, touch me," she whispers. I rub my fingers through her soft wet cleft, loveknot of flesh tightening under my touch; how do we know to touch each other like this? Countless centuries of skill flickering through me, instinct, hot light that teaches cat to lick her young, geese to depart and return with the rhythms of the sun. Light as hot and ready and ancient bursting in our bellies, our buttocks, the narrow caves of our vaginas, her sobbing, thank you, thank you, I moaning, unable to speak.

The tiredness, not quite able to believe what was sweeping us along, that rain made of light, that ocean of steam.

The quivering quiets. She bites my chin. I try to kiss her, she pushes me away with a giggle and darts back through the cold ferns to the stream. Laughing, I follow. Cold water, so wonderful, and her dark flashing eyes.

I wake to the dungeon's gift of cold and darkness and silence. It feels so good to lie with my cheek pressed against the cold stone of the dungeon floor. Stones are the bones of the earth, the strength of the earth. Gratefully, I absorb the strength of the earth's bones into my limp body. My tongue explores the hole left when one of my front teeth was knocked out. For a moment I am again six, seven, probing the holes left by my vanishing baby teeth with my tongue. Here, instead of a smooth hole or the edge of a new tooth coming in, there is a broken fragment of the old; sharp splinter of bone. Salty taste. My nose throbs; feels like it has been mashed flat but it's not so much a real pain as a pulsing heat. And I can breathe a little; cool air in my nostrils feels soothing.

I sense the young guard they call Ian outside the door, then hear the key in the lock, then the door groaning as it opens; clank of iron and creak of wood as it closes. The color pressing against my eyelids changes from black to a dance of orange as he sets a brace of torches against the walls. I drift off again into sleep. For awhile I perceive nothing. Then again I become aware of where I am. My body has not moved. Perhaps I was only asleep for a short while. Perhaps I am dying.

A mint salve is being held beneath my nose. I breathe it, and the coolness spreads, soothing my battered face from the inside. Ahh—it feels good.

"Little queen. . ." he whispers, "I have to cut your hair. Forgive me." Slide of cold metal against my head, a snip, and then another, the soft protective curtain of hair slides from my face. I start to cry. I have never had my hair cut and I know it means he is getting me ready to be burned.

How much it hurt when they put the hot irons on my body, how much more it is going to hurt when it is live flames eating me to ash. I want to be brave. Anu, Cerridwen, Nimué, I pray silently, do not let me die screaming. Help me be strong. But I am at the end of my strength, sobs held back until now burst through me. Ian stops cutting my hair and cups my head protectively with his hand.

"Oh, little queen, I'm sorry," he whispers.

The way his hand fits over the back of my head feels like Alain, the way he would pull my head onto his shoulder and hold me when I had my nightmares.

And I'm in Alain's sweet arms again, my forehead against his chest, his hand holding the back of my head, pressing me to him, holding me while I'm crying, patting me on the back.

"Fiona, tis alright, tis alright—it's only a dream—"

But it is this that is only a dream, this dream of being safe with my man, having my match, being loved and understood.

"There now. There now. There now," I hear him whisper. "My sweet girl, it's all right. I'm here. I'll not leave you, not until you come with me."

But he had left, and I feel overwhelmed with the loss of all I could have had if I had gone with him, knowing if I had gone that somehow I would have been able to survive Annie's death, that he would have held me like this while I cried until I had wept myself healed. I think about him holding Mark on his knee and how many times since then I had imagined him holding our baby that way—the thought of the babies that we might have made between us that we will never make now is more than I can bear.

As I cry, my body wakes up into pain, the burned places along my skin begin smoldering. Clutching the minstrel, physically feeling his shirt and the fur beneath it, clinging to him, not wanting his image to leave me. I try to imagine my body being the way it was when he last held me, not torn open and ruined as it is now. To lose my body and my life is unbearable; to lose the softness and power of this love is agony. I could have gone, I could have asked John to help me. In my mind I see myself crossing over the hills, walking with John who knew where Ross-shire was. I imagine coming into an unfamiliar glen and having the minstrel running to meet us, catching me tight in his arms.

"Forgive me for not coming to you," I sob. "Forgive me."

"You're here now," he says, holding me.

"Don't forget me." I press my brow to his. Still midnight blue of the starless place cradles us.

"Please don't forget me. I promise that in another life I will go with you; where you beckon I will come, what you ask, I will give you."

It is hard to be comforted by thinking of another life when I am losing this one, longing for his hands and his voice, his eyes and his mouth, his beautiful high cheekbones, the fur curling on his chest, in the hollow of his throat.

"Come back the same. Come back so I recognize you," I beg him.

"Horned One," I pray, "Shape-shifter, when we come together again let us come in such forms that each of us recognize the other. Lady of Love and Laughter, hold our hearts together."

The minstrel sings to me, his song falling into my spirit like the spring rain caressing and quickening the newly sown fields:

"My heart it will fly where thou art,
Bright star to its companion star.

I will love thee as well from afar,
I will love thee as well from afar."

Clipping of the shears resumes. As the guard cuts off my
hair, I start shaking. The cold of the dungeon is no longer comforting. He puts a coarse wool blanket over me. The hot, scratchy
wool feels like wire against my raw arms and throat.

I open my eyes. My heart twists with grief, seeing not
Alain's green eyes and beautiful weathered face, creases carved
by the sun and smiling, but the pale, unlined face and blue eyes
of a boy—no more than a boy, no older than me. His eyes are wet.
He looks at me with sorrow. I reach over, try to pick up the long
strands of my hair the guard has laid in a basket. My hand contracts in agony as I try to use it. I look at it, amazed at how
twisted and purple it is. I don't remember them crushing my
hands. The young guard holds the hair out to me. I stroke it fee-
bly. Much of it is matted and stiff with dried blood but some of it
is still soft and warm as a young animal.

"Give it to him," I say, imagining Ian giving my hair to the
minstrel.

"You want the young lord to have it?" he asks.

The young lord. Sean?

I shake my head. "Dreaming. . ." I mutter.

"I'll see that it is put—in the hollow of a sacred tree," he
whispers in my ear. "I'll return it—to the Mother."

I close my eyes again, willing myself to the starless place
where I can be with Alain. This time I hear a cry of agony. I have
never heard a man cry out like that. It is Alain, mourning me. I
hear him calling my name with anguish, as if his pain would
bring me back to him.

A vision comes. I see, as if I were a spirit not visible to him,
Alain sitting by the scrying pool, candles set to burn at the four
corners of it. See him cupping the broken fish necklace in his
hand, sitting still as stone, jaw clenched—staring not into the
water but into the black, ungiving air, into the roaring sound of
the River Inbhir crashing only a yard away, willing me to appear. But I am incapable of appearing to him. I can only watch,
part of the silent darkness, as he sits rigid, staring into the
night that brings him no visions or comfort.

Then I see him sitting on a gray horse, staring down at the blackened pyre that has burned me. Staring at the ashes, the round curve of bone that was my skull; another big piece that was my pelvis; the rest too small and charred to be distinguished from the blackened pieces of wood remaining.

A little breeze stirring up the soft gray ashes, all that remains of my body and the murdered trees. A dusky film settles on the pommel of his saddle and the hair of the curious children poking through the rubble. A few of the filmy wisps brush his face. He looks too shocked to cry.

And I see him older, his hair all gone to gray now, deep-carved lines etched in an unshaven face. I hear him singing songs, angry songs about the burnings and sad songs about the girl that he lost to them.

"A gypsy once told me," I hear him telling the crowd, "that I would find my love through a crescent of iron and lose her through a circle of gold."

And I see the circle of golden flames around the stake, and me vanishing at the center. Wondering if I will arise, as I did in my vision at the caves, as the fire-birds arose and danced out of the blood-fruits that I held in my hands during my vision at Initiation. Wondering if I will go through the pain and then into sleep, if I will be able to follow the minstrel and be a guardian spirit for him, knowing that Gran and Mina have always said how important it is for a soul to go on after it has died and to let go of its ties to the earth. Feeling how they have released me already; there is only this one tie with the minstrel that keeps me here, and but for that I am ready to leave.

Even the earth, as beautiful as it is—it is his beauty, the beauty of the strong muscled animals I feel in his passionate male body, the dance of the evergreen branches and swirling mists I see in his eyes. His kiss, his touch, his cock that is the bridge, the wand, the tree of life. The fire we conjured between us that spread from our genitals to our bellies, throughout our bodies, into the earth. The heart of the sweet creative fire of life. When we make love it is we who are the source, who are the dance, who are the Goddess and the God.

And again I feel this, feel how together we are the heart of the fire, the animals and the plants, the male and the female, the Goddess and the God, swirling together in one flame, one bright life-giving star.

Peace opens in me like a rose made of light. The heart of the fire, the core of the star, fills me. This fire is eternal. The fire that I face tomorrow will take me, and I will go through that fire to this one.

Hearing the voice of the Goddess again as I heard it in my heart at my Initiation:

"At the heart of the fire—lies the darkness.
At the heart of the darkness—lies the light.
At the heart of the light—lies the love.
At the heart of the love—lies the fire.
At the heart of the fire—"

. . . And in the heart of the fire I see the animals, the beasts and the birds, the hoofed and the horned, the feathered and scaled, the Goddess and the God in human form, all dance together, whirling into a single pillar of light.

In the heart of the fire, they are the same.

Epilogue

Fiona McNair died a tragic death, as did so many. And yet her spirit lives and sings in my bones. My Self is multi-dimensional, continuous. It spans across eons of time, through the prismatic mirrors of many personalities, through many levels and layers of consciousness. I am one with bird and creeping vine, cougar's grin, delicate footfall of deer, ripening fruit and new iris defying the last snows. In the heart of the fire, they are the same.

Hypnotic access to time travel is one shamanic tool among many from which we may heal our shattered sense of self, re-creating our awareness of continuity and restoring our knowledge of our sacred essence and its immortality.

I am grateful to my sister, Isis Coble, and the powerful magic we shared together, which enabled me to re-enter my lifetime as Fiona more vividly and completely than I had ever previously been able to do. In that lifetime, she was my teacher, Mina, and since she survived me by many years, she was able to provide me with her memories of what happened in Glen Lochlan after Fiona's death.

I did not understand why I had apparently been abandoned by my coven, none of whom chose to merge with me or provide comfort and support through the starless place while I was being tortured. Isis/Mina explained to me that she and my Gran had come to the barn while I was being raped to try to help me, but that my grandmother had been beaten unconscious and Mina had been left to drag her home. John Staghorn and William Winter had been out looking for lost sheep on the evening when I was taken and so were unable to be of assistance. The men had set fire to the barn and fled; only the Witch-hunter, McTavish and the Laird knew that I had been taken out the back rather than left to die in the flames. Since my coven had a taboo about contacting the dead, they made no effort to contact me, and when they felt me reaching for them they thought it was the unwillingness of my spirit to move on to its next place and so they cut cords to free me rather than allowing psychic mergence. Only Elana, my sister, young and psychically unshielded as she was, knew what was happening to me. She tried to tell the adults, but they would not listen. Soon after that she stopped speaking altogether. After a few years most people regarded her as if she were deaf and dumb and forgot that she had ever been able to talk at all.

The Witch-hunter did not return to Glen Lochlan. He did not have to; the spirit of the village was shattered. The rituals of planting and harvest ceased; camraderie was replaced by distrust. Most of the men who had hurt me felt self-loathing afterwards. The women of the village withdrew emotionally from the men, keeping their eyes on the ground when they were near. In Glen Lochlan, as in so many places, women began to repress and deny their sexuality and their power, in the hopes that they would not be singled out for the abuses suffered by so many of their sisters. This left the men with more apparent power in the world, but with a deeply undermined sense of self, and a fear that still deeply persists in many men's hearts; that women will never fully love and trust them again.

William Winter and Rose both died that winter, as they had predicted they would. My grandmother refused to heal from the beating she had received. She repudiated her magic and burned all of her magical things, including the nine wands we had brought back from Faery. She died the following autumn. This left only Mina, John, Peter and Sarah; they stopped meeting as a coven, although Peter and Sarah continued to secretly teach their children the old ways. Mina refused to give out herbs or do any more healing for the people. Eventually she moved to another village, living in anonymity as an "aunt" with a younger relative and her family. Sarah continued to deliver babies and give out herbs, continuing her life as a midwife with extraordinary courage.

Isis/Mina says that my mother never got over my death and she came to be regarded as slightly mad. My sister Eostre moved to another village when she was older. Ewan the blacksmith hanged himself in his barn several months after my death. Sean became so deranged that his wife left him and went back to her people. He disappeared several years after my death and never returned to the village. And so, left without an heir, Lochlan's lands eventually went to his old enemy, the McCleod.

The Minstrel came back, as he had promised, to find me dead. He continued to travel and wrote many angry and bitter songs about the burnings. Frequently he was only one step ahead of the authorities who would have liked to silence him, but always he received friendly warnings and managed to escape in time. About ten years after my death, he fell gravely ill in the Orkney Islands and was nursed back to health by a young widow. They married and had four children, and he settled down at last.

There are very few historical records left of any of the Scottish Witchhunts; during the English conquest and occupation of Scotland, they systematically destroyed as much of the history and culture of the Scottish people as they could. The records that do exist indicate that the Witchhunt which began with the trial of the Berkshire Witches in 1591-92 and ended in 1597 was among the most virulent. It is not known how many people died, but it is known that King James himself, a fanatical Witchhunter, ended the Witch-hunt in 1597 because he became aware that many, many innocent people were being accused, and so many people had been slaughtered, and the patterns of life so disrupted, that agriculture and trade were no longer able to function in any normal way.

"Everything lost is found again
In a new form, In a new way.
Everything hurt is healed again
In a new life, In a new day.

She changes everything She touches, and
Everything She touches, changes."

—Starhawk, from the *Kore Chant*

Afterword

A snake once told me a secret: "I am not my skin," he said,
"I am only a maker of skins." When my python friend Ananta
died, he came to me in a dream. In my dream, I saw him lying
dead beside his grave, which was shaped like a spiral. I was about
to lay his body in the spiral-shaped grave when I felt him
wrapped around me, hugging my body, holding me in the strong
spiral of his eleven foot length. "Don't be sad/afraid, little sister," his spirit whispered, "It is only a skin."

We grieve for our human tragedies. But there is a power
there. The power to recognize ourselves as co-creators in each moment. The power to own and acknowledge our unconscious choices. To make our unconscious choices conscious. The power to
change, to do things differently.

In that lifetime as Fiona I died because I chose to shut down
on my power, my awareness, my love for myself. I contracted in
guilt and apathy. When I first contacted Fiona's life, I believed I
had been killed for my beauty, my passion, and my power. But in
fact I was killed when I lost contact with those qualities, with

my essential nature. If I had been fully feeling, sensitive and aware, I could have taken a course which would have saved me.

It does not help us to judge painful situations in terms of guilt and blame and who deserves them. No one ever deserves them. When we choose to be aware of our power and our choices, then we become shamans, sourcerers.* Then we shape-shifters transform ourselves, and the world transforms with us. In this lifetime I have been highly committed to staying conscious, staying aware, developing my psychic receptivity, my ability to be present. I continue to fight to free myself from addictive behaviors, to come home to myself and be willing to see the truth, moment by moment. This is a gift I have received from my death as Fiona.

I have grown and evolved since my life as Fiona; many of the beliefs expressed in this book are no longer my understanding.

Traditionally in Goddess oriented religions like Witchcraft, the creative force is seen as primarily female. The male is seen as subservient, secondary; the son, the consort/lover, the sacrifice. Witchcraft as it was then and as it is mostly practiced today is a religion of will and body—direct knowing of the intuitive combined with the perceivable physical world. I believe that patriarchy, with all its attendant horrors, the wars and genocides, the fear and oppression of women, darkness, dark-skinned people, the will and the body, was and is a reaction to the milleniums old imbalance which saw men as having no intrinsic power. If men could not create life, they would bring death. And they would control and punish the life-givers, the powerful mothers, through rape, servitude, sexual control, and theologies which reversed the previous order by decreeing God the creator as male and women and the feminine as synonymous with the demonic.

True Christianity is a religion of heart and spirit. It offers such enlightening concepts as faith (even if you can't feel, touch or taste something, it is still there), forgiveness, and the awareness that all deities are one and that one is unknowable except through love. These are powerful, liberating concepts. Historically, the people who understood and promoted these concepts were branded as heretics and killed.

The church that dominated was a church of fear, a church of control and oppression. In my coven in Scotland, we saw Chris-

---

*My spelling of sourceress/sourcerer is intentional—a sourceress/er is one who acknowledges her/himself as the *source* of their experience.

tianity as being as monstrously perverse and evil as their dogma perceived us. The Christian Priests that we had contact with did not understand the message of Christ, and neither did we. True Christianity has the value and truth of spirit and heart, which balances the Pagan understanding of will and body. Each of us is all of these; body, will, heart and spirit; the degree to which we honor and integrate all these aspects is the degree to which we will be powerful, loving and free.

Collectively we have been acting our the fable of the blind men and the elephant, each feeling a part of the animal and quarreling about who has true knowledge of the beast. We are now at an evolutionary point where we can begin to listen to each other and start pooling our information instead of fighting as a response to our fear at the initial differences we discover.

It is beginning, this communication, this communion. Wherever the traditions of Africa, the Americas and Europe intermingle, wherever eastern mysticism and western shamanism connect and cross-pollinate, it is beginning. Whenever the enlightenment of the new age contacts the fertile endarkenment of the old ways, it is beginning.

Also beginning is a healing for men and women. For twenty years, women have been reclaiming the Goddess and redefining their power. Men have also looked for the Goddess within, contacting their own nurturing, soft, creative power. The will, the psychic, intuitive, sensitive part of each of us is reawakening, and with it the will of the planet is stirring to new life. And we are just now coming to a place where a new concept of maleness is arising; powerful and passionate, playful and primordial, the new masculine is rising, coming forth to meet and match and mate with the feminine.

For each of us, however sexually oriented or active, this Great Rite, this Sacred Marriage, takes place within. As we sense both masculine and feminine energies within us we will be able to receive other humans not as our opposite or our other half, but as whole beings, microcosms like ourselves. When this occurs, new realms of intimacy are born.

We are at the beginning of a time of partnership, the likes of which has never been seen on this planet. Never has there been a time where women and men have truly been friends, equals, and co-creators at the level which is available to us now. The possibility exists now for each of us to celebrate the Hieros Gamos, the sacred marriage of masculine and feminine, sun and moon, spirit and will, heart and body, within us. We are free to re-experience, in a new way, the old mystery: *The Goddess and the God are one.*

Glossary

Amergin—*The song of Amergin is an ancient evocation of the God.*

Ashtara—*Sexual Goddess cognate with Astarte and Ishtar. Goddess of Fire and Passion.*

Ashtar's Eggs—*Pieces of quartz polished smooth, about the size and shape of an egg. Left to soak in water they would impart a healing quality to the water which was then drunk to promote fertility and health.*

Athamé—*Black-handled knife used to represent the male principle and the element of air—used primarily in the mime of the sacred marriage and to draw magical circles and symbols in the air.*

Avalon—*Mysterious land of apples, or land of youth, where the dead waited for rebirth.*

Bairn—*Child.*

Bannocks—*Oatcakes.*

Banshees—*Faery women whose eerie wails, heard on the wind, prophesy death.*

Barrow—*Neolithic tunnels used for human burials and death/*

rebirth rituals.

Beltane—*May Day festival celebrated with bonfires, love-making, May-pole dancing and light-hearted play. Cross-quarter day across from Hallowmas/Samhain on the Wheel of the year, it is also a time when the veil between the worlds in thin and there is particular access to the land of Faery.*

Biolline—*Small white-handled knife used for carving signs and sigils on tools and candles, for cutting meat, bread or cheese.*

Blouwedd—*A legendary maiden Goddess who was formed of flowers and miraculously came to life. Goddess of youth, spring, beauty.*

Braw—*Brave.*

Bride, or Fest of Bride—*Celtic holiday known as Imbolc, Candlemas or Bridget. Held around Feb.2nd, it honors the first signs of spring, the lengthening days, and the Goddess Bride or Bridget, Goddess of poetry, smithcraft and healing.*

Brogans—*Shoes.*

Cailleach—*Dark aspect of the Goddess from which Caledonia, an ancient name for Scotland—was derived. Her full name is the Scotia Cailleach—she is a western version of Kali.*

Calling Conch—*A conch shell with the end cut off to form a trumpet to invoke the directions and other powers.*

Caves of Annuven—*Caves of the Goddess Anu that lie at the heart of the world; deep source of the Earth Goddess's powers of renewal.*

Cernunnos—*Mature Stag-God who periodically dies so that his blood may fertilize the earth, upon which he is reborn again.*

Cingulum—*Red nine-foot cord worn as a sash, used ritually to measure a nine-foot (traditional-sized) circle. Represents the umbilical cord.*

Cloved, The—*The Cloved refers to the God who is seen as hoofed and horned like the vital life of the animals he represents.*

Cone of Power—*Magical energy whirled into a cone-shaped vortex which may be directed to a specific purpose once it has been raised.*

Cony—*A young rabbit.*

Corn Dollies—*Weavings made of stalks of grain for magical symbols. They do not necessarily resemble dolls.*

Croft—*A small house.*

Crone—*Hag aspect of the Goddess; usually portrayed as an old-*

woman, sometimes kindly, sometimes terrifying. she rules death, rebirth, divination, prophesy, discernment, reaping, defense, the realms of trance and dream and winter.

Cunny Cheese—"Wise cheese," wisdom of sheep, goat, cow and human milk, mixed with the blood of menses or childbirth. Traditional first food for mothers who have just given birth.

Deosil—Sunwise, clockwise.

Druaderia—Gypsy tantra also practiced by minstrels and other heretics. Used to transform sexual energy into powerful magical and spiritual energy and as a form of birth control.

Elf-Bolts—Small arrow-heads said to be shot by faeries; probably remnants of Pict civilizations.

Esbats—Moon rituals, usually held at full moons.

Faery—A race of peoples similar in appearance to humans, generally mischievous, beautiful and wise. By the sixteenth century they were already more talked of than seen.

Familiar—Not a pet, but an animal a Witch merges consciousness with; both human and animal gain some of each other's power thereby. A symbiotic magical relationship.

Ganeesha—Elephant-headed God of India.

Gobbett or Grobbet—Malicious spirits.

Grimoire—Magical Book, a book of spells.

Guisards—People in ritual costume, often frightening in their "guises."

Gyves—Leather arm bands worn while hunting with hawks to protect against their claws.

High Toby—Highway Robbery.

Hotch-Potch—Traditional Scottish soup/stew.

Kelpie—Sea or lake "monster" such as the famous one found in Loch Ness. They are orms (snail-like creatures) with horse-like heads.

Kirk—Church.

Kyairthwen—Variation on the Goddess Cerridwen, Hag Goddess of transformation and inspiration, death and rebirth. Her symbol is the cauldron, her animals the pig, snake, cat and wolf.

Land of Apples—Beautiful realm of the dead, envisioned as lying over the western seas. See Avalon.

Leman—Lover.

Leviathan—Whale.

Litha—*Summer Solstice, also known as St. John's Day, which occurs on June 21st. Longest day and shortest night of the year, celebrated with bonfires, dancing, merriment and love-making. In our area people wore animal masks and disguises to call forth their own animal vitality. The power of the God in his forms of sun, oak and animals is celebrated.*

Lughnasad—*Harvest festival of the First Fruits celebrated August 2nd. Festival of Lugh, Lord of Light.*

Mabon—*Autumnal Equinox, celebrated around September 21st, day and night are equal length; night and the faery worlds rule after this time until Spring Equinox. Celebrated with a wicker or straw man sacrificed in flames, with baking, feasting and merriment.*

Maiden—*Young girl aspect of the Goddess, She who is one-unto-herself; virgin, but not necessarily chaste. Independent, innocent, joyous and untamed, She is the mistress and protectress of wild things.*

Mannanon and Marianna—*Mannanon MacLir and Marianna are the God and Goddess of the sea.*

Mother—*Aspect of the Goddess that is mature, full, fecund. She is fertility, mistress of the fields and orchards and domestic animals. Creator of the world.*

Morrigan—*A death and battle aspect of the Goddess.*

Need-Fire—*Fire derived from two people rubbing two pieces of wood together; also called New-Fire—considered essential for certain rituals.*

Ostara—*Spring Equinox, celebrated around March 21st, also known as Eostre, named for the Celtic Goddess of the Dawn. Celebrates the birth of the new animals and the coming of spring. Fields are worked and plowed as soon after as frosts will allow.*

Pan—*Hoofed and horned aspect of the God as animal; characterized as playful, youthful, lusty goat-footed God.*

Papists—*Catholics.*

Quadishu—*Literally, Sacred One; Priestesses who embodied the Goddess during sexual Temple rites held in the Middle East for thousands of years.*

Quern—*Grain and seed grinder.*

Ragni—*Spider Goddess; probably related to Greek Arachne.*

Raith—*Aura and/or astral body. Sometimes used to refer to a ghost.*

Reave/Reivers—*To steal; theives.*

Robin the Good—*Puckish woods God immortalized in the Robin Hood legends.*

Robin the Good's Minstrel—*Robin Hood had a minstrel named Alain-a-dale, legendary for his magical music.*

Sabbats—*Eight holy days of the Celtic-European peoples; Samhain, Yule, Imbolc, Ostara, Beltane, Litha, Lughnasad, Mabon. Together they form the Wheel of the year.*

Samhain—*Celtic Feast of the Dead, celebrated Oct. 31st. Often interpreted as the Witches New Year, it is a traditional time for divination and a time to honor the ancestors and the coming of winter. It is said that the veils between the worlds of the living and dead, past and future, human and other-worldly are thinnest at this time.*

Sasanach—*English.*

Scrying—*Using a glossy surface, most commonly clear crystal or water, to see visions, usually of the future but sometimes to see the present which is occuring at a distance.*

Seining—*Pagan baptismal ritual for welcoming a new child.*

Selkies—*Seals or magical seal-humans creatures who could mate with humans.*

Separationists—*Protestants.*

Sgian Dhu—*Small dagger used for defense and for the same purposes as the biolline. A biolline was a magical sgian dhu but the terms were sometimes used interchangeably.*

Sigils—*Mystical symbols drawn in the air or on magical tools. Each person also had a sigil representing their magical name or identity.*

Sooktart Machlana Shaumone—*A local child Goddess representing innocent wisdom.*

Talismans—*Charms carried for luck or protection.*

Taliesien—*Celtic Apollo/Dionysius, son of Cerridwen born with the gifts of music, poetry and prophesy.*

Tree Marriage—*The two pieces of different woods comprising the fire awl and cradle used to kindle the need-fire.*

Twelve, The—*Twelve Craft elders drawn from all over the Western Highlands. Their collective wisdom was made available to all the covens in the area.*

Waerlog—*Gaelic word meaning oath-breaker.*

Warlock—*Derived from Waerlog; an oath-breaker, traitor. not an accurate term for a male Witch (a male Witch is a Witch).*

Wheel of the Year—*The eight Sabbats and four seasons, visualized by ancient peoples as an ever-revolving wheel or circle.*

Widdershins—*Counter-clockwise movement.*

Yule—*Winter Solstice; Dec. 21st, longest night and shortest day of the year. Traditional birth of the God of Light, usually observed by an all-night vigil and fast, broken by feasting in the morning.*

ABOUT THE AUTHOR

Cerridwen Fallingstar is an experienced shaman devoted to synthesizing the best of the old ways with the new age, creating magic, ritual and relationships that work. She lectures, teaches classes, and offers individual sessions utilizing Tarot, hypnotherapy, and other techniques to support others in coming home to their freedom, power and love. She lives with her son Zachary in San Geronimo, California.

For information on classes, rituals and private sessions facilitated by Cerridwen Fallingstar, or to set up workshops and lectures in your area, write to:

Cerridwen Fallingstar
P.O. Box 282
San Geronimo, CA 94963